Praise for VICKI PETTERSSON's
dark and brilliant series
SIGNS OF THE ZODIAC

"[It] came out of nowhere and slapped me silly. Then it lingered days after I closed the cover. . . . Vicki Pettersson is a new voice that needs to be heard."

Kim Harrison

"From the one-damn-thing-after-another school of unputdownable books, [it] rockets into the air and explodes like fireworks, with nonstop bursts of action and imagination."

Diana Gabaldon

"Moody, fast-paced . . . blends fantasy, comic book superheroism and paranormal romance, but holds no promise of a happily-ever-after. . . . Imaginative. . . . [Readers] will embrace Pettersson's enduring, tough-as-nails heroine and anticipate gleefully the next volume."

Publishers Weekly

"[A] very exciting series . . . it'll keep you up past your bedtime."

Charlaine Harris

By Vicki Pettersson

THE SCENT OF SHADOWS
The First Sign of the Zodiac

THE TASTE OF NIGHT
The Second Sign of the Zodiac

THE TOUCH OF TWILIGHT
The Third Sign of the Zodiac

HOLIDAYS ARE HELL
(with Kim Harrison, Lynsay Sands,
and Marjorie M. Liu)

THE
TOUCH OF TWILIGHT
THE THIRD SIGN OF THE ZODIAC

VICKI
PETTERSSON

An Imprint of HarperCollinsPublishers

This is a work of fiction. Names, characters, places, and incidents are products of the author's imagination or are used fictitiously and are not to be construed as real. Any resemblance to actual events, locales, organizations, or persons, living or dead, is entirely coincidental.

EOS
An Imprint of HarperCollins*Publishers*
10 East 53rd Street
New York, New York 10022-5299

Copyright © 2008 by Vicki Pettersson
Author photo © 2007 Derik Klein
Cover art by Chris McGrath
ISBN 978-0-06-089893-9
www.eosbooks.com

First Eos paperback printing: June 2008

HarperCollins® and Eos® are registered trademarks of HarperCollins Publishers.

Printed in the U.S.A.

10 9 8 7 6 5 4 3 2 1

To my grandmother, Eva Mattingly.
Thank you for unconditional support,
ceaseless prayers . . . and for saying
I remind you of you.

Acknowledgments

In the time elapsed since the release of my first book, the audience that once existed solely in my mind has solidified into an enthusiastic core of readers, utterly surpassing my ideal. Specific thanks go to Joy Maiorana and Shada Adrianna for reaching out to me on message boards and allowing me to steal character names, and to Kim Castillo, who single-handedly kept this from being poorly titled *Book Three*. Of course, the series wouldn't exist at all if not for my exceptional agent, Miriam Kriss, and the enthusiasm, hard work, and dedication of my outstanding editor, Diana Gill. Emily Krump and Jack Womack have been on my side from day one, and Tom Egner's vision continues to astound me. Thank you all. There are others in the Harper family who've made me feel right at home, but names must naturally be omitted to protect the guilty (Rhonda Rose, Mark Landau, Donna Waitkus). Thanks always to Suzanne Frank—my partner-in-crime and literary BFF—the KWC girls, and continued gratitude to my husband, Roger, who remains my reason in All Things Good.

1

The country-western bar rocked on its pilings with music and conversation, laughter and line dances—and an obscene number of ten-gallon hats—all competing with the glint of the club's lights to obscure my sightline. It didn't matter. The scent of the Shadow alone was enough to alert me to her presence. Even the sweaty masses, with their perfumes and deodorants and soaps, could do nothing to mask the pungent rot of a demon masquerading as a human being.

A cigarette flared on the lips of a man to my left as I slipped smoothly across the straw-strewn dance floor, squeezing the grip on my crossbow through the open zipper of my designer clutch. Raucous laughter erupted ahead and to my right as bellies filled with the Jell-O shots that would eventually be blamed for this night's folly. The band rocked hard in front of a plate-glass window suspended beneath a slanted rooftop, and the lights of the Las Vegas Strip sparkled enticingly in the distance.

My awareness of all this was cursory. Acridness was building in the back of my throat, and the tang of soured skin made me wince as I neared the bathroom door, but I held my breath once there, stilled my movements, and steeled myself for battle. Regan—Shadow agent, astrological Cancer of our enemy Zodiac troop, and would-be rival for my true love's affections—possessed hearing so sharp she could make out wings beating in the air. She could taste unbridled emotion as if sipping from a cup, and given the chance, she could scent me too.

My nostrils flared as I breathed in deeply, and it was there . . . the petal-soft top note of singed roses powdering the air, just shy of cloying. The heart note like milk so recently gone sour a dulled palate wouldn't be able to tell the difference.

The base note of slick, hot vomit.

With aching slowness, I gripped my conduit in front of me, slipped off my kitten heels, then lowered my chin and widened my stance.

You are the Kairos, the fulcrum upon which hinges the paranormal battle between good and evil. Your every action is loaded with meaning, charged with energy, and linked to your legacy.

My troop leader's reminder fired like a rocket through my mind, and I shot back a mental rejoinder as I kicked open the door with a splintering crack.

How's this for action?

But the sitting area was empty, and I immediately sidestepped my way to the cluster of stalls, stopping short when something sharp and unnaturally shiny caught my attention. An ice pick lay angled across the vanity, projecting homicidal intent as clearly as a chalk outline. I recognized it as Regan's conduit, her paranormal weapon, the only thing that could truly destroy one of *us*. A blow from an enemy's conduit would slay you, and a conduit turned against its own controller would erase their existence so completely, they were scrubbed from supernatural history. Not even a footnote left to speak to their existence. And Regan's was lying right there in the open.

Stupid bitch. I took a step toward it.

"I wouldn't, if I were you."

I whirled toward the stalls in time to watch a slim, delicate, and deadly hand appear. It held one of the tiny, teasing devices I'd found littering my ex's modest tract home. It was the reason I'd come here to kill.

Lowering my own conduit, I stepped down. One mean twitch of her thumb, and a man would be blown to bits just outside these doors. *My* man.

"Come on, *superhero*," Regan taunted, coming into full view. "Show me your scariest super face."

Though expected, Regan's appearance always startled me. Her dark bob was exactly chin length, as if she'd measured it with a ruler while cutting it, and hadn't let it grow a centimeter since. Her build was more compact than when we'd first met, but then mine used to be as well, and that's what jolted me. That's who she'd been designed to imitate. Me. Before I'd been turned into a white-hot, slick-curved, brick-house blonde.

"Where is it?" My voice had turned unnaturally raspy for a woman. It happened when I was extremely pissed.

"His watch." She shrugged, watching me carefully, eyes lingering on my bare feet. "I told him I could get a great deal on a TAG Heuer. He loves it."

She sauntered across the powder room to perch herself on a stool designed like a mini-sawhorse, still holding the detonator aloft. I smirked as, one-handed, she began putting on lipstick in a shade I used to favor. Cute. She'd taken the blueprint of my former features—the way I wore my hair, the skin tone, and eyes—twisting the details in small ways to make them her own. The clothes she wore were still conservative, if a tad tighter than mine had been, and her jewelry was more dramatic, playing off deceptively delicate features.

Regan's beauty regimen, and her near-pathological need to test me, had her slyly setting the detonator down and whipping out a simple black compact. Not trusting that this too wasn't a detonator in disguise, I only watched as she used a cut sponge to reapply cover-up to a scar below her left ear. I wasn't privy to how she'd gotten that one, but I knew Vanessa had nearly caught her three weeks ago with her hinge-bladed fan, and sure enough, Regan lifted her shirt to reveal the still-angry scores above her waist.

Unlike wounds from mortal weapons, conduits always left scars . . . again, if we survived them at all. Ordinarily one had to work to conceal the raised scars, but this concealer went on smoothly and the scar vanished, leaving her belly flawless in its mirrored reflection. Whoever had mixed the compound, I admitted grudgingly, had known what they were doing.

"Isn't Ben even a little curious as to why his sweet 'Rose' has so many scars?" I asked acerbically. Now that my immediate plans for murder, mayhem, and revenge had been foiled, I decided to keep her talking until I came up with a plan B.

"Benny-boy sees what I want him to," she retorted, perching herself on the counter, feet on the sawhorse as she dabbed at her right calf. "You should get your lab rats to engineer a compound like this. Isn't it wonderful? Close to your coloring too."

I narrowed my eyes. It was *exactly* my coloring. The Shadow surgeon who'd turned her into a younger, stinkier version of the old me hadn't skipped any corners.

"So, am I doing a good approximation of you, Archer?" Since we were alone, she used my title—my sign on the Western Zodiac—openly.

"Please. You're merely poaching." I said, mindful of the device next to her as I watched her apply the makeup. It *would* be useful to have some of that for the mark on my chest. My glyph had burned me from the inside when I'd been captured in an underground cavern last month, and it still hadn't quite faded. Regan had been responsible for that Kodak moment too. "Hurt him and I'll finish the lobotomy your mother so clearly fucked up."

Regan stiffened; star signs and conduits were passed down via the matriarchal line. Regan's mother, Brynn

DuPree, had indeed been fond of performing psycho-surgery on known enemies with her ice pick . . . with an emphasis on the psycho. But, after a moment, Regan just continued smoothing on the concealer. "I can't hurt Ben any more than you already have."

Liar, liar. "Let me put it this way, then. If he even comes down with a cold, I'll punch so many holes through your body, it won't hold embalming fluid."

This time she paused in her dabbing, tilting her head my way. "But then Benny-boy would be suspicious, wouldn't he?" A theatrical sigh. "Not to mention brokenhearted."

"You flatter yourself."

"And you kid yourself." Her voice was harder now, lower and rasping like mine. She snapped her compact shut and dropped it on the counter, then picked up the detonator again, flipping it lazily in her hand. "You're going to lose him. It's only a matter of time."

"Is this where I get to say, 'To you and what army'?"

"You know what army. After all, you're a member."

I shook my head. "I'm only half Shadow."

"And I bet that wakes you up at night," she said, pushing off from the counter to stand. I couldn't let her at my back, so I turned and we squared against each other in the center of the room. "It's what drives you from your bed in the morning, and makes you want to carve your presence in this world. You want to step up and be someone. Leave a mark so that future generations remember your name."

She ascribed the ambitions to me, but the detail made me think she was talking about herself. Interesting. "I hate to tell you this, sweetie, but they're already going to remember my name."

"You sound like your father."

"Don't—"

"—call him that, I know." She rolled her eyes. "Get over it already. I've seen you in action, *Joanna*. I see the brutality that lives in your eyes when you look at me. You can't tell me you've never had a baser impulse. That you've never laughed when someone else took a tumble. Wished a person who blew by you in the fast lane would overcorrect an inch. Or that you've never seen a pedestrian on Las Vegas Boulevard and just wanted to *swerve*?" I opened my mouth to say, *No, I hadn't*, but she cut me off by holding up a hand. "I know you, and I don't just mean who you are beneath the gloss and the polish and the tits. I know *you*."

She knew my weaknesses, at least. It was how she'd tricked me before. But . . .

"If you really knew me, you'd walk away from Ben now."

"And speaking of," she sang, clasping her hands together like a schoolgirl, "you should check out some of his e-journals. Such a good record keeper, our little aspiring writer. There's some interesting reading there." She studied my carefully blank look, and laughed when the silence grew long. "Oh yes, I know you've bugged his computer. But if you'd read those entries, I doubt you'd be here. They're part confessional, part penitence. You might be particularly interested in his actions involving a dead drug lord last summer in an urban cage known as Dog Run."

Even the magic of overpriced makeup must not have been enough to hide my face draining of color, because Regan's grin widened like it'd been cleaved.

"Or the fate of a young boy named Charles Tracy. Remember him?"

I hadn't heard that name in years. Tracy had been a schoolyard bully who'd specialized in wedgies for the younger boys and used pudgy fingers to feel up any unfortunate girl in a skirt. Ben and I had ganged up on him at school, using the power of persuasion and our fists to make him stop. He'd dropped out of school altogether in junior high, and I hadn't thought of him since.

"I'm not interested in the lies you've planted in his journals," I told her shortly. She might have an advantage over me, but she had no right to touch on my past. "Or some fabricated story about a kid I haven't seen in over a decade."

"Aw, how sweet. Defending your one true love. Bad habits really are hard to break."

The need to amputate her smile welled, and I took a step forward before I could stop it. "You mean bad habits like planting bombs around *my* lover's house . . . ones you're going to remove before anyone even thinks of making them go bang."

She shrugged and pretended to study her nails. They were polished, but clear, as I'd have worn them. Another visual cue for Ben's subconscious to latch on to.

"Those bombs," she said evenly, "are less destructive than the anger and betrayal you planted by abandoning him twice. Do you have any idea how easy it's been to water that particular emotional seed? As much fun as my mother said it could be."

And Brynn DuPree had been a model Shadow agent.

"All it would take is one visit from me in my old skin, and you'd be nothing but a distant memory." Over Regan's shoulder I saw my reflection take another menacing step forward. It looked like someone else altogether; Olivia's bright, bouncy features had sharpened like they'd been whittled into angry points, the butter-soft flesh a delicate cocoon for the skeletal darkness threatening to burst forth. Welcome to my fucked-up dual existence.

"Maybe." She shrugged but it was jagged. She was fighting not to inch backward. "But then I'd have to spill your little secret."

"You mean reveal my Olivia identity to Ben? Or to the Tulpa?" I scoffed, though I knew the leader of the Shadow organization would offer a hefty reward to anyone who could do just that. "It's an empty threat, and you know it. You're too fond of the power and options that knowledge gives you."

"I take a certain pleasure from it, true." And she did step back, back and around to observe me again through the lasso-fringed mirror. "But I'm weary of glancing over my shoulder every time I visit the restroom. I want you to back off for good, and stop planting those fucking listening devices all around his house, or else Ben is going to learn of yet another secret his erstwhile ex has kept from him all these years." And then she mouthed a single, shocking word at me through the glass.

Ashlyn.

It changed everything. I'd have been less surprised if the floor had dropped from beneath me. Only one person could've given Regan that name, but I thought I'd killed him before he told anyone about my daughter. *Ben's* daughter.

Enjoying my reaction, Regan smiled. "Back off now, and I won't tell the Tulpa he has a granddaughter either. One that is of the Light." She laughed at the irony in her hoarded secret. The leader of the Shadows, a grandsire to a child of the Light. A leader, I knew, who'd kill my daughter all the more quickly because of it.

"Oh, your expression is priceless!" She laughed gaily, a sound like tiny bells chiming in the spring winds, before pretending to sober. "Though you should check it. I doubt your sister ever wore such a serious expression."

I pulled my gaze from her if only to hide the tumult inside, but looking at my image confirmed she was right. Olivia's eyes had always been bright blue—open, smiling, and trusting. Mine were light enough to look honeyed in the right light, a soft shade of brown Regan had very nearly duplicated, but they'd always deepened when I was angry. Right now they were flashing like polished jet in an expression that was as petrified and bright as the diamonds at my ears and fists. The earrings had been a gift from Xavier Archer, Olivia's father, and the man I once thought was also mine. But the eyes were from my real father, the Shadow leader, the being who either wanted me to belong to him or wanted me dead.

I waited to speak until I was steady enough to control my voice. "You don't know what you're talking about."

"Well, I don't know little Ashlyn's adopted surname, or where she ended up all those years ago, but it shouldn't take too long to find out. And even if it does, I don't mind waiting for the onset of her second life cycle." I opened my mouth, but she held up the hand with the detonator and shook her head. "Uh-uh-uh. Remember, I'm watching you too. And right now I'm going to watch you walk away with your tail tucked, while I enjoy a romantic two-step with your boyfriend."

I knew I was losing the battle for self-control when Regan's delicate nostrils widened, a sign that my natural pheromones were flaring, but I couldn't help it. My options were swiftly disappearing. Regan watched my face, drinking in the emotions she caught passing there, and as if thirsting for more, she leaned forward on the counter, gaze piercing mine through the mirror. "It's a conundrum, isn't it? Continue stalking us, and you risk pissing me off so much, I may snap and take it out on your childhood crush. Stop, and he might outlive his usefulness. Nothing to keep me from killing him . . . or making him wish he was dead."

I was clenching my jaw so tight my teeth ached.

"But, no. I'm not entirely without needs of my own, so I think I'll fuck him first." She tilted her head, and her pretty smile widened. "I'll make sure those listening devices are working properly so you can get off too."

I reached for her with a speed that still surprised me. Regan yelped, whirling and dodging as her glyph smoked hot on her chest, the realization she'd pushed too far stark on her face.

My face, I corrected mentally, and plowed a fist into it.

We were two opposing agents in our prime, and the fight was evenly matched, though it'd be a blur to mortal eyes, which is why the woman entering the restroom didn't register our presence until a stool crashed through the wall behind her, imbedded there like an oversized thumbtack. She also had to be severely inebriated. She stood in place, staring at the stool as the whistling and howling of wind—our blows and battle cries in flight—accompanied a blur of motion so fast, it was like a dust devil had landed inside. I rushed Regan, continuing forward when I should've stopped, launching up her body like it was a climbing wall to send a knee flying into her skull. She face-planted into the mirror she'd been sneering into only moments before, which gave me time to reach the mortal's side, gently pick her up, and deposit her back outside the restroom. Regan wouldn't hesitate to use her life as leverage, and I couldn't give the bitch an opportunity to harm anyone else.

"Keep guard," I told the woman, and waited for her dazed nod before the door swung shut. I turned around . . .

And had my stomach caved in by a driving skull. My ribs wrapped around my spine and the door splintered behind me so the yelp from the other side seeped through the cracks, but I was too busy learning to breathe again to worry about spillover into the mortal world. I was also pretty concerned about the ice pick arching toward the large artery in my neck.

"Fuck," I breathed, my glyph lighting in response to her conduit. Regan smiled.

Leaving my aching ribs exposed, I crisscrossed my arms against her weapon hand, and paid for it with a knee in my gut. My breath whooshed from me again, but I latched on to lift her wrists, reared back, and head-butted her. Twice.

Her arms went slack, my fingers scrambled; her hands wobbled, mine tightened, and the ice pick popped into the air like a champagne cork. One final swipe on my part sent it skittering across the sitting room and under the line of stalls. We both growled snaking sounds of fury and frustration, and redirected our assault.

An admittedly lucky left jab had Regan backpedaling, and I was back on her in two strides, a low kick connecting with her thigh, causing the muscles to contract in the mother of all charley horses. It was a tide-turning injury, and we both knew it. Regan's retreat was so fast, she looked like a spider scuttling away on too few limbs. I was just as fast, and had her . . . until sound erupted like a flash flood, waves of it careening over us both. We doubled over where we stood, hands pressed to the sides of our heads in a humorless parody of Munch's *The Scream*.

I tried to focus on Regan, but the narrow canals of my ears were closing up on me, like the cabin of a plane suddenly losing pressure. I cried out in pain, in silence, knowing what this was. This was stark elemental chaos, atoms and molecules compressed beyond anything this reality could hold, and the explosion of sound was as magnificent as an asteroid collision in space.

Except this sound wasn't set to a frequency in a galaxy far, far away. It was in a Las Vegas bathroom, next to me, all around me. *In* me. Someone—someone strong—was fucking with the vibration of matter.

I tensed in anticipation of the final concussion. Paranormal turmoil operated on a different wavelength than normal matter, its pulse detectable only by those equipped to hear it. So it was a good thing no one entered the bathroom just then, because Regan and I would have looked mighty strange writhing in the perceived silence. But instead of winnowing away like regular sound waves, the tremor swelled, similar to the bubbles blooming over the heads of comic book characters, and not by coincidence. Those who were supernatural could sense the forming of that bubble, the crest between the waves making up the vibration, the enormous size of its pressurized core.

And this was a big motherfucker.

A high-pitched whine wheeled through the air, refusing to be absorbed before oxygen dropped from the room, the city, and then the earth. Then the accompanying pop ruptured the void, ricocheting off my eardrums like a puncturing jab, and the collapsing vacuum ate my scream.

There was nothing but a low-grade buzzing for a good thirty seconds. I used the blissful silence to regain my equilibrium, trusting Regan was doing the same. My hearing returned on a single note, like the pluck of an untuned guitar string, and marked the ebb of the invisible tsunami of sound. It receded degree by degree, and when it was finally gone, Regan and I both straightened. Breathing hard, staring at each other across a distance of no more than a jab, we inhaled deeply.

The air was chalky and static, and sapped the moisture from my tongue as I tried to taste the highs and furrows created on the shocked air. Scent was equally obliterated, at least for a few seconds more, and then a sour putridity crept into the room. Regan's tensed shoulders dropped, and she found her smile again.

"What? Did you think we'd never fight back?"

The statement, and the stench, made it clear one of Regan's allies had done this. Somehow he, she, or they had punched a hole through the plane between realities, and it was my job—mine and my troop's—to fix it before the human element noticed. However, that wasn't what had my response catching in my throat.

It was clear from her words that Regan thought the recent series of vibrational outbursts had been caused by the agents of Light. They hadn't—and we hadn't been able to detect a source on the damaged air—but I wasn't about to tell her that. And I needed to go. This explosion was bigger than anything Regan threatened to make.

"No more bombs," I told her. "Or I'll send you to a place where hellfire feels like a spa treatment."

"And I'll bring Ben along as my cabana boy."

She surprised me then by retrieving her conduit and leaving first, without another word, but as I surveyed the shattered mirrors, the upended furniture, and the holes in the walls and door, my eyes fell on something tiny and girly and black. I picked up her compact, flipping it in my palm before pocketing it.

Then I left to find out what exactly was ripping at the fabric of our world.

2

I was surprised, though I suppose I shouldn't have been, to see the man as soon as I exited the bar. He was leaning against my black Porsche, dark eyes trained on me, and I sighed as I picked my way around the weeds and broken beer bottles scarring the dilapidated parking lot, gravel making little popping noises under my feet. Hunter Lorenzo, weapons master and fellow member of Zodiac troop 175, waited unmoving.

He normally wore tinted glasses when out about town, but had removed them in deference to the night. His hair was growing out—it was about the same length as Ben's now—but he sported a five o'clock shadow, which meant, though it was Wednesday, it was his weekend free from his cover job in security at the Valhalla Casino. Though not overly groomed, he was impossibly good-looking, and if you didn't know him, you might think he spent an hour in front of the mirror each morning.

Not that I should talk.

Not the same, I told myself as I flipped a curl over my shoulder. This silicone and self-tan and impossible *blondeness* hadn't been my choice of urban camouflage. My sister's appearance had been forced upon me.

"How long have you been here?" I asked as I came to a stop in front of him.

"Almost as long as you."

I crossed my arms, looking up at him. "I almost got my ass kicked back there. Why didn't you come in?"

He quirked one dark brow. "Because I don't drink watered-down beer or date horses."

I tilted my head. "You mean you ceased to have my back against one Shadow warrior—"

"And a bar full of twenty-first-century wannabe wranglers."

"—just because you didn't think you fit in?"

"I *don't* fit in," he said, wincing now. "Not unless I black out some teeth."

"Snob." He was joking, but I knew Hunter well enough to know his tastes ran to classical rather than country. In fact, in some ways I knew this man even better than the one I'd left inside that bar. Ben and I shared history, but Hunter and I had shared magic. We'd never sat down for a so-where-are-you-from? sort of discussion, but by once trading a soft-stream essence of breath tinged with a power known as the aureole, I'd seen into his soul.

We'd agreed to forget about this unearned intimacy, but that hadn't prevented Hunter from popping up on my mental radar in bright, jarring blips. I knew he felt the same. I could sense when his thoughts snagged on me as well . . . and it was a knowledge that wanted to burrow through my body, take up warm residence somewhere between my belly and pelvic bone, and part my thighs. It wasn't helping matters that Hunter seemed to be reconsidering our platonic pact, as evidenced by his appearance now. He'd been watching out for me as plainly as I'd been watching out for Ben.

"How'd you know they were going to be there?" he said, pushing from the car to stroll to the passenger's side.

How'd you know I was going to be there? I wanted to say as I disengaged the alarm and climbed in. "I put a trace on Ben's phone, surveillance software on his computer, and satellite on his house 24/7." Olivia had been a self-taught computer genius, a skill set that'd been lost when I took over her identity. Fortunately, I had the resources of a casino heiress's fortune at my disposal, and could buy as much information from her illicit contacts as I needed. The word in the underground was the hacker known as the Archer had gotten lazy, but the rumor was somewhat muted by great, flowing—and seemingly endless—stacks of green bills.

Hunter shot me an arched look as he shut the car door.

"What?" I asked defensively in the sudden, vacuumlike silence.

He tilted his head back, ostensibly to study the wide sky outside his window. "Have you ever stopped to think   "

"Not if I can help it," I interrupted smartly, revving the engine. I already knew I wasn't going to like the end of this rhetorical question.

"—that the fantasy of something, or someone, is often more vivid than the reality?"

"No," I replied immediately, shifting into gear as I lifted my brows. "Have you?"

His mouth quirked, but he shrugged one shoulder so his black T-shirt stretched across his torso. "You could just let him go," he said, his voice unexpectedly soft.

I looked at him like he'd grown a second skull. "Let the man I've loved since I was a teen be corrupted and tainted by one of the most evil beings in the Las Vegas valley?"

"Let the man you love," he said, emphasizing the present tense, "make his own decisions."

I turned back to face the road. That was the stupidest idea I'd ever heard.

Hunter was too close, watching me too carefully, and he smelled too damned good to be trapped in a car with a woman who had extrasensory perception. This wouldn't normally be so unnerving—men looked closely at Olivia Archer all the time—but Hunter knew what tight emotions lived coiled beneath the Botox and boobs. He'd seen and, more importantly, *felt* the sharp nosedive my nature took whenever I truly lost my temper. Not only did he seem not to care, it appeared to interest him further. Twisted bastard.

"Look, you didn't know me then," I said, before he could offer me any more sage testosterone-driven advice. "And despite what you think, you don't know me now. Ben does."

And while attraction was one thing, true knowledge of a person was rare enough that it was still celebrated with elaborate ceremonies—a church, a woman in white, a walk down the aisle . . . and, in those instances, only one man waiting at the other end of it to receive her. One man was all I needed, wanted, or could handle.

Hunter sighed audibly beside me, and the accompanying scent was a lacy pattern of spice and smoke. "You really know nothing of a man's reaction to spurned love, do you?"

"And you do?" I shot back.

"I'm an expert."

The quiet rejoinder made me wish I'd said nothing, and I shifted uncomfortably. When your senses were so keen you could sharpen knives on them, when you could feel life pulsing from the plant life around you, and the heat retained in the concrete even after a winter's day, the desire radiating from a person you were forever yoked to with magical power was like licking sunshine.

I'd be lying if I said a part of me didn't want to inciner-ate myself in that fire, to see how far and deep the con-nection could go, and if a physical joining could compete with, or complete, the breath-stealing intimacy of shared souls. Another, stubborn part of me said that wasn't fair. If I'd been allowed to share Ben's thoughts, if pieces of his soul and psyche could've been caught and interwoven with mine, I knew I'd feel the same intensity—probably *more*—for him. Hunter and I had simply crossed a frontier that Ben could never reach.

We remained silent as I gunned it down Boulder Highway, swiveling onto the 95 without slowing to head downtown. The stench of Shadow activity was as easy to follow as if it was transmitted through my GPS, and though it'd been less than a year since my extrasensory abilities had fired to life, using them was as natural to me as moving from sleep into full consciousness.

"It's not him, you know," Hunter said, after a bit.

I thought about Ben, probably two-stepping with Regan right now, holding her in a light, practiced hold. I remembered the way his palms had molded to my own back, and could almost feel them there now. *Mine first. Mine always. Always mine.* "Yes it is," I said sadly.

"That she wants, I mean," Hunter said, and I glanced over to find him watching me with stark compassion. "It's you. She wants to get inside your head and injure your heart, and you're allowing it. She knows she's getting to you."

He was right. My weapon hand twitched even as I nodded. I fought regret for the opportunities I hadn't taken. I should've killed her five months ago when she'd first approached me as a Shadow initiate, and said she wanted to "help" me. I should've killed her once I discovered she knew who I was beneath the identity that was my safety and refuge and only remaining link to my dead sister. I should've slain her before she targeted my lover, using him to get to me. What I'd done instead was barter her life in exchange for information about the one person who, at the time, I'd have done anything to kill.

But he *was* dead now, and with nothing left to haggle with, Regan soon would be too. I swore it.

"Something else is causing the vibrational outbursts," I said, changing the subject as we took the off-ramp down Casino Center Drive.

"Something else?" he asked, and I told him what Regan had said in the bathroom. Yet there wasn't anything else in the paranormal realm—there were Shadows, there were

Light, and that was it—and Hunter said as much as we veered north. I shrugged, unable to answer, knowing only that Regan's surprise, and ultimate relief, had been real. Maybe Warren would know more when we found him.

I pulled to a stop in front of a street-side meter and switched from my impractical heels into a pair of black canvas boots with silent rubber soles, Velcro securing them tightly about my ankles. I'd have liked to change out of my black skirt and silk top, but there wasn't time, so I locked everything but my conduit in the car, then took the lead on foot. I'd been a freelance photographer before my metamorphosis into a superhero, and had logged more hours on Vegas's back streets than any other agent.

We slipped past the four-block stretch still remembered by locals as Glitter Gulch. Though having undergone an extensive facelift—including a canopy of light, a name change, and an exodus of most elements of urban decay— the Gulch would always be grittier and more infamous than its temptress sister, the Strip, and for that I was pleased. Long live the ninety-nine-cent shrimp cocktail.

For now, we strained to see beyond the canopy of neon and into the scarred landscape of an in-fill site, the still developing Union Park. The city had bought the railroad land that'd been Las Vegas's original link to the rest of the world, and while the ambitious multi-use development promised to revitalize this historic urban center, right now it was a sixty-one-acre cross-hatching of cranes and gigantic mounds of earth. And a stark black void had opened up directly above the skeleton of one promising high-rise hotel and casino. I didn't say anything about our new beard being located at what seemed to be the center of all that opaque darkness because Hunter's stiffening posture told me he was thinking the same.

A beard was a mortal who acted as a front for troop activities. Beards—or goats, as the Shadows referred to them—were given gifts, usually monetary, in exchange for allowing us to own their lives. Most thought we were a new crime organization, while others were sure we were government special ops. Interesting that there didn't seem to be any perceptible difference. Naturally, some beards figured out the truth and ran to the press with fantastic stories about superheroes and monsters battling for the soul of the city, but the stories never ran. When you had your thumb on the pulse of the entire valley, it was easy to intercept one frantic, babbling mortal.

The Shadows, of course, had no qualms about torturing and killing our human allies in an effort to ferret out our secrets, and seeing this unidentifiable black cloud so close to one of our beards' outposts worried me. Meanwhile, they flaunted their allies, knowing we wouldn't harm them. The most notorious of them? The man I'd once believed was my father, the seemingly untouchable casino magnate, Xavier Archer. I had to admit, the first time I'd heard the term *goat*, I'd laughed. The thought of a heavyset, thick-jowled billy goat wearing Armani cracked me up.

But I wasn't laughing as we slipped past the construction fence into the old rail yard. The black cavity above the steel scaffolding appeared even denser as we advanced into the construction zone. Even the sky looked dry-erased around and above its field. Yet the structure below appeared sound, and more, the explosive particles that tasted like microscopic tin arrows on my tongue seemed to be drawing closer, pinging off one another with each breath, as if desperate to re-form whatever object had been obliterated. I doubted anyone inside that bubble of darkness could see a foot in either direction, but I covered my face with my mask anyway. I wanted my Olivia identity protected in the event that the particle-charged sac burst.

"You sure this is it?" I asked Hunter when he halted in front of one of a dozen construction trailers circling the shell of the high-rise. It was hard to tell one nondescript building from another in the haze.

"I'm the one who set it up," Hunter replied coolly, angling his head back at the giant structure. "I did the research, scouted the location, picked our man, set him up as foreman. He's in charge of this project in the day, and at night maintains visual surveillance of the entire downtown area from the top floor of that structure. His name's Vincent Moore."

Gone was the man whose deep gaze and subtle flirtation had made me squirm. Equally absent was the one who'd taken cheap shots at the urban cowboys. In front of me stood our troop's weapons master, the man who lived and breathed hand combat, weaponeering, and all the arts of martial command that so perfectly aligned with an Aries' natural physicality.

Physical talents aside, however, Hunter's greatest weapon was his mind. Ever the tactician, he was constantly assessing and planning, and was more at home in a combat situation than in a La-Z-Boy. Like a general marshaling his forces, he called on everyone to be their best, and if you fell short—and I had on occasion—the silent rebuke was deafening. In short, Hunter was the hero we all wanted to be.

"So then where's the top floor?" I said, straining to see any sign of life in the pitch-topped tower. Now that we were closer, I could make out filmy veils of ionized air draping to the ground from the thick nucleus in the blackened sky. They were like black flags hung up to dry in uneven layers from the top of the two-hundred-foot scaffolding.

"It was blown to smithereens about ten minutes ago."

We turned to find a filthy, greasy, soured, and tattered man approaching. His hair was matted with dreadlocks, and an authentic limp had him swishing and swaying in horror movie mode. "I can't see him," I told Hunter, "but boy can I smell him."

Our troop leader stepped closer and his features sharpened, as if drawn by a coal pencil. His sun-slammed skin was muted in the dark, but brown eyes pinpointed us in beady assessment. He was dressed in secondhand fatigues and a tattered trench coat, his standard vagrant guise, and one that'd served him well. Mortals found him too frightening to approach, and the Shadows found him too repulsive to scrutinize. "Better?"

"Not particularly," I said, eyes watering. Olfactory acuteness was both a blessing and a curse.

"It's about to get worse," he said, motioning us away from the base of the building. Sharing a confused glance, Hunter and I followed.

"I'm assuming you mean the haze," Hunter said, as we sped up. Warren's leg injury had done nothing to slow him down. If so, he'd never have ascended to troop leader, much less remained there.

"And the situation. Our contact was up there just before the corporeal explosion. Top three stories fell like hotcakes. Indication is they have him imprisoned on the same level used to gain access."

We all glanced up, then diagonally to the crane that any enterprising Shadow could traverse. And they were all that. Shit.

"How many?" Hunter asked, meaning Shadows.

"At least four from the way they've managed to secure all lower-level passages. But my guess is more than half a dozen." Warren smiled then, and I had to shiver a little. The look was off-center, brittle, slightly whacked, and thin. Don't get me wrong, Warren was one of the good guys, but he was the leader of a troop of paranormal beings who got off on this sort of situation.

"An ambush then."

"Their largest yet."

The troop charged with the paranormal security and safety of the Las Vegas valley was huddled beneath an isolated hydraulic crane. The sheets of destroyed wave matter, presumably fallout from the explosion, hung around them in tatters on every side. In the right-hand corner we had a doctor, a reporter, an oversexed college student, and a reclusive psychic. In the left-hand corner there were a dental student, a taxi driver, and a high school teacher. They all turned as one to watch as a bum, a security guard, and a socialite joined to create the whole of Zodiac troop 175.

Or what remained of it, I thought wryly. The Zodiac chart had twelve signs, but our Pisces star sign had been murdered last year after our troop had been infiltrated by a mole working for the Shadows. Our Libra, I thought, with guilt, had died only last month. Their star signs had yet to be filled.

"Movement, Felix?" Warren asked, falling in beside him.

Felix jerked his head in the opposite direction of our approach. "I saw the Shadows' Gemini. She was headed to the top of the crane."

"Sure it was her?"

"Only Dawn can wear a leather corset and still manage to look that sweet."

"Yes, she's so sweet," Vanessa said acerbically. Her hair was pulled back in a haphazard knot, soft curls escaping to frame her honeyed face, and she'd thrown on a mask similar to mine in style, because her reporter's profile might be high enough to get her noticed by the Shadows. "I almost never want to put a foot through her chest cavity."

"Violent," commented Felix, brow quirked.

"Only when I see her."

"You mean smell her," said Riddick, wrinkling his nose as he sorted through his set of oversized carvers and picks, deciding at last on a palm-length bar with double-sided hooks. Hunter had designed the set especially for him, as he did all our weapons. Fitting for a dentist, I thought. His was the only weaponry that gave me the heebie-jeebies.

"Did she see you, Felix?" asked Warren, steering us back on track.

Felix shook his head, and his hair fell over his forehead. He was older than me by a few years, but had the look of a college freshman, and his smile attracted coeds like bees to honey. He enjoyed his cover more than any of us. "Don't think so. But they've gotta know we're coming."

We always came when mortal lives were threatened.

"All right, here's the plan."

As Warren outlined our attack formation, I glanced at Hunter and waited. Feeling my gaze on him, he shook his head imperceptibly, so I returned my attention to the grouping of our combat positions. I'd asked if we should tell Warren about Regan's reaction to the initial blast, and that the Shadows hadn't been responsible for the plague of explosions upsetting the vibrational matter of this reality prior to now. He was telling me to wait; this particular event *was* the work of the Shadows, and it was all we needed to occupy our minds now.

I agreed. Though new to the troop, I was no longer the least experienced star sign. Jewell and Riddick had joined the ranks after me, and though *they'd* been raised in the troop's sanctuary, trial by fire inspired martial proficiency in a way a textbook couldn't.

Plus Jewell hadn't initially been tagged for the Gemini sign. Her sister too had died last year, and she'd unexpectedly inherited the post, like Riddick. A teacher by day, she turned into the quintessential Vegas party girl at night. The Shadows, we thought, wouldn't look too closely at the girl walking around with stamps marring the back of her hand. As for Riddick . . . he was exceedingly fond of those dental tools. I shuddered again.

Warren finished explaining our groupings: three tight triangular formations staggered and designed to interlock if we had to fall back to defend. Warren would go first, leading point, and his voice was clipped and strong as he told us to "fucking focus," before disappearing.

We palmed, primed, and honed our weapons in silence until Felix said, "I can fuck and focus at the same time."

Jewell laughed as she disappeared to back Hunter and Riddick, but Vanessa and I traded eye rolls. From somewhere in the haze to our right came Tekla's caustic reply.

"We're all well aware of your sexual prowess, Felix. And that you wake every dawn in a different bed."

"Hey, I'm like a good breakfast cereal," he called back to our Seer, causing Micah and Gregor to shush him. He whispered, "I help the ladies get going in the morning."

"Snap, crackle, flop."

I snorted as we headed out. "Speaking from personal experience, Vanessa?"

"Not in this reality," she scoffed, and when she saw me glance her way, quickly added, "Or any other."

Hunter's voice bloomed to the left of me. "Hey noob, keep that tooth hook away from me."

"Sorry," came Riddick's reply. "The gas in the air is disorienting."

"Just another day at the office," said Felix, but even he sounded muted. I suddenly noticed they'd all fallen back. Realizing I was leading a flanged assault with no backup, I immediately backpedaled.

"That's not cool, you guys. You didn't—"

I was going to say they hadn't given me a warning to pull back, but that's when I realized they were all moving in slow motion, their limbs wheeling forward as if swimming in Jell-O, straining with the effort. Hunter was trying to motion them back, but it was taking too long. I did it for him, then dragged Vanessa backward until I felt a second gravity field release around her body. A coincidence that the gaseous sheets lessened upon retreat? I think not.

I'd managed to pull Riddick from the smoky quagmire before the other teams reached our rendezvous point.

"The air's too heavy. It's like breathing in foam," Micah said, gasping. At nearly seven feet tall, he was by far the largest member of our troop, and seemed to be having the most difficult time breathing, though everyone was panting hard. Everyone, that was, but me.

"I can see well enough," Tekla said, bending over so her thin frame was almost hidden in her soft gray salwar-kamiz. "But I can only go so far before it feels like I'm being smothered."

I looked at the others, and they each nodded. So we huddled in silence until Warren popped up next to Tekla, his footsteps muffled in the heavy air.

"The air repel you too?" Gregor asked him, as Hunter and Micah swiveled to guard our perimeter, close enough to hear our words. Warren nodded, rubbing at red-rimmed eyes, and I realized that was exactly the smoke's purpose. We weren't meant to reach the center, our beard, or the detonation's origin.

Back against mine, Micah broke into a hacking cough. Alarmed, I put my hand on his great shoulder, and he spat on the ground at our feet. It was black. "Shit. This stuff is toxic."

Warren straightened. "Let's try it again together. I think it's just a wall, and not one thick enough to be sustained for any depth."

I glanced back up at the tight black nucleus sitting atop the fractured building and bit my lip.

"One large phalanx might breach it, especially if we focus our energies on a sole entry point. So on my count. Go."

We marched like Spartans . . . for a few feet. Then the others slowed, molasses-limbed, eyes bulging along with their lungs. Despite the foreign environment, I was breathing easily. So while the smothered coughs and gasps continued to vibrate feebly at my back, I faced the heart of the smothering sheets and drew in a deep breath. Blackness sank past the porous barrier of my skin, filling my muscles, replacing the water hydrating them with a density that made me feel like an outcropping from the earth itself. I was granite, with petrified veins and a solid heart that didn't need oxygen because it didn't need to beat. The air coated my tongue like wet ash, lining my throat until my not-breathing allowed it to harden and bake in my marrow. The others—still filmy, floating, fleshy beings—fell behind.

I caught Warren's gaze, his eyes large and white above the coat sleeve covering his mouth. He motioned me back with his head, an achingly slow movement, and one I could see pained him. We fell back, and I waited until they all recovered. This time it took minutes.

"We have to pull out," Warren said, sucking in great mouthfuls of breath. "Get masks and breathing apparatuses of some sort."

Masks would crumble like wadded paper under the weight of this concrete matter, I thought, rubbing an arm that felt like marble beneath my touch. I told Warren this, and what the air felt like inside me as best I could, adding, "The Shadows will make it impossible to clean up if we wait much longer."

There was a grace period before the mortal world recognized paranormal influence, almost like the interference had time sliding off its tracks so that it needed to stop, back up, and redirect. This period was less than twelve hours, and we could usually clear up whatever mess the Shadows had made before then. After that, time stitched the veil between our two worlds into a new tapestry, and the best we could do was cover it up with excuses and reasonable explanations, and make sure as few humans were affected as possible.

"I'll go," I said quickly. "If you guys cover the perimeter I can make it to the center."

I took a testing step backward into the curtained mire, and Warren's eyes widened. I dodged even before he reached for me, because if I waited until I saw him move, it'd be too late.

"Dammit, Olivia! There's too many of them."

"Warren, listen to me." I was only a few feet away, but utterly alone in the heavy air. My voice sounded leaden, and I knew the rest of the troop was hearing it seconds after I actually spoke. "Micah's right. It is toxic, but not for me. I promise I won't take any unnecessary risks, and if there's even a chance of being ganged up on, I'll turn tail immediately."

There was silence in the lag time, and then I could hear

Micah reasoning it out. "It's a power that shouldn't be denied."

What he meant was that it was all right for me to use the power of the Shadow side as long as it benefited us. Tricky argument . . . and one that'd been a sticking point within the troop ever since my emergence.

"Listen to my voice," I added, knowing a part of what was motivating me was a need to prove myself. Still. "I can be up and back with our guy before they even know I'm there."

Because if *we* hadn't known I could do this, they wouldn't either. I was that unpredictable, that new. More silence, this time a full minute passing before I heard a resigned sigh. I'd begun feeling cut off in a rich web of oil, and was surprised to find the weight heavy and comfortable, almost peaceful.

"You retreat if even one of them spots you," came Warren's reluctant orders. "Use your intuition—don't wait for your glyph to begin glowing before heading back."

"I swear it," I said, not reminding him that my glyph—drawn in comic books as a large letter or symbol on a character's chest—might start smoking instead. Yes, I was both Shadow and Light. My troop, even my leader, could often ignore the implications of that. I was finding more and more that I could not.

"And if I pick up a manual next week to find you've done any different, I'll save the Tulpa the trouble and kill you myself."

Surely that was hyperbole, so I nodded as I silently headed back into the swirling fog. Besides, manuals—and the activity they reported in such bright and meticulous detail—were the least of my worries.

I lowered into a crouch, preparing to charge the base of the tower crane. The lack of air was blunting my senses. I could see as I vaulted off the concrete pad and onto the crane's mast, but it was with a mortal's gaze, and tasting the air was impossible with a leaden tongue. Sound was stamped out under the heavy black boot of this particular mushroom cloud, but so was scent. My pace on the crane's mast faltered when I realized how vulnerable all this made me.

But the Shadows were laboring under the same circumstances, right? I hit the top of the mast and began to make my way across the crane's long arm. I couldn't help but wonder if my Light side would make me slower or less able than them. Yet it hadn't so far. Indeed, my dual sides seemed to fuel each other, and why not? I was the Kairos, the only one who'd ever been *both,* and could draw on powers no one else could. So then why were nerves winging themselves around in my gut like butterflies trapped in netting?

I patted the extra crossbow bolts I'd clipped to my waist, pulled my conduit so I was holding it upright, and continued to climb.

3

The density of the airless space lessened the closer I got to the building, and without it bearing down on—and *in*—me, I felt like I was suspended in space. Peacefulness threatened to slip over me again . . . until I glanced down to find the glyph on my chest warming like the coil of an electric burner, the razor-slim outline of a bow and arrow appearing like a beacon in the blackened sky. Warren was going to be pissed, I thought, before the prospect of imminent death pushed the worry from my mind.

Remaining perched on the jib wasn't an option, and I couldn't turn around and show my back. Backing up like a tightrope walker would take too long, and while I could feasibly jump to the platform below this one, even a cat needed to spot the ground. I couldn't see shit, and didn't see the purpose of breaking a leg just to flee an unseen threat. I might not heal in time to actually run away. So I continued forward, leaping to the steel scaffolding in a noiseless jump.

I ducked behind a bright red vertical beam, and had just caught my breath when a hoarse, off-key voice sang out over the lifeless air. " 'You are my sunshine, my only sunshine . . . ' "

Now I wanted to jump.

"Tulpa," I whispered, then charged the largest platform, dead center of the unfinished building. Not safe,
but safer. I slipped halfway and ended up straddling the
beam, my pelvic bone smarting under the weight of my
fall. Jostling my conduit, I fumbled it like a second-
string quarterback, and ended up lunging to catch it,
my thighs clasped tightly around the steel. I ended up
upside-down, thankful I wasn't saddled with a man's
more fragile parts.

A chuckle joined the name—and me—still hanging in
the air. "That's me."

It *was* him, I thought, righting myself. His description,
his title, and his identity all rolled into one distinctly foreign word. A tulpa was an imagined entity, one wrought
into being by thought rather than birth. For centuries
Tibetan monks had practiced and perfected the skill
of creating thought-forms real enough that they could
influence the mortal realm, though the man who'd created
this tulpa had been a Westerner. An evil one.

Even when drawn from the most benevolent mind,
the creation of a tulpa was considered a dangerous
accomplishment. Wyatt Neelson's original intent was
to use the thought-being for personal gain. The Tulpa
couldn't be killed. It could be sent into the most dangerous
situations, deal with the most nefarious beings, and come
out unscathed. Yet the Tulpa didn't want to come out, and
he quickly grew tired of the evil mind that had created and
commanded him. Once he was actualized in the world, he
began exercising his own will and judgment, and in the
process, became even stronger and more wicked than his
creator.

In short, the dude has some powerful fucking juju.

"You caused the vibrational chaos." It wasn't a question,
but the way the air suddenly moved about me, whistling
across all the empty floors below, I knew he'd given me an
answering nod. It also gave me his approximate location. I

angled sideways, putting a second pallet between us. "And there's no one else here, is there?"

I didn't need to feel the air shift to know the girl in the smoke—the one Felix had been so sure was Dawn, the Shadow Gemini—had really been the Tulpa. Able to take the shape and form of anyone he chose, he'd been reacting to Felix's expectations. Like I said, powerful.

"Disappointed? I can call in some backup if you'd like."

And do it with nothing more than a thought. "No, no," I said airily, and quickly. "Let's just keep this between the two of us."

It wasn't necessarily an improvement, but what were my options?

"Good. Because I think it's time you and I cleared the air . . . daughter."

I have mentioned this depraved, wrathful thought-form was my birth father, right? And he just loved to rub it in.

I tensed as the gases cleared around us, and peered from behind the pallet to find his outline materializing across from me, a breeze rushing in to surround his body, slowly expanding to leave a clearing on the unstable platform. From below it must have looked like a light had been turned on across the entire floor, though we were still standing in the pitch of night.

The first time my father had appeared to me, he'd been in the guise of an old-school casino boss; the Tulpa as Godfather—bada-boom, bada-bing. The last time, however, he'd been featureless as he threatened me in the backseat of his personal stretch limo. Knowing that he took the physical form of a person's expectations, this unnerved me most. It might mean I hadn't made up my mind about someone who believed manslaughter was a good tactic in getting your own way. Of course, he could have also been fucking with me. People loved to do that when you were new to the paranormal playing field.

So it was with relief that I realized he was the one doing all the projecting here. There was no disguise to soften the demonic visage looming across from me, though he stopped short of letting me smell the rot of his soul, and the organs stewing inside. Even the monsters, it seemed, were vain.

But he didn't try to hide the arching bones angling his ears into high horns, or the ashen skin stretching from the hooknose and over his hairless skull, all the way to his spear-tipped crown. I'd had a glimpse of the long talons curving his hands into deadly points before, so they weren't as shocking as they otherwise would've been, but the ropy, veined spikes impaling his shoulders and spine made me shudder. I swallowed hard and said the only thing I could think of. "Please tell me I didn't get your overbite."

His twisted lips curved even further. "It's a mask, daughter. Rather like the one you're wearing, though with a dual purpose."

"You mean you're actually uglier than that?" Note to self: work harder on controlling Shadow side.

"This veneer enables me to breathe normally when the cosmic dust from the black hole crowds back in around us."

So it was a black hole . . . of sorts. That explained why the others had been unable to locate even a molecule of oxygen to suck on. However, it didn't explain why the Tulpa could control it at will. Or how. "What happens if you take your mask off?"

His responding smile pulled his cheeks into sharp triangles, and my pulse began to hammer as he lifted his hand. But even before he ripped his own face away—the mucus and straining muscles tearing like the innards of a pumpkin—my vision narrowed to a pinprick, tingling darkness closing in fast. The air departed so quickly, blackness rushed in like the first tide of a monsoon, burying me beneath its pressurized weight. It held me upright as it closed in on all sides, and I suddenly realized I was going to die that way. It pissed me off. And I never did get to see his face.

My only consolation was that he was dying as well. Maybe he'd pushed too hard and the weight of the world was preventing him from returning the mask to his face, but a shudder like a sonic boom ricocheted through the unfinished structure as he fell to his knees. Ah well, I thought sluggishly. Taking out the leader of the Shadow side wasn't a bad legacy to leave behind. Too bad the breath had been crushed out of me, trapping that taunt in my thoughts.

That's what you get, I thought, fading. *Show-off.*

Then sound flooded over me like my head had been plunged under water. The weight lifted, I fell to my knees, and the Tulpa's greedy gasps for breath sounded like the wind over mountain steppes and plateaus, whistling and harsh, and with a whipping force.

He hadn't been lying, I thought in wonder, as my vision cleared so I could watch him struggle to his feet. We were somehow connected; I breathed because he breathed. The implication would've had me wincing just moments before. Now I found it a relief. He couldn't kill me without committing suicide . . . at least not that way. It bolstered my confidence.

"Is this where you try to convince me to come to the Shadow side or die in an airless, soundless vacuum?" I asked, grasping my conduit between both hands. It still hung limply from my tingling fingertips, not that it mattered. The Tulpa couldn't be killed even with magical weaponry. No one knew exactly how to kill him yet . . . which helped make these confrontations all the more disconcerting.

"No, because then this would also be where you deny me. Again."

I stepped out from behind the pallet. It wasn't helping against the Tulpa anyway. "Wow. Psychic in addition to being evil incarnate."

"Flattery will get you nowhere." His eyes narrowed, "Fast."

But bravado was the only weapon I had left. Almost every time I'd met this fucker I'd ended up beaten, bloodied, and broken. But he wanted something this time, and it was clear he wouldn't kill me until he got it. So could I figure out how to kill him before that?

Yet I'd have to be careful not to project my intention, or expend any excess energy in doing so. The Tulpa had a way of prevailing over, and gaining power from, the people who tried to kill him. Like Yoda, there was no *try*. You either succeeded or failed, and so far . . . well, the Tulpa had just grown more and more powerful. He wasn't anyone's imaginary friend anymore . . . and he had a fuse as short as a third-world dictator.

"Sit down." He waited until I found an upended bucket before settling across from me. Even crouching, he was over five and a half feet tall. A fine mist draped his lower stomach, where I assumed he kept his valuables, and I found myself uncommonly grateful for his discretion. I let my gaze fall to his barbed toes and wondered if the name of my pedicurist would be enough to let me live. "We need to have a little talk about vibrational resonance."

"I forgot to bring my notebook."

"I'll give you the Cliff Notes version."

"Okay, but my tutor won't approve."

A growl rumbled through his body, and the platform shook beneath me. "It's time for the third sign of the Zodiac to come to pass. The first sign was the revelation of the Kairos—the chosen one—*my* daughter." There was a note of pride in his voice, but the multiple attempts on my life rather blunted the charm. "The second was a cursed battlefield, which you not only managed to survive, but brought most of your current troop through in fighting form."

His emphasis of the word *most* wasn't lost on me. I gave him a look he probably recognized from his own mirror, because he chuckled again.

"Which brings us to the third sign. The reawakening of the Kairos's Shadow side."

I held up a hand to stop him cold. "I don't believe that's what it means."

See, these signs of the Zodiac had nothing to do with the astrological wheel, as one might initially believe. No, the signs were *portents* instead, indications that one side in the fight between good and evil was finally gaining dominance over the other, and doing it with my help. So while my willingness to switch to the Shadow side was theoretically feasible—with the gift of free will and a serious breakdown in my personal mores—what the latest portent actually said was that the Kairos's *dormant* side would soon reawaken. I didn't know exactly what that meant, but I was pretty certain I wasn't going to start acting against humanity any time soon.

Obviously the Tulpa disagreed. "Our mythology tells us that under Pluto's influence the woman born of the Archer sign will have a death, a rebirth, and a transformation into that which she once would have killed. Even though she begins her journey with the spirit of a dilettante, her light is soon eclipsed and given weight. There is a descent into the underworld, and she will soon see the unseen."

"Day-um."

His face froze, registering nothing. I swallowed hard. "I'm ready to forgive your adolescent dalliance with the agents of Light and extend to you, once *again*," he said tightly, "the offer to reign at my right-hand side."

The side, in history and mythology, reserved for the second-in-command. He was speaking literally too. I'd seen it in the Shadow manuals. A solid gold throne elevated on a red-carpeted dais. But still an underling. Still under his thumb. I nodded thoughtfully, before stilling. "Screw your mythology."

He surprised me by looking amused. It stretched that graying skin in all the wrong directions, and I found I preferred his scowl. "This is your final chance to reconsider. Normally you'd get only one warning, but paternal duty obliges me to extend one last olive branch before wiping you from the face of the earth."

"My lineage is matriarchal, same as anyone else's . . . no matter who my father is."

I was prepared for him to lose it, readied for a battle cry to sound across the sky, and tensed for his attack. But he merely studied me with sunken eyes before abruptly steering from the topic. "I understand my new Cancer is targeting your old boyfriend. She was dogged even as an initiate, raised by the ward mothers to be as cold and scheming as her mother. Yet I could stop her with a word. I can save your mortal love. I can give you Regan . . . like I gave you Joaquin."

My heart was pounding, and it took all the control I had to keep my face impassive beneath my mask. I held my breath until I was sure my desperation wouldn't be sensed on the next exhale. "You didn't give Joaquin to me," I said, bitterness bright on the air as I led him away from the subject of Ben. If the Tulpa found out I still cared for him, he'd be dead within the hour. "I took him for myself."

"So take Regan as well. She can be yours . . . for a small price."

"You mean my soul?" I scoffed like I didn't care about Regan or what she was doing. Besides, one didn't need superhero senses to scent bullshit. "Regan DuPree can't take out a want ad without tripping over her own nonexistent dick. I can kill her at will . . . and do it without reverting to my Shadow side."

One brow quirked like a dart. "Not yet a full year as an agent, and already so sure of your skills?"

"Trial by fire speeds along the learning curve."

"Call me a skeptic, but I'd like a little demonstration."

And he finally moved, not to attack, but like a stage magician conjuring his latest, greatest illusion. A flip of his wrist, those talons whipping upward, and an inky ball bloomed over our heads. The nucleus was controlled, but it grew steadily, eating up the air again with as much efficiency as a vacuum cleaner.

A speck appeared in the center of the hole, growing larger within the limitless void.

"What is that?" I whispered, my mouth dry, as the object took shape, first as a luminous five-tipped star . . . then as a splayed-limbed human being. I gasped, and found myself with a mouthful of rancid vanilla, a flavor that always accompanied the compounded scent of torment and fear.

"You mean who," the Tulpa corrected conversationally. "That's the man who agreed to be used as a tool against me."

"Where—?" I couldn't finish. Where had he come from? The man was full-sized now, suspended above us and rotating slowly, still centered in the ever-expanding void. His face was fixed in a pained expression, and though he was spinning, the shirttails of his plaid flannel shirt didn't sway. It was as if he'd been frozen in a block of black ice.

"He's been here the whole time, dear. That's part of the mystery, the magic, of black holes. He's been watching you from beyond the event horizon, even as he inches toward its center."

"Let him go."

"I can't. What you're seeing now is only a product of the curvature of space-time. This was him an hour ago."

"You can, otherwise we wouldn't be having this conversation." I began shaking my head slowly, then faster, unable to tear my eyes away from the petrified, lost mortal. "He's an innocent. He only knew how to work surveillance equipment."

"Ah, but you knew. And you enlisted him. Engaged him. Endangered him."

And the mortal was paying for our—my—hubris. "Don't hurt him," I whispered, not knowing if I was telling him or asking.

The Tulpa's face cracked in a grin, and he waved his

hand in my direction, causing molding vanilla to wash over me again, but this time it was charged, zinging in the air, stabbing at my skin like rusty darts. He'd already hurt Vincent; I just wasn't seeing it yet.

But then something went wrong. Perhaps the surrounding steel acted as a magnet for the Tulpa's force, like a lightning rod beneath a blistered sky, but somehow the wires got crossed, and instead of merely sensing the residue of Vincent's pain, I found myself on my knees, writhing with it.

Electricity spindled inside me, driven on a spiked axis through the top of my skull, splitting in my center, and arrowing out of the soles of my feet. Bolts of pain fired from my spine to cauterize my nerve endings, and the scent of something flash-cooking reached my nose before the membrane was seared and all scent blunted. But none of that was as painful as when the invisible axis was suddenly removed, like a flanged drill bit ripping through my center and out my skull. Minutes passed in long, blissful silence. When I could finally open my eyes again, the black hole blocked the entire night sky.

"That . . . that . . ." That was all I could manage. My tongue was singed. If I lived through this I'd bear the scars inside.

"Hurt?"

I gained my feet and shook off the brindled energy unsteadily, like a dog flinging water from its coat. "Felt familiar."

"It should. It's your power, inverted."

My stomach dropped, and my knees actually buckled. Not more than a month ago a good deal of my power had been depleted in an electromagnetic maze. I'd survived it, barely, but there were abilities that'd been stripped from me and transferred to the maze's creator, the Tulpa. It was why he'd sent me in there to begin with, and now the power he'd gained was being used against me . . . and an innocent.

I looked back up at Vincent, a man who'd lived a blissfully normal life until approached to be our cover, and the only thing I could think as I watched his slow rotation was, *I'm sorry.*

"You can't save him, Joanna," the Tulpa said, misreading my look. "Your power is what put him there, and nothing can escape the gravitational pull of a black hole. Besides, energy cannot be divided against itself. An *agent*," he clarified, his words damning me, "cannot be divided against herself. You are Shadow, and the sooner you accept it, the sooner your weaknesses will become your strengths."

I shook my head, refusing to be damned. "That is not my power holding him there. I would never do that."

"You already have," he said airily. "The reason this man is pinned up here like a science experiment is because of your hatred for another named Joaquin. A man, too, named Liam. Ajax and Butch before them. So the facts would seem to contradict you, Joanna. You have no qualms in dealing out death when it serves your purposes . . . you also seem to have a particular fondness for edged weapons."

"I have a *fondness*," I said sharply, "for eradicating evil from this earth. This man is an innocent."

"No, this man is an object lesson!" And now his voice arched like a rocket, burning into space. "He's here to show you how your own powers can be used against you when you are divided against yourself."

I clenched my jaw, and the unnatural red cast tinting everything the black hole hadn't eaten up told me my eyes, long black, had begun to glow. "Let. Him. Go."

Smoke began to pool around us. "Make me."

Which was what he wanted. He needed me to act against him so he could secure that energy too—expand it, invert it, use it against me. But Vincent was still in agony; I knew it. His petrified expression looked as though it was pleading with me, his bulging eyes begging for help. I wanted to end his torture, but I didn't know if he wanted to live or die . . . or if I even had the power to give him that choice.

"Help," I whispered, the word suffocated and ineffectual on the roiling smoke.

The Tulpa heard it anyway, and laughed. "Prayers, is it? And still you refuse to raise a hand." He raised his own, talons beckoning as his laughter veered into a rumbling command. "Bend your knees and bow, Joanna. The only way to overcome is to succumb. Every person who has ever made a mark on this world had to first descend to the underworld."

I glanced around at the encroaching smoke, at the black hole above, felt the emptiness below, and realized the elaborate lengths he'd gone to draw me here. A scheme, I suddenly realized, revealing an obsession. He'd told me what would happen if I continue to refuse him. We'd become enemies. He'd hunt me down. There'd be a war. Actually, I thought, biting my lip, the term he'd used was *apocalypse*.

"You're not courting me," I said, returning my gaze to those soulless eyes. "You're targeting me."

The explosion had been to draw me here, the smoke a way to get me alone. The mortal wasn't targeted because he'd been a front for the Light, but because the Tulpa was going to make me choose. My life or his. Shadow or Light.

I sent up my prayer again, silent this time, forcing myself to look at Vincent. *Somebody help me.*

"I've lost my patience," the Tulpa said, now that the realization someone was going to leave here in a body bag was plain on my face. "You can either join me or perish. But the fence you've been straddling, this effort to best me, must cease. One way or another, I will stop these chaotic outbursts."

I did a mental double-take at his words. I knew my thoughts were coming slowly, the horror of seeing a man ripped from this world into the weightlessness of a minicosmos had made me sluggish, but this still seemed an abrupt change in subject. I studied the Tulpa and saw . . . well, nothing he didn't want me to see. But there was another component to his measured dialogue, an accompanying aromatic flag that had my eyes fluttering shut and my nostrils automatically flaring.

Fear.

My eyes shot open, and the Tulpa growled. What could possibly scare him so much he'd rather kill me than have me know it? And how could I get him to tell me what that something was without our little therapy session turning into a bloodbath?

"Make a decision," he said, vocal cords tight, brows pinched, mouth thin. "His life or yours. Shadow or Light. Now."

"You can't kill me this way," I said as smoke continued to roil in. The weight was returning to the air, but it was different from before, ashy but not ionized, thick but not dense. "Take off that mask and you'll suffocate too."

"Oh, this?" he said, waving his hand through the air so he cut it in ribbons. It formed again in a thin, gray film. "This isn't suffocation . . . it's insulation." And the lazy tendrils of smoke suddenly snapped like bands, congealing to form a barrier on all four sides so that I was in a solid box . . . and it was getting warm.

I looked up and found the sole means of escape. He hadn't tried to obscure the black hole.

"I was very lucky to find this building," the Tulpa said conversationally. "Anything other than steel would incinerate in this kind of heat."

Including me. Moisture was being pulled from my body so fast, I was sweating in places I didn't even know I had pores. I used my shirt to wipe at my eyes, but it felt paper-thin and hot, like it would burst into flame at any moment.

I glanced back at the Tulpa, who looked impossibly cool. "I, of course, can withstand this heat because of the protective shell I'm wearing. Not a mask, mind, but a swirling cloak of kairotic power."

My power, I thought as my organs began to ache.

"See, the vibrational matter you're so fond of manipulating can also be used against you . . ."

Still going on about the chaotic outbursts, I thought, tilting my head. It was getting hard to think—it felt like I was standing inside an oven—but it wasn't any great mental leap to measure it against Regan's earlier words. They thought we were responsible for the recent spate of vibrational outbursts. He thought *I* was. "It's not me," I told him, but he was on a roll and not listening.

"And like any vibration," he explained as if he actually possessed patience, "the high crests and deep troughs create waves of radiation in a confined interior."

Oh my God. Not an oven. A microwave. "But it's—"

"Generated by heat and light." He cut me off, smiling scathingly. "Faster, hotter, shorter . . . like a boiling ocean tide." I gasped as he made that happen now, but the air was sucked from me. He growled his satisfaction. "Well, you're the one who said 'trial by fire.' "

My body screamed for cool air and water and escape, and damned if that black hole wasn't looking good. He wanted that too. Me to either jump into oblivion, or choose him. If I did the latter, I thought, a swallow catching in my dry throat, I'd have to let Vincent drift away in a slow death to cement that choice. "Look, someone else is causing the vibrational outbursts."

"Bullshit!" He spat and his eyes sparked red.

"I don't know how to manipulate matter!" That was it; my voice was gone, drier than dust, and fatigue began to smother me. There was no more sweat.

"Your scent is all over it, Joanna! I want you to dismantle her energy, and maybe then I'll consider sparing your life."

"Her?" I croaked.

He growled, and I cooked.

I struggled past the *literal* heartache, past my desire to rip my mask and clothing from my body, to rend my very skin from my bones if it meant relief, and focused all my remaining energy into building a cocoon around me, constructing a place inside this inferno where I could safely disappear. But as my walls began to shimmer, a mocking look passed over the Tulpa's face, and I knew the big, bad wolf didn't even need to puff to blow my house down.

"You'd trade my life for the destruction of . . ." I pretended to falter, waiting for him to fill in the blank. At best I could relay the information to the rest of the troop later. At worst I'd know what I'd died for.

But the Tulpa wasn't in a helpful mood. "I'm not offering a trade. I'm telling you to come with me and begin the systematic breakdown of the double-walker—"

"The wha—?"

"Or make yourself comfortable."

Think, Jo, Think or fry. "But it's not—"

"Liar!" He didn't even let me finish, and his red eyes gained heat, twin coals fired by unyielding fury. I knew how that felt, the blinding anger fueling that gaze, so I also knew he was past reason. Heat soared, burning and agonizing, and my litany of prayers dissipated until only one word remained. *Please, please, please . . .*

"Break down the double-walker!"

My mouth was so parched I had to be spitting ash. I tried to speak again and choked. My sandpaper tongue was expanding in my mouth. My organs shriveled inside me. "Don't know how—"

"I do." And with those two words, air rushed over me, lifting sweaty strands of hair from my neck as two hands clamped down over mine. Relief was immediate, like I'd cannonballed into a cold plunge pool.

I sucked in a delicious breath, as deep and thorough as I dared, then did it again. On my next inhalation, I glanced up to find that the Tulpa was no longer fixed on me. I twisted to follow his gaze, and discovered a surprisingly slight woman just behind me.

She was short, barely five feet tall, and so pale her skin sparked off itself, causing her to glow with a soft radiance.

If she was wearing clothing it was spandex-tight, merely rounding out her curves and muting her sex like a naked Barbie. Her hair swung down her back, snapping in effervescent waves, and I watched as a droplet fell to the floor, where it reflected the light blazing from the Tulpa's eyes before it sizzled and was gone.

Behind me the Tulpa roared. "Break it down!"

The woman smiled . . . with sparkling spiked teeth. "I have a better idea."

And though she looked too fragile to resist a blown kiss, much less the Tulpa's anger, she effortlessly scooped me up at the waist, her translucent, shiny fingers winnowing their way down to my ankles. I was so disoriented—and so relieved to no longer be cooking from the inside out—it took me a moment to realize I was floating. "Shit—wait!"

The Tulpa protested too. "You can't—!"

"Just did." Her voice, like her hair, was effervescent and snapping sharp, the syllables of her words running together in churning ripples to reverberate off one another.

"It's a law!"

"Meant to be broken." She waved the Tulpa away, and flashed those pointed teeth again, more pearl than white. She glanced up to find me watching. "Come. We must hurry."

"The mortal—" I began, flailing as she shifted her feet.

"—is already dead." She was studying the distance between the floor and the top of my head, and said it without emotion. "The Tulpa is animating him with residual energy."

"It's an illusion?" I took my eyes off her long enough to gaze up at Vincent again. He was still rotating slowly, drifting closer to the center of the black hole, but too far removed now for me to make out the expression on his frozen face.

"Yes, but the heat melting this building is not. Let's go." I'd floated higher, and she pulled me beneath the center of the black hole, straight-armed, like I was a kite. Wait a minute . . .

The Tulpa objected as well. "You can't shield her forever!"

"Don't need to," she muttered, almost sounding bored. She grabbed my other ankle, steadying me, the coolness from her palms spreading through my body, though I knew it was unbearably hot. Even the steel beams looked to be sweating. "Creating and sustaining a black hole burns a massive amount of fuel. You're running out of energy at an alarming rate, am I right? Besides, I could just take her back to Midheaven with me. You'll never touch her there."

I didn't think it was possible for the Tulpa to blanch, but he did, and wondering what, and where, Midheaven was, I looked up.

That's how I saw Vincent's body suddenly stretch like spaghetti, his head whipping back in a sharp centrifugal swirl. For a moment I thought the rest of him would follow, but people weren't meant to enter black holes, and in the next instant his body was rent by the tides of gravitational force, snapping, dissipating, destroyed so thoroughly, it was as if he'd never been. I swallowed down a scream. The woman and the Tulpa seemed not to notice.

"Now scoot along, tulpa," And she said his name like she would say *cat* or *dog*, like he was a thing and not a person. The black hole wobbled in the sky, and the Tulpa let out an infuriated but hollow yell.

The woman turned her back on him and whispered to me, "Are you ready for this?"

"No, no, no!" I said, suddenly panicked, knowing what she was thinking. "I was never good at science, but I know if you get too close to a black hole, there's no escaping it. So maybe we can talk about fighting or shooting our way out of here instead. I-I'm really good at that."

"Okay, shooting. We'll do that." She turned her wicked grin on me. "I'll be the propulsion. You're the rocket."

And she bent her shimmering knees and shot into the air with an explosion to match the Tulpa's initial blast. I—we, because the woman was still anchored to me—shot past him so fast, he was still staring at the spot where we'd been standing, and the vertebrae in my neck cracked with the pressure of our ascent. There was a sucking sound, the breach and subsequent burst of the black hole disintegrating behind me, and then we were free, darting through the crisp night, Vegas spread below us like a hard, glittering pool. Wind whipped my hair and whistled in my ears, and through the weight of the night air I could hear the woman screaming delightedly behind me. At least someone was having fun.

And then, as we slowed to an apex, the Tulpa's words revisited me. Glancing down, I realized what basic universal law this woman had broken.

Gravity, I thought frantically, and immediately began falling.

4

The great planets revolving around our sun are subject to the same basic law that had an apple thrumming Newton on his brilliant beaner. We—an iridescent woman who scoffed at the Tulpa's empowered rage, and me—had broken that law, and while I was sure there'd be cosmic hell to pay for the breach, I was hoping it wouldn't be due until well *after* we'd landed.

And yet I couldn't help but be awed. Supernaturals could jump—damned high too—but we couldn't fly. Outside of a steel bird, I'd never seen the entire town spread below me like a bright LEGOLAND replica, and my cannonball shot over its center made me feel momentarily possessive of everything below me, and unreasonably proud. The city's peace in the clear, cool night put me in mind of a snow globe at rest, all the glitter and sparkle winking up at me from the earth's floor, as if the world's orderliness depended only on perspective. Wind rippled in my mouth as I smiled back . . . and then, with only a hundred feet left between the ground and me, that bitch let go.

Fifty feet, thirty feet—the descent more dizzying than the initial blast—I felt my hair fluttering like a banner behind me as I streaked toward hard earth. I acclimated

myself enough to know where we were heading—a swath
of dirt outside the old rail yard's fence—but that wasn't my
most pressing interest. As the ground rushed up at me, the
speed had my once-mortal instincts recoiling. I pinwheeled
in the air, anticipating the crash, wondering if bent knees,
proper form, and superhuman healing was enough to get
me out of this one, and so the movement spied from the
corner of my eye barely registered.

It was the woman, or possibly just part of her, slipping
beneath me to break my fall like a trampoline. I spotted
the nucleus of a glimmering sheet of . . . well, *something*,
and trying not to think too hard about what that something
was, I landed as hard as I expected . . . right into its pil-
lowing middle. It shot me back up, dangerously high, so I
endeavored to return to its middle upon each subsequent
bounce, and when I was bounding only as high as a single-
story building, it disappeared entirely, so that I landed in
a bone-jolting crouch on the gritty earth. When I looked
up, the pale pearl of a woman, still ethereal and pretty and
radiant as an opal, was standing beside me.

I opened my mouth, but she cut me off with one word.
"Portal."

So we weren't out of danger yet. My mouth snapped
shut, and I followed her back into the tight weave of city
blocks, both of us canvassing the doorways and windows
for a small, variable star. I watched her sail along in front
of me, knowing I should think of something intelligent to
ask or say, but she didn't seem inclined to talk until we
were well away from the Tulpa, and that was fine with me.
My insides were still raw and bruised and burned.

Lately I'd been trying to avoid using the portals. I'd last
accessed one during a training session where we were at-
tempting to spot false entries, which we'd discovered had
been set around the city like mousetraps to ensnare us until
the Shadows could check them, and kill us. Although it'd
been daylight on this side of the portal, the sun had flipped
around on itself on the other side of that supernatural gate-

way, and I walked into a replica of the street I'd left, but for the darkness blanketing the earth while the heavens were spotlit by the sun. The alternate reality was colorless, with a silver-gray haze reducing everything to a shadowy line drawing. It had also been bitingly cold . . . unbearable to a desert rat like myself, and the whole experience had totally creeped me out.

Yet I was the one who spotted our first portal marker positioned above a planked-over window, and I veered to it. I'd already ripped the wood from the casing when I felt the woman's cold hand on my back, causing me to jolt. It reminded me of that alternate reality, and I shuddered.

"Not this one," she said, her phosphorescent features shifting with eerie undulations, like breath over the surface of a bubble that wouldn't break. "Too close."

I wasn't sure why that mattered, as no one could follow once the portal closed behind us, but she was already moving away, so I followed. Maybe she was a part of that reality, I thought as I hurried to keep up, because her touch—never mind her look—wasn't human. And maybe she'd been in the threshold of a nearby portal when she heard my frantic prayer, fighting boundaries and barriers to come to my rescue. I couldn't imagine how many laws *that* would be breaking.

"Need to get back immediately?" she asked, whirling on me suddenly. I backed up two paces, nodding. Warren and the others would be worried. She inclined her head like she'd expected that and turned away, motioning for me to follow again. Normally I didn't do passive, but after my rescue I was inclined to let her take the lead.

"Thank you," I blurted out, speed walking to keep pace as the image of Vincent roiling helplessly in space replayed itself in my mind. "It's not enough, but I don't know what else to say. You saved me, you outplayed the Tulpa. I've never seen a black hole before, so I wouldn't know how to escape it . . . and how'd you do that flying—?"

"Dear, you're babbling." Shimmering, she cut me off with a slanted look, and I took a deep breath, not caring if she could scent my relief, my shock, and my exhaustion on the exhale. One side of her gleaming mouth quirked, but she kept those sharp teeth hidden as she jerked her head to the left.

"Sorry. I've never been rescued by an angel before," I said, as I sniffed at the air. Warren left a trail like a skunk . . . deliberately, though. He knew I'd recognize it and head in his direction, and right now it smelled like he'd moved to the nearby outlet mall where he liked to window shop after a long day of panhandling. I started that way, but paused when the woman doubled over in her tracks. Laughter caused her to literally froth at the mouth, spume also slinging from the ends of her constantly rejuvenating hair with every jerk of her tiny body.

I smiled uncertainly, then ducked my head as she motioned for me to keep heading forward, though I remained aware of her behind me—the angle of her body, the pressure of that cold palm on my back again—as we hiked along Charleston Boulevard. I thought about blowing a breath in the direction of the shops to let the troop know I was coming, but didn't in case the Tulpa was still in the vicinity.

"Who are you?" I said, when the woman had finally sobered. She was still smiling, those teeth like dazzling white stones, her marble eyes catching the streetlights to dance.

"Do I look like a 'who' to you?" She glanced away as she scoffed, then did a double-take at a run-down auto shop. "Oh, look," she said casually. "There's our portal."

I glanced at the dilapidated building, seeing nothing but chipped paint, rusting roll-doors, and a pile of stripped tires breeding black widows in the side lot. "I'm sorry. I don't know what you're talking about."

"Between the fence and the paint booth," she said, nudging me closer. "Soften your gaze."

I stared again at the auto shop, letting everything at the forefront of my visual perception blur. Then, like a lighter being flicked, a canary yellow portal popped out at me from over the glass door. After a moment, however, it slowly bled over into a deepening burgundy. The woman moved closer when I gasped in surprise. "What's wrong with it?"

"Nothing. Why?"

"It's just . . . I've never seen one turn that color before," I said, gaze lingering on it before I turned fully to face her. "I thought they all looked like tiny stars."

Under the spotlight of the streetlamp, I could see her hair beading, constantly re-forming at the root, sliding down the shaft in effervescent droplets, and fracturing at the tips to keep it blunted below her glistening shoulders. More surprising, however, were her eyes. They lacked irises or even a tint of color; pure orbs as white as carved out pearls, though brightly alive. She returned my intent look, almost as if drinking me in, and I drew back a bit, reminding myself that while beautiful, as well as my rescuer, she was also extremely powerful.

"It's fine," she said, her lips repositioning themselves on her face as she smiled at me. It wasn't just her expression altering, I realized. It was her whole face, constantly forming and re-forming. "Come."

I hesitated. If there was one thing I'd found in my short time with the troop, it was that limitations were placed on us for a reason. We learned of things when we were meant to, and too much knowledge could skew one's actions in the same way going to a psychic could alter mortal behavior. I bit my lip, not wanting to offend her—*owing* her—but not wanting to go somewhere my troop leader couldn't find me. She smiled, noting my reluctance.

"Just a quick peek," she encouraged, hand again guiding my back. But this time it chilled to the spine.

I angled away from her touch. "Why would you want me to look inside there?"

"Because I want to help you." Now she gripped my arm. "The Tulpa was right about the fallout of disjoined energy. A person cannot be divided against herself."

And anyone who thought the Tulpa was right needed to not be touching me.

"No, thank you." I placed my hand over hers and firmly pulled it away. She didn't resist, just angled her head so a gossamer glob dropped from her hair. "I should get back. My troop will be worried."

"Your troop, is it?" Her beautiful laugh turned brittle when she saw my mind was made up, and she pointed to my face with one disconcertingly honed fingernail. "My goodness, is that a mask or blinders that you're wearing? Either way, it works brilliantly."

But peer pressure did not. I squared on her and put some distance between us. "Why did you save me from the Tulpa?"

"Now you're asking the right questions." But the edge in her voice reminded me of steep cliffs, sharp rocks, and divers poised tenuously on the edge. She was going somewhere with this, and I wasn't sure I wanted to follow there either. "Well, obviously it wasn't out of the goodness of my heart."

And she crossed her heart in a playground promise, those razor-sharp nails cleaving layer after radiant layer of glistening skin to reveal a gaping cavity where there should've been organs.

"No heart," I whispered, half to myself. She was like a balloon twisted into shape by a circus clown, with only a translucent outline to define her as a woman. Horrified, I glanced back up into her face. Now I knew what her sparkling achromatic eyes were swirling with. Air. What I didn't know—and what suddenly bothered me all the more—was why her teeth were so sharp.

She tilted her head, the innocent movement clashing strongly with the severed chest and that razored grin. "I thought maybe you'd let me borrow yours."

I was already backing away, so when she lunged I tripped over an abandoned crate, which was all that saved me from a vertical autopsy. The first swipe of those ice-hook claws took a chunk from my left breast, but I dodged the second. She shot forward and secured one bony hand around my throat, and I scrabbled at those tensile, opalescent fingers as her other palm fell again to my chest, firing my glyph, too close to its target. Her fingers dug in and I head-butted her, causing both her hands to loosen. I got one more in before her frigid hand clawed onto my shoulder again.

"The spirit of the Kairos shouldn't be shackled to a body with damaged *chi*," she snarled, and returned my head butt, sending shards of icy white light firing through my skull. Then she dragged me toward the portal. I scrambled, digging in my heels, the nonslip soles catching until she leveled one of hers down on top of my left foot. She was as strong as I was, but suppler, bending and reshaping to form in front of me or beside me or behind me at will. I struggled harder against her fluid grip, now positive I really did not want to go through that supernatural doorway.

Still, she was making slow and steady headway, and so focused was I on the bloodred portal that the cold sprawl of that homicidal hand crawling over my face was a complete surprise. "Time to remove the blinders, Kairos."

And she did what no one else had been able to before. She yanked my mask from my head so the straps tore at my earlobes, threw it to the ground, and drank in my Olivia identity, my most prized secret. I drove my left elbow straight up and connected with her chin, though it immediately shifted. Judging the number of steps and direction the blow would send her, I sent a flying kick to await her there. But she didn't show up. The next thing I felt was her knee connecting with my already bruised kidney from behind.

Well, she had me bested there, I thought as I crumpled to the ground. I couldn't very well return the favor when she didn't have any organs.

When she could dissipate like smoke only to reappear behind you . . .

No, I thought, balling up as she flipped me over. Nobody could do that. I just hadn't been seeing clearly.

But I was seeing clearly now, and her whole body was shining and ethereal and luminescent as she straddled me. "Divided energy, Joanna. Divided looks . . . and a divided heart, no?"

I swung my legs up behind her to link them beneath her arms and propel her to her back.

The scent reached me first, more of my blood being spilled, though pain came close on its heels, an eruption of nerve endings telling me something had just destroyed my spleen. I squeezed my eyes shut, arching backward as sound gurgled in my throat. I was on my back again, and this time she dropped her knees to my shoulders, pinning me, closing the distance between us.

"You asked why I saved you from the Tulpa." The froth bubbling up in her voice wasn't as enticing now. She nudged my chin and waited until I could look at her. "It was for one reason only, Joanna. You're the real target in both my worlds. You're the Alpha and Omega of the spectral plane. You, my dear, are the golden ring."

"And let me guess," leveled a voice from behind me. "A pretty lady like you likes your baubles."

A light flared through the rent in her chest and I had a moment to think, *Glyph*, though before I could identify it, her weight was gone, layer after layer of her morphing into flight, breaking laws with bubbles, delicately straddling worlds. Those in my troop who had projectile weapons fired them into the night sky. Hunter's whip coiled up in a resounding snap, but caught nothing but disturbed air. My glyph died on my chest, but the pain was still coming in regular, if less intense, waves. When I looked up, Felix was looming over my head.

"Dude," he said, boyish face implacable. "I totally thought you were going to throw a seven."

Hunter punched him in the arm as I struggled to my knees. "Good to see you too, Felix," I grunted.

Micah put his arm around me and lifted me to my feet. Grateful, I leaned into him. "No injuries? No permanent damage?"

"I might need a new boob job . . . and I think my spleen's missing." God, it would suck if that sharp-nailed, no-organ bitch had taken off with my spleen.

"Who, or what, was that?" Vanessa asked, handing me my mask.

"Oh that." I waved my hand and mask in the air, still unable to straighten fully. "That was the lady who saved me from the Tulpa's giant microwave, only to try and eat my heart with her spiked teeth. She's impervious to the law of gravity"— *I think she dissipated and reappeared behind me*—"and she wanted to show me what was on the other side of that bloody portal."

I jerked my head in the direction of the fixed star, proud of myself for how calm I sounded about the whole thing. So why were the others gaping at me with expressions of disbelief? All except Warren.

"What was she wearing?" he wanted to know. That was Warren, always picking up on the important stuff.

I rolled my eyes. "Nothing that I could see. Maybe a bodysuit, but it was made out of the same material as her skin."

"Which was?" he prompted, like he knew there was more.

"Bubbles." I winced at how stupid that sounded and amended my statement. "Maybe bubbles. Maybe Saran Wrap, I don't know. It was hard to tell. Ouch." I doubled up again.

Warren began mumbling to himself, his homeless mien taking on an authentic aspect, before his head snapped back my way. "Tell me what happened again, from the time you first saw her to the moment we scared her away. Don't leave anything out."

So leaning against the greasy auto shop fence, I re-counted everything I could about Vincent's death, our gravity-defying escape, and the way the woman made a point of bringing me to this portal. My chest was still on fire when I finished, but my breathing was even again, my glyph had faded, and the pain in my side was gone. Maybe I'd kept my spleen after all.

Warren grimaced, turning his sun-baked features into craggy ridges. "So she could have removed you from this plane earlier, but chose to bring you here first."

"And I bet that's the reason why," Tekla said, jerking her head at the star shining like a ruby above the doorway.

I glanced from Warren, clearly disturbed, to Tekla, who only appeared resigned. Then I noticed the others were doing the same, curiosity as bold as question marks on their face. The whole troop, I realized, was seeing a colored portal for the very first time. And Micah—the most senior troop member next to Warren and Tekla—was studying it fervently.

"What is it?" I asked, able to straighten now.

Warren didn't answer, turning away, running his hands over his head, but Tekla sighed heavily, her large eyes like dark globes in her thin face. "It's a breach into the other reality. It's the cause of all our vibrational chaos."

"Which means?" Riddick prompted as he scratched his goatee.

"It means we've found the cause of the elemental out-bursts." Warren whirled again, rubbing at the back of his neck. "This woman, this being—"

"The Tulpa called her a double-walker," I offered.

Tekla and Warren looked at each other. "This double-walker," he said evenly. "She's been tearing holes in the fabric of our reality instead of using the portals. There have to be a half dozen of them."

"You mean that's not a portal?"

Warren shook his head. "It's an open wound."

Limping forward to get a better look, I was breathing normally by the time I reached the shop's door. My side had closed up too, which was a great relief. I wouldn't die, at least not today.

Up close, it was easy to see why Warren called it a wound. The portal's blazing light was as steady as any other, brilliant but for the deep red sheen that continually ran over its surface, like blood dripping, though it never fell. Yet the outline was less starlike the closer one drew, its edges jagged as though ripped. I reached up . . .

"Olivia! No!"

And gently rubbed a fingertip over the star.

Tekla was there, slapping my hand away . . . too late. A crack sounded as the star clamped down over my hand like a Venus flytrap, and my fingertips immediately went numb, dozens of stinging barbs puncturing the printless pads. An acute and tortured scream echoed across the parking lot. Then, just as abruptly, the tiny star released me, and all five points curled in on themselves, a fundamentally protective gesture.

We all stared questioningly at Warren, clueless superheroes, down to the last.

Warren looked like he wanted to scream as well, but instead blew out a breath and leveled a maddened look at me. "Okay, so this is the point where I tell you all not to peel off the scabs of the wounded reality."

"No," Tekla corrected sharply. "We passed that point about a minute ago."

Warren shot her an equally livid glare . . . and another at me.

Ew, I thought, glancing back. Was that what I'd done? "Sorry," I muttered, to him and the Universe.

"Why can't we touch it?"

"You said there are others?"

"What's a double-walker?"

"Well, that perked them right up," Tekla said, walking away.

Warren sighed again, then looked off into the sky as if the answers to all our questions were written there. "Come on, then."

"Where to?"

"Someplace safe." And as he began limping away, I thought I heard him add, "With lots of alcohol."

5

We reconvened at the Downtown Cocktail Lounge on Fremont Street, a touchstone in Vegas's emerging entertainment district that was helping turn the promised downtown revitalization into less of a long-standing joke. The surprising thing about DCL was its refusal to cater to tourists. With a dim interior, low-key vibe, and not one overpaid celebutante or slot machine in sight, everything about it screamed "locals' bar" . . . including the hidden front door.

However, watching tourists scratch their heads as they tried to find their way in was only part of the location's appeal. It was also a newly designated safe zone, which explained why we were meeting there. We couldn't be ambushed by Shadow agents in a safe zone—or tulpas or hopefully bubble beings—so they were good places to while away the hours between dawn and dusk. It was only in the fractional seconds of the sun and moon's momentary truce that we could cross over into the safety of a true alternate reality, and not merely the flip side of this one.

There was also no better place to gather than one that served stiff cocktails and funky world beats via the DJ's laptop 24/7. That too kept the children away. Warren put his hand in the air to call over the waitress as we settled ourselves around the large communal table. We spoke of nothing in particular until drinks were served, at which point I sucked down half the tonic-laced vodka before telling the others about the mask connecting me with the Tulpa, how it'd enabled us both to breathe beneath the massive weight of the black hole, and how his anger had been tinged with fright for the woman who bent gravity to her will.

Micah tilted his head, his analytical and scientific mind clearly whirring. As our troop's Seer, Tekla was as sharp as they came, but even she looked perplexed. However, Warren, who'd taken time to change and shower so the DCL employees didn't move the hidden door entirely upon his approach, perked up at this. "Olivia, I need you to think. Can you tell me what this being smelled like?"

"Sure," I said, and closed my eyes to strengthen the memory. My sense of smell had dramatically improved with my metamorphosis at the age of twenty-five into something superhuman . . . but it hadn't stopped after that. Experience and applied practice had increased my ability to distinguish textures and patterns in the delicate dance of air molecules, and I was developing a better language and vocabulary to describe sensory nuance.

My encounter with the woman was still fresh, so I easily picked apart the medley forming her essential scent. Despite the frightening encounter, it was a pleasure, for once, to dissect something not reeking of rot and decay. "The top note was herbal, like fresh-cut chives or sweet green onion, but lightly so, as if dug up too early. She was empty inside, so maybe that's why it's not more potent, like the scent could disappear with a puff of breath . . ." I trailed off, thinking of dandelion spores drifting in the wind, but didn't say it. She wasn't human, and so her genetic makeup would be different, but I had a hard time thinking of it as insubstantial. She'd clawed at me with sickle-sharp nails. She had substance . . . but what was it?

"And the heart note?" Warren pressed.

The most important and telling scent, that of her soul.

I frowned, trying to pinpoint it, but shook my head after a minute. It just wasn't there. "It's like a big white space in my mind. I can't even locate the aromatic clues."

Warren remained silent for so long, both looking at me and not, that I started to think he didn't believe me.

"What was she, Warren?" Jewell asked, twirling around a strand of soft brown hair in one delicate hand. She was so silent I often forgot she was there, and I knew she felt out of her element, like she'd come so late to her star sign that she'd never catch up. But what she lacked in natural talent, she made up for in perseverance. The confidence needed to back it up would come with experience.

"Isn't it clear?" Riddick, also new to his sign but lacking Jewell's reticence, tapped his fingers on the polished tabletops. Light from the red votive candles made his smooth fingertips shine. "It's the double-walker the Tulpa was talking about. The one he wanted Olivia to destroy."

Nice to know he—and the Tulpa—had such faith in me, I thought as I gingerly fingered the claw marks still scoring my chest. It was both itchy and sensitive to the touch, and my palm felt wonderfully cool against the wounded flesh. I stilled my fingers when I realized Hunter was watching, but every other head was turned toward Warren.

"So what's a double-walker?" Vanessa asked, reading my mind. "Someone who can walk freely on both sides of reality?"

"A logical conclusion," Warren answered, absently swirling his glass. "But no. Its more common name is doppelgänger. Do any of you know what that is?"

"It sounds German."

Vanessa arched a brow at Felix. "Got something against the Germans?"

"Well, the umlaut thing is kind of annoying."

"Can we please focus here?" Warren muttered, stirring his whiskey.

"Don't be shallow," Riddick told Felix. "I love the Germans."

"You're an American who's never even left this city, much less the country," Felix countered. "What do you even know about the Germans?"

"I know they're not French."

"Focus!" Warren's yell silenced the whole lounge. Even the DJ's beat seemed to momentarily pause. Riddick had the sense to look abashed, and the rest of us averted our eyes, but Felix—no stranger to his leader's admonitions—only sipped at his rummed-up Coke.

"Okay, geez. Double-walker, doppelgänger . . . no clue. Enlighten me."

"A doppelgänger," Micah informed us, "is a living person's ghostly twin. Usually evil."

They all looked at me.

I choked on my drink. "Who, me? A double of me? No way—that thing didn't look anything like . . . either one of mes."

Though not everyone knew I was Joanna Archer beneath Olivia's glossy exterior, they did know I wasn't the ditzy socialite I presented to the rest of the world. With them I was the Kairos, purported savior of the paranormal realm, steadfast troop member, with a sharp demeanor and acid tongue to match. Basically I was myself . . . but cuter.

"No, but it smelled like you." Warren smiled grimly. "As a double, it's still shaping, taking its clues from studying you." I recalled how hungrily the woman had watched me, and how she could form and re-form at will. "The more impatient doubles, those most greedy for life, have been known to attack their living counterparts."

I nodded wryly. "You mean eating my heart would be a good way to more fully materialize in the physical world."

He shrugged. "In short."

Great. So I had two strong, evil, ethereal beings after me. I signaled the waitress for another drink.

Sitting with her hands folded in her lap, Tekla took up the lecture. "Most doppelgängers aren't this strong. Their sphere of influence is limited to causing confusion in their double's life—appearing to family and friends, haunting their double, mimicking them, or at best giving bad advice. They're the paranormal equivalent of a knock-knock joke."

"Well, anyone who thinks that thing is funny didn't stick around for the punch line."

Brown eyes swimming with sympathy, Vanessa put her hand over mine.

"Here's what I want to know," Hunter broke in for the first time. "Why was she trying to convince Olivia to enter that particular portal?"

Warren nodded at Tekla to continue.

"A doppelgänger can't just walk into this reality if she didn't originate here. She has no opposite or negative. No flip side. Her energy—or lack of it—doesn't register, and so the portals won't allow her passage."

"Okay, but what's she doing over there? Or over here?"

Well, the "over here" was apparent. She wanted me, whom she'd dubbed the golden ring. *In both my worlds* . . .

So, then, as to the "over there" . . .

"That must be the other world she was talking about." I sat up straighter, looking at Vanessa and Hunter, Felix and Riddick in turn. "She told the Tulpa she'd take me with her. That he'd never touch me in the middle of heaven."

I remembered this because I'd looked up into the sky then, searching for her meaning, and watched a man disintegrate instead. I closed my eyes now, but opened them again in time to catch the rest of my troop exchanging strained looks. I shifted my gaze to find Hunter frowning at me. "Do you mean Midheaven?"

I didn't know—did I? I frowned back.

"But that's not a world," Jewell blurted out. "It's an angle in the birth chart."

"Right," Felix added, sprawled in his chair. "Basic astrology. It's located in the house of reputation . . . what we want to be known for."

"The Tenth House," Tekla confirmed, nodding.

"Well, it's what the bubble lady said," I retorted, a little too sharply before slumping. These people had been raised in the sanctuary, trained in fields of astronomical study—including astrology—from birth. I didn't have that advantage. My mother had shielded me from any knowledge, study, or course that might attract the attention of the Shadows. Or help me now.

Vanessa blew a dark curl from her forehead and leaned my way. She had a way of imparting information like she was telling a secret, and it'd served her well as a reporter. Shoot, I knew what she was doing and it still worked. "I think she was messing with you, Olivia. Midheaven as a place is a myth. As Tekla said, it's nothing more than an angle on the astrological chart . . . an important one, but it's not a physical location."

"Then what is she doing over there?" I asked slowly, thinking the question obvious. I was a little behind in my astrology lessons, but my critical thinking was up to par.

Half the troop looked to Warren. Tekla closed her eyes. Hunter, who never drank anything harder than water with bubbles, merely swirled his glass thoughtfully.

"I don't know," Warren said after a moment.

We looked at Tekla, who also shook her head.

I wanted to run. Or scream. Or both. I'd been attacked three times in one night, and if the senior members of the paranormal troop I belonged to couldn't tell me why, nobody could. Hunter reached over and placed a hand on my knee, staying it. I hadn't even known it was twitching. Then I realized Vanessa had taken my hand again and I was squeezing hers, my own like ice. I shot her an apologetic half smile and loosened my grip. I nodded at Warren, who was watching carefully to see that I could relax before continuing.

"One thing is clear," he said, leaning back again. "Whatever the doppelgänger's doing, it has the Tulpa on his heels."

"Why would she be any more important to him than to us?" said Micah, shifting his large frame, though he still couldn't have been comfortable on the narrow bar stool. "The destruction of matter affects the Shadow side as much as it does us. It could be he simply wants to stop her before it's too late."

"Too late for what?" I asked.

Reluctantly, Jewell whispered in my direction. "For the world to heal. Each successive explosion, or breach, that the doppelgänger carves into our reality weakens the fabric of our world. Haven't you noticed them getting longer? And more debilitating?"

"So it's like dynamite? Each one builds on the one before it?"

"And the last will be the capstone," Hunter said tonelessly.

I looked to Tekla. "And she doesn't care?"

She shrugged her small shoulders. "She's neither Shadow nor Light. She has no conscience—she has yet to draw that from you—and cares nothing for that which doesn't somehow feed into her plans."

"So let me see if I have this straight," I interrupted, feeling a selfish but mounting need to prioritize. "This creature, whom even the Tulpa is afraid of, can blow holes through realities, has no conscience, and can lay waste to both sides of the Zodiac—not to mention the mortal realm—and she's after me?"

"Sucks to be the Kairos," Felix muttered in his cup. Hunter punched him. I didn't feel a bit sorry as the breath whooshed from his chest.

"Look, the doppelgänger didn't find you. She found the Tulpa's black hole, and you happened to be there. There's no reason you can't remain active, living your life, continuing your work."

"What kind of work?" Riddick asked Warren, leaning forward so his rangy frame obstructed my view of Felix. "I mean, what do we all do in the meantime?"

Warren, in turn, leaned back. "We count on the Tulpa being distracted by the doppelgänger. So no more efforts to merely balance the Zodiac—this time we target him as well."

We all stared at him in baffled silence. Warren's stance had always been that our job was to maintain the balance of the valley's Zodiac. Twelve of them and twelve of us. His mission was to keep the peace, allowing the mortals in the realm we patrolled to make their own choices, ones outside the unfair influences of people who were stronger and had more knowledge than they did.

What was yin without yang? he liked to say. *How could you know good without knowing evil?*

Even as the Shadows continually sought to upset that balance, Warren held us to a higher standard of responsibility. Our power, he claimed, made us accountable.

But something in this conversation had him abandoning this long-held stance. I'd told him of the Tulpa's initial threat to kill me weeks ago, and we hadn't gone on the offensive then. I glanced around the table to find varying expressions of surprise and wonder . . . and also sniffed out a burgeoning skein of excitement.

But I tended to be a bit more cautious when it came to Warren's motives. Sure, he could just be looking out for the good of the troop, but what if that wasn't all? What if he secretly agreed with the Tulpa and thought the third sign of the Zodiac was the rise of my Shadow side? Because if that was Warren's real fear, he'd never say it out loud. He'd just give orders and expect them to be followed.

Like he did now.

"So this is how we're going to play it. We break up into pairs. I don't want anyone out there alone. Felix and Jewell are a logical duo as they can canvass the party cir-

cuit most thoroughly. Vanessa and Hunter will join forces
. . . a reporter and a security guard aren't necessarily the
most natural match, but sometimes there's no accounting
for taste."

"Thanks a lot," Hunter mumbled, and Vanessa leaned
over and gave him a playful peck on the cheek. I felt no
jealousy at that, just a wave of relief at not being his partner. I didn't need the additional distraction.

"Micah and Tekla should make a handsome older couple,
though we'll have to find a different occupational cover
for you," he said directly to Tekla. "A physician wouldn't
likely find himself in accord with a psychic."

"You mean the opposite, I'm sure," Tekla said, tone im-
perious.

"Ouch." But Micah slung a big arm around her diminutive shoulder, and lightly squeezed. If they made an odd
couple, I thought, it wasn't because of their vocations, but
their sizes.

"I'll pair up with Riddick since he's working on his self-
control . . ." A snicker rose, and I hid my own smile behind
my glass. Riddick had gone after the Shadow's Capricorn
in full mortal view, causing a ten-car pileup on the 15,
which took a cleanup crew half a day to set up as a semi
driver's loss of control. But at least he'd taken some heat
off me for a while. It was nice not being the only troop
member to get busted for overreaching.

"So I get Gregor," I said, and tapped Gregor's fist with
my own—and he only had one; his other arm had been
cleaved off above the elbow.

"Nope. Gregor needs to be available to us all. He can
use his cab to ferry us to drop points, as we'll be spreading
out to canvass the city." He nodded, addressing Gregor directly. "But I don't want Gregor alone either, so I'm going
to bring in Kimber."

Kimber was an initiate I hadn't yet met, but I ignored
that. My stomach did a steep pitch and roll as I realized
who that left. "Wait, wait. That means—"

"Don't argue with me on this, Olivia," Warren said, holding up a hand even.

"But then how will you know how very wrong you are?" I said, though it was only for form's sake. He'd already made up his mind. I thought of Chandra, the only one left in our troop, even though she wasn't a full-fledged star sign. I thought of how she hated me, how I didn't much care for her either . . . and how our pairing would be like mixing oil with water.

"It's not wrong. You were both born under the Sagittarius sign. You're on the same side. You want the same things."

Which was precisely the problem. Chandra had been raised believing she would be the next Archer in our Zodiac. She'd only had a year left until her metamorphosis when I arrived on the scene; unexpected, uninvited, and the Kairos to boot. Naturally she hated me.

"I'd be happy to pair up with Chandra," Vanessa said, and I whipped around to stare at her. "Or Olivia. It doesn't matter."

"No, Warren's right." Tekla was unmoved as my mouth fell open. Shaking her head, she said, "It's time these two put their childish games behind them and started working together. You're both a part of this team."

I noted she didn't say *troop*—she couldn't, because as long as I was alive, Chandra would never be a true troop member, but it was clear she wasn't going anywhere. And neither was I.

"What about the doppelgänger?" Hunter asked pointedly. It, she, was still on all our minds.

Warren acknowledged it with a nod. "We have an advantage there. Because we now know of the breaches, we can triangulate them and find out exactly where she's based on the flip side. Next time she breaks through, we'll be waiting."

"To do what, exactly?" Felix asked, breath recovered.

Warren and Tekla looked at each other again. "We'll work on that."

"But one thing is sure," she added, so seriously we all fell still. "She has to be stopped, for all our sakes."

After a spooky moment where we all silently pondered that, we ordered another round. Then we spent the rest of the evening hashing out details—how we'd smoke the Tulpa out, how we'd target any establishment with the Archer name on it, and what we'd do once we were confronted with the Tulpa himself. We sat there until our table was littered with empty glasses, until the graveyard waitresses had gone home, bleary-eyed, and the day-shift girl appeared, less interested in why our motley group was still drinking at five in the morning than if she was going to get a tip. The splitting dawn found us all crammed, knees to chins, in Gregor's cab as he ferried us to the Neon Boneyard, a yard filled with dilapidated signage that also served as cover for our sanctuary. We crossed the alternate reality, crashing through a brick wall that immediately congealed behind us, then left the cab in the middle of the yard and hoofed it to the chute tunneling to our subterranean sanctuary. Before I got there, however, Warren cornered me privately.

"You need to put last night's loss aside," he said so bluntly it made me wince. It was as if I'd been gingerly fingering the memory of Vincent's death, and he'd come along and ripped off the scab. I didn't look at him as I ran my hand along the rim of a giant fiberglass coin. It'd once spilled from a neon slot machine high above one of Vegas's first bars. Warren stilled the movement by putting his hand over mine, but I didn't look up. "I know the Tulpa wants you to believe Vincent's death was your fault, that you could've prevented it if you'd gotten there faster or acquiesced to his will, but you weren't and you couldn't. And that guilt you're carrying around can be scented a mile away."

"Again?" I thought I'd been hiding it well. He nodded, and I sighed. "He told me there'd be a war if I didn't join him. This was the first victim."

"We're already at war, Joanna." Warren's use of my real name startled me into looking at him. It always surprised me to see him like this, clear-eyed and serious, probably because he'd been manic and verging on the psychotic when I first met him. I still wasn't sure the crazy bum persona was entirely an act. "He murders mortals because he enjoys it, and he toys with them first because he knows it'll affect us. It's always been that way. We can't save them all. We simply have to prioritize, and you come first."

I sighed, knowing he was right, but hating the gross randomness of it all. Someone was waking this morning, showering and dressing as they always did, and might end up dead by day's end because some powerful, immoral being willed it. I had a hard time being at all objective about that. Maybe because I'd once been that person.

"Then let me ask you something else, Warren. I know you said this other world, this Midheaven, doesn't exist—"

"It doesn't, and she's not there, Jo," he said quietly, and this time the understanding in his voice made me wince. "The myth that is Midheaven, the fairy tale? It's like something out of a horror flick. It's a twisted place, as the story goes, a giant pocket of distended reality, and it changes people. If it did exist, and if your mother had been there all this time, she wouldn't be the woman you once knew. She wouldn't even be someone you'd like to know."

"But how else could she so thoroughly drop off the face of the earth?" How else could she have left me so completely?

"She didn't. She's a mortal. She's on this plane, and I think she's still in this city."

I leaned in, my eyes searching his face in the dark. "Can you scent her?"

"No." He shook his head. "But she's still out there. She's working on behalf of the Zodiac in some way. She's doing some small part—whatever she can in that mortal skin—to help us. I know that."

"How?"

This time he was the one who drew closer, and his voice was surprisingly fierce. "Because I know her, and that's what she does. She'll never stop. Not until she's dead."

But was he only saying that so I wouldn't be tempted to look for her myself? I could never tell with Warren.

My goodness, is that a mask or blinders? Either way, it works brilliantly.

I shook the doppelgänger's voice from my head and squared my shoulders.

"Okay," I told Warren, lifting my chin. "But I have one other thing to ask of you."

He looked wary until I explained myself, then smiled as if he understood. He couldn't—he didn't know what it was to love a mortal—but he swore he'd look into Regan's account of what had happened in Dog Run, and I was satisfied enough with that. I had to know that the thug I'd left lying unconscious in the dirt of that ghetto alleyway, alone with Ben, had still been alive when the cops had arrived seconds later.

However, Warren did have one condition. He made me swear not to go after Regan again until our business with the Tulpa, and the doppelgänger, was resolved. After agreeing, I followed him to a building-sized shoe made of silver fiberglass and light bulbs, the only thing separating our sanctuary from the rest of the world. I donned the mask that barred the supernatural security system from detecting—and attacking—the Shadow in me, and followed Warren down the steep chute.

My fingers remained crossed the whole way down. Regan might be a lesser worry than the other two nefarious beings angling for my life, but with a little rub of my metaphorical heel, she'd soon get smaller still.

6

I'd never had to explain myself to my sister, and that was one of the things I missed most after she died. Olivia alone had known me in and out; she knew what had driven me to learn to fight, she knew the reason I'd picked up photography and the safety I felt hunched behind that lens, and she understood why I took both skills onto the neon-slicked streets at night. Olivia knew both why I hunted and why I cried.

And when our mother left us when I was sixteen, and she three years younger, Olivia alone had known how much that had truly hurt.

Percentages and statistics abound about the disorders shadowing abandoned children into their adulthood, and they're not pretty. For a long time it looked like I'd end up one of those depressing statistics. By the time my mother disappeared I'd also endured assault, near death, and an unwanted pregnancy. I was then raised by a man who blamed me for all those things, one who piled my mother's abandonment on top like a little something extra. In short, my entire youth was an emotional Molotov cocktail, but with Olivia's consistent, gentle help, I had picked the fucker up and thrown it right back at the world.

Surprisingly, during this time Olivia's worldview hadn't altered much at all. She was considered a flighty creature, her naïveté and mercurial nature attributed to too much beauty and money and an inherited position at the top of Vegas society. But I knew my sister as well as she knew me. She was lively but she was also stubborn; she stuck when my mother ran, and nursed me back to health with a powerful combination of admonishment, challenge, and tough love. She'd cried and begged and yelled, forcing me to climb from my sickbed if only to get away from her.

She'd been there in the beginning, when as a preteen I'd first fallen in love with Ben; she'd been there in the middle—with me in the desert when I was attacked coming home from his house—and she'd been there at the end, alive long enough to see it all come full circle, when time and maturity erased the guilt and shame keeping Ben and me apart, and the romance we all thought had been lost forever was reignited.

The only thing Olivia never knew was that I was the reason she had died.

That night, the genesis of my twenty-fifth year on this earth, had marked the onset of my metamorphosis into the supernatural realm. Opposites attract, and when my pheromones flared with my burgeoning powers, I was tracked by my enemies—the Shadows—and marked for death. They succeeded only in killing the kindest, purest love I'd ever known, sending Olivia to her death in my place.

Warren had saved me, and then begun schooling me in the finer points of paranormal warfare, but along the way they'd had to arrange it so my former life—and everyone in it—was wiped from existence. My sole constant, my sister, was dead and gone. My life as Joanna Archer was over.

But my obsession with Ben was not.

What can I say, except the man haunted me? He invaded

my consciousness in the same way the ocean washes up on the beach, with sweeping tides of longing and regret, and with such power and raw force, I often woke with the taste of salt from my tears clinging to my skin. I'd be lying if I said I wasn't bitter over what I'd lost . . . twice. Sometimes, even awake and allegedly in control of my emotions, I'd be scouring this city like an avenging angel when a glimpse of dark curls, broad shoulders, and an easy gait would cause my breath to hitch painfully in my throat. Each time it was like a fresh wound carved over my heart, reminding me again of what was no longer mine.

The shared dreams, entrusted secrets, and heartfelt promises. The softest lips, hardest body, and sweetest tongue. The man who promised to love—always and only—me.

Because, Regan aside, *I* was to blame for the dark turn Ben's life had taken. If not for my death the second time, he wouldn't have thrown off the constraints of his badge, his shield, to become a P.I. And if I hadn't let him know I was still alive, only to disappear on him yet again, there'd be no bitterness shellacking his gaze, turning it into a cold, hard thing. No, if Ben was susceptible to Regan's machinations, it was because I had injured him, enabling her . . . and now I needed to do something about it.

Once again, I turned to Olivia. I clicked on her computer, and bent over the keyboard, my face awash in the bluish-green light. I was intent on finding out for myself if Regan's words were true. A part of me couldn't help thinking I should let him go, that the kindest thing I could do for Ben Traina was to allow him to fade into the ebb and flow of a normal life and erase my existence from everything but his past.

But I needed to know if he was capable of killing a man in cold blood. And no matter what I found—because I was a hero, because I was responsible—I then had to get him back.

* * *

Olivia Archer—heiress, minor celebrity, and Louis Vuitton addict—was also a computer genius. Self-taught, she had run an underground website operating as a sort of clandestine cocktail party for hackers world-wide, a soiree that put some serious weight behind the term *networking*. She'd been able to circumvent top-level security systems with no more effort than it took to apply liquid mascara, while I still had trouble seeing the need for either. My way of getting around computer passwords was to punch a hole through the center of the screen.

Fortunately, Olivia's more obvious talents had recently come to good use. Two months ago I'd managed to secure the contact information for a well-known hacker in Switzerland, and had flown him in on Xavier Archer's private jet, plied him with wine and women and other latent adolescent fantasies-come-true, and a story about needing a partner in my expanding business. Actually, I could've probably spoon-fed him SPAM and sent him back to Europe on a dinghy, and still met with the same enthusiastic results. He took one look at his voluptuous "partner," a second at the bankroll, and readily agreed. So we determined he would take over the web business while I would meet with the big players in person, if needed. We spoke once a month by videophone on a scrambled line, and whenever he geeked out and starting talking over my head, I just leaned forward and gave him a nice cleavage shot.

Sorry, Olivia, I'd think, as he stuttered off into silence. *But it was just so easy.*

So Maximus X had set up a satellite security system I could access by remote, though I'd still had to go in and plant a camera and audio in Ben's house by hand. I had full access to Ben's accounts, and if he was pissed at me now, he'd be livid to know I could view his every keystroke with one click of my mouse.

But it was for his own good, I thought, sighing as I typed in *Rose*, gaining immediate entrée into his private journals. At least that's what I told myself.

I skimmed through the early entries, a faithful retelling of a young boy's turmoil—the emotionally absent mother, an abusive father—because it was a story I already knew. I lingered over the words detailing the dark side of his work as an officer—what he'd seen and what he'd done—and how both could climb inside you if not for the badge acting as a barrier for your soul.

However, that line of thought had abruptly ceased when he quit being a cop, and it was then that a darker, more cynical Ben emerged. Leaning close to the screen, I could almost see in the pixels the downward spiral of his mental health, the story written between the lines. He'd once told me he wrote mysteries as a hobby, but the incoherent ramblings filling the screen looked more like horror to me. I had to close my eyes a handful of times, consciously willing myself to breathe, before I could continue. This was torment *I* had caused. Not Regan, not his parents, but me. I had to stop reading altogether when he said he'd had to get it all out on paper just so it'd stop burning him on the inside.

I skipped forward and began reading again on a random page when his heart had clearly hardened toward me. I should've known Regan was telling the truth about that. She *was* getting to him—drawing on his bitterness, bringing anger to the forefront of his psyche—because that's what Shadows did to humans. It was like watching a cat bat at a single-winged moth, toying with a life just for amusement.

Similar, I saw, to the way Ben and his brothers had toyed with Charles Tracy.

I leaned forward and began to read the entry with Tracy's name. It chafed that Regan knew about him, this childhood bully Ben and I had known, though she'd probably discovered it from this very account, an entry detailing one week in my fourteenth year, right after Ben and I had banded together to make sure Charles never victimized another child in our school again.

Of course, Ben hadn't really needed me. I might have already developed a healthy sense of right and wrong, but I wasn't yet physically strong. Meanwhile, Ben came from a military family; his father was retired air force, one older brother was in the reserves and working as a mechanic, the other in the marines, though at the time of this incident he'd been on leave. I'd remembered all this well because Ben hadn't been able to hide the bruises on his torso, and though he'd grinned at me when recounting the antics of his older brothers, he'd done so with a split lip, his front tooth missing. He'd told me with a crooked smile that he didn't care—it made him tough and built character but then Charles Tracy made fun of him in front of a student assembly, and Ben didn't show up to school for three straight days. It was okay, though—or so I'd thought then—because neither had Charles.

And now I knew why.

Ben's father had served in Nam, and when he wasn't using his family as a punching bag, he'd regale his boys with stories of his non-government-sanctioned activities. When Ben came home from that assembly, pissed and humiliated about Charles's taunts, his brothers decided to test the effectiveness of wartime tactics on a thirteen-year-old. They abducted Charles on the way home from school, told him they were going on a little desert camping trip, and pulled out a sleeping bag to prove it.

They used military grade twine to bind him inside that bag, laid him out at the base of an old Joshua tree, and rigged a water cooler to release one icy droplet at a time onto the center of Tracy's forehead. According to the entry Ben didn't have a hand in this, but he didn't try to stop it either. It was only water and it couldn't really hurt, right?

Besides, it was just as likely he would end up in Tracy's position if he said anything at all.

Who was the bully now? his brothers wanted to know, laughing as they prodded the immobilized Tracy with sticks from their campfire. By morning Charles was unable to form words, moaning incoherently, and he had a welt on his forehead the size of red walnut. While the elder Trainas brewed instant coffee and ate bacon over a campfire grill, Charles still begging and moaning like an animal behind them, Ben was sick behind a giant saguaro.

The following week rumors of torture circulated around school, but the Traina brothers denied it, their father backed them, and Ben said nothing at all. I finally cornered him in fourth period gym class and asked him about it outright. He looked me in the eye, sincere and earnest and intent, and he lied.

Charles Tracy, once one of Olivia's greatest tormentors, returned to school like a ghost of his former self. His harassment of her—of everyone—abruptly stopped, and I'd thought it was because Ben and I had finally set him straight. Eventually I'd stopped worrying about him, stopped seeing him as a threat, and finally—like a ghost— he disappeared altogether.

So what did this confessional entry say about Ben's actions? What explanation did he have for allowing the torture, then lying about it afterward? Had he hidden the truth from me because he was afraid I'd judge him or because he was ashamed of what he'd done?

No. He'd hidden it because he wasn't.

"It's exactly what Regan is looking for," I murmured, lacing my fingers beneath my chin. These words were the smoking gun Shadow agents looked for in the mortals they targeted as beards, allies, or victims. And yet I was having trouble reconciling the boy portrayed here with the man I'd left sleeping in my bed a month earlier. As for the drug dealer in Dog Run, I didn't care what it might look like—what this entry alone might hint at—there was no way Ben could kill another human being, take a shower, and then make love to me only hours later. It would mean he'd been caressing me with lethal fingers, and that just didn't compute.

But the entry on Charles Tracy forced me to consider one thing that'd niggled at me since Ben's reintroduction into my life. What else, in the name of justice, had Ben decided to take into his own hands? What else had he done behind the shield of his badge and not felt ashamed about? And did I really want to excavate the answer to those questions?

You're going to lose him. It's only a matter of time.

I could feel the chaotic energy balling inside me, and swallowed hard, closed the file, and calmly shut down the computer. I sucked in a long breath, holding it before letting it spiral out of me like a string of yarn, then left the room to put on some tea. I was determined to put the issue aside until Warren could do his research to confirm for sure the dealer, Magnum, was dead. I walked back to Olivia's bedroom, reasoning that even if he was, Warren's account would be markedly different from Regan's. Opening the closet doors, I stepped inside to the scent of cedar and expensive leather, and gently pushed aside a wall of little black dresses.

Then I punched five holes through a false back, the report muffled by the clothes and soundproof foam I'd installed four months earlier.

I didn't know what had happened in that dark alleyway last month, but I did know this: Ben was the victim here.

I'd opened the door to his life and Regan had walked through it. She was like her mother that way, insinuating herself into the life of the vulnerable and unsuspecting, and filling his mind with ideas he'd never have otherwise had.

Five more fucking holes. Plaster crumbled on thousands of dollars' worth of shoes.

I knew what it felt like to be a pawn in someone's twisted game, and it was my job to keep that from happening to others, mortals, Ben. And. I. Would. Not. Fail.

Because there was also the issue of that unwanted pregnancy I mentioned before, the one I'd once believed had been the result of violence. Ben had a child out there he didn't know about, and I'd be damned if Regan was going to be the one to reveal that.

"She won't tell him," I swore, breathing hard, "and she won't tell the Tulpa."

And, of course, there was only one real way to ensure Regan's silence. I'd have to make it look like an accident to keep Ben from suspecting my involvement, and I'd have to act without the troop's knowledge too. They weren't yet aware of Ashlyn's existence either.

But Rose/Regan *would* die. She'd walk in front of a cab or bus, drop down an elevator shaft, or fall prey to a mysterious illness. And Olivia would be there to console Ben.

And, eventually, when he was ready, so would Joanna.

A harsh glint of red rebounded off metal hangers, belt buckles, and far too many sequins and crystals as I left that closet, but my blazing eyes didn't concern me. Neither did the smoke trailing behind me like a wispy, lashing tail. I didn't worry or fear that the third portent of the Zodiac really did mean my Shadow side was rising up to overshadow the Light in me. This was the real world—one with superheroes and demons and the soul of the city at stake—and brutal machinations demanded brutality in return.

And mothers, I was discovering, did what they had to to protect their children. I had a daughter who would some-day ascend to my star sign, the Archer, though like me at that age she didn't yet know it. But when she did finally find out, she'd want to know who her real father was, and

I'd be damned if I told her he was once a good man who'd been tainted and tormented and turned by the Shadows. I was determined to protect them both from that possible future.

Because the story of a little girl with a monster for a father had already been told. It was ugly, and it was mine.

7

Even though it was the final stretch of the year, and the rest of the country was gearing up for cold nights, blazing hearths, and the holidays, those of us who'd just endured a blistering summer season were only now settling into the welcome balm of fall. There was no changing of leaves or need for scarves and gloves and down jackets in Las Vegas. Burning candles was a waste of wax; with a sky so blindingly blue, the flame stuttered feebly in comparison. In short, Las Vegans were experiencing the summer the rest of the country still yearned for, our seasonal marathon of blazing heat over for another year.

Of course, the Strip bustled all year long, so it was with amusement that I kept one eye on the ever-entertaining flux of tourists gawking at one another in the cavernous halls of the Forum Shops, and the other on Chandra as she was fitted with custom couture tailored to her strong, stocky frame. Frankly, people watching couldn't compete with the entertainment value of seeing the robust and athletic Chandra polished and fawned over like a well-heeled society maven. And it was close enough to Halloween that I wanted to toss her some candy.

"Enjoying yourself?" she hissed when the tailor briefly left the room, already knowing the answer.

I widened my innocent blue eyes as I opened my Balenciaga bag, rummaging inside, though instead of lipstick, I pulled out a syringe and primed it. "You can't waltz into Xavier Archer's house in Doc Martens and fatigues. In fact, your walk alone is enough to clue someone in on your rustic pedigree."

As soon as I tapped the pressurized needle, the room filled with a chemical designed to mask my true biological odor. It was indistinguishable to mortals—pheromones always were—but through the mirror I saw Chandra's nostrils automatically flare, picking out the delicate texture of the synthetic component, a masking agent that blotted out my natural chemosignals.

Next came the perfume spritzer. It was Olivia's favorite scent, but the pheromones copied from her biological blueprint were mixed in with the freesia and blue orris enclosed in the small vial of cut crystal. In addition to being a biological barrier, these precautions also acted as a sensory shield for my emotions. Particularly strong feelings, like love, hate, jealousy, or desire, could lead an enemy agent right to your door. Regan knew who I was, but the other Shadow agents did not, and I wanted to keep it that way.

Chandra was eyeing herself in the mirror uncertainly. "There's nothing wrong with the way I walk."

"Sure," I agreed, returning her dead-eyed stare through the three-way mirror. "If you've just been deployed."

I'd mistaken Chandra for a man when we first met, and even though she wouldn't have liked me anyway, that little faux pas had sealed the deal. I'd come to the conclusion there was no way she and I would ever be friends, so instead of holding out the olive branch, I took my pleasure in baiting her.

Though, watching as she twitched beneath the tailor's steady hand, I had to admit she'd begun looking better lately. Had she always had those strong legs, or was the tailoring tricking my eye? While it was true she would never be a size zero, that wasn't a bad thing; she was predisposed to curves, and would've looked like a lollipop head if she even tried. Her chestnut hair was now past her shoulders in a long, graduated bob, and it played nicely against her warm eyes . . . though only because I'd gotten the best stylist in town to do both.

Still, she looked pretty damned great. Since I'd eat glass and spit shards before letting her know it, I let the thought slip away, and pulled out the compact I'd stolen after my little run-in with Regan in the ladies' room. It was nice to see I hadn't imagined its previous efficacy. It covered my scars as effortlessly as it had Regan's, and each time the tailor left the room I applied more, silently impressed that even my glyph's outline, burned into my chest, was obliterated from sight. I had to get more of this stuff.

After leaving the shops, we drove straight to the home of Xavier Archer, the-man-formerly-known-as-my-father. It had been a shock to both Olivia and me to discover we were merely half sisters, though Xavier must have long suspected I wasn't really his. *His* reaction had been primarily one of relief. Unfortunately, masquerading as Olivia meant I was still very much a part of the bastard's life, though that was coming in useful. As I mentioned before, Xavier was the Tulpa's chief mortal ally, and visiting him gave me an opportunity to canvass his home for clues that might lead to the Tulpa.

I told Chandra to hurry before she fell apart again, and she told me what I could do with my fashion advice, so by the time we arrived at Xavier's compound, our silence had escalated to cold-war–style tension. In fact, the only point at which we acknowledged each other's existence was when an explosion blasted through the temporal plane, so strong and close it was as if it'd gone off inside the car. I screamed as one of my eardrums ruptured inside my head, and veered from the road so quickly, the cars around me swerved and honked their horns as I spun to a halt in a sandy ditch. When we'd finally come to a stop, and minutes later when we were both able to straighten in our seats, Chandra and I looked at each other.

"Longer," Chandra said, referring to the doppelgänger's latest explosive breach.

"Oh yeah." I sighed, envisioning another bloody wound on the world as I restarted the car. Hands shaking, eardrum healing, I eased back onto the roadway.

"So why didn't you bring that useless piece of fluff along today instead of me?" Chandra asked, changing the subject as we approached Xavier's compound. "Bless her little tabloid heart."

She'd put a hand to her chest the way Olivia's best friend Cher would, and her voice took on the lilt of a Southern belle, though I noted it wasn't totally steady as I scowled back at her.

Chandra had stopped disparaging "Olivia" when she found out my bombshell exterior was a cover, but my sister's flighty, frivolous, mortal friends were still fair game. "I've sent her and her mother on an all-expenses-paid vacation to Fiji. Just in case Regan changes her M.O. and decides to annihilate anyone and everyone Olivia Archer is associated with."

Last I'd heard, Cher was desperately missing her latest romantic conquest and Suzanne had come down with a mild cold, but that was better than them being cast into a black hole like our friend Vincent. Besides, it was a relief not to worry about being Olivia so convincingly for a while. I may have known the wider parameters of Olivia's worldview, but that was nothing compared to the minutiae of private details and thoughts Cher had been privy to.

"Must be nice to be able to buy all your friends."

"I'm sure you'd find it helpful."

Little had changed in the weeks since I'd last been to Xavier's, and I felt a familiar roll in my gut as I sped up the long drive. I hated this place. Despite the gilt and grandeur, it had always been my personal prison. I'd fought like hell to get out of this gilded cage, and walking back in—even in Olivia's skin, even with her welcome—was like voluntarily shackling myself again. Still, Xavier was my best chance of getting to the Tulpa.

"Does Xavier know we're coming?" Chandra asked as we headed up the palatial white steps leading to the umbrella portico and the front door. I shot her an arch look.

"Olivia Archer doesn't need an invitation to visit her own home," I said loftily and grabbed the big gilt door handle. I pushed in. It didn't budge.

"Hm," Chandra said, crossing her arms over her chest as she leaned against an ivory pillar. "But perhaps she needs a key?"

I looked up at the camera with its steady red light. When had they begun locking the door? Between the guarded gate, the attack dogs, and the extensive electronic security system, there had never been a need. I raised my hand to knock but the door swung open, cutting Chandra's laughter short.

"Ms. Archer, so good to see you again."

I held back a sigh as a man the width of a flagpole popped up in front of me. He wore a double-breasted suit sagging in all the wrong places, and looked as if a stiff wind could blow him over. For all that, he was impossible to evade. I knew. He'd practically shadowed me when I was growing up here. It made him the perfect butler, a loyal sycophant . . . and an eternal pain in my ass.

"Mr. Deluca," I said, voice pitched somewhere in a soprano's upper register. "Why, you look more handsome every time I see you. Have you lost weight? Done something different with your hair?"

He straightened visibly as my eyes scanned his body, belly inverting so quickly, I thought he'd pop a lung. "Well, I have been exercising a bit more lately."

"I'll say," I said, pinching his biceps between two fingers. He might've flexed beneath my touch, it was hard to tell. "You look fabulous."

Deluca blushed, a grand feat if you considered that I'd never even gotten him to crack a smile. "Thank you, Ms. Archer. Is there anything I can do for you this morning?"

I stepped forward, insinuating myself into his personal space so that he had no choice but to step back, and put a delicate hand on his chest to keep him doing so. He edged backward like we were dancing the tango. "I was in the neighborhood, and thought I'd pop by to see if Daddy was in."

"He's on a conference call to Macau. Looks like construction is back on schedule."

"Marvelous," I said, like I gave a shit about Xavier Archer's expanding empire.

"Would you like me to tell him you're here?"

"No," I said, too hurriedly, and had to cover with a frilly little laugh as I handed over my sweater and handbag, dropping my keys into a crystal container on the marble-topped console. I motioned Chandra forward, and she did the same. "Don't you dare. I know how he gets when he's interrupted. We'll wait in the drawing room until he's finished up."

Deluca made no effort to hide his relief. "I'll get your refreshments."

Refreshments? Chandra mouthed to me when he'd walked away. I turned my back on the follow-up eye roll, and led her into the living area.

The room had recently been redecorated. There was new cream-colored paint and white casings on the floor-to-ceiling windows, new curtains in a burnt orange to match the season, a color that was picked up in the silk pillows angled along the milky chenille couch. The tables were all glass, the fixtures chrome and crystal. Xavier had been remodeling a lot lately, taking the house apart piece by piece and putting it back together in a different, though unimproved, state. I think it was his equivalent of a sports car in a midlife crisis. The only thing that'd remained were the trio of oil portraits he'd commissioned of Olivia in different years of her life, but the portraits were glossy and posed—hardly personal—and the furnishings had been appointed by a decorator with a modern sensibility and a blank check. Still, Chandra was impressed.

"No wonder you don't have a job," she said, dropping onto the couch, sinking into the tangerine sea of pillows.

Actually, Xavier didn't want Olivia to have an opinion, much less a job, and only barely tolerated her charitable activity. He was happiest when she was flitting mindlessly about town, a theory I'd recently tested by going on a shopping spree at Mandalay Place that made her credit card look as lethal as an Uzi. Despite the danger to his bank account, Xavier had all but applauded. It was sick.

But the twisted family dynamics that'd had Xavier shunning me, coddling Olivia, and forbidding anyone to mention my mother, ever, wasn't even his worst offense. Nothing could top his ingratiating status as the Tulpa's pet, which made him indirectly responsible for his own daughter's death. If it were up to me, I'd have made sure he knew it. Why should I be the only one grieving over her daily, or shouldering the responsibility of having failed in my obligation to protect her?

Yet rubbing salt in that wound would accomplish nothing for the troop, so instead I'd sworn to make him pay for his spinelessness. From his pocket, I thought, staring up at the final and largest portrait of Olivia. From his soul.

But first he was going to make himself useful. We'd only get one sweep through the mansion, and it'd be a surface one at that, but a feeble mind wasn't one of Chandra's innumerable faults. It would be a start.

Deluca returned bearing a tray of tea and scones, and after he'd poured, he excused himself and backed out of the room. I remained where I was long enough to take an obligatory sip, then rose and motioned for Chandra to do the same. "Come on. I'll take you on a tour."

If the room was bugged, and I already knew it was, Olivia's offer to show her new friend around wouldn't attract suspicion.

I led Chandra through the upper levels—there were three—purposely skipping the rooms that used to be mine. It'd been years since I lived there, but residual emotion was a funny thing; someone with Chandra's keen perception might be able to scent me in there. She mixed the compounds covering our natural scents, and had almost certainly memorized the hooks of my genetic makeup. One sniff and she'd figure out my secret.

More, I didn't want to risk releasing more emotion into that room. The furnishings were different from when I'd lived there, but I knew the secrets it contained. The hidden compartment behind one floorboard, another tucked into the northeast corner of the crown molding. The vows I'd etched on the tops of the doorframes. If I walked in that room, my thoughts would flit to those things like heads turning toward a car accident, an unwilling act of compulsiveness. One Chandra would sense.

"Your fucking photo is everywhere."

I glanced at Chandra, but she was gazing around, her words apparently sincere, momentarily forgetting that I wasn't really Olivia Archer.

It was then that we hit the wing housing Olivia's childhood bedroom, and even I had to wince in embarrassment. It would've been eerie even were she alive, but with her dead it was a virtual mausoleum. The three giant portraits downstairs were only Xavier's favorites. The rotunda leading to her suites was lined with photos from every year of her life, the antique accent tables lining the hallway topped with the less formal snapshots.

"Come on," I said, hurrying through the passageway and into the common areas before Chandra could sense my sorrow. "Xavier should be ready for us."

We took the elevator back to the ground floor and Xavier's private office. There was a time when Xavier Archer had been hounded by the press, so he'd had an office suite and conference room built at home so his associates could come to him. But all that was before, when he'd been the primary figurehead for his empire. Nowadays Olivia grabbed most of the headlines, and Xavier was content to let her. He still spent the bulk of his hours secluded at home, but fewer employees and investors were stopping by. He'd begun to prefer taking his meetings by conference call instead.

Chandra gasped when we stepped from the elevator. I gave her a moment to look around, not bothering to hide my matching awe. We hadn't decamped into the most opulent room in the manor, but it sure did make a statement.

The room was floor-to-ceiling white marble, with three high unadorned windows letting in specific amounts of light. Its interior was supposed to resemble a Tibetan stupa—an elaborate mound built in ancient Tibet to house the remains of great lamas—which was a fancy name for tomb. The highlight of the room was a museum-worthy exhibit containing the first complete English translation of *The Tibetan Book of the Dead*, which, as far as I knew, Xavier had never even cracked open, but the objects that really attracted one's eye was the vertical phalanx of prayer wheels leading to a red-carpeted dais. A giant, overly ornate throne had been added since I was last here, solidifying my suspicion that Xavier wasn't just egomaniacal . . . he was psychotic.

When I'd been an angry teen living among this physical anomaly I'd only wondered what the hell a gaming mogul thought he had in common with Tibetan meditation masters, and merely decreed the whole thing creepy. Now that I knew the link, that this place of worship had probably been forced upon Xavier as a condition of the Tulpa's patronage, the room sent chills up my spine. However, I still didn't know exactly what the area was for, why there was a throne, and what the room's only ornamentation—a half-dozen ancient masks; some wooden, some plain, some copper, some ornate—signified, if anything at all.

"Come on," I said, gesturing to the opposite side of the stupa. "That's his office."

I knocked on the great oak door and waited for the familiar bellow to either welcome us inside or tell us to go away. The only response was a lengthening silence, so I knocked again, louder.

"Do you hear music?"

I wouldn't have if I'd still possessed mortal hearing. But there was a thread of low and resonant drumbeats, and the faintest tinkling of chimes. I tilted my head and furrowed my brows. "Xavier always works in silence."

Chandra stared at me for one long second before doing something no one else had ever dared. She turned the handle on the office door and let herself in.

I expected an explosion of fury and outrage to erupt from the other side of that threshold and was already scrambling for an Olivia-esque excuse . . . but the bellow didn't come. There was just that steady, thrumming beat and the continued tinkle of chimes. The beautiful and unexpected scent of sandalwood had my eyes widening in wonder. If Chandra hadn't pulled me inside the office and shut the door, I probably would've stood there, dumbstruck, until the music stopped to effectively break the spell.

The only thing familiar about the office was its layout. The desk was where it should be, and the floor-to-ceiling shelves lined one chocolate wall with their stiff-spined books, but even those familiar features were hard to distinguish in the cloying, curling smoke. Heavy burgundy drapes had been pulled tightly over the glinting windows of lead crystal, and the lamps had been extinguished in favor of one great corner candle. But it was neither the dimness that made me squint and strain to see around me, nor the incense, though that didn't help. And smoke usually derived from flame, from heat, from the disintegration of something substantial, but this was more like the cool waves of mist that wound about a Scottish highland . . . except these tendrils weren't rising from the ground to overtake the landscape in a heathered glen. They were coming from an opening in the far bookcase, where the steady flame of another candle called to us like a beacon.

"I take it he's no longer on a conference call with Macau," Chandra whispered, unable to take her eyes from the hole in the bookcase.

And together we stepped forward, through the faux barrier, and into a room I'd never known existed.

8

Xavier Archer was on his knees, chanting, which was probably why he didn't hear our approach. He was holding something that reminded me of a child's rattle, but when I inched closer I recognized it as a handheld version of the prayer wheels in the stupa outside. Its handle was wooden, but there was an ornate metal cylinder at its apex, with a ballasted chain helping the cylinder whirl around with a deft flick of the wrist. His mouth moved as he repeated his mantra over and over, but it didn't sound like Xavier's voice. It was too low and respectfully resolute.

"Praying?" Chandra asked, so lightly only I could hear.

I shook my head. Xavier didn't pray. "No. It's more like . . ."

"Worshipping."

Centered on a colorful rug, he leaned over in a practiced move to pick up a mallet, striking the side of a bronze bowl without losing beat with his prayer wheel. A warm bell tone overtook the tinny chiming in the room and resonated through my body, making the spot on my chest where the doppelgänger had nearly rent me open pulse lightly. I lifted my hand, wanting to rub the feeling away.

I also wanted to back out of the room, ponder what this could mean far from the compelling smell and sound of ritualistic Eastern prayer, but Chandra was inching closer to Xavier. I caught up with her as the even spin of the wheel stopped and the tonal notes died in the air. The room fell to complete silence. We didn't dare breathe in the unearthly stillness, and even Xavier's mouth moved soundlessly as he set aside the first singing bowl and mallet, and picked up a second, larger one, placing it directly in front of him on the carpet.

He held the hollowed disk with straight arms, as if proffering it to someone, and I had just enough time to think: *No, not a bowl. A mask.*

Bending his elbows, he drew the mask toward his face in an exaggerated motion. It was too small for his bullish mien, its bowl delicate and shallow, and obviously a totem meant for ritual ceremonies, clearly not intended to be worn. Yet as Xavier drew the plain wooden artifact parallel to his features, the ancient wood startled and sprang to life. He cupped it to his face as the wood pushed against itself and began to flatten, grain thinning with a high-pitched noise. It attached itself to Xavier's skin, caressing his cheeks in a jagged slide, seeping like wax beneath his hairline to add Xavier's coiffure—down to his cowlick—to its inanimate features.

It went fast after that, like the wood was once again living and vital, anchored in the earth, and not merely a hollowed out husk. Xavier was already statue-still, but once the mask encompassed the whole of his face, I heard a sharp click—the animate wood meeting and fastening at the nape of his neck—and he went absolutely rigid.

Ash flew from his mouth to thicken the air in a blackening haze. I leaned forward, waving a hand before me, but the effect was temporary; the air was too heavy, molecules pressed so tightly together they were almost sticky. The whole scene took on a dreamlike aspect, as if what I was seeing was taking place inside of my lids. I took another step forward, and with a second I spotted the candle burning like a focal point in haze. A third step and Xavier became visible again.

Smoke billowed from the mask now, soot coating and darkening the walls of the room. If the smoky mixture had been cloying before, it was oppressive now, and it coated my mouth in wafer-thin layers with every inhalation.

"Only one thing tastes like toasted anise," Chandra murmured, her face scrunched in disgust.

"What?"

"Parfum de personne." She waved her hand in the air to look me in the eye. "It's his soul essence."

"But what's he doing with it?"

She squinted, returning her gaze to Xavier. "It looks like he's giving it away."

"Well, that was a tad freaky."

Chandra and I backed from the office, shutting the door silently behind us, and I made a face as I tried to clear the cloying sweetness from the back of my throat. Was I going to have to walk around all day with Xavier's soul essence clinging to my clothes? "Let's get back to the drawing room. We'll wait for Deluca there."

We started back through the giant stupa, neither of us seeing it this time, still mesmerized by what we'd just witnessed. I was so lost in thought, it wasn't until Chandra called out to me that I noticed she'd fallen behind.

I walked back to her while she continued to stare into a sunken alcove, so taken by what she saw there that she actually touched me when I reached her side. We both jerked away out of habit, but her eyes stayed fixed on the wall across from her. "Do you see what I see?"

I turned my head, and though I'd passed by it hundreds of times before, my gasp was real, and immediately smothered. Of course! I did a mental head slap. "More masks."

Half a dozen more. And they'd been hanging on these

walls so long, they'd only ever registered as creepy, not significant. But they were. Clearly antique, and bearing a freakish resemblance to the one Xavier had donned, the one in front of me looked frighteningly like the mask the Tulpa had been wearing when he'd tried to microwave me only days earlier. I looked around, pointed to another, and we crossed the room in implicit silence, standing before it like it was a caged animal. It was simply, even primitively carved, and painted entirely red, like it'd been shellacked with fresh blood, but for the black line painted down the bridge of the wide nose. I'd just reached out to remove it from its wall peg when a voice behind me went off like a firecracker.

"What do you think you're doing?"

I whirled, hand falling like it'd been slapped. Recovering quickly, I performed the eye roll I'd perfected in front of the mirror last month, and crossed my arms, tapping my fingers impatiently.

"Buffy," I said, quickly thinking up the name for Chandra's socialite alias. It was cute, and it'd piss her off. "This is Helen, our long-time housekeeper."

And if Xavier had been the devil when I was young, Helen Maguire had been his succubus. Her looks were ordinary enough; she was mousy, in fact, with hair that was neither curly nor straight, and a long, sallow face framing eyes that were slightly hooded. But beneath the lids that made her look like she was dozing on her feet were sparrow-bright eyes. Apropos, as I'd always had the feeling she stored away the dramas of the Archer dynasty like shiny baubles to line her own emotional nest. She gleaned information about other powerful families as well, and after every party Xavier threw she could be found in the camera room, eyes devouring the video as she replayed recorded conversations.

And what did she do with those tiny bits of gossip she scavenged and studied? She marked them as experience, and counted them as her own.

If bothered by the way I'd pointed out her position in the household, Helen didn't show it. Probably because she considered it a title, like mistress or duchess or queen. After my mother had left, I thought wryly, she'd certainly acted like it.

"I asked what you think you're doing?" She took a step toward me, a laundry basket with crisply folded sheets resting snugly between an arm and one flaring hip.

"Dusting, Helen," I retorted before I could stop myself. "Someone has to."

She reddened under the implied criticism, and for what may have been the first time, really looked at the woman she thought was Olivia. The look softened after a moment; she'd never treated Olivia as anything but a fluffy piece of lint and was obviously still unimpressed.

"Don't touch the artifacts, Olivia."

"Don't tell me what to do in my own home, Helen." I glared at her. She took a step forward.

"What's going on here?"

For a moment neither of us acknowledged Xavier's presence. Then duty overcame Helen and she started babbling. "Sir, Olivia is manhandling the relics. I just want to be sure they don't come to harm."

"Daddy!" I said, and raced to throw my arms around him. His clothes reeked of charred spice, and I jolted upon realizing he didn't fill out the custom-made suit as well as he used to. Pulling away, I saw dark smudges circling his eyes, and though a two-hundred-pound man couldn't be considered gaunt, his cheeks were sunken and his skin sallow. I pretended not to notice, and shot him a blinding smile. "I was telling Buffy about your world travels, and how there's a story to the way you acquired each of these masks." I reached out and stroked the one nearest his office and heard a quickly indrawn breath behind me. Interesting. "But the hired help told me to leave."

Helen stuttered. "I didn't—!"

She hadn't. But maybe it was time the brownnosing

sycophant learned Xavier wasn't the only Archer in this household. Gain for Olivia in death a little of the respect denied to her in life. I shot her a blazing look over my shoulder before turning back to Xavier with a brilliant smile. "Of course, I've forgotten most of the stories behind these masks, so I was hoping you had time to tell us one of them."

Xavier closed his eyes, pinching the bridge of his nose between thumb and forefinger. "Olivia, I'm awfully busy today."

My bottom lip shot out. "You're always busy."

He looked from me to Chandra, assessing her so quickly, I could practically see the ticker tape rolling across the screen of his gaze. I was glad I'd insisted on her makeover. Finally he sighed. "Five minutes. That's all I have."

"Thank you, Daddy!" I squealed, and clapped my hands wildly as I grinned at Chandra, who gave a good shot at giggling back as Xavier turned away. My apparent giddiness drained when my eyes stalled on the house-keeper, who was still staring at the hand I'd returned to the wall next to the mask. "Oh, you're excused now, Helen."

The impulse to stay where she was flashed like lightning in her eyes, but died just as quickly. Her lips thinned to a single line. "If you need anything," she said stiffly, and left it at that.

Xavier had already disappeared back into his office, and Chandra whispered as we followed. "Does it seem like a little more than coincidence that she arrived just then?"

"Cameras," I muttered, gesturing to the one above the study door with my head. "Helen seems to have a knack for popping up at the most inconvenient times."

"Curiouser and curiouser."

Maybe, I thought, and maybe not. When you grew up in a house of secrets and unspoken resentments, even oddi-ties seemed normal. I suppose that's what had kept me from seeing the masks before, and at the moment I had to admit Warren had been right. Partnering up had been a good idea. As annoying and spiteful and untrustworthy as I found Chandra, she was no idiot.

"You know," she said, in a voice so low it couldn't be picked up by a mic, "Hunter has mentioned before that Valhalla has a room full of Asian artifacts, tribal pieces reportedly collected while searching out Viking artifacts to accessorize Valhalla. I bet these are more of the same, but even more valuable."

"Viking artifacts in Asia?"

I looked at Chandra—saw the same dark knowledge tingeing her gaze—then around at the room I'd both seen, and somehow hadn't, my whole life. Thus a plan was born. Warren might kill me for not running it by him first, but he was the one who'd told us to go on the offensive. I had to start seeing the physical spaces that had occupied my old life in a new way—even when Chandra wasn't with me—including my childhood home. Including Valhalla.

"Stay here," I told Chandra, and headed back to Xavier's office.

She caught up to me. "But—"

"I have an idea," I told her, and shut the door in her face before she could say any more. Xavier would be too aware of her presence, his pride and self-consciousness acting as barriers to seriously considering my words, and I had to get what I needed from him in the same way Olivia always had. By appealing to the soft side of her beloved, doting father.

In retrospect I could appreciate that the years I'd considered myself trapped, confined, and caged under Xavier Archer's roof hadn't been heartbreakingly traumatic. He could be accused of neglect, but not abuse. He had never injured me physically, though his words, and even his silence, had possessed a whiplike feel to them. Compared to the way some people terrorized their children, Xavier could even be called benign. But back when I was sixteen—traumatized, alone, abandoned, frightened, pregnant—I didn't have such a wide frame of reference. I only knew that he flinched when I walked into a room, he refused to let me speak of my mother, and he ignored both the physical and mental scars of my attack, so that I felt shamed in my own young body.

So fuck him if he was having trouble sleeping lately.

The office was normal once again, oversized furniture returned to the room's center, desk spotless, wood gleaming like it'd just been polished. Even I wouldn't have been able to scent out the lingering incense if I hadn't known it was there only minutes before. The Tulpa had set Xavier up with some seriously powerful hoodoo. Which begged the question. *Why?*

"Where's your new partner in crime?" Xavier said, jerking his chin at the door as it swung closed behind me. His word choice threw me for a moment, but I relaxed when I saw he meant it figuratively.

"Outside. We're just hanging out until Cher gets back from Fiji. But I wanted to talk to you alone."

He motioned to a high-backed chair across from him, before settling in his own.

"I'm going to get a job," I announced brightly, crossing my legs, and sitting up straight so I looked innocent and eager. Maybe my bright smile kept Xavier from recognizing Olivia Archer's first ever act of defiance. When, after an awkward moment, he realized I was serious, he laughed anyway.

"We've discussed this before, Olivia," he began, his tone patently patronizing, one most people used with domesticated animals and toddlers. He picked up a thick fountain pen and began twirling it in his fingers.

"No, you dictated before. I don't remember ever discussing it."

"Well, the answer is still the same."

"Except this time I'm not asking," I said, my voice both high and sweet. His fingers stilled. The incongruity between my words and tone seemed to baffle him, and I widened my smile, probably confusing him further. "I've been doing a lot of reevaluating the last few months and have decided I need to change some things in my life. I need a purpose. A rhythm to my days. A reason to get up in the morning."

Xavier didn't move. I realized I was going to have to sugar him up, so made sure my gaze wasn't challenging when I met his eyes. "Like you, Daddy. You get up in the morning and you know exactly what you want from your day. I want to be like you."

A number of emotions passed over his face in quick succession, fatigue overlaying them all. That might have softened me toward him if the very first emotion hadn't been derision. If it had been Olivia sitting here, she would have seen it too. I consciously unclenched my jaw.

"Honey, I don't think that's a good idea."

"Why?" I asked, imbuing hurt I didn't feel into my voice. "You don't think I can do it? That I don't have the ability to learn?"

"Why would you want to?" he asked, skirting the questions. "I give you everything you want. If there's something more, tell me. I'll get that for you too."

I leaned back in my chair. "Okay. How about self-respect?"

When he only sat there, those fingers still and brow drawn, I thought, *You bastard.* He'd always done this, regarding Olivia from a distance that reduced her to a single dimension. A pretty picture he could hang on his wall, imagine as he wished, control and attend to at his whim. "Nobody who's given everything they desire without having to work for it," I inserted into the silence, "can truly possess that."

I was talking about him, about the way the Tulpa dangled carrots to control him, but naturally he didn't realize that. "Self-respect doesn't come from what we do, Olivia. It comes from who we are."

"Who we are?" I repeated slowly. "You mean an Archer?"

"Yes. Exactly that."

I nodded my head slowly, like him, then stopped. "I don't know, Daddy. Sometimes the title feels like something I'm wearing. A brand upon my skin. Like I belong to someone, rather than *am* someone. Like I'm a puppet in the . . . Archer's organization."

And there it was. Humiliation had him wincing. Anger thinning his lips. Hopelessness lowering his eyes. The blended emotions smelled like used fuel and the soul he was so cheaply giving away. "That's ridiculous. Now, you're not getting a job and that's final."

I stood. "It's not final."

"You're not getting a job."

"Fine." I angled my body around the chair. "Then I guess I'll have to—"

"What?" he finally snapped, rising to his feet and turning away at the same time, only to whirl on me again two feet later. "What will you do, Olivia? Go on a spa strike until I give you your way?"

I let that hang between us to see if he could hear how ugly it sounded. He did, and shame dueled with stubbornness to have him turning away. He paced over to the window to regain his composure, but I wasn't going to give him time for that.

"I was going to say," I said softly, "that I guess I'll have to leave."

He stiffened, and half turned. "What?"

His face was sallow in the harsh daylight, and he suddenly looked fragile despite his bulk, or what was left of it. I didn't care.

"Leave," I repeated, clasping my hands in front of me. "Leave the city, leave the West Coast if that's what it takes. Leave the Archer dynasty."

"I'll cut you off like I did Joanna. Is that what you want?"

It was an automatic response; the ruthlessness and nerve that'd propelled him to the top of the competitive gaming world had him calling my bluff while countering with one of his own. Usually it served him well. But not now.

I shrugged. "I'll survive."

"How?" His voice was a tad hoarse, and he cleared his throat, adding a sneer to his words. "How will someone like you survive? You have no skills, no real education, you've never even won a talent contest."

I pressed my hands against his shiny desk, leaning forward to keep the bitch-slap with his name on it from knocking him off his feet. "And why is that, Daddy? Why have you always been hell-bent on keeping me in my place, a box marked, 'Look, but don't touch.' A pretty one, but a box no less?" I straightened as his eyes widened. He was finally facing me fully. He was finally listening. "You never hear or see me. You refused to even consider I might have an opinion, and now look at me. I'm like a property you acquire, wealth you hoard, a company you collect because you can."

"You're becoming hysterical."

I was acting like Olivia, but speaking for myself . . . and he'd never seen my kind of hysterical. I lifted my chin and returned his earlier sneer. "Mother would have never allowed you to do that to me."

And that was said for both of us. Xavier was breathing hollowly now, much like when he'd been chanting, his movements measured as he returned to his desk and deliberately lowered himself into the soft leather chair.

"But she did allow it, Olivia," he said, leaning back, eyeing me from the relaxed pose of an attentive tiger. "She allowed it by her absence. By abandoning her family. She left and never looked back. I wanted to make you into a better woman than she was, that's all."

So that's the lie he told himself so he could sleep at night, I thought. One of them, anyway.

"You made me," I said evenly, as Joanna, as myself, "into a shadow of what I could have been."

Xavier didn't even blink. "I've given you a place in this world. Is that really so bad? If your mother had been more like you—"

"—she wouldn't have left you," I finished for him, amazed it had taken me this long to see it. That was it. He'd smothered Olivia with money and baubles and coddling because he didn't want to lose her. In some corner of that useless heart, he might even love her. It was nice to know . . . but for the fact that his involvement with the Tulpa made him indirectly responsible for her death. "She couldn't have left you."

He didn't deny it. "I just want to keep you close."

Inhaling deeply, I pretended to consider that. Though anger had me shaking inside, I was used to holding my tongue around Xavier, and as I angled around the desk to take his hands in mine—careful not to let him feel the unnatural smoothness of my printless fingertips, or the tensile strength in my palm—I smiled.

"And I want to be close to you as well." *Because you're going to lead me to the Tulpa. And someday I'm going to see you pay for all your countless sins.* "So where better to begin my career than at Valhalla? Surely your premier property isn't below me? Plus you can keep an eye on me while I learn a skill. Surely there's a way, Daddy, for us to both get what we want?"

He was silent for so long, even the house seemed to hold its breath around us. There was almost an audible exhalation when he finally said, "Tell me again why you want this?"

"Because I want to be like the parent who raised me. The one who stayed and stuck. I want to be like you."

He rubbed a hand as large as a ball mitt over his face, and I knew I'd won. "I'll think about it."

"Thank you, Daddy," I said, and exited his office before my eyelids caught in a permanent flutter. I had finally gotten him thinking, and that was the best I could hope for right now.

Or so I thought.

Chandra was back in the drawing room, seated awkwardly on the window seat, but she stood to fall wordlessly into stride with me as we exited. We skipped down the palatial white steps, hopped into my car, and I rolled the engine over, still silent. I glanced up to find Helen's pinched face peering at us from the living room windows, though she drew back when I waved, retreating into the house that so completely defined her existence. The gates were already opening as I gunned down the drive, though I waited until we'd left the compound and had reached the first stoplight before turning to Chandra. "You look smug."

"It's all that goop you made me put on my face."

"And?" Because there was more.

And she lifted the handbag I'd made her carry, opening it wide enough to reveal a blackened face stretched in a long, silent scream. The light changed. A car honked behind me. I looked from the mask in her purse back up into her face. And for the first time since we'd known each other, Chandra and I exchanged real smiles.

9

The derring-do of both sides of the Zodiac was recorded in comic book form. While that might seem imprudent, there were fail-safes in place to keep information from one side leaking to the other. For instance, the Shadow agents couldn't read the manuals of Light, and vice versa, thereby eliminating the possibility of one side gaining dominance over the other that way. This prohibition didn't apply to me since I was both Shadow and Light, but I'd recently taken the opportunity to compare the manuals written after my arrival with those written before, and noted a lot more detail being left out these days, or delivered in more obscure terms than in the time prior to my arrival on the paranormal scene.

Of course, agents on both sides of the Zodiac had attempted to glean knowledge from people known to follow one series of comics or the other, but all had found that those mortals inevitably gave out misinformation, enthusiastically relating the wider worldview of the Zodiac to a competing agent—information they already knew—while blithely forgetting the specifics of the latest manual. It was our micro-universe's way of keeping the battle between Light and Shadow squared and properly balanced.

The kids who frequented Master Comics, however, weren't just any mortals. They knew the stories and characters they were following were real, and were willing partners in our paranormal battle. They thought and spoke and dreamed of us, picked sides, and taught the other younger children the mythology of the Zodiac. As they grew up, leaving the energy and belief of their youth behind, our legacy then continued in the minds of the next generation. However, if they failed to pass this knowledge on before maturation, we wouldn't merely be in jeopardy of losing the battle against our enemies, we'd actually cease to exist.

All the mortal children who know of our world gathered at a comic book shop called Master Comics. Therefore it wasn't only a natural place to look for back issues containing clues that might lead to the Tulpa's demise, it was also a hotbed of exuberant fandom. Chandra and I swung into the store prepared for a preadolescent pop quiz. Instead we were met with dead silence.

"Smells like geek central," Chandra said, glancing around. "Looks like geek central. But where are all the geeks?"

The comic and manga titles were ordered obsessively on floor-to-ceiling shelves, with a DVD section on the back left wall, a gamers' paradise on the right. But the store was otherwise eerily empty. "I'm getting ghost-town vibes."

Chandra was still standing just inside the door, looking ready to bolt if she had to. But Master Comics was a safe zone for all agents, neutral territory, so I moved farther into the shop, albeit warily. "Maybe they're out buying Halloween costumes," she said.

Except every day was Halloween in Master Comics. I shook my head. "I don't think so. Carl's already had his costume for six months."

She glanced over at me. "What's he dressing as?"

"All he'd say was it would be totally unexpected and out of character for him. My guess is he's going as a normal kid."

Chandra snorted. "Well, maybe they're all at school."

"Shut your mouth," I scoffed, picking up an independent comic. "Besides, what about Zane?"

Zane was the owner of Master Comics, a loner in his late twenties who still hung with kids, but who was the creator of the Zodiac's manuals as well. Anything going on in Las Vegas's paranormal underworld would end up on the shelves within two weeks, depending on how quickly Zane could process and translate the storyline. The aforementioned boy-who-would-be-normal, Carl, was the series penciler.

"What the hell do you want?"

I jerked so quickly I dropped my comic, and frowned less at the sudden appearance of the kid who'd addressed us than at his tone.

"Excuse me?" I asked, bending to pick up the comic as I took in a beanpole body, wild hair, and fists hinged on bony hips. He was looking me up and down like I was rabid, and Chandra snorted again behind me.

"I said what are you doing here?"

"Well, I wasn't looking for a dressing-down by a twelve-year-old," I said, straightening.

"You must be the Archer," the boy sneered, eyes cataloging me again. "Smart mouth, wall-to-wall tits—" Chandra snickered beside me and he whipped his gaze to hers. "And you're the pretender. You probably followed her to a safe zone so you could take her out without anyone reading about it later. Crazy bitch."

I'd have laughed but the little fucker was already on my nerves. "And you are?"

"Your worst nightmare."

"Sweetie," I said in my most condescending voice, "you clearly haven't read about my nightmares."

He feigned shaking with fear. I thought about throwing him over my knee and giving him the spanking he fully deserved, but knew how the episode would be depicted in the manuals. We may have violence, crime, and gore, but it was still primarily an American adolescent audience. Gruesome death was fine. Sex, verboten. "Where's Zane?"

A new voice bloomed from the back of the shop. "I was giving a tour to the new changelings."

Zane lumbered from the tunnel leading to the storeroom that doubled as his personal library. His apartment was located above the store, and between those three crucial amenities he never had to leave Master Comics. If his social skills were any indication, I thought as he passed by me with a grunt, he probably never did.

"New changelings?" Chandra asked, sidling up to the register. "Is it time already?"

He stared at her until she removed her hand from the glass case, then rubbed a rag over the whole thing. "It flies when you're waiting to take over a star sign, doesn't it?"

"What is it, asshole hour in here today?" Chandra asked, turning to me.

"Two-for-one special, apparently."

Zane made a face, but before he could reply, a handful of children tumbled from the tunnel and into the shop. I didn't recognize any of them, but they had no such problem, and they crowded around us like superhero groupies, firing questions as they grabbed at our clothing. *How old were you when you learned to fly? When did you get super strength? What's harder to break, a chair back or a spine?* I glanced over at Chandra, panic mounting until I saw Carl saunter from the storeroom. He was dressed in unrelieved black, hair dyed to match and plastered to his head. Matching black eyeliner was meant, I was sure, to drive his parents nuts.

"Hey, Archer," he said, pushing the younger kids aside,

and smiling at my obvious relief. "Didn't know you cared."

Neither had I. But even though he was a hopeless mess socially and fashion-wise, he was both knowledgeable and helpful, and had been a good friend to me. "New change-lings?"

"'Fraid so. Nobody older than nine."

I looked around for a couple of bald heads. "The twins?"

"Lost to the horrors of puberty," he said dramatically. "Their voices started cracking and they shot up an inch in one month. A week later it was as if they'd never known us. These five are the next batch, preordained to continue serving the Zodiac by spreading the legacy among others of their kind!" He grinned when I rolled my eyes at his rhetoric, and pointed out each of the children. "This is Dylan, Sara, Kylee, and Kade. That's Douglas over there."

Chandra and I nodded at each of the kids, who'd finally calmed, though Dylan was sucking hard on an inhaler, eyes wide. Beyond keeping the secrets of the Zodiac, changelings held a special place in our mythos. If agents from opposite sides of the Zodiac happened to appear in the shop at the same time, they turned into peacekeepers, using the ability to physically morph into a living shield—and the clever use of fangs—to deter the opposing sides.

But even they eventually stopped believing. I noted the absence of Sebastian, the changeling who'd acted as protector of the Shadow agents, and glanced again at Douglas, still sneering at me from the far corner of the room. "Sebastian's replacement?"

"Better the devil you know than the devil you don't, huh?" Carl grinned, but I dismissed the kid now that I knew he was naturally antagonistic to the Light, and began searching for a little girl whose adoration of me bordered on idolatry, and whose natural inclination to help the Light, and me in particular, had proven priceless. I was already regretting not getting to say good-bye when she suddenly sauntered in from the hallway. I took in her crisp schoolgirl uniform, stumpy black pigtails, and smiled in relief. "Jasmine. You're still here."

She was followed by a smaller version of herself, a round-faced, glossy-haired, pixielike child who perked up as soon as she saw me.

"Yeah," Carl said, nervously looking over at Zane. "We were going to talk to you about that."

I motioned for him to hush and waved the two girls over.

"What's up, Jas? How've you been?"

She looked up at me from beneath dark lashes. "Do I know you?"

"Oh, Jasmine," her miniature replica said, voice trembling with excitement. "This is the Archer, esteemed member of troop 175, paranormal division, anti-evil, and preordained savior of the Zodiac!"

Jasmine whirled around and smacked the smaller girl upside her head. "I swear, if you don't stop with that superhero shit I'm going to beat it out of you."

The younger girl rubbed her head, fat tears welling in eyes as big as moons. "But, Jas, you're the one who told me about the legacy of the Kairos and how the portents signaling her chosen side's ascendancy over their enemies were already under way."

"Yeah, I also told you the tooth fairy was real. Sucks to be eight." She raised her hand to smack the girl again, and I grabbed her wrist, spinning her toward me. I let her jerk away, and she crossed her arms over her chest and proceeded to glare at me with unconcealed disdain.

"Jasmine. What's happened to you?"

Zane cleared his throat behind me. "Why don't you read the manual she's featured in and find out?"

A changeling featured in the manuals?

I turned in time to catch the comic he'd flung at me,

fumbling it against my body before drawing it away to study it. My picture was on the front, drawn in black and white against a livid red background, and I scowled at Carl—he'd drawn me top-heavy again—before flipping to the last page. Why read it? I'd lived it. It was just a question of where this issue ended.

Yet the last page was blank, as was the one before that. I skipped back until I finally found some text, Carl's bright panels coming to life a third of the way into the issue. The new changelings oohed and aahed as they realized they were standing in the room where I'd first confronted my then arch-nemesis, Joaquin, but the panels ended abruptly, right as Jasmine was seen taking on her changeling form. I closed the manual and waved it at Zane. "How about finishing it first?"

"It is finished."

Alarm skirted through me, and I scented a fresh wave of it springing from Chandra as well. "You're not going to write the series anymore?"

Surely I'd misheard. That would mean disaster for my troop, and Zane would probably be drooling and babbling incoherently by week's end. I'd seen what happened when he was blocked before. It wasn't pretty.

"Of course I'm going to write them." He held his hand out, motioning for me to return the manual. "Why should my head explode because you refuse to make amends?"

Power-hungry asshole, I thought, rolling it up and slapping it back into his palm. Was that what this was about? I'd asked Jasmine to use her shielding abilities to help me outside the confines of the shop last month, something Zane instructed the changelings never to do. "So you're going to keep the kids from reading the manuals just because you're holding a grudge?"

"I'm not the one keeping them from reading them," he said, and tossed me a second comic. "You are."

I snatched it out of the air, and the kids crowded closer, necks craning. But I looked down to find this one entirely blank. It was bound like a traditional comic, but even the cover was a glossy white sheet. "What's this?"

"That's the latest manual of Light. See where you're confronting the Shadow Cancer in a classic honky-tonk bar?"

I flipped through the blank pages. "No."

"Well I wrote it. It's not my problem if it isn't there." And he went back to polishing the glass top, whistling as he worked.

"Let me see that." Chandra yanked the not-manual from my hands. "Olivia, what did you do?"

"I didn't do anything," I said, wracking my brain. Had I?

"Actually," Carl began, and I whirled on him. He shrugged sheepishly and spit it out. "You fucked up the evolutionary *chi* when you took off with Jasmine's aura. It's time for her to hand her post over to Li and move on like the twins, but she's unable to mature without the whole of her aura. We told you not to wear it for too long."

"We told her not to leave the shop with it," Zane corrected from across the room. His head was still bent, but I could tell his teeth were clenched.

"You said not to wear her aura for over twelve hours. I gave it back well before then, undamaged." The changelings' ability to shield an agent from harm was due to the tractability of their aura. They could release their aura to us, allowing it to mold itself to our bodies so our true identities were seen, while our corporeal bodies remained protected. That's why I'd borrowed her aura. It'd enabled me to appear to Ben as myself—looking and feeling exactly the same as he remembered me—so I could give him a kiss that'd probably saved his life.

It'd worked too. While the frail shell of Jasmine's aura-less body had been safely cocooned back at my high-rise condo, I revealed myself and my continued existence to Ben. The idea had been to simply comfort him, assuage the grief he'd been feeling over my apparent death, and kiss him in parting. But I'd miscalculated both his grief and mine, and after finding solace together, I'd left in the middle of the night, sneaking away without explanation, thinking it best. Treating him, I realized now, like he was a pawn. It was a gross understatement to say Ben had reacted badly, knowing I was alive, but furious at me for returning only to disappear again. That fury was what had opened the door to Regan, who'd been more than happy to let herself into his life.

But as much as I was to blame for that botched effort, I hadn't screwed up when it came to Jas. I'd been extraordinarily careful to get her aura back to her under the twelve-hour mark. Her body hadn't wasted away, her soul hadn't expired.

"Wait a minute. Did I miss this issue?" Chandra yanked the comic from me, flipping through the pages faster as if that would make the story appear. She almost looked frantic.

"Come on, Chandra," Carl said, holding his hand out for the manual. "You know how these things work. The events directly affecting the battle between Shadow and Light are withheld from Zane and me until the time when revealing it won't tip the scales in favor of one side or the other. We didn't know she'd caused irreparable cosmic damage, and therefore you didn't either."

"But we all know now," Douglas said, and he laughed like he should be wringing his hands and twisting a mustache.

"So what does this mean?" I asked, ignoring him and motioning to the manual no one could read.

"It means you'd better fucking fix it," Chandra said, causing Douglas to laugh harder. This time we both turned on him, and he instantly sobered. Chandra turned an equally dark gaze on me. "If they can't read it, we don't get their thoughts or energy or any of the good juju enabling us to do our job."

I bit my lip and looked hopefully at Zane. He gave a

short jerk of his head, knowing what I was asking. "You were clothed in the aura of the changeling of Light. The Shadow manuals haven't been affected."

I closed my eyes. Fuck. So while the Shadow mythology would continue to be written, their legacy continuing to grow, the agents of Light were stuck in a sort of supernatural moratorium. We would fall behind degree by degree, and eventually we'd lose ground in the fight for the city.

"Fix her!" Chandra yelled, frantic now.

I opened my mouth to yell back, realized my frustration, though equal, was misplaced, and whirled on Jasmine. "Leave!" I said, pointing to the door.

She scoffed, snapped her gum, and pulled out her iPod.

Carl pulled up beside me, looking up in dark exasperation. "That's not going to work, Archer. You broke something inside her. Li is supposed to assume her position, but she can't until Jasmine matures, and for that you have to repair her."

I threw my arms into the air. "Well, what am I supposed to do? Order her to have her period?"

The boys around us started gagging. Jasmine reddened to a lovely rose-colored shade. And Li continued gazing up at me adoringly. Shit.

I sighed and knelt before her. "Jasmine. You really don't remember who I am?"

She gave me a hard stare, and for a moment I thought I saw a flash of regret, the girl I knew waving at me from behind those deep oval eyes. Then she lifted her chin. "I know who you think you are. And I don't think it's appropriate to promote that sort of pathology in trusting children."

I drew back at that, straightened, and found myself face-to-face with Chandra's pointed glare. Again. "What?"

"You haven't told anyone about this, have you?"

"I didn't know about it until now!"

She began shaking her head madly. "It's something a Shadow agent would—"

"Oh, don't fucking start that again," I interrupted, voice lifted to drown out hers. "I'm getting so tired of people saying the third sign of the Zodiac is the rise of my Shadow side! I'm not going to do anything to harm the agents of Light!"

"Except maybe you can't help it. It's like these kids hitting puberty and having to pass into adulthood. They may not want to, but biology helps determine one's destiny. You may not want to be part Shadow but that's your nature, as well as the Light. The sooner you start respecting that your compromised physiology has made you different—"

"She means a freak," Douglas edged in.

"The sooner you can start approaching aberrant situations from a new beginning point."

I wasn't hearing this. I wasn't a mutant, I wasn't weird. I wasn't a freak. "It was an accident!"

"It's suspect," she said simply, and I had no answer for that. She shook her head as she turned away. "You want me to believe it was accidental, you'll have to make it right. Or else we'll all pay the price."

"Chandra, wait," It rankled to call out to her, but she knew more than I did, and I could use her help on this one.

"No. I have to let Warren know about this." She pushed open the front door, bells muting but not completely drowning out her muttered "Someone does."

Some partner, I thought, watching her walk out the door, but I didn't follow.

"Forget her, Archer. She's deadweight."

No, she was more than that. She was right. But I'd deal with Chandra—and the rest of the troop—later. Right now I needed to stay focused and use my gifts—gifts, dammit!—to read both the Shadow manuals and the Light. Given time and luck, I knew I could find clues to the original manual, which contained the secret to the Tulpa's immortality. Killing him wouldn't just fix the problem with

Jasmine's interrupted development, it would forever settle the question as to whether I could overcome *my* biology. After all, wipe out the Shadow and all you were left with was Light.

"Here's the way I see it," Zane started, when the door had shut behind Chandra.

"Oh God," I said, turning to find him staring at me impassively. Zane made conspiracy theorists look like cheerleaders.

"You conned an impressionable young girl into giving you her aura, stole her *chi*, and broke the manuals detailing the exploits of the agents of Light. Your strength will grow because of your inclusion in the Shadow series, while the others in your troop will grow weak and impotent, and you can now rise to the head of your troop unchallenged."

It almost seemed plausible . . . if you were a complete nutcase. I leaned onto his newly polished glass top. "Cute theory . . . and dead wrong."

"Is that right?"

"Hey, Mr. CSI, why don't you let the agents worry about the detecting work, so you can continue playing armchair quarterback in this particular playing field?" I straightened and he dove for his Windex. "Now I'm looking for—"

"The original manual, blah, blah." He sprayed fervently, and I took a step backward as he tapped his head with his index finger, rag in his hand. "You don't think I already know? It's not here, we don't have it. Move on, little girl. Go play in someone else's sandbox."

He wished, I thought as he dismissed me with his frenzied polishing. Zane's lifelong quest was to find and possess the original manual, but no one knew exactly why. Certainly he'd be able to auction it off to the highest bidder, making himself a multimillionaire and incurring the debt of the Tulpa's slayer in the process . . . but I didn't think he was after mere money. He was too passionate about his work, and when he wasn't drawing manuals, he was poring over them; studying them, dissecting them. It made me wonder if he'd ever had the opportunity to hold out on us; if maybe there was something Zane knew that had never made it into the written text.

"You're a dick," I told him lightly.

"Yeah, well at least I'm not an evil, *chi*-stealing bitch."

My hand was on his throat before I even knew I'd moved and there was a sooty cast to the air, not unlike the smoke that'd swirled in Xavier's lair, though this didn't have the overlaying trail of incense to soften the odor. Glancing down into the spotless glass case housing *Star Wars* collectibles, I saw a fabulous hairdo and two eyes glaring like burning black marbles. I loosened my grip on Zane's neck.

"No," I said, dusting his shoulders, though he was wearing a ratty *Farscape* T-shirt and not a suit. I ignored both his flinch at my suddenly deep voice and the surprised exclamations from the group of the kids now backing away from me. I cleared my throat, but I was still angry, and my words scratched at my larynx. "You're not a bitch. You're just a mortal with a God complex. So remember who the fuck you're talking to."

I didn't know if it was fear or anger that had him shaking, but his hands were unsteady as they knocked mine from his shoulders. "You touched me," he said, in an incredulous whisper. "You're not allowed to touch the record keeper!"

Obviously.

Carl put a hand on my arm now that the smoke had literally cleared. "Hey, Archer. Look, maybe you should go."

His rebuke shamed me. I glanced around at the wide-eyed kids—including Jasmine—and frowned. What was I doing?

"It's the rise of her Shadow side!" Douglas called from behind a carousel displaying the entire Anita Blake series. "The third sign of the Zodiac is coming to fruition!"

"Wait . . . I can feel it," I said, turning his way and putting one hand to my chest. Douglas's head popped out, eyes going wide. "Yes, here it comes . . ."

Carl stepped forward. Zane stepped back.

"It's amazing," I said loudly, my face going slack as I stared into an unseen distance. "It's here . . . oh my God, it's the rise of . . ."

An unnatural hush overtook the shop.

"My middle finger."

I smirked at Douglas and he scowled back.

"Bitch!" he yelled, before ducking back behind the Executioner titles.

"Evil, *chi*-stealing bitch," I corrected, before turning again to Zane. He was looking at me with renewed disgust. This is what we, in the grown up world, call irony. "Can I go look in the archives now?"

"Whatever," he muttered, picking up his pencil. "Just don't ask me to help you."

I didn't; instead I told him to do something anatomically impossible as I whirled to the storeroom.

"You can go alone, and you may even look at the covers of the ancient ones." He made them sound like artifacts rather than comic books. I'd have laughed but I wasn't so sure that they weren't. "But if you even think about slipping one from its protective cover, I'll know it, and I'll charge you. Handsomely."

I sneered back at him and pulled out a wad of bills Xavier had thrown me in hopes that I'd forget about my pipe dream of getting a job. "Take cash?" I said, and smiled prettily, turning away before he could answer.

10

Despite my bravado and anger over Zane's accusations, I was shaken by the news about Jasmine, as well as Chandra's reaction to it. It wasn't her threat to tell Warren what I'd done that had me daunted. I screwed up pretty regularly around these paranormal parts—the product of a youth misspent as a mere mortal—and we were all used to that. But messing Jasmine up to the point that I'd effectively blown up the system keeping our world in balance . . . well, it was obvious that hadn't been done before.

One mark of the Kairos was the ability to do things others could not, such as reading both the Light and Shadow manuals. This was a physical manifestation of my ability to act on behalf of either side of the Zodiac, and it was why—despite repeated assurances to the contrary—the Tulpa still hoped the strength of his bloodline would win out over my mother's. Messing up the cosmic balance to cataclysmic proportions certainly qualified as such, I thought wryly, and fueling the angst of a teenager wasn't far off either. Threatening the record keeper—and, worse, feeling no remorse over it—was probably also a big supernatural no-no.

And even though I knew Zane's analysis of the situation was off, I wasn't so sure my troop leader would pause long enough to hear my side of the story. I *was* certain Warren would be pissed.

"Drama, drama," I muttered, trying to push the worries aside as I headed down the surprisingly long, dark, and cold tunnel leading to the storeroom. We'd find a way to fix Jasmine, I'd get Zane to tell me which of the thousands of manuals would lead me to the original, then I'd kill the Tulpa, escape my doppelgänger, pick up the dry cleaning on the way home, and we'd all live happily ever after.

And that highly probable plan hinged on the elusive treasure of knowledge buried in the storeroom.

Taken one by one and read on their own, the comics recording our adventures were nothing more than paranormal parables, anecdotes to entertain the masses, a product to engage the imagination of readers in illustrative and written form. But together they formed a comprehensive map leading to the master manual. There were clues planted throughout the manuals supposedly leading to the original's location, especially in the earlier ones. As time went on, the clues were spaced farther apart, but there was always something a knowledgeable reader could piece together. A template leading backward, all the way to the beginning.

Since the earliest manuals were created prior to the widespread use of the printing press, each major world metropolis possessed only one handwritten and highly coveted edition. I didn't expect to find one of those here; if there were such a treasure on the open market, it would be secured behind a case of unbreakable glass, protective wire, and a laser-tripped alarm. Frankly, I didn't know why I thought I could find something nobody else had, including the Tulpa, but at least I was doing something.

I paused at the entrance, letting my eyes adjust to the dim room, its accompanying length and width, and its surprising decor. It had more in common with an eighteenth-century English manor library than an urban shopping center. The perimeter of the room was lined with mahogany shelves, filled with manuals and studded with index cards sporting dates and which side of the Zodiac was grouped there. Still, you could cram an awful lot of comics into shelves that soared from floor to ceiling, so finding one with a recognizable clue was a long shot, and it would take considerable time.

I skipped past the foursome of leather easy chairs in the center of the room, resisting the urge to drop into one of them and fall asleep with my feet propped on the hearth of the ever-roaring fireplace. The last time I was here it'd been the peak of summer and the room was stifling with heat, but this time the fire shooting up the suspended flue was welcoming . . . and distracting.

And I bet that's why Zane had it here, I thought wryly. Invite the agents in, set them down for a warm cup of cocoa, and keep them from asking for help in pirating his beloved stash.

So I circumvented the fireplace, scooted past the half-full shelves holding the latest issues, including those telling of my arrival on the paranormal scene, and slipped deeper into the storeroom. I slowed as I hit the section I knew held tales regaling readers with my mother's exploits. There was the story of the way she'd killed the Tulpa's creator, which I'd already read, but loads more that I hadn't, including one everyone kept telling me about called "The Harvest." Warren had promised me its issue number, but conveniently kept "forgetting" it every time I asked. I could search for it now, but again, there was time to consider. I also knew Zane had some sort of silent alarm alerting him to any disturbance, and had no doubt he'd do as he said and charge me an exorbitant amount of money for anything I touched. With a wistful sigh, I left those shelves and continued to the back of the room to begin my search for something leading to the original manual.

I hadn't been at it five minutes when a voice bloomed behind me. "Well, isn't *this* an interesting coincidence?"

I whirled, then narrowed my eyes across the length of the storeroom as Regan DuPree stepped inside. Douglas followed her, though he'd now assumed the form changelings took when acting as protectors for their agents. His body looked like it'd literally been pounded into putty, his skin taking on the sheen of light reflecting off blackened water, blinding me to what was going on inside that pliant body. His jaw was misshapen, the softly curving cheeks of a preteen replaced by a hinged mouth the length of my skull. *All the better to eat you with, my pretty*, I thought, peering at the elongated teeth everybody in this world seemed to come equipped with but me.

For now Douglas only flanked Regan, swaying in a slightly nauseating motion, but if she needed protection from me he'd throw his aura over her like a supernatural cloak. Her true form would then appear, replacing this pseudo Joanna she'd donned for Ben, and Douglas's prepubescent body would fall to the floor, emptied of his life force, nothing more than a vulnerable shell until his aura was returned.

Jasmine appeared then, looking bored and put-upon, and pushed past Regan without looking up from her cell phone. I couldn't help but compare the sullen teen in front of me with my memory of the girl who had once been eager to help me, and had even consented to lay lifeless and fragile in a sea of jewel-toned pillows while I flitted around town wearing her aura. But whatever was broken in her was not on the outside. *I'll fix it*, I silently swore, even as her gaze locked on mine, resentment clear in those giant eyes.

Li, my would-be changeling, followed her sister so closely, she kept trodding on Jasmine's heels, clearly trying to get her to hurry. Jasmine slumped when she finally reached my side, and Li bounced on the tips of her tiny feet. Douglas snickered, a soft squishing sound, like slugs underfoot.

"A little sense of urgency would be nice," I told Jasmine.

She rolled her eyes. "Maybe you should've snapped your fingers and whistled."

"Why are you even back here if that's how you feel?"

"It's the rules," Li provided, obviously anxious to help in some way. "We're obliged to assist our agents in the designated safe zone where we derive our powers and have sworn to do our part in keeping the Zodiac balanced."

Good to know. I turned back to Regan, who'd drawn closer, and just seeing the smug look on her face made my blood sizzle. "How'd you find me?"

Regan hesitated as she considered allowing me to go on wondering and worrying about that, but her changeling had already dug a cell phone from his pocket, holding up the answer in one blackened, gelatinous hand.

"Is he allowed to call her?" I asked Jasmine, as Regan bawled him out about waiting for her signal before answering questions, and hit him upside his head. The slap made a juicy sucking sound as she yanked her hand away.

"Boys." Jasmine watched in disgust as his skull wobbled back into place. "You'd be amazed how much mileage you can get out of a wine cooler and a tittie magazine."

"Actually," Regan corrected, "it was a six-pack and a subscription."

"Maybe I should start bribing you to do your job as well."

"Why?" Jasmine said, studying her nails. "She already knows who you are."

"Good point," Regan said, studying her own. "And I also took down the license plate number of a car left overnight at a country bar on the outskirts of town. Know a guy named Lorenzo? Hunter Lorenzo?"

I froze momentarily, then quickly remembered he used a different surname as the head of security at Valhalla. His identity there was still safe, but if she could find that out so quickly, what else did she already know?

My hesitation made her laugh. "Relax, Archer. I'll uncover his alternate identities eventually. But discovering this one was easy. After all, it's plastered all over town."

She threw a stack of loose-leaf flyers at me, hard enough to pelt me in the chest, though most went flying through the air, colorful as confetti. I shot Jasmine an annoyed glance as she picked away a flyer plastered to my chest. It was one of the street rags advertising sexual entertainment, peddled to tourists along the Strip. There had been a county law restricting the practice at one time, but the ban had been deemed unconstitutional, and the peddlers were as aggressive and ubiquitous as ever. I didn't recognize the phone number printed below the "direct to your room" statement, but the man whose chest it was superimposed upon was definitely Hunter.

"Ew!" Jasmine dropped the flyer and kicked away another plastered against her Skechers. Li squeaked and covered her eyes with tiny hands.

"I take it from the look on your face that Olivia Archer didn't know she was going around on the arm of a professional escort?" Regan giggled maniacally. "My God, what will happen when that news breaks? 'The Heiress and the Call Boy' would make a great cover story, don't you think?"

Xavier would have a stroke. I tried to cover, though. "You think you're telling me something I didn't already know?"

And did Warren, or the others? Was I the only one in the dark about Hunter's erotic side work?

"Oh, I *know* I am. Though you have Benny-boy to thank for that priceless spot of dirt. All I gave him was that plate number. Superior detecting skills for a mortal, that one, and for some reason he's highly protective of his dead girlfriend's little sister." She tilted her head, the spark in her eye hardening to flint. "In fact, he's now so determined to find something to take to the authorities on Mr. Lorenzo, you'd think he was worried the man might be after her inheritance."

Which told me she was about to plant that seed in Ben's mind, further aggravating his suspicions.

The shop was technically a safe zone, but these changelings were still green. I was willing to bet I could drag her outside and pummel her to pulp in the parking lot before they even knew what was happening. It was worth a shot, and I transferred my weight onto the balls of my feet.

Regan thought I was straightening up. "Oh, the Kairos gets angry. Could this be the 'rise of your dormant side'— the third sign of the Zodiac come to life? Take notes, Douglas. We're in the presence of greatness here. Are you shaking in your high tops?"

Douglas actually looked down. Regan rolled her eyes. "Breaking in new changelings is a bitch."

I made a face, though I happened to sympathize.

"Guess that leaves me to sum up the situation without the wisdom of the adolescent set. So how's this for a pithy little roundup?" She sauntered to the center of the room, and I angled to keep her in view as she dropped her weight on the arm of one of the chairs. Douglas shadowed her. "Your real boyfriend is about to hop in the sack with your mortal enemy, and your fake one is getting horizontal with everyone else."

"That's just nasty," Jasmine told me, leaning against a bookshelf crammed with Shadow manuals.

"But the surprising thing is that a man like Lorenzo would need to pimp himself out at all." Regan took a slow breath. "After all, I'd do him for free."

"Even that would be charging too much."

Regan's left eye twitched and she rose to her feet before she could stop it. I closed the space between the fireplace and me and saw alarm flash in her eyes. Steady, I thought, staying myself where I was. I didn't want to spook her too soon.

"Jasmine!" Li pulled her sister into view, straining with the effort. "Help her!"

Jasmine yanked away and Li toppled onto her butt. "Get bent, runt."

Li looked up at me in bereft helplessness.

"Don't worry, Archer. That lazy bitch can't help you in any way that matters."

"Hey!"

"Oh, *now* you protest?" I muttered to Jasmine, who was suddenly standing attentively beside me. "And do I look worried to you?"

Regan's brows rose. "If you're not you should be. Your cover identity is starting to unravel at the edges. It's only a matter of time now."

"Does that mean you're ready to show your hand? Let the Tulpa know his daughter is posing as . . . " I mouthed, *Olivia Archer*, erring on the side of caution, not wishing to risk the information leaking into the manuals. Paranoia, one of the few superstitions we *did* entertain.

Thoughts, actions, and even conversations with an enemy remained private unless the acting agent willed their actions to be known. Otherwise we'd never be able to make love or have a meal, or even go to the bathroom without worrying it would end up on the glossy cover of a graphic novel. Our private moments and thoughts, the same ones mortals kept secret from others—and sometimes themselves—those things remained hidden. Right now these confrontations between Regan and me were parries and thrusts of a personal nature, but if she ever chose to truly strike, the world would know it.

"Not quite yet." She edged herself back onto the armchair and shot me a sly look. "Though I could tell him about *other* family members."

My teeth clenched, but I relaxed when I realized she would only hint at my daughter's existence as well. She didn't want to talk about Ashlyn in front of the changelings, and wouldn't risk the girl's name showing up in the Shadow manuals either. An empty threat then, I thought, relaxing marginally.

"Or," she continued, " I could make this really interesting. Even the playing field a bit. Show you *my* true identity."

Why? I wondered, instantly distrustful. "You'd better not. You'll scare the children."

She remained undaunted. "But don't you want to know what exactly Ben is fucking, say, this time next week?"

That was why.

She gestured to Douglas before I could answer, and he completed the transformation from jellied shadow to roaring monster. His outline wavered as if a chill wind had swept over him, and the scrawny preteen frame thinned even further. He was the width of a dime as his mass expanded outward and upward to mirror Regan's. He looked like the ugliest paper doll I'd ever seen. Then he pivoted in front of her, she took one step forward, and their bodies married. His husk—all the parts she didn't need—fell away, hitting the ground like stoneware. He didn't move again, and the new Regan, the real one, grinned.

In relative terms, she was pretty. Joaquin, our enemies' Aquarian, was the last Shadow I'd glimpsed from behind the viscosity of his changeling's aura, and he'd been all ebony bone and rot, skin hanging from him in blackened strips of aged decay. Regan, in turn, was merely skinless, like some barbaric beauty treatment had shaved it all away, and her blood had dried around her muscles, making her look like she'd been dipped in a thin layer of burgundy candle wax.

Her glittering, pale blue eyes stood out against this dull sleekness, though I spotted a section near her collarbone where the blood had scabbed over unevenly, like a human's would. It was trailing fresh blood and pus, and when she saw I'd noticed, she began worrying it with her fingers, icy eyes daring me to react. I spotted the white bone of her elbow peeking at me through the ruins of her flesh, still smooth but with a hairline crack, and knew that fissure would widen. Every time she moved, some other muscular system popped open and began to bleed, and though she was meaty—unlike Joaquin—she was still rancid. The wriggling I saw pulsing inside her chest wasn't from a beating heart.

I decided to wait and drag her from the shop when she wasn't so gooey. "Let me guess? You guys start decaying as soon as you metamorphose into full-fledged agents, am I right?"

"Duh," Jasmine said to me. "I could, like, totally smell her from here. And I have allergies."

"I'm not decaying," the living corpse said evenly. "I'm becoming more deific, like my ancestors before me."

"No," I said, playing along. "You're simply not aging well."

The insult was right up Jasmine's alley. "I'd recommend a face lift . . . if she had a face."

"Now, Jas," I chided. "She's better off sticking to the basics. Eight hours of sleep, plenty of water . . . multiple skin grafts."

Under the "Rose" persona, Regan's reaction would've been no more threatening than a hair toss. But now she snapped her head back and forth, like a snarling dog, her emotions as exposed and raw as her mucus and muscles. As she struggled to regain her composure, I wondered again why she would show me this. I found out as soon as she resumed looking like a mere zombie, instead of a psychotic zombie. "I have a message from your father."

I sighed. Of course she did. And that's why she'd sought me out . . . though it still didn't explain the freak show. "Let me guess. He wants to make good on all the back payments on my child support?"

Muscles ruptured as she clenched her jaw. "It's about the doppelgänger that saved your life last week."

Which confirmed Warren's suspicion as to who, or what, the woman was. And that the Tulpa knew it too. I quirked a brow at Regan. "And he sent you?"

That didn't make sense. If the Tulpa thought Regan knew where to find me, he'd have pummeled it out of her and come after me himself. At that point my Olivia Archer cover would be moot.

"He sent a message-by-minion."

Li put her hands to her cheeks and gasped. Jasmine groaned and pulled out her cell phone again, checking out. I stood blank-faced, pretending I knew what that was.

"I just happened to be the first one to find you." Her shriveled lips quirked. "Imagine that."

From her words I gathered a "message-by-minion" was something that applied to all Shadow agents, a mandate that couldn't be disobeyed. Apparently it also meant Regan had to take her reluctant revelation a step further. Literally. She widened her stance, lifted her arms in the air so the muscles split and bled, and took a moment to steady herself before lowering into a backbend. Her decaying spine cracked in five places.

Jasmine glanced up from her text messaging, unimpressed. "There's a girl at my school named Cindy who can totally do that. She's been in tumbling and gymnastics since she was, like, three and can touch her nose with her . . ."

Regan shuddered, and her ribs ruptured in her chest cavity. They splintered upward, jagged edges pricked with scraps of muscle, while toothpick-sized bits sprang out like thorns to keep enemies at bay. Unnecessary, I thought, swallowing hard. I didn't want to get any closer. Her exposed ribs swung like they were on hinges, knit together on the opposite side, and her head rotated a hundred and eighty degrees on her neck.

Jasmine's mouth snapped shut as the Regan-thing turned. "Cindy can't do that."

In turn, Regan's mouth sprang open. A wet, guttural cry rose from the emptiness of her ravaged core, and bloody tears began to stream down her face. Those pale orbs widened, then protruded so I could actually see the tendons connecting them as they strained from their sockets. The Regan-thing blinked—or I thought it was a blink because even though her lashes and lids had wasted away, her eyes rolled three hundred and sixty degrees in their sockets—but when they appeared again, they were tar black and smoking.

"Shit . . ." Jasmine's curse morphed into a howl and her jaw dropped open, elongating into a gaping maw. The rest of her skin softened, shimmered, and thinned, and she was suddenly as rubber-limbed and tensile as Douglas had been. Skittles, a Hello Kitty coin purse, and lip gloss littered the floor as she spun, whipping around to position herself before me. Her remaining aura deepened her skin color to near opaqueness, and her outline shimmered at the edges as her body expanded to my height and width, concealing me fully.

Apparently Li had been right; she had no choice but to help when I was truly in danger because she took two rippling steps backward, and I closed my eyes, stockstill, and felt coolness sweep over me, like a wave of air fresh from the sea. When I opened my eyes a second later, the world was awash in a pastel lavender hue. Jasmine's body lay at my feet; knees tucked into her chest, eyes pinched shut. I sensed Li's form prone on the ground next to her, but didn't dare look for sure. Instead I carefully stepped over my changeling's shell to face off against my father.

"There you are." The Tulpa brushed at an invisible speck of dust on one bloody entrail. "I've been looking all over for you."

"You don't say," I said dryly.

His eyes canvassed the room, passing over the shells of the changelings, lingering longer on the shelves over my shoulder, the question he wasn't asking clear as they landed again on me. "Leave it to Regan to locate you first. Though when I sent out the message, I thought she might. She despises all agents of Light, though her hatred for you is almost toxic. Don't know why."

He was waiting for me to elucidate. I did. "Because she was born under a mushroom cloud?"

"Because she likes her luxuries," he countered. "My agents are forbidden to eat, sleep, fornicate, or shit until a transmogrified message has been delivered—"

"Those are luxuries?"

"I sent this message out three days ago."

"So Las Vegas is teeming with a troop of hungry, horny, sleep-deprived, bunged-up psychopaths?" No wonder the crime rate had spiked in the last forty-eight hours.

"I've decided to give you a second chance."

"A second chance *again*?" I let my eyes widen into saucers and his—hers—narrowed. "What? You're the one who declared apocalypse and tried to microwave me in your supernatural funk." And he hadn't been wishy-washy about it either.

"I've had a change of mind."

"Obviously." My eyes roved over his head in distaste. I didn't even want to know what that membrane was covering all that coiling gray matter.

The Tulpa held out his hands—or Regan's—in supplication, but the gesture wasn't as winsome as he intended. Each digit was dripping with fresh blood. "We need to talk."

And I was willing to bet Regan's mention of the doppelgänger had something to do with that. Knowing that gave me an edge. "All right. Let's talk about why you're so afraid of a woman made of bubbles."

He reached out and slapped me so fast, I gasped from

the shock as much as the pain. He wasn't supposed to be able to touch me in a safe zone and he sure as hell shouldn't be able to reach through Jasmine's protective shell. I put a hand to my stinging face, and felt wetness there.

The Tulpa brought his claws up in front of his face, smiled, and licked blood from his fingers. I didn't know if it was Regan's blood, Jasmine's, or mine . . . probably a bit of each.

"Or you could choose the subject," I said, like I thought I had a choice. He inclined his head. Easy to be agreeable when you knew you would get your way.

"I made a mistake," he began, surprising me, though his sharp look had me holding back my first response. I didn't feel like finding out what would happen if he *really* wanted to put his hands on me. "I thought you were . . . in league with the double-walker. It seemed likely after the way we last parted that you'd attempt to attract a double-walker for additional protection against me."

Ye-ah. Because I knew exactly how to do that. I didn't say that, though, choosing instead to play dumb. It wasn't exactly a stretch. "Well, she can't be my doppelgänger because she tried to disembowel me. And she doesn't even look like me."

"But she smells like you," he said, and it came out a hiss because of his torn tongue. Those black eyes widened. "I wasn't lying when I said your pheromones were all over her. Every disturbance caused by her unnatural passage into this realm sends up a cloud of eau de Joanna."

"I've never seen her before in my life."

"So? Consider what you know of supernatural phenomena—or more exactly, what you *don't* know." He smirked, and I thought: *Sure, rub it in.* I couldn't argue, though. "Due to the rather *surprising* circumstances of your conception and birth, who's to say there weren't once two of you?"

I blanked at his meaning, not because I didn't under-

stand what he was saying, but because the idea was so foreign to me, and what I'd always known about myself, it
took a moment for his words to sink in. Finally, I managed,
"A . . . a twin?"

"One—the strongest, the Kairos—survived . . . while
the other became a ghost."

I blanked again. A twin. Was it possible?

"Too bad Zoe isn't around to ask," he said, echoing my
own thoughts . . . though he could've been reading my
expression. I'd been shocked into transparence. A twin.
"Stranger things have happened," he said, motioning down
the body he temporarily possessed. "In any case, this
double-walker has focused on you. The more interaction
there is between the two of you, the easier it will be for her
to *become* you."

"But why?" I thought, so taken with the idea, I let my
attention momentarily wander from the Tulpa. "Why now,
I mean?"

"Why not?" He shrugged, the movement causing Regan's shoulder to tear in three separate spots, and I tried
to ignore the fresh blood staining Zane's Persian carpet.
Explain that one to the steam cleaners. "You're the Kairos.
You've finally come into your supernatural powers, something a double-walker seeking corporeal expression would
find irresistible. But I saw your face when she appeared at
the top of that scaffolding. You were as surprised as I. And
you and your troop have as much to lose."

So the others were right. He was just as worried about
the doppelgänger's increasingly debilitating explosions
as we were. Further proof that she had to be stopped, and
soon. "She tried to rip my heart from my chest before escaping," I admitted, watching for a reaction. It was difficult
through the decaying tissue and twitching tendons, but his
eyes narrowed and his voice softened.

"Did she?" The hint of protectiveness in his voice might
have warmed me if *he* hadn't already tried to kill me multiple times as well. "It's because a double-walker needs a

fleshly relic from their chosen prey in order to fully manifest in the physical realm. Organs are best, they contain the most condensed inner energy, and a heart, as the center of your life force, is the most symbolic as well. They'll do anything to achieve full material form. Of course, there hasn't been one in this valley for years. I won't allow it. But this one is strong . . . and smart. She gains admittance by circumventing the portals, and she'll soon attempt her vitalistic shift into a natural state."

"Which means?"

"It means she's going to kill you, my dear." He smiled at me like I was a child, before offering his twisted version of a helping hand. "Unless we work together."

I jerked, like a horse spooked at the reins. Work with the Shadows? Zane's accusations came flying back at me, and Warren's unspoken fears that I'd do just that surfaced in my mind. I suddenly felt filthy just for speaking with the walking dead, and pulled myself straight. "I don't know how many times or different ways there are to tell you. I'm not coming to the Shadow side. Ever."

"I'm no longer asking you to," he said, startling me again. He spread his hands in explanation, fingers cracking at the knuckles. "You're a target for a doppelgänger, Joanna. Your *chi* is fouled, and the gifts you might potentially bring to the Shadow side are blunted by the risk you pose to those around you . . . and yourself. Besides, until you get rid of this double-walker, this dualistic version of you, everyone around you is in danger."

"And you care why?"

"About the agents of Light?" he scoffed, and pulled at a clump of skin hanging from his neck. "Clearly I don't. But I do care about the possibility of them gaining unfair advantage during one of these chaotic outbursts. We should work together to eliminate this third party so the fate of the valley will be won or lost independent of some ghostly creature's whim."

I was silent, weighing his words for deceit, but I couldn't

see any other reason for wanting to work together than the one he'd given. I didn't say the words, but my prolonged silence was apparently enough to convince him of my agreement.

"Think about it, and if you decide to take me up on my offer, think about *me*. Envision me coming to you, do it in a 'safe' zone if you must"—the mocking in his voice wasn't lost on me, and it sent my injured cheek to pulsing, but I said nothing—"and I'll come to you through the nearest agent, like now. Work with me, Joanna. It's the only way we can banish this chaotic life force."

And before I could agree, or not, his blackened eyes were snuffed, smoke rising from empty sockets before the whole of him caved back in to Regan's chest cavity. Douglas's aura stretched like a sail away from Regan's body as soon as it flipped inward, as if anxious to be away. Regan straightened, and I saw organs rearranging themselves in her middle, her rent skin stitching itself back together as if being zipped up before she bent to touch her changeling's shell, a little more roughly than necessary. Douglas gasped as his aura ripped from Regan like tape, adhering back to his shell to prevent any permanent damage. He lifted his head and shook it as if dazed. I couldn't blame him.

"The Tulpa always has such a compelling argument," I said to Regan as I stroked Jasmine's pale face and watched as her aura sloughed from me like soapsuds under water. Her cheeks warmed with my touch. "He'd make a great lawyer."

Regan spared only a brief glance in my direction but said nothing as she smoothed over her peasant top and patted her hair back in place. I watched her fuss with the bow on her top, and smothered a smile. She'd heard nothing of my conversation with the Tulpa.

"So," I said slyly, studying her carefully for a reaction. "I understand you live in a townhouse south of the Strip."

Her head shot up, shock blanketing her face.

"And that you drive a red Audi, two-door, cute, though it's been in the shop twice this month. You might want to think about replacing that. And how'd your visit to the dentist go last week? Other than the filling in your upper left second molar?"

Obviously I'd gotten Maximus X to dig up the info on "Rose," but if Regan thought the Tulpa had provided me with the information in exchange for something he wanted, who was I to correct her?

"What does that mean, do you think?" I asked her, tilting my head. "That your leader had so much to say to me in private?"

Regan hesitated, left eye twitching again, and I knew I'd spooked her. I smiled because I'd also just discovered her "tell." Unable to trade barbs since she suddenly had no idea where she stood, she deftly, and not so subtly, changed the subject. "You know, Ben's taking me up to Mount Charleston for the weekend. We're going to rent a cabin, drink spiked cocoa, and cuddle in front of a log fire. I think it's time to take our relationship to the next level." She tilted her head wonderingly. "What do you think I should wear? A white baby doll or a red one?"

A tremor, like an animal stirring to life, moved through me. "Ben will never be with your pulpy rotting ass as long as I'm alive, clear?"

That eye twitched again, her mouth thinning. "Well, we can fix that, can't we?"

My eyes slid to her changeling, who'd picked something slimy from his hair and was studying it closely, trying to figure out what it was. My gaze found hers again, and I thought, *Fuck it*. The leader of the underworld had made me an offer I couldn't refuse. A doppelgänger wanted to eat my heart for breakfast. What was one more little war?

I ran at her so fast, my fist was flying toward her face while her hands were still motionless at her side. The crunch of her nose was less satisfying now that I knew how rotted out her insides were . . . and besides, it wasn't enough to kill her.

Momentum had me somersaulting over her head, but I anticipated, and was twisting in the air above her, readying a second assault even before I'd touched ground. She turned into me, I blocked with my right, and the sharp tip of my elbow sailed downward to bury into her left eye socket.

Douglas had finally found his feet and had again co-agulated into the grotesque, rubberized monster meant to protect the Shadows, but I ignored his snarl, dodged his lunge, and thrust my foot into his solar plexus. It sunk through to the other side, and would've pierced his body if not for a membrane wall as clear and thin as a yolk sac. He screamed as I yanked my foot free, but the interruption had given Regan time to retreat. She moved so the blazing fireplace was between us.

"Don't." I circled closer as her eyes flicked to the door. "You'll never make it."

She shifted too. "What are you doing? You can't kill me here."

"This is just practice, Regan," I said, stalking her. "A taste of things to come."

She pulled out her conduit, even though it was useless in the safe zone. "Is that what the Tulpa told you when he took a chunk out of your cheek?"

My face still ached with the residual sting of the Tulpa's slap, but I shrugged. "That was before we came to an agreement. And I'll heal."

"Sure," she said, feigning unconcern as her gaze darted sideways. "But will your changeling?"

"I'm fine," Jasmine said, but she was guarded, clearly worried Regan would seek retaliation for my attack on her changeling.

But Regan hadn't been looking at her. "Jasmine . . . where's Li?"

"She was here a minute ago," Jasmine complained, and

she backed away to peer under the freestanding bookcases separating the back of the room into rows. "I swear, if I lose her again my mother is going to . . ."

"Oh God." My eyes found Li at the same time Jasmine's did. I was vaguely aware of Regan's laughter—laughter and footsteps as she ran from the storeroom—but I bolted in the opposite direction, and dropped to my knees next to Jasmine, who'd been closer and had gotten there first.

"Wait, Jas!"

But she was already turning her sister over. "Li, how many times do I have to—"

We both gasped, momentarily stilled by the china doll cheek scored with three deep claw marks. It looked like she'd been attacked by a pit bull. Her beautiful skin hung in tatters, and blood pooled on the floor around her. Even once the bleeding was staunched, even when the furrows were stitched back together under a surgeon's gentle hand, the child would be scarred for life.

But when she looked up at me, there was none of the loathing I expected in her watery gaze. There was no room for it with pain and fear and hope all jostling for space. "I did good, right? I protected you?"

The lump in my throat turned into a mountain. "Yeah, baby. You did great."

She smiled with the good side of her face. I turned to Jasmine and found the piercing accusatory glare I deserved.

"Happy?" she asked, voice breaking.

God, no. I certainly wasn't that. "I-I didn't know."

My voice cracked and a tear slid down the cheek that mirrored the injury to Li's . . . except mine would heal. Jasmine looked at me in a length of charged silence, and for a moment I saw something akin to pity flickering behind her gaze, but she snuffed it out in the next. "Whatever."

"I'm going to fix it." I reached for Li.

"You'd better." Jasmine said in a voice round with fury and disbelief. "*Hero.*"

But there was only one heroine present, and I lifted her in my arms and gently carried her from the storeroom.

11

I drove Li and Jasmine to the emergency room, and left only after their mother had arrived, assuring her all medical costs would be covered by the Archer Children's Foundation. She thanked me repeatedly for "saving" her baby's life from a vicious dog's attack, while Jasmine sat in a plastic chair, swinging her feet back and forth as she alternated text messaging on her cell phone and glaring pointedly in my direction.

I wanted to tell her it wasn't my fault. I hadn't expected the Tulpa to attack, and I didn't know how the injury had been transferred to Li instead of me or even her. But intentionally or not, I really had broken something vital to the balance of the supernatural system, and now not only were the manuals not being written, but a seven-year-old's life had been permanently affected.

It was too late to return to Master Comics. The shop was closed and I'd received instructions to meet the rest of the troop at eight o'clock to examine the mask Chandra had stolen from Xavier's. It was seven-thirty now and I still had to get across town in the rush of Friday night traffic, but at least it gave me time to think of a way to tell the others about Li, as well as ponder the smorgasbord of trouble now filling my plate. Okay, so it wasn't all bad news. I'd learned the doppelgänger's appearance had spooked the Tulpa enough to have him willing to bargain with the Light. I'd also learned Regan's left eye wigged out when she was nervous, that she was overly sensitive about turning into a walking corpse, and I could best her in hand-to-hand if I played my cards right.

The news about Hunter having a side gig as a sex worker wasn't what one would call *good*, but he always had a reason for what he did, and surely he had one for keeping it from the rest of the troop. Since I was exceptionally curious as to what that reason was, it was convenient to find myself swinging in front of the warehouse that served as his workshop with almost a quarter hour to spare. We were meeting here because we weren't sure what would happen if we tried to take Xavier's mask back into the sanctuary with us. Anything related to the Shadows was instantaneously incinerated as it slid down the secured chute leading to our hidden underground lair. I shuddered as I recalled the sole time I'd attempted entry without donning my protective mask. In contrast, we didn't know if *this* mask was inherently evil—though there was something determinedly not right about a piece of wood that came to life and sucked out a person's soul essence—but we couldn't risk it being destroyed before we had a chance to examine it further.

Hunter's workshop was as safe a place as we could hope for on this side of reality. It wasn't a designated safe zone like Master Comics or the Downtown Cocktail Lounge, and was technically accessible by mortals and Shadows alike, but Hunter had the place so booby-trapped, the unfortunate Shadow who attempted a break-in here would be skewered, rotisseried, and served up to his or her enemies faster than you could say, *Would you like fries with that?* I'd seen him construct a weapon out of nothing more than toothpicks and twine, but the devices buried about his workshop were more than that; they were lethal works of art. Hunter did like his toys.

The steel bay door was open on the easterly side, and I assumed all alarms, traps, and missile systems had been turned off, so I pulled my Porsche to a stop next to his Ford Mustang, noting they were the only two cars here as of yet. Also convenient.

Clicking the alarm on my car, I glanced at the red Mustang and wondered if he used it for his security cover or if it was the ride for his side gig. What did a call boy drive on a date, anyway? And why, I asked myself as I shook my head, should I even care?

The workshop was housed in an isolated commercial district where the Strip's biggest names in magic stored their props. Burton, Copperfield, Penn and Teller; they all had storage buildings the size of airplane hangars, so if our place ever *was* broken into, the templates and drawings and odd contraptions could be explained away as yet another magician's illusionary trove of tricks.

What it was, however, was a place to plan, design, and test the weapons we used against the Shadows as we vied for control over the valley. The conduits designed to complement a specific agent's talents, temperament, and training were conceived and honed to lethal perfection here. However, that was a relatively rare task—agents, with any luck, tended to live a long time—so the rest of the time it was a place to run sims and defensive programs meant to counteract our enemies' machinations. Even the tools used to clean up a location affected by a paranormal battle were contained in raw form and made here. And Hunter's hands crafted them all.

I'd once heard the Eskimo languages had dozens of different words for the concept of *snow*. Agents, I decided, should have the same extensive linguistic flexibility for the qualities of smoke, because the scent I inhaled upon entering the warehouse wasn't the Shadow stench of incinerating flesh and hot ashes, and it wasn't the suffocating fallout that had squeezed all the air from the molecules in the pseudo black hole the Tulpa had created downtown last weekend. No, Hunter's scent was more natural, like the wisps rising from an isolated forest campfire, when the breeze was up and there was no other person for miles around. I located him by inhaling the heady mixture of clean sweat and a spice as identifiable as a sliver of ginger on the tongue, and my belly flip-flopped inside me. It's true what they say, I thought, rounding the corner to find him shirtless, bent over a sliding table. Where there's smoke, there's usually fire.

And this man was scorching.

He wasn't overbuilt like a gym rat; his physicality was more raw and far less self-conscious than that. He was sleek in the fashion of panthers and fast cars, built for performance, with latent power almost quivering beneath that compact frame. Still, the first word that would spring to mind if you ever saw him backlit, in silhouette, would be *man*. I especially liked the way his shoulders rounded, how they rolled high and smooth, like statues on display, clearly the force behind his fist. I'd seen him pummel through a concrete barrier with a careless backslap, and couldn't help but compare that to the way I fought. I had never solely used the torque of my shoulder. I used my wide hips, my long thighs, my agile mind. As a woman, my whole being had to be the force behind my fist.

And back when I was a *mortal* woman, Hunter was exactly the type of man I'd study from behind the lens of my camera. I'd see them moving across a room with unconscious, predatory grace, and wonder what it would be like to be that powerful. What did it feel like to be able to run faster, jump higher, hit harder? To feel synapses firing in split-second bursts beneath the skin, testosterone making me jumpy?

Those were, of course, the covetous thoughts of a girl

who'd been victimized in a way most men could never imagine. Back then, before I was a hundred times stronger than all those men I so jealously and suspiciously studied, I equated physicality with power. I thought the stronger you were, the more you controlled your own body and destiny. I even remember swearing in the abyss of night that if I'd been born with a male body I would never let it get out of shape or allow it to be less than what it could be. I'd have sculpted it until David wilted beneath his fig leaf in comparison. I'd have taken up as much space as possible. I'd have run just to feel power pumping in my thighs.

I hadn't felt that envious twinge since my metamorphosis, but it struck me now, and surprise had me holding back as I studied Hunter from my location beside the wall cabinets. I'd never seen him without his shirt before, and the ambient light from the low-hanging bulbs captured the cuts and grooves of his muscles as he worked. His skin was burnished like faded copper . . . the result of sporting beneath the desert sun, not worshipping. More, there was a tattoo high on his back, above his right shoulder blade, and when he shifted again I crept closer to inspect it. It was a perfect circle of ink so black, his tanned skin looked pale in comparison. One side of the circle was shaded, the other left naked in the classic design of yin and yang. But the artist had left enough skin bare on the shaded portion to spell one potent word: *Desire*.

On the naked side? *Fear*.

"You're in my light," he said, not looking up. He knew my scent too. In fact, every fresh encounter between us strengthened that knowledge, and soon those silty layers would be thick enough to form a solid bedrock of intimacy. If a team of archaeologists could dig up the emotions lying between us, unearthing the beginning of my relationship with Hunter, the aureole we'd swapped and shared would mark a distinct altering of the hostility that came before it.

It was hard to hate someone when you'd stood not just in their shoes, but the very seat of their soul.

And right now, with his scent invading my pores and the sight of him with fewer clothes on than I'd ever seen before, my vision clouded. All I could see was that damned tattoo, like some of those emotions I'd experienced while inside him had been inscribed on his skin. I could all too easily recall the slide of his lips beneath mine as I passed him the aureole, the power in both his body and mind mingling with mine. It was a memory I didn't want.

And starting an argument, I decided, would be a good way to push it away.

"I'll stand over here, then," I said, before pulling out one of the flyers Regan had pelted me with and dropping it in his line of view. It landed at the toe of his left boot, and he merely shifted his eyes, the rest of him still as he remained bent over his work. "I mean, this *is* your good side, right?"

Now he did look up. "Where'd you get this?"

I crossed my arms. "They're plastered all over town."

Now he did straighten, stretching blithely, which annoyed me for some reason. "And when did Olivia Archer become a patron of the smut peddlers?"

"Actually, Ben discovered it. He's decided he doesn't like you."

Hunter turned back to the pencil and scale he'd been working with. "Oh, I'm real worried about the mortal who keeps stepping on his own dick."

"Hey!" I straightened, indignant.

He waved my protest away and kept working. "Big deal. So Ben told the little sister of his not-dead ex-girlfriend—who really is his ex—that he doesn't like me. Meanwhile he's dating her sworn enemy. Stop me when this gets ridiculous."

I circled to the other side of the table and leaned forward so I really was in his light. "You mean ridiculous like pissing off a P.I. so badly, he shared everything he's learned about Hunter Lorenzo with his new girlfriend?"

That had him looking up. "What?"

I shot him a grim smile now that I had his attention. "Ben didn't show that to me. Regan did."

I saw his mind working, body still as his eyes wandered the floor, mentally covering all the angles as I had. The Hunter Lorenzo identity, the odds of Regan tracking him to Valhalla. Finally his tensed shoulders relaxed. "It doesn't matter."

"It does if she ever sees you at the casino. What are you going to say, security is your side job? Or hooking is?"

His jaw clenched, but he still offered no explanation. "You worry too much."

He meant I asked too many questions. Feeling my temper rise, I linked my hands to keep them from curling into fists, and worked on keeping my tone light and even. "I'm not worried, just curious. I mean, what kind of women call you? Desperate? Homely? College girls come to Vegas to party? Doctors' wives left alone too many nights in a row?"

He turned away again. "Business etiquette prevents me from speaking of my clients."

"How quaint. An escort code of honor." I held up my hands as his gaze whipped up to mine again. "Hey, I'm interested. I mean, do you go to dinner? Dancing? Or is it straight to the bedroom for horizontal gymnastics?"

He almost smiled, and I realized my voice had risen. "Whatever they want," he said coolly, twirling his pencil lightly between thumb and forefinger. He was watching me carefully now. "Each woman's needs are a unique and fragile thing."

"Don't go all new age call boy on me," I snapped. "Warren doesn't know about this, does he?"

Hunter shrugged. "He wouldn't care. As long as I'm discreet."

I glanced back down at the flyer with his face plastered across the cover.

Hunter's jaw flexed as my eyes returned to him. "Not that it's any of your business."

I was in no position to argue; I'd turned him down repeatedly, and made it clear we would never be an item. Sure, I was physically attracted to him, but the imprint stomped on my heart was Ben-shaped, and it'd been there long before Hunter came along. No matter how honed that capable body and mind might be, he would never fit into that space.

"Fine," I said agreeably, backing up a step. He watched me for a moment, sniffed, then pulled the cap off a bottle of water, downing it in practically one gulp. "So what are you working on?"

He wiped the back of his hand across his mouth, then tossed the empty bottle into a lined trash bin without looking. "A new conduit."

And anyone could see that designing the weapons each agent carried into battle was his true passion. Two oversized drafting tables took up the warehouse's nucleus, and both were littered with sketches, pencils and erasers, rulers and flow charts. He then cast his experimental weapons in foam templates, though that didn't mean his work was tentative. The weapons master prior to him had been an exacting teacher, breaking Hunter's inferior efforts underfoot until he'd finally learned to abandon caution and rely solely on his warrior's instinct. For every conduit created there were a dozen more abandoned—as evidenced now by the two full bins of discarded foam—but the result was weapons with responsiveness and punch, a harmonic blend of stiffness and tenuity that coupled with the individual agent's personality and talents. These martial creations were a big factor in our troop's success.

"For whom?" I asked, picking up one of the foam templates from a metal bin next to his drawing board. It was probably one he'd discarded for something better, and too bad, because even carved in foam it was very nearly sleek. It looked like a gun with a barrel as long as a spine, but somehow the palm-sized butt was still easy to handle. Probably ballast at the end; I turned it over to look, but Hunter snatched the template from my hand, gave me a hard look, and tossed it back in the bin. I held up my hands until he backed away. *Passionate* could be another word for freaky.

"It's for Kimber Marshall. Her official metamorphosis is on the nineteenth. There will be a new moon, it'll be a new week, a new Libra. Marlo's old sign."

I waited for him to say more, but the mention of Marlo was enough to tell me Hunter still blamed himself for her death. Sure, he hadn't been responsible for the virus lying dormant in her young body, but he was there when it'd sparked to life inside her. He'd been the one to ignite it . . . but I'd been the one responsible for it being there in the first place. Time to change the subject.

"Why a blowgun?" I asked, glancing at the vellum paper splayed over his largest drawing table. The hollowed-out tube was represented there in different dimensions and angles, as were the darts. "I mean, how do you choose this weapon as her conduit?"

Conduits were like prosthetic limbs, extremely personal and individually fitted for the wielding agent. Mine was a miniature crossbow, bequeathed to me by my mother, as conduits often were. But Marlo's lineage had died along with her, which meant a new dynasty could lay claim to the Libran star sign. Yet because Marlo's ancestors had been here since the birth of the troop, there were no other Librans of Light in the valley. We'd sent a message out to the troops nationwide, a sort of supernatural want ad asking for a second daughter of good lineage. Our succession was matriarchal, and second daughters were rarely called into duty, but that didn't mean they weren't well trained or ambitious. And if a family could have two daughters serving the Light in two different cities, it served to strengthen their legacy and interests.

After receiving replies from a number of interested parties, Tekla had cast lots and compared birth charts to determine which of the proffered daughters was fated for the job. It didn't hurt that Kimber's birth date was closest to Marlo's, and she would metamorphose—coming into her full powers as an agent—in only a couple of weeks. We needed the manpower now, and she had the added advantage of coming from an allied troop. We regularly sent our initiates for fostering in Arizona; the desert climate meant they faced many of the same physical challenges we did, but they also returned with new ideas and skills gleaned from the leaders of that troop. As an initiate Kimber could still cross state and city lines, but after her twenty-fifth birthday that ability would be stripped. If she remained in Arizona, she'd merely serve on an auxiliary basis. But by coming to Las Vegas, she would become a full-fledged agent, and she would belong to us, leaving her life there behind. She would also need a conduit.

"I don't choose them, at least not consciously." Hunter told me, opening a giant chest to pull out the blowgun in question. It wasn't the crude weapon brought to mind by Pygmies and rain forests and silent ninja crouched on shadowed rooftops. The tubing gleamed unnaturally, not silver but not black, with a mouthpiece and guard matching in opaqueness. A fragile glass cylinder rested on top, presumably the dart quiver. "But I start fiddling around in the workshop, touching this textile or metal or stone, and as I handle all these resources that can be fashioned into weapons, I think of the agent's gifts—talents and temperament and tendencies—and the right material always speaks to me."

"Speaks to you." I raised my brows, tucking a loose strand of hair behind my ear.

"Not literally, but yeah." He gestured to a sheaf of papers tucked on the corner of his table, which I immediately recognized as a birth chart, probably from Tekla. "For instance, Kimber is the Libra, an air sign known to be calculating and cool, but with a passion for balancing injustices. Yet she's also near the Libran/Scorpio cusp, which gives her a touch of bravado and some impulsiveness. A distance weapon would fit her well, but not something requiring close contact. Anyway, when I pick up the raw material my fingertips, I don't know, tingle. I think of her doing the same, envision her body, her particular strength exerting a specific force on the object, and this helps me determine the weapon, its stiffness and density, its design and shape. If I piece these elements together correctly, that tingle turns into a full-blown pulsing when I fire or wield the weapon."

He'd rubbed his fingertips together when he said it, so I held out my own hand, asking, "You can actually feel if the design is right?"

He nodded. "Firing a weapon is an act of acoustic vibration. A perfect weapon unleashes energy at a frequency that allows for easy manipulation of world matter, and then the throwing or shooting or stabbing or whipping takes no effort at all. Some people call it being 'in the zone.' All that violent energy is absorbed by the body; there's no kickback or impact."

I snorted. "Tell that to the target."

He inclined his head, a small smile visiting his lips, and I was glad I'd changed the subject. He was happiest when he was talking about war. "But—and here's what's important to understand—a perfectly constructed conduit also manipulates the agent. Firing it releases acoustic vibrations that oscillate back and forth between controller and conduit. A weapon's shape, therefore, acts as a funnel for the will of the agent, but it also reinforces the agent at the same time. That's why they must be uniquely matched . . . and perfectly paired."

More vibrational theory, I thought, with a wry smile. Explosions destroying molecules, black holes eating up matter. Now violence that resonated in the soul. I shook my head, and stared at him for long seconds. "What are you up to, Hunter?"

He looked at me to clarify, and I would have if I could put my feelings into words. Maybe it was the same sort of power that gave him the ability to study a weapon as if it were a person, though more likely it was the aureole still humming between us. Yet for all that, he was still a mystery. And even though I wanted to know why he'd taken up another identity—in the sex industry, no less—the way he was looking at me now, like I should already know, had me squirming like a bug. I broke eye contact. Maybe some things should remain unspoken.

Apparently Hunter didn't feel the same. "You know, someday you'll come to me. I'll wait, because I'm a gentleman, but you will come. Again and again."

"That is gentlemanly," I quipped, but he smiled when he saw me swallow hard. I turned to walk away, but he was suddenly there, spinning me back. I yanked my arm away but he only strengthened his grip, and I knew he'd leave bruises. I shook my head, pissed. That big, powerful body, I thought glaring up at him. Making me feel like a mortal again. But I could still fight him with words. "I should tell everyone about your side gig as a sex worker."

His hands lowered to mine, still powerfully twined, though his thumb played lazily against my palm. "And I should tell everyone about your daughter."

Now he was trying to piss me off. "Then I might slip and mention yours."

"Then I might slip also, and call you Joanna." He drew closer, testing me.

I remained where I was, and though the only thing touching was our hands, the heat from his body pooled around him, resonating against my skin like the sun. "Wow, blackmail and threats on top of manhandling. You do know how to woo a girl."

"Well, you don't seem like the flowers and chocolate type."

"Is that your *professional* opinion?"

"Honey," he said, eyes narrowing as they fastened hard on mine. "Were I a celibate monk secluded from the fairer sex my entire life, I'd still know your type."

"Really?" I snarled. So much for his lip service to everyone being unique; now I was a *type*. "Which is what?"

Angling forward, his chest touched mine. It was like setting a match to oil, and my nerve endings burned with it. "Mine."

The warehouse door slammed behind me, and I heard voices talking, calling out, bantering, but I was afraid if I moved, it would be into him. I looked at his body again, running my eyes over it like water.

"We had an agreement," I whispered feebly, hating my fluid emotions, the pull of both desire and anger, the reaction to his mere physicality.

And knowing how he affected me, Hunter winced like he was apologetic, bent . . . and ran his lips over my cheek. "Well, now we're going to agree to disagree."

I jerked away as Felix rounded the corner, followed by a girl with thick blond hair, dreaded and hanging halfway down her back. Each was carrying three boxes of pizza, and the scent of cheese and pepperoni presumably masked the emotion coming from Hunter and me because neither of them looked alarmed.

"I've got eats, yo, but I'm not paying for everyone—poor college student, remember?" Felix threw his pies on top of Hunter's drawing table, and wiped his hands on his jeans as he shot us his wide, trademark grin. "Pony up the bills, kids."

I batted my lashes and flipped my hair back over my shoulder. "Sorry, Felix. All I've got is my American Express Black, but Hunter will cover me." I regarded him with a raised brow. "He gets paid in cash."

12

In addition to booby traps, and bombs, and anything one would need to manufacture indestructible weaponry, Hunter's workshop boasted a panic room. If Shadows ever found the warehouse, an agent could retreat here until backup arrived. It's where we went after everyone else had arrived, chatting about nothing in particular until we'd all gathered in the weapon- and soundproof room.

An old-fashioned card catalog was shelved along one of the shorter walls, and another two drawing tables were pushed together as a center workspace. A blow-up bed, currently deflated and stowed in a giant cabinet, could be pulled out in emergencies, but the room was otherwise utilitarian, without even a chair to sit on. We spread out along its perimeter, and I leaned against one of the cabinets used for archival storage. This one held meticulous records of Shadow appearances and attacks, tracking their movements and dates, and triangulating their positions.

We also kept duplicates of the valley's street maps here, the residential roadways as well as the main thoroughfares, though they differed from maps that could be bought at the corner gas station in one very significant way. These pinpointed the location of previously known portals, when they opened and closed, who accessed them, and where they led in Vegas's corresponding flip side. These records were constantly updated, usually by Gregor, whose cabdriver persona gave him the most obvious pretext to canvass the streets, though we all kept daily logs of our encounters that went to Warren at the end of the week.

But the personality of the room, the thing that made it come alive despite a lack of warmth or personal effects, came from the flat stacks of hand-drawn maps in the climate-controlled case beneath the drawing tables. These historic depictions detailed the Las Vegas known to previous generations, all the way back to the early 1700s, and an independent agent who'd been tagging along with a desert expedition led by a Spanish scout. He was the one who'd dubbed this fertile swath of land "The Meadows."

Of course, Las Vegas hadn't become large enough to warrant a true troop until long after that; first came the fort that acted as a refuge for the original Mormon settlers, then the trading posts and railroads that brought saloons and prostitution and, eventually, the workers who'd labored over the Hoover Dam in the nearby Black Canyon. No, it wasn't until the Second World War was over, and tourism turned a sole dusty boulevard into a flashy desert oasis, that the true battle for Vegas's soul began. So the city grew, our troop formed, and the maps reminded us of how far we'd come, and in a way allowed us to pay homage to those who were here first.

Our generation's map was splayed like a banner over one full wall, the population boom of the early nineties penciled beneath the expansion in the millennium and the mid-decade rise of the city as it began to spread up as well as out.

Warren rolled up the giant sketch currently splayed

across the tables and stuck it in an upright file so that Felix could deposit the pizzas on the center tables. The rest of us fell on the food like we'd chased it down ourselves. The troop pecking order was made clear in the process. First Warren, then Tekla and Micah; Gregor and Hunter were followed by Vanessa and Felix, then came me, Riddick, and Jewell, with special allowance made for Chandra due to the time she'd served with the troop. The last to come forward was the girl who'd entered with Felix, who accented her blond dreads with a nose piercing, black nail polish, and quotidian black clothing. This was presumably Kimber, our soon-to-be Libra, and I inched over to give her room next to me, but she backed away to prop herself up by the door instead.

Tekla, who was only picking at her pizza, wasted no time in getting to the point. "Chandra told us about the changeling at Master Comics. How you broke her, halting the publishing of our manuals."

I'd figured as much, though a part of me had held out hope that I could be the one to tell them. Yet the way Tekla said it, matter-of-factly and without an ounce of anger, and the way Warren went after a third slice of pie, reassured me it could be fixed. I glanced at Chandra and smirked. "Thanks. Partner."

She scowled back.

"She also said she was the one to steal this." Warren roused himself enough to pull Xavier's mask from somewhere behind him, tossing it onto the drawing table next to the now-empty boxes. Nobody moved, though a shiver jackhammered its way up my spine as the mask stared up at us, a scream captured in its throat. Which was exactly where the pizza I was swallowing caught as well. I lifted my gaze and was startled to find a maniacal glimmer of barely contained excitement alive in Warren's. "Why didn't you bring it, or one of the many others hanging around that house, to us sooner?"

I forced myself to take another bite and shook my head.

"These masks have been hanging in Xavier's home for years. I told Chandra that."

"And you never connected Xavier's peculiar love of Tibetan art with the culture that created the Tulpa?"

Surprised, I looked over at Kimber like she'd suddenly sprouted another dreadlock. "And the fuck you are is who?"

Vanessa and Riddick, closest to Kimber, both took a step back.

"Okay, okay," Warren said, moving into the vacated space, wary eyes on me, but addressing Kimber. "It's not something that would be readily apparent to someone new to our troop. Olivia's had her hands full these last few months." That was the understatement of the year. "And she's still learning. She just needs to be more vigilant in the future."

"Oh, I will," I said pointedly, noting that Kimber and Chandra had almost unconsciously moved closer together.

"For now," Tekla said, from her corner, "tell us your version of what happened when you entered Xavier's office."

Warren looked like he was going to object, but Tekla shot him an arch look that had his mouth snapping shut, so I told them about the music and scent and smoke roiling in the air of the attached room I'd never before seen, then of Xavier's strange behavior, and how when we spoke afterward he'd somehow looked . . . smaller. "I've never smelled anything like that before, but Chandra said it was his soul essence being sacrificed to another."

"She's right. It's what the Tulpa demands of his acolytes," said Warren, unable to contain himself any longer. He rocked forward onto his toes, eyes on the mask that he'd barely been able to stop studying during my telling. "But now—"

"But now we need to know what you saw when you entered the office a second time," Tekla interrupted sharply. "Alone."

Warren stepped back with barely contained impatience, and I looked at Chandra again. If there'd even been a sparking hope that we could work together as partners, if not friends, it was gone now. She'd no doubt told them of this second visit to the office in order to cast suspicion my way, so that I again had to deflect it from my own allies. I sighed, and threw my half-eaten pizza back onto the table in disgust. "The masks littering his home made me wonder what might be housed in his giant resort. I asked Xavier to give his darling daughter a job in Valhalla so I could find out."

"No."

All heads turned toward Hunter, who looked like he wanted to yank the single word back out of the air, his jaw clenching reflexively as he turned to Warren. "The place is overrun with Shadows. It's too dangerous."

"*You* work there," I pointed out, eyes narrowing.

Calm now, he faced me again. "I'm not as visible as you are . . . in either of our worlds."

I pursed my lips, wondering why he was really objecting. If there was ever a time to play the call boy card it was now, but Warren spoke up before I could pull it out of the deck, actually agreeing with me. That was enough to have Hunter's mouth falling open and mine snapping shut.

"It's a good idea, and a natural step for Xavier Archer's sole heir," he said, speaking quickly. Tekla was frowning in disapproval, but he ignored her this time. "She'll most likely be assigned to the executive offices, and can keep an eye on upper-level management while you scout the blue collars. The more agents we can plant in the Tulpa's den, the better our collective data will be."

I didn't even need to shoot Hunter a victorious look; my satisfaction could be sensed like it'd blown in on a spring wind.

"For now let's go back to the changeling."

The wind died in my sails. Hunter smirked.

"I did a little research after Chandra came to us with this information." Warren pulled out the last manual drawn, one that had come out two weeks earlier, and showed Tekla bringing down hellfire in an abandoned warehouse. "You did indeed return Jasmine's aura to her on time. You obviously meant no harm, so your motives are not in question."

"Yet it's a serious problem, Olivia," Tekla said, stepping forward. Her face was drawn, and she took the manual from Warren and placed it behind her back, clearly wanting to forget its contents. "If the manuals aren't written, the children can't read them, in which case we don't receive the energy generated from their imaginations. Which means eventually—"

Warren stayed a hand on her arm. "Eventually I'm sure we'll get to the bottom of this and reverse the process."

Both Tekla and I gaped. Warren's tendency was to over-react rather than the opposite, and though one needed only to know his family history in order to understand this, understanding didn't make it any easier to weather his emotional storms.

I looked around to find everyone else similarly non-plussed. Even Kimber looked like she was waiting for the other shoe to drop. I turned my attention back to Warren, who shrugged philosophically. "Changelings are an un-deniably important piece to the supranatural system, but they're still mortal, and thus fragile creatures."

For once Warren was sticking up for me—first with Hunter, then with Tekla—and I was going to blow it by telling him how serious the Jasmine problem was, and how the Tulpa, through Regan, had managed to reach out and touch me in a safe zone. So I did it quickly, explaining how Li had somehow absorbed the injury. Warren's face was more appropriately grave when I'd finished.

"Is there anything else, Olivia?" he said, vocal cords tight with control. For a fleeting moment I considered leav-ing out the Tulpa's offer to work with me to find the doppelgänger. The third sign of the Zodiac was the rise of my dormant side. The Tulpa thought that meant my Shadow side, and while I knew that was bullshit, who was to say my troop didn't believe that as well? If not, the Tulpa's offer to work together might turn them into believers. But I'd kept information from my troop in the past, and though it'd seemed like the right thing to do at the time, the results had been disastrous.

"We had a doppelgänger in Phoenix," Kimber said, as soon as I'd finished. "It was years ago now, I couldn't have been more than seven or eight, but he took out almost a dozen mortals while trying to get to a particular agent before he was stopped."

"Children too," Jewell added grimly. "I know this story."

"Not children," Kimber corrected. "Embryos. In particular, their developing pink spinal cords."

I couldn't help myself. "What?"

"Concentrated energy," Tekla provided.

"How'd your troop finally stop him?"

Kimber looked at Hunter. "They didn't. He was targeting a Shadow agent. The Shadow Zodiac just handed that agent over, and afterward took in the fully realized doppelgänger as their own."

"Oh my God," said Vanessa.

"Wow. With friends like that . . ." Felix began.

"Who needs an opposing Zodiac troop."

And if I'd ever seriously considered joining the Tulpa's organization, the image of someone devouring another man's quivering spinal cord would've cured the impulse.

"All right, then," Warren said, after a moment, but I had a feeling he said it less for my sake than his own mounting impatience. "Let's move on." And he eagerly picked up the mask. "Has anyone seen one of these before?"

"I have," Kimber said immediately, then cleared her throat and came down off her toes when Riddick groaned next to me. I smirked. "In my studies, I mean. All of my electives for the past five years have been in Tibetan myth and culture. Animism, the belief everything has a soul, is a big part of it."

She looked at me, and I had an unreasonable urge to shoot a spitball into her dreads. *Teacher's pet*.

"That's right. The Tulpa is a diehard animist. Someone who believes wholeheartedly in imagined entities, and that souls inhabit ordinary objects as well as animate beings."

I snorted. He was an imagined being who'd turned into the leader of the paranormal underworld. Of course he believed it. And that's what mattered. His belief would spur his thoughts into actions.

"I too have seen masks like this one before, though not in texts." Warren held the mask in both hands as he stared down into its screaming face. "They direct soul energy from the wearer and convert it into raw energy for the Tulpa. I expect he ordered Xavier to meditate, though I doubt he told him why."

"Didn't we destroy an entire cache of these things a decade ago?" Gregor asked, the first to step closer to the mask.

"All but one," Warren said softly, causing Gregor's head to jerk in surprise. "But it was plain wood, not decorated." He looked at me, waiting for me to indicate that Xavier's mask had been plain as well, and I nodded my reply. Eyes shining, he fought back a smile. "If I'm right, this one is special, and infinitely more powerful."

Gregor ran a tentative finger over its shell. "I remember making a bonfire of those masks. They screamed as they burned."

Warren nodded as the memory played itself out in his mind as well. "It was the same night we destroyed the Tulpa's home. It was why he built Valhalla, with its guards and security and cameras studying every person who enters the place."

I shook my head, wondering if Xavier had known what he was getting himself into when the Tulpa approached him with his offer. Selling one's soul for money wasn't a new concept, and even though Xavier had more cash than one man could ever spend, I remembered how he'd looked with smoke billowing from his masked face, and would have even felt sorry for the guy . . . if I thought he'd had a soul to begin with.

"So if this isn't one of those, what is it?"

Now Warren smiled.

"This is a tool. An animist's mask designed to show the wearer his greatest desires . . . and the means to achieving them. I believe it's also how the Tulpa has been able to anticipate our moments, foil most of our plans, and stonewall us at every turn."

"The one of legend?" Tekla stepped forward to stand beside him, all her previous annoyance gone.

"The same. See the stylized curve of the mouth? The mismatched brows? I studied the texts after Zoe left . . ." He paused, quickly addressing me. "She was a fervent student of animism—"

"As she had to be," Tekla added, "living with the Tulpa."

"This is where he gets his omnipotence, his seeming omnipresence," Warren took over again, with the fervency of a zealot. "But he *isn't* godlike. He isn't even that powerful. He simply had the right tool."

And the satisfied smile that swelled on his face said what he did not. *And now we have it.*

"So what are we supposed to do with it?" Vanessa asked, picking up the mask between a thumb and forefinger. Her straightforwardness made me smile. I liked her because she was quick, witty, and unerringly practical. She was also tough without sacrificing her femininity, which had gone a long way to helping me feel more comfortable in my sister's curvaceous body. Where I'd once dared people to point out my femininity, Vanessa had never been at war with her body. It was simply hers to do with as she pleased, like her mind or her time; and while others sold, squandered, or cheapened these gifts, she owned and improved upon them, and took joy in every return on her investment. I felt more comfortable with her than any woman since my sister's death.

"We try it on."

"Oh, hell no." She tossed the mask onto the table, obviously unconcerned about the spirit trapped inside. "I'm not letting my soul essence ooze out of me like air from a leaky tire."

"It doesn't work that way. I know this legend too," Kimber spoke up.

Of course you do, I thought, as she stepped forward and leaned on the table to peer into the face of the mask. "You're already aware of its purpose, and you have a will strong enough to match the spirit buried within the wood. If your wills are opposed, the only thing that will happen is a sort of private interchange, like a song heard by someone wearing headphones. I suspect Warren wants us to try it on in order to learn the secrets it already holds, am I right?"

"Very good." Warren inclined his head, then picked up the animist's mask and held it out to her. "And since you're the resident expert, we'll start with you."

Her sure smile wobbled, and I snorted, crossing my arms. Nobody likes a know-it-all.

Unsurprisingly, Kimber didn't back down. She bit her lip as she reached for the mask, chipped black polish running over the painted features before she raised the mask to shoulder height, a move that looked stiff and overly formal—like she'd studied but never performed it—and brought it to her freckled skin.

If I hadn't been looking, I'd have never seen the wood grain shifting, though her quickly indrawn breath as the carved ears bent inward would have betrayed the activity.

"What do you see?"

Her fingers splayed to begin her explanation, but nothing came out at first. "I see myself . . . except it's not me. It's a future me. I've metamorphosed into a full-fledged agent and I'm holding a blowgun. I've slain the Shadow Scorpio with a dart to the artery in his neck."

I glanced at Hunter, and he at me. I'd seen the template for the conduit she mentioned, but I could tell by his face that she hadn't. He hadn't even finished making it yet. After another few seconds where she was left too breathless to talk, she lifted her hands and removed the mask. Her steel blue eyes seemed to catch all the light in the room, and her face was glowing with excitement. "It was just like the textbooks said. All you have to do is stare through the eye slits, but use your mind to see what's on the other side, not your vision. I could feel the other spirit residing in the mask, but it was peaceful, almost welcoming. It wanted for me what I wanted most. We were in harmony for as long as I chose to wear it."

Warren only grunted, and I was relieved to hear skeptical consideration in the sound as he motioned Kimber back and prepared to lift the mask to his own face.

"Stop!" Tekla shouted suddenly, rushing forward. She grabbed his arm so roughly, he fumbled the mask. Offering him a half-apologetic smile, she pulled away, and said more calmly, "It's not that I don't believe Kimber, but I'd like a little more proof before my troop leader dons an obvious totem of spiritual power. It may be what . . ."

What the Tulpa wants. She didn't have to say it. Warren had been targeted before, and none of us had seen it coming. So everyone understood Tekla's concern, but nobody stepped forward to take the mask from Warren's hands.

Tekla smiled and reached for it. Warren outranked her, but the troop's Seer was given an equal amount of respect, and a good deal of leeway for what was kindly described as her more erratic behavior. "I'll go next."

"Your mind is as valuable as mine," Warren began, but Tekla turned away, shielding the mask from his reach with her body.

"You've survived without me before. You'd do so again."

Not too long ago Tekla had turned away from her visions, her gifts, and her star sign. She was newly returned to her position, so while her skills and power were stronger than ever, her confidence was shaky. There were times she could be heard ranting in the astrolab, screaming at the domed sky above her, arguing with the fates. Other times she disappeared into her room in the barracks, unseen for days.

But now she was hooking the heel of her hand upon the chin of the mask to bring it to her face one-handed. A small click, the pinning of the wood behind her ears like sunshades, and she fell utterly still.

"Tekla?"

"Oh my," she whispered, clasping her hands tightly together in front of her. "That's just . . ."

Warren was immediately by her side. "What is it, Tekla? What do you see?"

"Wonderful," she breathed, and an almond-soft scent bloomed in the room. Hope. "My son's spirit is at rest. There's a new constellation forming even as we speak, born of his goodness and purity and potential. Moving past his death has given me the ability to read messages born of this new star system. Shadows will die because of it. My son will still fulfill his legacy as a member of this troop. I can see it all as if it's happening right now."

Tekla fell silent, and when it became apparent she wasn't going to remove the mask without prompting, Warren put a gentle hand to her shoulder. She startled, jumping like she'd forgotten where she was, and when she removed the mask, her face was wet with tears. She let Warren take it away, expression disoriented and mildly disappointed as she stepped back again, tucking unsteady hands into the sleeves of her robe.

Three more people tried on the mask and three times it showed various predictions of success; Vanessa's vision spoke of love, Jewell's of worthiness, and Gregor physically overcame a Shadow agent he didn't recognize, besting the giant man even with just one good arm. When it came time for Hunter to reveal what he saw, he only said the others were right; it was most definitely the near future. And though the look on his face was benign enough, I sensed chaos swirling through his bloodstream. I studied him as he avoided my gaze, but by this time even Warren was displaying uncommon excitement. He turned to me, eyes gleaming.

"Your turn, Olivia."

I didn't want to. I knew it was my almost pathological need for control, a knee-jerk reaction caused by past helplessness that had me mentally rearing back when he held the animist's mask out to me, but I thought I saw the wood twitch in his hand, and it didn't look benign to me at all. It looked anticipatory. It looked hungry.

You're safe, I told myself, taking the mask, feeling nothing but smooth wood in the weight against my palm. I was in the warehouse, in the panic room, surrounded by my troop. What could happen?

The magic slipped on easily, dimming my awareness of my surroundings like a sun visor, and the muscles in my thighs twitched as a facsimile of me strode forward to knock on the door of Xavier's home office, a reproduction of my conduit loaded and locked.

The door was ajar and swung open like every horror movie cliché I'd ever seen. Apparently none too bright, the faux me made my way through the smoke of the exterior office to the hidden room beyond the far bookcase. I stepped through the threshold . . . and onto the roof of the tallest hotel in Vegas, recognizing the view from the apex of Valhalla. It was night, and the Strip was spilled out below me like a blinding waterfall, headlights and digital billboards cascading to and fro in a rapid river of activity that couldn't reach me up here. Even the wind had been muted, I noted, looking around, which was when I spotted the two chairs balanced on the hotel's ledge.

Not chairs, I thought, drawing closer. Thrones. Goldplated, cushionless monstrosities I'd seen before, and I tilted my head as I slipped in front of the larger one, lifting my bow when I saw the Tulpa reclined there, dressed like a mafia don. I'd been anticipating him.

He tracked me with his eyes, the rest of him still, balanced on that ledge. I edged over to the smaller throne, and took a seat opposite him, my left foot dangling off into space. I wasn't afraid, and I don't know if his smile was because of that or in spite of it.

"All of this," he said, motioning below, "Can be yours."

I looked at the vibrant city, and despite the zinging neon, random flares, and bustling crowds, saw peace. The smooth currents of air rippling over the quiet desert made me homesick, if only because I was so clearly removed from it. "If?" I asked, returning my gaze to him.

He chuckled in answer, and bent forward to pick up a brown paper lunch bag. His throne wobbled, one gilt leg halfway over the ledge. Bulging at the bottom, the bag snapped open crisply, and he lifted out a sandwich wrapped in foil.

"Split it with me?"

The city danced below us. The air continued to swirl. I glanced back at the sandwich and after a moment more, inclined my head. A truce, if possible, would be nice.

He handed me half, not a barbed claw in sight, and I unwrapped it, first the foil, then plastic wrap.

"Meat, tomato, cheese, lettuce, and mustard . . . your favorite, right?"

My eyes came to rest on the bag now perched on his golden armrest, and I caught myself mid-nod, mid-bite. The bottom of the bag was oozing blackly. The sandwich pulsed once in my palm.

The Tulpa crossed his legs at the knee and smiled. "A divided heart, get it?"

I lunged, and knew from the air's current that my throne had toppled from the ledge. Horns honked as it turned into a missile; mortals screamed. The Tulpa tried to get away, but his teetering throne banked, and he threw himself toward the rooftop . . . right into my arms. His jugular called to me, as brightly pulsing as the city below us, and I grabbed for it. I saw the seams only because I was so close, and ignoring the rest of his body, I squeezed. Two muted pops sounded, like snaps coming undone, then another jaw appeared above my pressing thumbs. With a howl of rage I tore the Tulpa's face away, lifting so tissue and tendons ripped . . . and the doppelgänger gazed up at me with a smile.

"It's better this way," she choked the words out, strangling. "A person cannot be divided against herself."

I squeezed harder. Her smile widened. And in the moment the light left her eyes, her shining skull popped like a balloon, suds and frothy bubbles flying everywhere. I yelled out in victory. The sun took to the sky like a comet . . . and revealed one more face beneath my clenched palms.

The jaw was slender and heart-shaped, the fragile skin smooth and too white. Frantically I wiped away the foam . . . and stared down into my mother's waxy, sightless face.

I pivoted . . . and found the city rotting like a carcass beneath a scorching desert sun.

I could only stare as all the people I knew rotted with it.

"Olivia! Olivia! It's off, stop struggling!"

It was only then I became aware of my voice, a sandpaper scream sawing through my brain. *Get it off! Get it off! Make it stop!*

A white-hot pain arched around my jaw as my cheeks parted from my bones, as if cleaved with a burning, jagged blade. "God! Oh God!"

"I had to," said an unfamiliar voice. No, not unfamiliar. New. I opened my eyes, blinked back stinging tears, and saw Kimber staring down at me with those hard blue eyes. "The textbooks say it's the most effective way of separating joined psyches. The skin should grow back."

Skin? And *should?* I panicked, but then Micah pushed her aside, and my vision narrowed on him. His reaction would tell me whether I should worry, whether the biting cold all around my jawline was as serious as I thought. Whether the ripping of my own skin from my bones should be cause for alarm.

He wouldn't meet my eyes as he spoke in an overly soothing voice, "It's going to be fine."

"Oh shit . . ." I began to cry.

"Shh." He lifted his hands, fingertips pressing gently across my face. I was numb, and didn't feel them. "No, it is. Your magic is already grafting the skin back in place. You'll be as good as new in a few minutes."

It would have been like consulting with any other doctor if he hadn't used *magic* and *grafting* in the same sentence. Laughter wanted to bubble up out of me, except it couldn't get past my throat, past the skin rent from ear to ear. I squeezed my eyes shut, and both wished for, and dreaded, my complete healing.

Because then I'd have to tell them of the vision contradicting all the premonitions they'd experienced. I opened my eyes and found Tekla ushering everyone from the room. Chandra was the last, and she looked back, met my gaze, and shuddered.

The sooner you start respecting that your compromised physiology has made you different, the sooner you can start approaching aberrant situations from a new beginning point . . .

Fuck you, Chandra, I thought, and let myself cry again. Just fuck you. Fuck the Tulpa . . . and fuck me too.

13

Half an hour later I was alone with Warren in what amounted to a crow's nest above the cavernous expanse of Hunter's workshop. There was a bed pressed against two walls near the back, a simple presswood desk pushed against the forward railing, which was where I was seated, and nothing but a tattered rug in between. Hunter didn't use the place often, preferring instead to return to the sanctuary each evening, crossing realities as faithfully as most people put in their nine-to-fives.

Half the troop had left, though Vanessa and Riddick were talking in low voices as they waited for their partners, while Hunter showed Kimber the conduit he was designing for her. I watched her gesture excitedly below us, beaming, no doubt telling him it was just how she'd envisioned it while wearing the animist's mask.

The evil, life-sucking mask.

"It started with the Tulpa," I told Warren, hands cupped around a cup of coffee so bad it was soothing for its heat alone. I'd shifted the chair so it was sideways to the desk, and Warren stood, cross-armed, five feet away, near the ladder leading below. "I distinctly saw him sitting in a throne above the entire city. He offered Las Vegas to me, said it could be mine."

I told him the rest, the multiple masks, my mother's face beneath. My mother who'd handed me a heart. My mother, whom I'd killed.

"Hm . . ." he said, like that was significant, looking out over the cavernous workshop.

"Hm, what?" I asked. Warren's eyes were tight, whatever scene he was playing out in his mind superimposed over the inactivity of the workshop, but then they relaxed and he turned to face me.

"You can't let what happened with the mask scare you. You're a good person, Joanna. Even when you act impulsively, even when you've gone against my orders or spoken out of turn—"

"Who, me?"

He ignored that. "You're doing so from a moral seat. More importantly, even if the third portent of the Zodiac is the rise of your Shadow side, I believe you'd find a way to overcome that and do what's right."

"I want to believe you," I said, shaking my head, palming my cup. "But I just had a vision where I killed my own mother by hand, and I know myself—even this new version of myself—by now. The rage and exultation when my hands were around her throat . . . that was real."

"And so was the horror when you realized who it really was."

"Yeah, but by then it was too late!" And that was my constant fear. That no matter what abilities my kairotic powers gave me, my late entrée into this paranormal morass would leave me flat-footed when it mattered most. That was why I had problems sitting on my heels, waiting for direction. Besides, eight months of the strongest supernatural support couldn't erase a decade of self-reliance. Other than Olivia, the people I'd counted on most had always abandoned me.

He leaned against the railing, reminding me of the way the Tulpa had shifted, his throne tottering on that thin ledge. Seeing my shudder, Warren winced, sighed, and dug into the pockets of his long, filthy duster.

"I wasn't going to give you this yet. But since you seem to be a slave to that which you've seen both in visions and reality—"

"Hey!" I said, jerking so hard I spilled coffee over my hands and knees. I sat the Styrofoam cup on the desk, and flicked droplets from my wrists before wiping them against my pants. "The things I've seen could make grown men weep, then drool, then do nothing but rock in a corner for the rest of their lives."

"Exactly." He pulled out a crumpled stack of papers stapled together at the corner and handed them to me. "I checked into Regan's account of what happened the night you left Ben alone with a man named Ernest Thompson, a.k.a., Magnum, in a barricaded alley called Dog Run. As you asked."

I narrowed my eyes and cautiously took the papers from him, then scanned the first page. A drug dealer named Magnum had been found facedown in the dirt of a public housing lot, a single bullet to his head. The report called it self-defense, but I knew that wasn't possible. I'd left Magnum knocked out at Ben's feet just as the sirens from his backup came wheeling around the corner. There was no way Magnum had woken up and threatened Ben in those intervening seconds. The report began to shake in my hands.

"Why are you showing this to me now?"

"Joanna," he said softly, and I shut my eyes so I didn't have to see if the look on his face matched the pity in his voice. "Your back has been to the wall so many times I'm surprised you don't have a permanent imprint there. But the person who did this had a choice and still took the lesser action, and that's what a person's Shadow side is.

The wrong decision even under the right circumstances."
He paused, thinking by doing so he was letting that sink
in, but what filled the gap was another denial. I hadn't seen
it, so maybe Ben wasn't the one who decided to be this
man's executioner. Warren took a breath. "You need to let
us erase his memory. It's the best way to get rid of Regan.
It'll be a fresh start for Ben. And for you."

I wiped at my eyes. "No."

"Joanna—"

"No!" I screamed, crumpling the report in one fist.

The warehouse stilled below, but Warren didn't let the
sound or sudden blooming smoke bother him. The alarm
clock across from me reflected red-hot eyes in the glass
front, but he didn't let that scare him either. He waited,
cross-armed, until my breathing had evened again, the
smoke clearing. "I don't have to ask your permission, you
know."

I knew. He could take chunks of memory away and Ben
would become the person he'd have been if I'd never entered his life. And he wouldn't think or speak or dream of
me ever again. I pressed the palms of my hands to my eyes
until I saw black spots, then pulled them away as a sigh
stuttered from my chest.

"What's the first thing you do when you wake up in the
morning?"

I don't know if he was more taken aback by the whimper in my voice or the change in subject, but Warren only
stared, eyes jumping around my face like it was a puzzle
he needed to put together. I managed a tired smile and
smoothed the report back out over my knees. "You don't
have to tell me every little detail . . . in fact, don't. Just your
first thought."

He shrugged after another moment. "Okay."

"Now let me guess. You don your superhero cloak. You
pound your chest. You yell, 'Up, up, and away!' and run
from the Batcave, catapulting into the air."

"You're mixing up your superheroes."

I looked at the man who was both troop leader and bum. That was the truth.

"If I'm on the streets," he began, crossing his legs at the ankles, leaning back and humoring me, "I take a piss and try to find some food. If I'm in the sanctuary, I take a piss, a shower, and then try to find some food."

"I told you not to tell me." I winced, and he laughed, and it was suddenly a little easier between us. "The point is, you don't wake up thinking, *Hey, I'm going to save the world today!* Right?"

He lifted a brow. "Do you?"

"No," I said, but before he could ask anything more I leaned toward him, lowering my voice. "I wake up and think, *There's some fucker out there with a knife in his pocket. He's going to go a little postal today. And he might do it around Ben.*"

I licked my lips, aware of Warren's gaze on me now, absent of humor. I stared back, equally serious. "I think about the people out there with too much artillery and too little brains and how today they might start firing, again, around Ben."

"And what about the other two million inhabitants of our fine city?"

"Do *you* consider each and every one of them every time you intervene in human drama?" I replied shortly. "Maybe you should, and maybe I should too, but I'm too preoccupied with the one who best represents goodness and fairness and kindness to me, who represents them all."

Warren slid the photo of Magnum back under my nose, a reminder that after an intervening decade I might not know Ben at all. But that wasn't true . . . because if I didn't know him, I couldn't love him. And I did.

One side of Warren's mouth turned up in a wry, humorless smile. "And what if you wake up one day and *he's* the fucker with the knife and the mean opportunity?"

I shook my head. "I tell myself the truth. He's under the

influence of Regan, who comes from a long line of women who enjoy destroying the virtue in a good man. And then I remind myself that he spent years before that under *my* influence, and I don't mean to let him get away without a fight."

"So it's a game?" he said quickly.

"Sure," I said lightly, though it wasn't. "A game of chance. And I want mine. Because I know if I can get him to talk to me I can fix this." Because no matter what was printed on these pages or what Warren thought Ben might have done to another mortal on a night when he was cornered like a wild animal . . . I knew he'd listen. And if he listened I could alter whatever Regan had fucked up inside him already.

Warren shifted where he sat and I found I couldn't meet his eye, not with tears in my own. I glanced back down at the warehouse, and saw Hunter placing the foam template I'd handled earlier in a locked cabinet shoved against a concrete wall. When I'd finally recovered my voice, and was sure it wouldn't crack in my throat, I whispered, "Not yet. Please."

I saw him stiffen from the corner of my eye, shift uncomfortably, and knew I'd said the wrong thing. Pleading was a weak emotion, and Warren responded best to the logic of the mind. "You need to focus on the Tulpa."

I started to laugh. The sound spiraled, escaping me in a raw and wild vortex, like a tiny tornado tearing through the workshop. The agents below fell silent again and looked up, trying to see what was so funny. It made me laugh even harder.

"Focus on him," I gasped, wiping at my eyes, then bent over to pick up the papers I'd caused to splay all over the floor. More calculations and drawings, more templates, more weapons. I tapped them on the desk in a halfhearted effort at neatness before tossing them down. "Every one of us is so fucking focused it's like living under a microscope."

And I told him what the Tulpa said about the doppelgänger being fixed on *me*, that a fleshly relic—my heart—would allow her full physical manifestation, and that she'd stop at nothing to get it. I also told him the Tulpa no longer wanted me as one of his Shadows. "I have ill *chi*. He said we could work together to kill the double-walker because I had as much to lose as he, but that's all he wants."

I picked up my now-cooling coffee, and thought again of my unyielding hands around my mother's neck. Maybe the Tulpa was right. If that's what the future held for me, maybe I was a danger to everyone around me.

Warren had straightened during my telling and was absently running a hand over the scruff at his neck. "And he claimed to scent your pheromones every time the doppelgänger ripped a hole into this world? Did he say exactly what that smelled like?"

Of all the bits of information to latch on to. I rolled my eyes. "Are you listening to me? The Tulpa asked me to work with him."

Warren's eyes found me again, and he shrugged. "Then you have a decision to make."

"What?" I drew back so suddenly, my coffee sloshed in my cup. I was making a mess of the crow's nest, I thought, rubbing at the wet floor with my shoe. Warren offered a handkerchief, but I took one look and knew if I touched it I'd add vomit to the mix. Did he have to take his vagrant persona so seriously? "Okay, Warren? Not to shoot myself in the foot here, but aren't you at all worried the third sign of the Zodiac is the imminent rise of my Shadow side? Isn't that your greatest fear right now, what with my biology permanently on the fence and all?"

"Why? Because the Tulpa wants you to work with him?" He leaned against the railing again, rubbing at his bad leg. "I'm not concerned with what the Tulpa wants. It's you I'm concerned with. And, Jo?" He leaned forward to loom over me. "You've proven yourself, okay? Sure, you fuck up regularly, and you're stubborn, and your quest to keep Ben in your life is one of the stupidest—"

"Thank you," I said loudly before he could screw up the rest of his compliment.

Warren smiled. "Besides, the Tulpa is obviously more worried about this doppelgänger than he is about you."

"He said she could be some long-lost twin of mine. He told me one of his agents would have to meet with me if I decided to work with him to get rid of her."

That unseeing look came over Warren's face again. Suddenly he was backing down the wooden staircase. "I have to go."

I threw my hands up into the air, palms up. "Oh, sure. Don't mind me. I'll hang out here. A sitting target for heart eaters and other things I never knew went bump in the night." My voice had escalated with true panic, so I wasn't surprised when his head popped back up.

He tilted it, sighing. "Jo. I am worried about you. I don't like that Regan was the one to find you in Master Comics. I don't like that she knows your true identity, and could spill the Olivia/Joanna connection at any time. I'm scared to death of the way the Tulpa managed to touch you in a designated safe zone."

"Don't forget the way an animist's mask had to be ripped from my face," I said, rubbing my jaw. It was sensitive— aching as if there was a scar there, though the damage couldn't be seen or felt beneath my fingertips. Micah was right. I'd already healed.

"That too," he said, not unkindly . . . but not overly solicitous either. "But unless you're willing to be locked up in the sanctuary for the foreseeable future—"

"Hell, no."

"Or give us leave to reconstruct Ben's memories?"

"No."

"Then I need to get on with the running of this troop."

"But . . ." But Zane's words had gotten to me. I could

admit it here, alone with a man who'd overcome his suspicion of me before. "You know I didn't break the changeling
on purpose, right?"

His irritation instantly disappeared. "Of course not. The
others don't think so either," he added, because it was clear
that's what was really bothering me. I'd been outside the
troop's good graces before, more than once. I didn't want
to go there again. "The new manuals are being written,
even if they aren't being read. We'll find out how to fix Jasmine—which is what I'm going to go research now—and
then all those written words and images will bloom to life,
bringing a fresh wave of energy and force to our cause.
Supply and demand at its best.

"Until then, the children who follow the Light side of
the Zodiac can feed their insatiable imaginations with the
older manuals. Those can sustain them, and us, for a long
time." He pushed back his trench coat so it billowed out
behind him, and began descending, mindful of the leg that
gave him so much trouble.

"Warren?" I said suddenly, and the top of his head
appeared again, eyes mildly irritated. I rushed through
my question, but mostly because I needed to. "Why don't
you erase Ben's memory without asking me? I mean, you
could, and there'd be nothing I could do about it."

He leaned forward, feet on the staircase, elbows on the
floor, to stare up at me. "Because I know what's involved
in a slow good-bye. The release of long-held dreams is a
kind of death, with all the emotional stages that go with it,
including anger, though you're not quite there yet. It'll be
hard enough once you are, and I'd rather it not be directed
at me."

"I see. A selfish ploy to avoid the brunt of my wrath."

His smile was tight-lipped. "You'll release him when
you're ready."

I wouldn't. Not ever. But I sat prim and proper as he
finished his spiel.

"Just try to prepare yourself to do it sooner rather than later. For his sake. For yours. And for ours."

Not even for all the inhabitants of this city.

A wry smile flickered at one corner of Warren's mouth, and he shrugged, still thinking I was in denial. The belief bought me time, so I said nothing. Without another word, Warren did disappear beneath the sightline then, reappearing seconds later on the ground floor below me. I followed him with my eyes, relieved I'd come clean about the Tulpa and what he'd asked of me . . . but curious about Warren's reaction.

This was the guy who freaked out at the slightest perceived imbalance in the Zodiac. So why wasn't he freaking out now? The changeling of Light was broken, the manuals couldn't be read, my *chi* had apparently become the supernatural equivalent of foot funk, and the Tulpa suddenly wanted to be friends. And what the hell had he been thinking when I told him how the Tulpa planned to rid this world of the doppelgänger? Because the expression that'd slipped over his face had looked like excitement, not concern.

Below, Vanessa glanced impatiently at her watch. Kimber still fondled her unfinished conduit, looking younger and friendlier and dreamier than any future Shadow killer should. I couldn't blame her. Her metamorphosis was scheduled two weeks from now, and it was the event an initiate looked forward to from the time they first learn of their preternatural destiny. I glanced at Hunter, thinking I should've told Warren about his call boy identity. If he was telling the truth, and Warren wouldn't care, there was no reason not to mention it. Except I owed him. He'd kept my Joanna identity from those who didn't already know it, as well as the bigger secret Warren knew nothing about—my daughter.

So I sat back in the crow's nest and watched Vanessa finally yell at Kimber, who reluctantly handed the weapon back to Hunter before disappearing through the bay doors. Then I sucked in a deep breath filled with the warmth of toasted fruit, so heavy and round I wanted to take a bite. The scent of Hunter.

He glanced up at me sharply before he relaxed, and a languid smile visited his face. *I'll be your secret keeper,* he'd once said to me. But he'd said it with heat, looking at me the way he was now, meaning that and so much more.

"I'll be your secret keeper too, Hunter," I murmured, pushing away the memory even as it rippled through me. "But that's all."

14

I used my Shadow manuals often. Most had belonged to my first enemy, the man who thought it was fun to attack little girls on steamy desert nights. I now possessed them because our diminutive, assessing, and steady troop Seer, Tekla, had gone apeshit on his putrefied ass, literally shredding him to bits, saving my life . . . and saving a bit of herself in the process as well. The next week Joaquin's extensive stash of meticulously organized Shadow manuals had somehow shown up in the sanctuary, though whether he'd bequeathed them to me, knowing I'd continue the work he'd started—finding a way to kill the Tulpa—or whether they'd somehow been appropriated on my behalf, I still couldn't say.

I also didn't walk around advertising my possession of them, not with the third sign of the Zodiac looming over our heads like a giant question mark. So I waited until the next day, when most of the others had been called to clean up Shadow activity on the East Side, before pulling an armload of them from my locker, and taking them with me back to the barracks for some late night reading.

It was in one of these that I found an account of the last time the Tulpa had sent his agents out via "message-by-minion." He hadn't been kidding about the missive's hold over his troop. The manual depicted his investigation of one of his own, a Shadow agent named Tripp who'd balked at orders to murder his own family. Instead he'd warned them, and they all rabbited. Their effort to escape the Tulpa, a plan that revolved around some rumored underground for former agents, was foiled by a long-forgotten confidence in the Shadow Gemini, whom he'd told about his safe house in nearby Mount Charleston. Though the Gemini was, in truth, a genuine ally, after a month of no food or sleep or the ability to eliminate bodily functions, his will was thoroughly broken.

The family's slaughter a week later—three generations of Shadow Aquarians—had shaken the foundations of that side's Zodiac. It was a brutal act even by the Tulpa's lofty standards, and the final panels showed a meeting—sans Tulpa—swearing it would never be allowed to happen again.

It must have pissed off Joaquin too, I thought as I left my room, because the manual was dog-eared, and he'd even scrawled in the margins, using that strange hieroglyphic alphabet I'd seen lining the walls of his underground cavern. These, however, were punctuated with giant exclamation points.

So why would the Tulpa impose a message-by-minion again, and once more risk alienating his own agents?

"The doppelgänger," I murmured, sinking to the floor outside another barracks' door and rubbing at my chest where the woman had scrabbled for my heart. My wounds had healed, but every so often it was as if dozens of ants marched beneath my skin, tiny legs scrabbling over muscle and tendons, and below it, my beating heart. I pulled my hand away, and attempted to push that image out of my mind.

But what was it about her that spooked *him* so much? The message-by-minion, the knee-jerk willingness to kill me just because we smelled similar, the offer to work together to eradicate her existence . . . it all spoke to a fear far greater than his hatred for our troop. Greater, even, than his paranoia at my ascension as the preordained Kairos.

What could he find so threatening about her existence?

"Must be my lucky day."

I glanced up, already smiling as Gregor approached his room in the barracks, dropping the manual back into my shoulder bag as I stood. It was just after dawn now, and the troop was trickling in. Though he'd be going to bed soon, Gregor held the day's first cup of coffee in his one arm because he first had to attend a meeting about the night's mission in the debriefing room. He showed neither surprise nor alarm to find me waiting for him, just motioned me aside with his head so he could reach inside and gather his warden, Sheila. She went everywhere with him on this side of reality, and she bounded from the room to rub up against his legs before flicking her black tail dismissively in my direction. I could have sworn she was also deliberately trying to trip me up as we wound our way through the sanctuary's concrete halls. Cats.

I'd given Ben's address to Gregor after my run-in with Regan at the bar, and had asked him to stop by, poke around, and see if she'd planted any more bombs. Gregor was more objective than I was, and could canvass Ben's home with perspective, a practiced eye, and without leaving behind an olfactory trail. I couldn't trust myself to do the same.

I'd tried to be patient, but I was obviously anxious to know what he'd found. Fortunately, he didn't make me wait. "So I did a drive-by on the mortal's house and saw nothing unusual. I returned later when I was sure it was empty and found this."

He handed me a slip of paper with Rose's name and address. I'd been looking hard for a secondary location where Regan stayed outside her troop's sanctuary, so this would've been a *Eureka!* moment . . . if I wasn't so sure it was a setup. She'd given me an address in the past. Going there had nearly killed me. "She must think I'm an ass to fall for the same ruse twice."

"Doesn't hurt for her to throw it out there. If you're looking so desperately for the complex hoax, you might fall for the simple one." Gregor's hoop earring glinted as he handed me his coffee cup and bent to lift Sheila. Completely devoted to Gregor, she was purring before he'd even scooped her up. She regarded the competition, me, with cold assessing eyes. "She was probably also feeling reckless. Pissed off to find so many bugs planted around the place."

I smiled back grimly. Placing the listening devices around Ben's home had been a cheap and silly mortal's trick, but they'd seemed to annoy her, so I'd had Gregor do it again. The possibility of falling for something stupid went both ways.

"Thanks, Gregor."

"I also found this." He balanced Sheila on his shoulder and rustled in his jacket pocket, coming out with a photo of Regan in a crystal-studded, heart-shaped frame. She was in Rose mode, so there were enough visual cues to suggest a likeness to me without fully reviving me in Ben's mind. It was one of the Shadows' more subtle ways of luring in their mortal prey.

One of the *less* subtle ways was attached on the back, via the crystals.

I took it, studying the plastic backing Gregor had obviously pried away. "Another bomb," I said, as my stomach dropped to my toes.

"More like a hand grenade, and one activated by a sound signal."

"So she can hit a button in one location . . ."

"Or blow a dog whistle, whatever she has the receiver set for, and it'll blow wherever she's planted it."

I licked my lips slowly, and gently held the grenade back out to Gregor. He laughed, and waved it away before tucking Sheila back under his arm. "I called Hunter immediately and he told me how to disengage it. See the wire next to the photo hinge? Plug it in and you're live again. Thought you might want it."

I shook my head in disbelief. "I don't get it. She's had plenty of opportunity to come after me herself. She could plant bombs around my condo, in my car, on my cat—"

Gregor winced, nuzzling Sheila. "Don't say that."

As if she'd ever be able to touch Luna, I thought, but gave Sheila an apologetic rub under the chin anyway. Our feline wardens could slice Shadows to bits. Of course, their canine counterparts could do the same to us. "All I'm saying is if the goal is to get to me, why is she going after an innocent? A guy who clearly has no knowledge of me or my world?"

"Because that apple didn't fall far from the tree," he said wryly, and Gregor would know. He'd been the one to drive a mace into Brynn DuPree's chest. Yet before that, Brynn too had targeted an innocent man. She'd seduced a priest, conceived his child, and used that to blackmail him until he was as corrupt as she was. Though it wouldn't surprise me to find Father Michael had been depraved long before Brynn DuPree had come along. The Shadows were experts in telling which humans had nefarious potential living beneath their skin. But Ben was different, targeted solely because I loved him, and I said as much to Gregor.

"And I don't understand why she's so fixated on me, anyway," I added as we passed walls studded with mythological symbols and astrological shapes. "Why doesn't Regan go after you?"

"That's my girl," Gregor replied jauntily. "Sugar and spice."

I tilted my head. "You know what I mean."

Killing Brynn had made him infamous on both sides of the Zodiac. The infamous man shrugged lightly. "She can't come after me because I believe in luck, not love, and that's something she doesn't know how to twist."

I frowned, halting in my tracks. "What do you mean?"

He turned to face me, and the stripe zinging through the hallways to light our way stopped with him. "I mean the one great lesson imparted to Regan before I could relieve her mother of her worthless life was to use a person's love against them. She believed there was no room for love in a heroic life, so she broke her daughter of the habit immediately."

"How?" I asked, jogging to catch back up as Gregor started off again. By my calculation Regan had only been ten when Brynn died. Most moms hadn't even initiated the birds-and-the-bees talk by then.

"She made an example of Regan's first love, of course. And by then he was already serving life in prison."

"Oh," I said slowly, realization dawning. Her father. That made sense. "What did she do?"

"Once Brynn realized Regan had feelings for her father, that she wanted to get to know him and have some sort of sustained relationship, she sent pictures of a young Regan to the man who'd been convicted of stalking children, replacing Regan's introductory letter with a love note she'd penned herself." Gregor's mouth twisted in distaste, and he must have tensed because Sheila squirmed in his grip. "When he responded with a letter more suitable for a lover than a daughter, Brynn simply told Regan there was no such thing as pure love. It was a weakness, one that always came with strings attached."

"Why would you do that to your own daughter?" I mean, Shadow agent aside, wouldn't any mother want to protect her daughter from that sort of flattening disappointment?

"I asked her, you know." He nodded vigorously at my surprised expression. "I did. Right before I killed her. She said, 'You agents of Light worship the idea of love, but we Shadows kill anything we feel the slightest affection for.'"

"She loved him?"

He nodded. "She said she did. And he loved the church . . . could've loved Regan. One thing Brynn couldn't ever abide was competition."

I remembered that; Regan taunting me over defending my lover, saying bad habits were hard to break. Brynn had certainly succeeded in her quest to twist her lover, and her daughter. And now Regan was using my first love against me. "Effective," I murmured darkly, but strangely not feeling a bit sorry for Regan. Go figure.

Gregor looked at me sharply.

"I didn't say it was right," I said, fingering the palm-sized frame I'd dropped in my pocket, "just effective."

And it confirmed something I'd already suspected. If there was something Regan couldn't have—a place in her birth father's life, a love to share that life with—then she wasn't going to let anyone else have it either.

"Do you have a rash?"

"Oh, yeah." I glanced down. The skin above my V-neck T-shirt was red to the point of being raw. I must have been scratching it for a while now. "I might."

He glanced at my chest where the doppelgänger had swiped at me, moving his eyes along the rest of my torso, pausing at my left arm where even I hadn't noticed red bumps popping up over a new, and still sensitive, scar. "It's spreading. You should have Rena make a salve for it," he said, then grinned and imbued his tone with motherly censure. " 'I swear, sometimes you full-fledged star signs are worse than my initiates.' "

I grinned back. It sounded just like her.

But our levity dropped away when we reached the briefing room, where it was immediately clear there'd be no meeting today.

Tekla was there, but she didn't note my arrival, nor did the others surrounding her. She was prone on the floor, and at first I thought she was crying, but then I saw she was only there for support. A keening rose from the circle, the bubble of people shifted as one, and I caught sight of Kimber, sobbing and splayed on the floor like a broken doll. The animist's mask was lying on the ground beside her.

"I wanted to see my fate again . . ." Kimber was saying as Micah held her. Vanessa stroked her hair. "I didn't think it would attack me. I didn't know her ill *chi* lives in the mask . . ."

The *her* in question backed out of the room unseen and unsensed, ears roaring with blood while everyone else's horrified attention remained fixed on Kimber. Even Gregor seemed to have forgotten me, and I placed his coffee on the ground outside the door before I ran.

My mind ticked with possible routes of escape: bone-yard, cantina, locker room, other reality . . . no, no, no, *no*! Thankfully my movements were as rote as my thoughts, and I turned automatically to my sanctuary within the sanctuary.

Throwing open the door to the sparse, utilitarian room, I tossed my messenger bag on the large platform bed, but remained standing, palms to eyes, emptiness pressing in around me. I'd added little of myself to the room, choosing instead to leave it as it was when my mother lived here. The walls were white, relieved only by chunky end tables and floating mahogany wall shelves. Granted, there wasn't enough room to do much more, but I could have added color in the form of a painting or photos or a rug overlaying the concrete floor. I could have added life in the form of a plant or a vase of flowers or mementos that would've truly made it mine, and I didn't need a psychologist to tell me why I didn't. The clothes I left hanging perfectly spaced in the closet—clothes not mine—told me I was in a hold-ing pattern, a moratorium, waiting, still hoping *she* would come back.

"She's not going to rescue you, Joanna," I muttered darkly to myself as I rubbed a hand over my face, then jerked it away as I thought of the mask in the dojo. Rescu-ing wasn't what I needed anyway. Tough love, the kind my Krav Maga instructor, Asaf, had used to bring me back from the walking dead, was more effective. Yet all I had was *self*-love, and a tenuous thread too. But I could fake tough. I could be my own trainer and mentor, wear yet a different hat for the time it took to see a way out of this trouble. Again.

Rescue yourself.

Okay, I thought, opening my eyes. I would do that. I strode into the bathroom and leaned into the mirror, trying to see any difference than there'd been a month ago, before the third sign had been revealed. I didn't *feel* like I had bad *chi*. No stiffness or soreness, no loss of equilibrium or sudden bouts of vertigo. And wouldn't there at least be something to indicate some sort of imbalance? Maybe not physically, but if I was destined to, oh, say, kill my own mother, there'd be something to indicate the predisposition, right?

Then again, did the Shadow agents wake up with heartburn every morning just because they had the desire to exterminate the soul of humanity? Did humans who killed other human beings spend their days feeling like a walking meat suit, unable to process emotion unrelated to their violence? I had to at least concede the possibility that just because I didn't feel it didn't mean it wasn't there. If anything, I'd learned how to strip past the layers of my multiple identities and get comfortable analyzing my own interpersonal neuroses.

So what about Kimber's accusation, her injury? She said it was bad *chi*; the Tulpa had rescinded his offer to allow me to join his troop for the same reason. Even the doppelgänger, with her deadly focus on me, "the golden ring," had said the spirit of the Kairos shouldn't be shackled to a body with damaged *chi*.

I didn't know. The only clear thing was that of all the problems plaguing me, the doppelgänger was public enemy number one. Get rid of her and I'd nullify the danger posed to everyone by the chaos brought on by her violent ruptures of the fabric of our world. But would that entail having to work with dear ol' dad?

I had to admit, if anyone knew how to move seamlessly

along different realities, it was the Tulpa. I'd seen him call someone to his side with nothing more than a thought; disembodied, he'd once assaulted me using nothing more than the windy torrent of his breath. He clearly knew how to access alternate planes, what was possible as well as what was limited. And even given all that, he thought he needed my help. But at what cost to myself?

Meanwhile, I still had to figure out what to do about dear, sweet, smells-like-a-carcass-marinating-in-a-putrid-swamp Rose. In the past few months Regan had manipulated my relationship with Ben, made me infect my allies with a deadly virus, had me chasing my enemies—and my own tail—and nearly cost me my place in the troop. I could be philosophical about all this if she'd done those things just because I was Light. If she'd just killed me . . . or tried to. But she hadn't, which made this personal. She wanted more than my death, but what? And why?

Learn that, and I could anticipate her next move. For now I prioritized: doppelgänger, Regan, and then Tulpa. Eliminate these one by one, I thought, tapping the side of the sink, and surely my ill *chi* would take care of itself.

15

The next day found me back in mortal reality, sans Chandra. Despite Warren's orders that we all remain partnered up, I no longer had to work to ditch her, probably because she'd suddenly—and not so subtly—paired up with Kimber, whose hear-me-roar girl power had fizzled into a feeble whimper. The initiate refused to even look at me as we all piled into Gregor's cab for dawn's crossing, and hid her face behind her thick blond plaits and shaking hands. I'd anticipated at least a modicum of resistance to my going it solo, but it seemed Kimber's run-in with my ill *chi* had the others wanting to avoid the same, and though Warren didn't confront me about what'd happened to the new initiate, he clearly hadn't stuck up for me either. The others went their way, and I went mine.

After Gregor dropped me off at my condo, I showered and pulled on a cashmere turtleneck and pinstripe trousers. The ensemble was expensive, but nondescript enough for everything I had to do that day, and as I dressed I decided I didn't need so-called allies who didn't believe in my inherent goodness. Going it alone also meant not having to fight with anyone about returning to Xavier's. I wanted to put some pressure on him about the Valhalla job, and as much as I wanted to believe that was because of Warren's blessing, I knew Hunter's objection to my employment was equally motivating.

I called Cher's hotel room in Fiji on the way to the mansion, but was asked to leave a message by some man at the front desk with overpolite mannerisms and a thick, lovely accent. I sighed wistfully, gave the clerk my name and number, thinking a long vacation with nothing more complicated than frothy mixed drinks sounded divine. Given the benefits my new powers and strengths afforded me, my inability to leave the valley was an insignificant limitation, but it still chafed. At least the mortals most likely to be affected by my current troubles were temporarily safe. All except Ben, and I'd be taking care of that exception soon.

Reaching Xavier's estate, I batted my lashes at the guard dozing in the gatehouse, then gunned the Porsche's engine, knowing my arrival was being phoned in even as I drove. I screeched to a stop outside the mansion, raced up the white, palatial steps, and used the key I'd remembered to bring along with me this time to open the door. I didn't want to be stalled by Deluca, accosted by Helen, or spend more time in this gloomy mausoleum than I had to.

I hurried through the servants' quarters and used Xavier's private hallway to access his office. I still had to walk through the stupa, with the throne identical to that in my rooftop vision, and with the animist's masks I now knew were aching to glue themselves to my face. I controlled a shudder by moving fast, though the spirit I'd felt living inside the one I'd worn wasn't in evidence in any of the grainy faces staring back at me. However, there was a glaring blank spot where it'd once hung, and I knew Helen would've noticed its absence by now.

All the more reason to hurry.

I skipped the customary knock on the office door and flung it open, taking a deep breath to airily explain my unexpected intrusion. But Xavier wasn't glaring up at me from behind his gigantic desk. The tinny jangle of foreign chimes once again filled the air, muting my steps across the Persian rug as I inched toward the gaping mouth of Xavier's secret room. I'd misjudged him, I thought wryly, shaking my head. Because if he was spending this much time siphoning off his soul energy, he must have had a soul to begin with.

But my dark humor abated as I peered around the bookcase and into the hidden chamber. Xavier was kneeling again; his hair disheveled like he'd sprung from bed, still clothed in pajamas that showed more of his frame than his custom suits would allow. A tremor of shock moved through me. The once-giant man was absolutely gaunt.

But this time he wasn't meditating or lost in prayer. Helen loomed behind him, hands on his shoulders, thumbs on his neck. They weren't, I noted, placed there in support. In fact, her entire demeanor had lost the solicitousness that'd always marked her servitude in the Archer household. Instead it looked like she was holding Xavier in place; stilling his shoulders as they twitched beneath her palms, grounding him like he might float away.

"It hurts," he was saying, head bowed, snaking wisps of incense twining around him. "I feel like my ribs are going to pop. Look, they're still bruised from the last time." He tried to pull up his pajama top. "They're bruised from the inside."

She pushed his arms down, shushing him. "Because you're holding your breath."

"No, it gets trapped inside and expands like—"

"No, it doesn't!" she snapped, her arms straight as she levered him forward again. "The matter is pouring from the mask like a smoky waterfall."

"But that's not my breath! It belongs to the one who lives inside."

"Just put it on, Xavier. You don't want to make him angry, do you?"

I thought he whimpered. "No, but—"

"He wants more."

"It hurts," he whimpered.

"Put it on!"

Helen's roar was so loud I didn't hear my phone ring, but I felt the accompanying vibration, and acted instinctively, darting from the room before the ring tone could sound again. The theme to *Gilligan's Island* just didn't fit the mood.

I knocked on the door as I swung it shut, knowing they'd both hear that. My heart was pounding as I backed away from the door, and I whirled to give myself time to regain my composure, answering the phone in the middle of the next refrain. As the office door whipped open behind me, I turned with a bright grin on my face, held up a finger in Helen's glaring one, and giggled into my BlackBerry.

"Cher, honey, let me call you back. I'm at Daddy's, and you know how he likes my full attention." I paused, then laughed cheerily as Helen shifted on her feet, the hands that'd been stilling Xavier now planted firmly on her nonexistent hips. "Oh, I know! That humid island air hates me too. Just tell your momma to make a Nyquil smoothie and she'll feel all better in the morning."

Helen cleared her throat impatiently.

"Oh, darlin', gotta go. There's a shark outside Daddy's door too." I laughed again at Cher's reply as Helen's hooded eyes narrowed into slits. I blinked prettily after I dropped the phone back into my handbag, though it didn't have the same effect on her as it'd had on the guard at the gate.

"Your father's busy," she said before I could ask for Xavier.

"Helen," I said, batting at her like she'd told a joke. "You know he's never too busy for his favorite daughter. Just be a gem and tell him I'm here."

I made a move toward the office, and her hand shot out, palm on my chest. "You don't understand me," she said firmly, letting a cool gleam enter her gaze. "He's not well, and can't see you now."

"Not well?" I exclaimed, stepping back from her touch.

She let her hand fall, and I put a hand to my face, covering the deep breath I allowed to coat the bridge of my mouth, my teeth, and throat. I closed my mouth, ran my tongue over thc fresh air molecules, exploring their texture and taste. "Then I must tend to him!"

"I'm tending to him. It's my job, remember?"

I tilted my head. "I remember you telling me to take care of myself because you weren't anybody's nurse."

"That wasn't you. That was your sister."

"Oh," I said, nodding slowly, before straightening. "Well. It was still bitchy."

Her nostrils flared. I was careful not to breathe. "Either leave now or I'll throw you out myself."

I fell still and serious, and finally met her eye. "Oh, Helen. You're making a very grave mistake."

She snorted, rolling her own. "I'll tell your father you stopped by."

I bit my lip like I was confused about something, then turned away as she wanted. I felt her watch me as I crossed the throne room, and knew she continued to watch on the office monitors as I left the house and climbed back into the car. It was only after I'd sped through the gates that I let out my own scentcd breath.

"A very, very big mistake, Helen Maguire."

And it was either the first one she'd made in the twenty years she'd been employed in the Archer household, or else I simply hadn't had the tools to notice such a slip before. But I had them now—skin so sensitive to texture I could pick up the marble-smooth fingertips even without seeing them. A palate so refined I could taste decayed emotion. And an internal alarm alerting me to Shadow agents, one that currently had me smiling to myself . . . and sharpening my metaphorical knives.

I returned Cher's call en route to Master Comics.

"We're comin' home," she said without preamble. "Momma's not getting any better and I think the humidity is fermentin' her lungs. Why do people live in places where your hair can get all frizzy?"

"Spoken like a true desert rat," I told her before growing serious. "What are her symptoms?"

"She's wheezing and has a fever that causes her to break out in sweats and cry out in her sleep. She has the weirdest dreams . . . our cabana boy stars in all of them."

Was that out of character for Suzanne? "Has she seen a doctor down there?"

"Are you kidding? The local medicine man would probably kill a chicken and splatter its blood in a circle around the bed. They're hospitable enough, but I wouldn't call them civilized."

"Cher," I chided, narrowly avoiding a tourist who'd eschewed an overhead walkway for a shortcut that'd take him twice as long. "That's so ethnocentric."

Cher gasped, offended. "I am not a bit religious, and you know it."

"Look," I said, blasting through a reddish stoplight. "She doesn't sound well enough to travel right now. Why don't you call Dr. Porter and give him her symptoms. He might be able to prescribe something over the phone and fax a prescription to a pharmacy down there."

"You think?"

What I thought was that the last thing I needed was for those two to come back to town, setting up two more big bull's-eyes for Regan to train her sights on. What I said was "I sometimes manage it, yes. Call me if Suzanne gets any worse. And give her a big smooch from me."

I didn't just say it because Olivia would have. Both Cher and her mother had grown on me, and I was as protective of them as if they were my own family. Natural, I suppose, since I didn't have any left. Keeping them out of Vegas wasn't just necessary because of Regan; now I had the doppelgänger to contend with. If she knew about me she might know of Olivia's friends as well.

The next call I made had to be done in person. It was almost closing time when I walked back into Master Comics, and I'd intended to head straight to the storeroom—flipping off Zane on the way—only pausing long enough to pick up this week's Shadow manual, the Light presumably still not showing up. But one look at the little girl peering up at me with wide and hopeful eyes was enough to have me dropping to my knees.

"Oh, Li," I whispered, cupping the soft oval of her face in my hands. There were no bandages covering the claw marks marring her face, an effort to get the wound and stitches to dry out, and my heart broke as I wished I could help her heal faster.

"It doesn't feel as bad as it looks," she said, in an attempt to be brave, tilting her head so her straight hair swung over the angry red slashes. The fissure in my heart widened.

"Yes it does," Jasmine cut in sharply, standing at Li's right side, one hand dropped protectively on her shoulder. It reminded me of Helen's hands on Xavier, though I didn't know why. "She screams when my mother cleans it, and now the rest of her skin is starting to crack. She looks like Humpty Dumpty."

Li blushed furiously, which only accentuated her scars and made the cracking Jasmine was talking about more noticeable. She was right. Li's once pristine skin now resembled a chaotic inner city road map. Blue veins and red vessels had risen to canvass the thinned-out skin, and I noted her eyes were beginning to bulge a little too.

Jesus, I thought, it even looked like the muscles beneath the skin were thinning. How did I fix this?

"You know you should be a little more sensitive," I told Jasmine. "This could kill you too."

"I'm not the one with draining life energy, and besides, I'd rather die as a hero than live as a weak mortal. I'm never giving up my powers."

"You're not superhuman, Jasmine. I am."

"Really? Then how can I do this?" And she bent over and lifted me from the ground as easily as I would a suckling babe. With one arm.

I blinked, bit my lip, then asked without turning around, "Carl? How can Jasmine pick up a hundred-and-twenty-seven-pound woman?"

"One-thirty-two," he corrected, and Jasmine nodded as she balanced me. Bitch. "Part of the broken changeling deal, Archer. You've blitzed a chunk of her humanity and replaced it in the changeling vessel with your own *chi*. That's why the manuals aren't being written. Her personal energy is registering as yours, and Li's isn't registering at all. You could always try to convince her to give it back, though."

I raised my brows, peering down at Jasmine. In answer, she dropped her arm and I landed on the ground. Crouching, I peered up at her. "Not even to save your sister? An innocent?"

"I'm superhuman," she clarified, before gesturing to me with her too-strong hands. "You're the superhero. You fix it."

"She's going to die if you don't help her!"

That gave her pause, causing her little jaw to tighten, but only for a moment. "She's mortal. She's going to die anyway."

I shook my head in disbelief, and glared at her so hard and long, she finally looked away, pursing her lips. "You're right," I whispered. "You're no hero."

I bit my lip and turned back to Li. "I'll fix this, sweetheart. I swear I will."

She nodded without hesitation. "I know."

Tears staining my eyes, I thought about Regan's black makeup compact settled in the bottom of my bag, but Li and I had vastly different coloring, so it wouldn't do her any good. I'd ask Chandra, and see if something similar couldn't be made for the changeling. "You should go home and rest."

"But you might need me." And, more faithful than Old Yeller, she followed behind as I made my way to the counter. Zane was there, studiously ignoring the goings-on in the shop as he ran a pencil across a sheet of paper, the marks disappearing as swiftly as they were made. The half-dozen changelings, save Jasmine, crowded around me, shouting out questions about what Zane "saw" and suggestions on how to make the ink appear. Zane ignored them out of habit; I did so because I couldn't get Li's tattered face out of my mind.

I leaned on my elbows to peer up into Zane's face. His nose twitched.

"We're about to close," he said, moving his papers aside and continuing his work.

"Get ahold of the Tulpa for me."

He didn't even look up. "What do I look like, your local operator?"

"I know you can get ahold of him." My voice hardened. "Now help me."

He flipped his greasy hair back from his forehead, equally greasy. It immediately fell into his eyes again. "I don't have time to help you work out your daddy issues. Now get out of my light. I'm busy writing a manual you'll probably never get to see."

I folded my arms. "Look, Zane, I don't know what happened to the changeling. I wore her aura but I got it back to her on time. If you have any idea what I can do to fix it, you should tell me."

He sneered as I pulled back, so I decided to try appealing to his morality. "Fine, don't do it for me. But look at Jasmine. Shit, look at Li—"

"I see them every day!" he screamed back in my face, gesturing widely with his writing hand. "While you're out trying to figure out who to screw, I practically live with the little kids your bad decisions are destroying!"

Spit flew from his mouth, and my own fell open, while the kids in the half moon around us froze, unnaturally silent. Zane threw down his pencil, swallowed in an obvious effort to control himself, and when he got his breathing back under control, he said, "I want to help them, I do. But you're the only one who can mend the changeling."

I let his previous remarks go, and said in my own heroic show of control, "How?"

He chewed at his bottom lip like he was struggling to hold back words, and had to munch down on the syllables to stop them from pouring out. Finally, in a strangled voice, he managed, "That's not the right question."

"Then give me the answers and we'll work backward from there."

"This isn't *Jeopardy.*"

"No, because that's a game. *This* is about a little girl's life."

He stared into my eyes for a long moment, frowning like he was using telepathy on me, willing me to understand his thoughts, and when I only stared back he finally shook his head. "I can't help you."

I sighed, deflated, then pointed to the manual he was working on as I turned toward the storeroom. "Why don't you pull up an armchair while you write those things?"

"Fuck you."

"Trite," I shot back over my shoulder. "Good thing you're not thinking up the dialogue too."

I bent, ordered Li to stay at the front of the shop despite her protests, then bypassed the walls of anime, manga, and comic book carousels. I stalked past the cabinet containing the Zodiac manuals. Two members of the pimple brigade followed.

I entered the long hallway. They shadowed. I exited into the library-esque storeroom. More of the same. By the time I'd scooted around the fireplace I'd become almost paranoid in my awareness of them. Then I made the mistake of making eye contact.

"Hey, lady. Can we talk to you for a minute?"

"I don't actually speak Klingon," I muttered, scanning

an eye-level shelf with my fingertips. I wondered how many silent alarms I was setting off for Zane, and decided to touch every manual on every shelf. Fuck him.

Undaunted, the kid introduced himself as Kade, his friend was Dylan, before continuing. "See, here's the thing. Halloween's coming up, right? And you're going to be out canvassing the city, right?"

"Why are you asking me questions you already know the answers to?" I retorted distractedly. I was nervous about what I was going to try, but I didn't see where I had a choice.

"So, with the changeling of Light broken and the manuals of Light going unrecorded you could technically switch sides, and align yourself with the Shadows without anyone knowing the difference."

Was swatting him like a fly out of the question? "For the last time, I'm not a Shadow."

"But you could appear as one on the outside . . . even if you weren't feeling it on the inside, right?"

"Wrong."

Dylan piped up, breathy with excitement, verbally punctuating his sentences in all the wrong places. "Yeah, cuz, like, once I was reading *National Geographic*—"

Kade punched him. "You were looking at the boobies."

Dylan reddened, and spoke faster. "And they had these little Thai dudes who dressed up like women and not only did no one ever know the difference, they were better-looking than most real women."

"Minus the boobies."

He nodded vigorously. "So we were thinking you could do the same."

I blinked. Faced them fully. Blinked again. "Dress up like a Thai woman?"

"No," said Kade. He had a habit of speaking primarily in questions. He was a bit taller than Dylan, blonder too, while Dylan possessed a bit of a lisp. "I mean, pretend you're something you're not in order to fix the changeling, but without the paranormal boundaries levied on the agents of Light. Because you're already dual-sided, kinda like Storm and Mystique, right?"

"More like Clark Kent and Superman."

Their mouths dropped open. "You mean you're a dude too?"

My jaw clenched. "I mean I'm already two people at the same time."

"Nice," Dylan said, looking me up and down appreciatively.

"Not as good as those Thai dudes, though."

"I'm not a—" Forget it. I wasn't going to get into a conversation about transgenders with a kid who read *National Geographic* for the boobies. "Was there something you boys wanted?"

"We've been doing a little reading, catching up on the Zodiac history, right?"

"I'm sure."

"And we think we found a way to help Li. Did you know someone else broke a changeling before? This manual shows how he fixed it."

"Really?" I accepted the Shadow manual to stare down at a giant of a man with biceps twice the size of my neck. He was dark-skinned, so his blond crew cut was obviously dyed, though his penchant for girly grooming didn't make him any less fierce. I didn't recognize him.

"Yeah, man. Jaden Jacks totally iced the changeling of Light." Jaden Jacks. What was that, his porn name? I wondered as Dylan pointed to a panel where Jaden was half shadowed, beckoning to someone from in front of Master Comics. "He coaxed the kid away from the shop late one evening, disappeared around the corner next to the sandwich shop, and the other changelings never saw him again."

I flipped the comic shut. "You want me to kidnap Jasmine? And what, keep her in my superhero locker for all of eternity?"

"No, dude," he said, flipping it open again, pointing to the last series of panels. "You gotta kill her. I'm sure there's still some square footage left in this desert that doesn't already have a body in it."

I narrowed my eyes as Kade and Dylan high-fived. Catching my look, the little aliens sobered. "Don't worry. We won't tell."

"Yeah, she's been a real bitch lately."

I heard a snicker, and glanced up in time to see the Shadow changeling duck back into the hallway. Nosy little eavesdropper. And what a juicy nugget to report back to the Shadows.

"I'm not going to kill Jasmine," I said evenly, loud enough for Douglas to hear.

"But she's been using your superpowers for evil! Yesterday she wrote, 'I will rule supreme' over all the Warcraft gaming tables!"

I thought of the way Jasmine had lifted me in the shop, effortlessly, and with more than a little misplaced pride. She was definitely growing stronger, and apparently the more power she gained, the less sympathetic she grew to her sister's plight . . . and the less likely it seemed she'd willingly release the power as well. Not good. But I didn't know what to do about that yet, and I certainly wasn't going to kill her. "Look, guys, intentionally causing injury to someone weaker than yourself is evil. You don't kill someone because it might help your cause down the line. Understand?"

"Yeah . . . but she made Li stand on the table and repeat it a hundred times."

"What?" My head jerked, and Kade nodded as he worried a zit under his chin.

"Well, it makes sense, doesn't it?" he said, stretching his neck. "Li is a threat to her burgeoning superpowers. If Li becomes the changeling of Light, then Jasmine will have to accept her mortality. She'll have to grow up. She'll have to get married and have babies."

They both shuddered where they stood. I heard Douglas groan from the hallway. The little shit was still there.

I glanced back down at the Shadow manual. Jaden Jacks had killed the changeling downtown. I recognized the garish skyline. "So you guys are saying if I kill Jasmine, Li will become the changeling, the manuals of Light will be printed once more, and all will be balanced and well again?"

They looked at each other. I caught Kade's eye and lifted my brows. "Right?"

"Well, we're not sure. Jacks either disappeared or took a new identity immediately after. There's no way to follow up when the manuals omit those sort of details." Omit them so neither side of the Zodiac gained leverage over the other. "But, hey, if you're really two people at the same time, then you can let your Shadow side come forward, off the little bitch, and then your Light side can take credit for healing Li, right? You can totally keep this identity."

I sighed and handed the comic back. "I can't kill a little girl."

Neither of them reached for it. "Hey, either Jasmine dies or Li does, but one way or another, this shop is going to be down one less Chan come the end of the year."

So that was how long I had. Two months to figure out how to fix Jas. Why couldn't Zane let me know that?

That's not the right question.

I bit my lip. "Do you guys think you could do a little research for me? Try and find out what became of Jaden Jacks after he killed the changeling?"

"We could try. Zane doesn't charge us for looking at the manuals. Not if we return them without stains."

I closed my eyes and lowered my head, pinching the bridge of my nose between thumb and forefinger. "All right. Thanks."

"Don't mention it," Kade said, obviously pleased to help. The boys couldn't tell me anything that would unfairly unbalance the Zodiac, but it wasn't as if there wasn't anything in here I wouldn't eventually discover for myself. I could read all the Shadow manuals; it was just a matter of time, and of looking in the right place. It would help to have a few extra pairs of eyes on the manuals . . . and on Jasmine. "Do you want us to send Jas back?"

"Yeah," said Dylan, patting his jeans pocket. "I brought a Taser in today. I could prod her skinny ass down the tunnel."

"No. That's okay, I have it covered," I said, shaking my head free of the image. The two boys left, I heard them scuffling with Douglas in the hallway, their voices growing fainter as they returned to the shop, and I tucked the manual in my bag without looking at it again. I'd find a way to fix Li without killing her older sister. Maybe what I was going to do next would help, I thought, pulling out my mask. But I didn't want to risk further injury to Li if the Tulpa injured me through Jasmine's aura again. I'd just have to trust the mask I was donning now would do its job. So I slipped it over my eyes, and began envisioning the Tulpa crossing the threshold across from me.

16

"The last time I saw you," I said to the Shadow agent who entered the storeroom, "You were hemmed in by a bunch of children who were using you as an electric pincushion."

Zell Trexler didn't know I was there, and if my voice hadn't caused him to jump and nearly fumble the ax he'd drawn in the adjoining hallway, the words would have. Though a senior Shadow agent, Zell was afraid of me. Or at least very wary. The first time we'd met he'd been absolutely certain his leader, the Tulpa, knew all. But the Tulpa *hadn't* known of my existence, and Zell had been further blindsided two months later when it was prophesied that if the third sign of the Zodiac came to pass, he would die at the Kairos's hands. My hands. I knew this because of my ability to read the Shadow manuals, so even though Master Comics was a designated safe zone, he still blanched when he saw me striding his way. I anticipated his instinctive reaction to run, and shifted my eyes to the threshold, throwing up a wall to block his path.

The Shadow Scorpio nearly peed his pants. "You can't hurt me here!" From the nerves straining his vocal cords, it sounded more like he was trying to convince himself.

"Then why are you backing away?"

"What do you want?" He put a cart with all the latest manuals between us, the glyph on his chest sparking to life despite the lack of danger. His cheekbones pressed against the thinning skin of his face, an aggressive reflex to fear, like a cobra's flaring hood.

"A sense of purpose, enthusiasm for my work, and a good retirement plan," I told him, leaning against an aisle divider. "What about you?"

He smirked, licking his lips as he visibly calmed, though that also could've been because I was talking and not shooting. "What do you want?" he repeated more coolly.

"An audience with your leader."

"The Kairos wants to convene with the Tulpa?" he sneered, but I could practically read his thoughts like a ticker was inching its way over his forehead. *The rise of the Shadow side.*

I rolled my eyes. "The third sign is the rise of the dormant side. It doesn't mean I'm joining the Shadow side."

"What else could it possibly mean?"

Good question, but I didn't let him know I thought so. "It means the Shadows need to find themselves a new Seer. The whack job on the corner of Sinatra Boulevard gives more accurate prophecies than your psychic."

He swallowed hard. He was wearing a suit, and I wondered what he'd been doing when I "called." "So what do you want with him?"

I looked at him like he'd just flatlined.

Zell folded his arms over his deceivingly slender chest. "I'm not calling him until you tell me why."

I sighed like he was testing my patience. "Let me tell you how this is going to play out, *Zell*. The Tulpa wants to talk to me. I've decided to talk back. You, a peon prewired to do his bidding, are here to facilitate that conversation. So you can channel the fucker now, or I'll call him to me with my mind, and he can climb through your chest cavity to reach me. *Capisce?*"

Zell swallowed hard, and I gave him a couple of moments to swallow that hard pill. He was a senior Shadow agent, I wasn't even half that, yet I could usurp his authority at will. I could ask for his death, and for that of all his allies, and if it meant my coming over to the Shadow side, chances were the Tulpa would grant it. It was clear he hated me for it; he stared at me without blinking for so long it was as if he'd frozen there, then he cracked his neck in preparation, first one side and then the other. I backed off and took a seat in one of the leather armchairs.

Two minutes later I was still sitting there as Zell continued limbering up. "Is this going to take long?" I asked, smoothing a wrinkle out of my pinstriped slacks.

He cracked an eyelid, annoyance burning in his gaze. "Hey, you try rearranging the organs inside your body to host another person. It's not exactly comfortable."

I wanted to say, *That's called pregnancy, you big pussy,* but I didn't want him wondering how I knew. Besides, a pregnant woman's body had nine months to rearrange itself. Zell had fewer minutes than that, and watching the way his chest cavity unnaturally gave way to the roiling going on in his belly gave me the heebie-jeebies. But when he finally did settle himself, I watched. I shuddered as his cry roiled over the high-ceilinged room, and scratched lightly at my own skin when his ripped, beginning at his bottom lip, straight down his middle like he was being butterflied. Finally there was nothing recognizable of Zell in the mass of pulsing organs and skinned bone, just the flaps of skin falling open and shut like fish gills against a skull that had whipped a full circle on his neck stump.

Inside out, the bloodied lids fluttered over the crimson orbs and I could practically see Zell's thoughts extinguishing as the Tulpa took over his consciousness. "Ah, Mr.

Trexler. It figures he'd be the one to receive your call. He regularly canvasses the shop by loitering in the adjacent alley. He likes to spook the children as they leave. I'll have to tell him to cease now that I've told you of it."

"I'm sure he'd appreciate that. Zell doesn't seem too fond of me."

"You're not an easy person to like."

I smirked. "Thanks, Daddy."

"I take it you've reconsidered my offer to work together? Rid this plane of the double-walker? May I ask what prompted this change of heart?"

I smirked at his emphasis of the word *heart*. "I'm sure you'll agree that it's in everyone's best interest to get rid of the doppelgänger as quickly as possible."

If he'd had lips they would've pursed. "She scares you more than I do. I think I should be offended."

"This plane is going to collapse under her continued attacks, and besides, she scares you too. I keep wracking my brain, wondering why, because I know it's more than her ability to unbalance us all, not that I expect you to tell me. I'll have to do a little research into the history of tulpas and doppelgängers."

"So until then we join forces." A bloodied stump of a tongue darted out to lick those nonexistent lips.

"Under one condition."

Surprise twisted his features. "You're making conditions now?"

"You can't tell anyone we're working together," I said flatly. "I want this to be between you and me alone. We combine our powers and work together to eliminate the doppelgänger, but I don't want anything to do with your troop."

That was true enough, but it wasn't all. What I really wanted was to keep this agreement between us from Regan. She'd been content to keep my Olivia identity to herself because not only did it give her an advantage over the other Shadows in securing my death, it gave her a sense of power to know something the Tulpa didn't. However, she might spook if she found out the Tulpa and I were speaking. She might tell him about Olivia. She might kill Ben as a warning to me.

"I already told you," the Tulpa said, scratching his rib cage. "You're no longer welcome in my troop."

I inclined my head. "Then you have no problem keeping your Shadow agents out of the loop."

"Only if you're kosher with abandoning the agents of Light for the time being."

"I figured that was a given."

The muscles in his cheeks stretched into a grin. "Agreed, then. So I'm going to give you a mantra that speaks to her natural frequency. The next time you see her, you must say it three times exactly the way I tell it to you. Saying it once will call her to you. Twice will bind her energy in place. The third time will bring me to your side."

"I can do that?"

He chuckled darkly. "Oh, the things I can teach you, daughter."

I went wide-eyed beneath my mask. "Like how to play catch? Roughhouse on the living room floor? Lessons on how to fend off unwanted advances . . . though it's a little late for that, isn't it?"

I hadn't forgotten the Tulpa's culpability when it came to the destruction of my entire adolescence, and he needed to know it. We might be working together now, but it was as a means to an end, and didn't mean I liked it.

He folded one claw over the other. "Anybody can do it, provided they know how. This specific combination of words is set on the same vibrational plane as her energy."

More vibrations, I thought ruefully. "And you know what that is, how?"

The answer flashed over his face. "I read it the moment I laid eyes on her."

I grunted. Of course he had. "So it's a spell."

"You can think of it as a prayer if it makes you feel better," he said, his smile mocking. "But it's really alchemy."

"Alchemy that can kill her," I clarified.

He rolled his eyes, causing bloody tears to form in the inverted ducts. "You haven't been listening. She's pure energy. She can't be killed. But she can be absorbed back into the universe, made harmless, dissolved back into raw matter like all spirits upon death. Then our world will regain its original cosmic resonance."

And we could go back to killing one another. So, then, the equally important question was "And what about me?"

"You're free to leave as soon as she's bound. No need to stick around."

Which was fine by me.

"Yet there is one more little thing."

I folded my arms over my chest, but inclined my head so he'd continue.

"A condition of my own." He lifted his chin, and I saw red beads, like sweat, rolling down his throat. "If you use this mantra to get rid of the doppelgänger, then as soon as I exterminate her, you must come willingly to the Shadow side. You come into my domain, learn what I have to teach, give me a chance to show you everything you didn't know you were missing."

I suddenly felt like a fish on a line. "You mean if I use it, I belong to you."

"It makes sense, doesn't it? I'll have saved you, and the world, from her cannibalistic designs, her basic destructive force. You'll owe me."

And it was a good way to facilitate the rise of my Shadow side. I shook my head. "I'll never owe you a damned thing."

"Not if you're dead," he quickly agreed, narrow tongue darting out to lick at the corners of that inverted mouth. "The only other way to stop her chaotic attacks on this reality's plane is to give her what she wants. You watch, each time you run into her and don't bind her with my magic, she'll have taken on more of your appearance, your mannerisms, your aspect. The collapse of this world aside, wait much longer and you won't even have the ability to choose sides. She'll just take over your life. A new model . . . one that will make the old one obsolete."

He watched me steadily through Zell's blood-slicked orbs, but I said nothing for so long, he must have despaired of an answer at all. He shifted on his feet. I sighed and met his gaze. Just because I had the mantra didn't mean I had to use it. And at least using it was a known risk. So much about my double—my twin, as he called her—was still unknown. I finally nodded.

"Good. I figured you wouldn't be willing to speak in a foreign language—"

When the words were powerful enough to bind another being into place? "You got that right."

"So I've translated the mantra for you from the original. You must repeat it exactly as I do." His eyes rolled back into his sockets to show only white as he pulled the words from memory. " 'I, Joanna Archer, pledge . . .' "

"I, Joanna Archer, pledge—"

"Not now!" The irises whipped forward in his skull, flaring red. "You don't want the energy released before its time. My God, the things you don't know! Just repeat it silently over and over again. Memorize it."

I did. But as I did, I thought. He wanted me to bind the doppelgänger so he could come along and destroy it. Yet basic science held—and he'd said himself—that energy could never truly be destroyed, only transmuted into a different state. The Tulpa had called it alchemy, stressing that inflection and tonal intonation were important. I didn't know anything about mantras, but I did know they had to be directed at something . . . someone.

"So what do I call her?" I asked, thinking the damned thing might backfire on me.

"Call her nothing. Her name isn't needed for the spell to work."

"You mean the *prayer*?" I said dryly.

The remark didn't require an answer, and he didn't give one. He just turned away and began to head toward the long hallway.

"Wait! Aren't you going to . . ." I waved up and down at the length of his host body when he turned to regard me, one hairless brow cocked.

He smiled, dripping blood. Zell's suit was shot. "Not quite yet."

I watched him walk out, dripping fluids, and moments later heard screams of terror pinging within the shop front. It sounded like a roomful of children were being massacred. I rolled my eyes and removed my mask, pulling down my tight bun to run fingers through my hair.

As the screams died out front, I wondered why the Tulpa was being so reasonable about all this. Agreeing to disagree wasn't in his nature, and I could feel the synapses in my brain aching to fire, but the new connections weren't being made. There was something he wasn't telling me, something he needed me for beyond binding the doppelgänger. Who knew? Maybe Kade and Dylan could help me figure out what that was as well. Until then, agreeing to work with him to rid our city of the doppelgänger was the only constructive thing I could do.

Zane didn't even look up as I left the Master Comics. He'd flipped the sign to CLOSED on the glass door, and enlisted those changelings who hadn't fled to help him clean up the blood Zell's entrails had smeared over the stumpy blue-gray carpeting and—more disturbingly— the front window. I didn't know exactly what the Tulpa had done out here, but it looked like he'd wiped the place down with his pancreas. And though I didn't think it was entirely fair, the dark looks of the remaining changelings had me acknowledging I had released a force I couldn't control upon them. Even Li merely shot me a closed-lip smile before throwing a blood-soaked paper towel in a lined wastebasket. I silently swore that next time I had to call on the Tulpa I'd do it in a different safe zone. One with fewer preteens to scare.

I drove north, figuring I'd head downtown to scout the location in the Jaden Jacks manual before heading back to Olivia's high-rise apartment. Sure, the Shadow agent's trail had long gone cold, but I knew better than most that you could see the most amazing things if you just followed the streets.

Besides, I thought as I raced down Paradise, I couldn't get back to the sanctuary tonight anyway. Dusk had already split, and if Warren wanted me to return at dawn he'd call, though I didn't think that would happen. Not after Kimber's harrowing experience with the mask-o'-death. I didn't care what he'd said in the crow's nest about trust; I knew the welfare of the troop came first with him. The care and feeding of my ego was no match for his sense of duty, and they'd probably all been relieved to find Gregor's cab one occupant short when they'd crossed over at dusk.

He'd help you, a small, needy voice said inside me.

Yes, Warren would help me if I asked. But I'd told the Tulpa I wouldn't involve my troop, and had no doubt he'd know if I reneged on the promise. The mask we'd stolen caused me to wonder about the other tools at his disposal. It made me question, too, how he'd learned of the mantra he'd given me to use against the doppelgänger.

I was so taken by this riddle that I passed right by the Holsum Design Center before I realized it was First Friday, and that parking would be impossible along any of the side streets. I whipped a U-turn to park at the Government Center on Grand Central Parkway, and waited there with other pedestrians for the trolley to come along and ferry us to the heart of the event.

First Friday was a monthly art festival, billed as a block party for the artistic set. Once a month the historic downtown area morphed into a showcase for street performers, local bands, fledgling restaurants, and antique stores. Old railroad homes once housing nuclear families were now rented by sculptors, photographers, and painters, and the city-funded trolley clanged along a circuit of exhibits, bars, and vendor booths that acted as an urban showroom for local talent.

To say the crowd was eclectic was a gross understatement. Teens sporting a decades-old punk rock look they thought they'd originated bumped hips with aging hippies and chic soccer moms for whom bohemian sensibility was more of a fashion statement than a way of life. I'd attended First Friday religiously before becoming Olivia and had even considered using one of the low-rent artists' cottages on Colorado to showcase my photography, but alas. Saving the valley from noxious, demonic monsters had taken precedence. Scratching lightly at the rash underneath my turtleneck, I fought off nostalgia for a time when my greatest preoccupation had been framing and capturing the injustices mortals inflicted on one another. Ah, the good old days.

Most of the pedestrians hopped from the trolley at Antique Row, where the majority of shops and galleries were located. I waited until we'd picked up steam again, heading farther into the urban weave of surface streets until I saw a brightly lit building I remembered from past visits. It wasn't a designated stop, so as soon as I was sure no one was looking, I jumped from the back of the trolley, hitting the wide parkway, immediately altering direction. Had anybody been looking, and blinked, they would've missed it. Paranoia: my new art form.

I arrived at another building, this one from the seventies that the city was billing as historic, right next to one from the fifties that almost was. I paused there to take in the scents of grilled veggies and salsa wafting from the nearby Mexican restaurant, and remembered the time Ben and I had come down here as teens. The block across from this had been one giant souvenir warehouse then, and we'd emptied Ben's pockets of change, divided it, and split up to search out the perfect gift for each other . . . one that could be had for $2.73 or less. I'd gotten Ben a wallet with a faux sheriff's badge, and he'd given me a plastic ring with a diamond the size of my earlobe. I still had it—or, at least, I knew where it was—stuck inside a secret cubbyhole of an antique desk in Xavier's mansion.

Now *his* prison, I thought, as a lone cab inched its way past the building and up the street toward the beehive of activity on Antique Row. And revisiting it, and Helen, was something else I needed to get to. Though it wasn't at the top of my supernatural to-do list, even if Xavier had looked ill. He'd phoned in his fate upon accepting the Tulpa's patronage. Giving up your soul essence to help keep another being animated was bound to take it out of a person.

The souvenir warehouse was gone now, and sections of the boxy brick facade had been painted by different artists. The bright canvas was then divided into three stories with a red steel staircase perched off one side. There was a glass-blowing studio at street level drawing a big crowd of onlookers, a tapas bar on top, which would see its best business as an after-party to the event, and an infamous tattoo parlor sandwiched in between where some pop starlet had made one of many mistakes on a drug-fueled binge that'd landed her at the drive-up chapel after this . . . and on the cover of the tabloid papers by sunup.

I gazed up at the wide, open windows of the ink parlor, idly wondering where Hunter had gotten the tattoo I'd seen on his shoulder. It was intriguing that he believed fear and desire were flip sides to the same coin, as if one couldn't exist without the other. Did I believe that? I wondered, as a burly man leaned over the windowsill, saw me looking, and waved at me to come on up. Hunter had made no secret of his desire for me, so it made me wonder if there was a bit of him fearing me as well— or, at the very least, the intensity of the attraction. So, then, was his recent decision to pursue me in spite of the danger . . . or because of it?

I pointed at my watch, signing to the man I had somewhere to be, and waited for another cab to pass before crossing the street, annoyed by the way my thoughts had flitted back to Hunter rather than sticking on Ben. I knew what was bothering me, what kept my psyche sliding from the thought of him like wheels over an oil slick. Warren's report and Ben's alleged homicidal turn had coupled with his refusal to speak with me, and I suddenly felt like I didn't know the man at all. Distance and bitterness and whatever had crawled into Ben in the years since I'd first known him had me unable to guess what he wanted anymore, so it wasn't any surprise Hunter's relatively simple desire to bed me was easier to face in comparison.

I reached Casino Center, pulled out the manual the boys had shown me, and held it up, aligning the skylines. There. The exteriors of the surrounding buildings had changed, but the streets had not. The same alley disappeared behind the artist's tents now pitched before Third Street, across from one of the city's most popular antique stores, The Funk House. The first changeling had been killed in that alley, and I needed to slip in there. But it'd be best to approach it from its opposite, less populated, side, so I headed out onto Main Street, where I slipped past Dust, an edgy gallery with contemporary exhibits, and had just passed a store devoted to overpriced urban footwear—a DJ working two tables, the minimalist concrete room packed with teens—when I saw the cab again. I knew it was the same one because there couldn't be two drivers canvassing this area with a wool jeep cap turned backward. This time, however, he wasn't doing a slow crawl; impatience wafted from his open window as he waited for the pedestrians to clear, the backseat of his cab empty. That's how I knew I was being followed.

I dove into the next doorway I came upon, a bar with gouges in the floor, team trophies lining the walls, and an inexplicably large jar of pickled pigs' feet next to the register. Two men holding pool cues over a neglected table straightened when I came in, but I ignored both them and the stares from those who swiveled on their red patent leather stools. I wasn't looking for a game. I needed a way out.

I headed straight to the back of the bar and pushed through the kitchen entrance. The slit-eyed cook never looking up from his portable television as I exited into the back alley. My nostrils flared as I first pivoted left, then took off in the opposite direction, following the scent of decay.

Following Regan.

It wasn't hard to put together, and I did it as I ran. The little shit in Master Comics had called Regan again after overhearing my conversation with Dylan and Kade about Jaden Jacks, and Regan had either tracked me, or correctly guessed I'd research the events in the Jacks manual immediately. My money was on the latter, as we all knew fixing Jasmine was a priority.

So Regan DuPree knew I was here . . . but I knew she was too. I knew her scent as well as I did my own, and offensive though it was, it would take a miracle to dislodge. Regan, I decided as I rounded the block, didn't have another miracle left in her.

I blew by an apartment building, wind at my heels, knocking over a child's bike, leaves and debris rustling in my wake. I flattened myself against the building's short side, double-palmed my crossbow, and eased into the adjacent side street.

She was picking her way through the street's middle, a

dark figure with a sharp, swinging bob, and I was pleased to see her looking tentative. Her scent was the same as it'd been in the shop, and in the bathroom before that: smugness like smoky marshmallow, crazy like cheap liquor, and as spoiled as fermented flesh.

I thought of all the times and ways she'd eluded me, how she'd pawed Ben so possessively, and threatened to either blow him to bits or shrivel his soul until it matched her own. As she neared the last quarter length of that alley—nearly safe—I thought of what Gregor told me about her parents and decided that playing fair was overrated. Her death, I thought as I lifted my weapon, would be a relief to us all.

The damned toddler was what saved her. His screech as he ran from the street festival announced his arrival at the mouth of the alley, a tiny bolt of flying limbs accompanied by his mother's panicked, exasperated cry. I lowered my weapon as they appeared in quick succession, the frantic mother whipping him back to her side where he cried out again. They drew lines in their battle of wills, right there between the two bland apartment buildings.

Regan didn't slow. In fact, her confidence lifted at the sight of them, and why not? I'd never attack with witnesses present. Their arrival also gave her options, other lives to play with in this cat-and-mouse chase with me, and I decided right there and then: not again.

I rushed her. It wasn't as fast as an arrow through the heart, but the timing was perfect. I cleared twenty yards in the seconds it took for the mother and child to slip from view. Regan hadn't taken three steps before I was on her, momentum driving me too close for a fully extended punch. I settled for the more lethal elbow to the temple, driving downward with all my supernatural might just as she shifted, brows furrowing . . .

On a face that wasn't Regan's.

I pulled up short, but it was too late. The blow still connected and the woman fell, probably without even knowing she'd been hit. *Not a deathblow*, I pleaded silently, my breath sounding loudly in my ears. *Please, please not a deathblow.* But through my pleading, and as I cradled a clearly mortal body in that ragged silence, I battled back confusion. I could still scent Regan on this woman, in her, a sensory record of a life touched by Shadow. And when I coupled that olfactory knowledge with the woman's appearance—a build similar to my old one, the blunt hair exact, but a face that was nothing like Regan's or mine—my confusion was snuffed, and my blood went colder than the thin stream of that which was trickling from the mortal's ear, onto the ground.

It's you she's after.

And she'd use anything and anyone—including an inno- cent—to get to me. I'd have bent to study the track marks I knew studded the veins in her arms, but Hunter's reminder sounded again, more insistent this time.

It's you she's after.

I dove to my left, only because I happened to be lean- ing to my right, just as the bell-like laughter sounded down the alley. Luckily there was a jumble of shopping carts and construction debris to block me from view, but still my heart pounded, my own emotion now up and easily scented, and I looked back at the woman sprawled in the middle of the street regretfully. I hated to leave her, but I had no way of knowing if Regan was alone.

Back to the wall and using the construction material as a shield, I shakily inched my way again to the bar's rear exit. I'd come full circle, but it was the knowledge that I had to get out of here now that had me light- headed.

The moment I touched the handle of the kitchen door, it rocked into me with a force that should've been impossible on spring hinges. My skull cracked on the steel doorframe,

then with one good yank on my arm, I was pulled inside.
I let my knees buckle—they wanted to, anyway—and
narrowly avoided a blow to the head. I could have also
eluded the foot in my gut if my attacker was mortal, but
the blow nailed me true and square and sent me sprawling
on the kitchen floor, joining the unconscious cook and an
obscenely large cockroach scuttling past my head. All I
could think as Regan squashed it beneath her boot, was
Clever bitch. She'd predicted I'd recognize the cab and had
made the driver drop her off in front of me on his previous
circuit, along with a woman she'd probably culled from the
herd of mortals days ago. Why was it only clear now, when
it was too late?

"You . . ."

She'd plucked an innocent from the world, one she made
sure looked like her—me—from behind, then marked her
with her own olfactory scent. She made me kill the mortal
because watching that would be so much more fun than
doing it herself.

Regan just nodded to all those unspoken accusations,
her other boot pinned at my neck. "And you thought I was
just another pretty face."

"You made me . . ."

"Puh-lease shut up. For once take some responsibility.
You did it yourself."

The tinny scent of the woman's blood burned the lining
of my nose, causing my eyes to tear up.

"Besides," Regan went on, increasing her weight. "I told
you not to fuck with me anymore. I thought the threat on
Ben's sad little life would do the trick . . . but then I found
this."

I glanced at the bugging device in her hand, less concerned about that than the ice pick poised at my heart
while my conduit still lay unguarded outside the kitchen's
back door. "Maybe you missed it before."

"I did not miss it!" Her hand disappeared into her pocket,
and before I could speak again she withdrew it and pegged

me with five other devices . . . all the new ones Gregor had planted. They stung my skin, fell harmlessly to the floor, and I lay extra still, trying not to look like I was planning to attack her.

Trying to figure out a way to kill her where she stood.

"What did I say about backing off?" She placed her hands on her hips, her conduit fisted in her right. Ben should see her now, I thought, eyeing her black on black street wear—perfect for the First Friday crowd—her hair slicked back behind her ears, looming over me with homicide in her eyes.

It'd be unrealistic if I played too nice, so I voiced my first thought. "Gee, Mom, I don't know. What did you say?"

"I told you I'd kill him. But first I'll tell him about your ugly secret, the daughter you don't want him, or anyone, to know about."

Yet here she was talking about it again. So, even prone on the floor, glyph glowing brightly beneath both boot and conduit, I wasn't as scared as I probably should have been. I also wasn't dead like the mortal in the alley, and even though my bones had risen to burn through my fragile skin, Regan read the thought.

"The Tulpa has said you're not to be touched." She ground her teeth together, and a smile began to spread over my face. "Not for a while anyway."

Her left eye twitched, and I whipped my legs up, somersaulting backward to avoid the coming blow. Gotta love knowing someone else's tell. "This is not touching?" I said, flipping my hair from my eyes as we circled each other again.

"It's not killing," she said, tone harder now as she tried to figure out how I'd anticipated the blow. "You can't prove I touched you. The evidence is fading already."

"So it seems we're on equal footing once again." In more ways than one, I thought, circling.

"You forget I know who you are, where you live, what

your daughter's name is. And I still have the man you love."
She licked her lips when she saw I wasn't going to argue—
all those things were true—and went on. "Have you looked
up what I told you about Ben and that street thug yet? Read
the account in his journal of how you appeared in a ghetto
barricade, disarmed a criminal, then left Ben alone to mete
out justice? I guess that makes you an accomplice to that
murder as well, huh?"

Magnum hadn't been an innocent, not like the woman
still warm in the alley. He'd probably been born bad,
yet he was mortal all the same, so technically under
my protection and care. And I *had* left him sprawled
on the floor of that barricade. But. "Ben didn't murder
that man."

"Oh, Joanna," Regan sighed, flipping her conduit in her
hand. "Can't you see? It's not hard to push a man to his
breaking point. Ben will kill again if I tell him to. In fact,
his finger is already on the trigger. All I have to do is tell
him where to aim."

"He's a good man." My voice came out in a whisper.

Regan smiled. "A good man with a stain on his psyche.
One you put there. And the longer I'm with him, the wider
and deeper that stain will spread.

"Yes, I have plans for ol' Benny-boy," she went on, smiling. "He's going to help me accomplish some of my long-
term goals. And when I'm done with him he'll be a cracked
shell of the man you once loved."

The bones beneath my lotion-soft knuckles fisted, the
rings on my tensed fingers glinted, and Regan's eyes widened. I hit her so hard, one of my diamonds was imprinted
on her cheek, the memory of something precious carved
into her fouled skin. Her ice pick fell as fast as a dart to
connect above my knee. I crumpled, and she was spinning
in the air, her left foot in my face as she whipped around
me on her way out the door. My head knocked back, but I
lifted it in time to see her fist lowering again. See it, but not

stop it. The scream of panic and rage welling in my throat scuttled off like a roach in the light as my temple took the full force of the blow. There was a slow, almost arduous dropping, then nothing after that.

17

Light pricked at my vision in shards, and I groaned to send them slicing through my brain. The fluorescent bulbs above me coalesced, and the smell of grease anchored me back in time. *Regan. Damn. Bitch.*

When I could do more than form one-word expletives, I picked my defeated ass off the floor, and found my bag in the alley, though, unsurprisingly, not my conduit. Regan, I knew, would use the crossbow as soon as the Tulpa lifted his protective ban on my life. And then she wouldn't just kill me, she'd obliterate my memory and legacy from the manuals, our history, and the earth.

It's you she's after.

I limped over to the body still lying sprawled in the alley, vision wavering as I placed weight on the leg Regan had stabbed. I slid down the grimy wall to drop next to the woman. Of course she was still there. Regan didn't care about her, the mortal had served her purpose, and it was more tortuous to leave the body for me to deal with.

My nose felt lopsided, and I didn't bother wiping away the blood yet. My eyes, probably both blackened, watered as I popped my nose back into place, but ten more minutes alone and no one would ever know. At least my extensions had held, I thought, feeling the top of my head. Yay for bonding glue and hairspray.

And then I began to cry.

Shit. Regan was right. I had to start taking responsibility for what I'd done, and now *I'd killed a mortal*. And what about what I was allowing to happen to Ben, and possibly to this entire mortal plane?

What the fuck was I doing? I thought, gazing through the tears at the woman's body.

At the involuntary twitch of her thumb. My sniffles died in my throat and I was next to her in a millisecond, belly on the ground, cheek over her mouth, but otherwise entirely still. The softest breath, like a baby bird's first, warmed my ear.

"Oh my God." Alive. *Alive.*

And to keep her that way I had to get to the hospital quick. Not one of ours; Micah was tucked in the sanctuary until dawn, and she couldn't wait that long. So one of the mortal hospitals, then, I thought, lifting her. But I'd have to drop her at the emergency entrance, unable to risk the paperwork, the questions about my involvement and appearance, the certain leaks of both of those to the Shadow side . . . leaks Olivia Archer couldn't risk.

But this mortal would live. She had to. And after I saw her safe, I would get cleaned up, find a replacement conduit for the one I'd lost, and retire to someplace safe until I could cross to the sanctuary at dawn.

And there was only one place to do all that. Unfortunately it wasn't until after I'd left my fragile package beneath the spotlight of a streetlamp at the city's trauma unit, until after I heard cries of surprise and yells for assistance, and until well after I'd entered the shell of the warehouse and its arsenal of silent, hidden alarms that I thought about what exactly it meant to be alone with Hunter Lorenzo. In the depths of night and in a building only he could arm and secure. It really hit me when he swung open the side steel door and I found myself face-to-face with those muscles rounding beneath his white wife-beater, his fresh sweat so heady my nipples contracted. He looked great, yes. But, more, he looked safe.

If Hunter noticed the hitch in my breath he didn't say. Instead his eyes widened as he took in my face.

"What the hell happened to you?" he asked, yanking me inside.

"Haven't I healed yet?" I asked, patting at my face.

There was nothing seductive about his touch as he dragged me to the center of the warehouse, positioning me on a high metal stool next to his drawing table to assess the damage. But he wasn't looking at my face. He'd scented my blood the moment he saw me, and had torn the seam of my slacks aside to reveal the wound above my right knee. It looked like a splash of red paint against a flawless ivory canvas.

"It's nothing," I told him, swallowing hard at the sight. One more scar to hide, I thought. Olivia would be appalled at the way I was treating her body. "Just a scratch."

"From a conduit," he said, his concern not lessening. "I wouldn't call that nothing. Whose?"

"Guess," I said wryly, as he yanked open a drawer on a cabinet-length toolbox to reveal emergency medical supplies. You had to hand it to the guy. He was prepared.

He whipped his gaze up to mine. "Again?"

"Don't look at me that way!" I bristled, stood, and bristled again when he pushed me back onto the stool. "I'm not seeking her out, I'm not losing control of my emotions, I'm not even going near Ben. She's like a poisonous mushroom. She keeps popping up whenever the conditions are right."

"You mean when you're alone and vulnerable and not suspecting her attack."

I flipped my hair back and focused on the alone part. "Hey, it's not like I'm trying to keep Chandra from accompanying me—"

"Anymore," he added quickly, but I ignored that too, gritting my teeth as he swabbed the cool, stinging alcohol over my knee.

"Besides, it doesn't seem to matter where I go or who I'm with. She's locating me almost at will. I can't figure it out." I scratched at my chest, and Hunter gently pulled my hand away so he could reach my forearm. I hadn't even realized it'd been nicked.

"Tell me what you were doing when she found you," he said, pushing up the long sleeve.

"She didn't," I said, swallowing hard. "I found her."

I told him about the woman in the alley, what I'd done, where I'd left her, and felt his eyes on me when my voice broke, his work slowing. Without looking at him, I quickly moved on to the Tulpa's decree that I not be killed, though he stopped bandaging my arm altogether when I said I'd lost my conduit. It was a moment longer before I could look him directly in the eye, but when I finally managed it, I found none of the disgust or anger I expected . . . or that I felt for myself.

"Oh, Joanna," he said softly.

"Don't," I said, tearing up. "You'll make me cry. And I can't cry." I scratched at my other arm and wished for my room in the barracks.

"Okay," he said, drawing the word out as he rewrapped a length of gauze. "So you said you think the Shadow changeling told Regan where you were going?"

I nodded. "I know it. Douglas heard my conversation with the other kids. They wanted me to kill Jasmine, if you can believe that. They said it'd been done before by a guy named Jaden Jacks . . ."

I started to rise to grab the manual the boys at Master Comics had given me, thankful for something to do, but Hunter stilled me with a palm on my thigh. "And did it actually look like Regan in the alley?"

"God, yes! You think I would've struck her otherwise? But it was dark and she'd marked the mortal with her own scent, I'd know it anywhere, and I tried to pull back but it was too late and—"

"Shh." Hunter's hands stilled my own, which were moving faster and faster in the air with the telling, and I took a deep breath, realizing I was close to hyperventilating. We both waited until I was calm enough, and then my gaze met his. His voice matched it in softness. "So if you know Regan so well, how can you not see she's been planning this forever? That woman's injury wasn't your doing."

"It was," I argued. "It's because I know her so well that I should have seen it coming."

"So now you're responsible for all the evil in this world as well?"

Take some fucking responsibility . . .

I shook my head, loosening Regan's words, but unable to keep from recalling how soundly my elbow had cracked against that woman's flesh. I scratched my chest absently, tears threatening again. "All I know is Regan possesses knowledge of my old identity and my new. She has my past, my conduit . . . my number. And she can find me at will. I just don't know *why*."

Hunter straightened, eyeing me narrowly, and I froze in mid-scratch. "What?"

"What are you doing?" His voice was low, modulated, and suspicious.

"Playing patient to your bossy-ass doctor act," I said, scratching again as I indignantly pushed off the stool. "What does it look like I'm doing?"

He pushed me back down. "Allowing your skin to breathe."

"What?" My hand stilled on my arm as he reached for my sleeve and ripped it. I was about to yell that cashmere didn't come cheap when I glanced down at my bare arm. At first it looked like flaking skin to me, but then Hunter was peeling it away in strips, like dead skin lifting from a healing sunburn, but in neat, even rows. "What the—?"

The bronzed slivers lifted, and the scar I'd gotten four months earlier from a Shadow agent named Liam Burke appeared. I realized immediately I hadn't seen it since applying the makeup Regan had left in the ladies' room. I'd barely been aware of the itching since then; it'd been as subtle as the bite of a mosquito in summer, something to be slapped at, but not concerned with.

"Shit." She hadn't left it by accident. "It's the makeup."

"It's a tracking device," Hunter clarified, and peeled a thin, flexible strip from my arm.

I was a fucking idiot.

And Regan made a brutal man named Ajax, and a psychotic one named Joaquin, look like kittens at play. *Of course* she wasn't going to come at me with guns blazing. Women fought differently. I knew that.

Hunter pulled out a knife and a pair of goggles from the stacked tool chest next to us, and I sat stone-still as he cut a giant cross through the center of my turtleneck, then angled the blade toward my chest. The cool tip whispered against my skin until it caught on the edge of the compound. Hunter picked at the edge carefully, close enough I could feel his breath on my earlobe as he worked, the dark hair that was only just growing out again falling across his forehead in front of me. The blade scratched, moving between us, and I kept my hands clasped in my lap. Yet with his head lowered, eyes covered and his hands busy, I could allow my gaze to fall to his lips, slightly parted as he concentrated on my skin. *Damn.*

"There are microscopic wires embedded in the compound. They flattened as you spread the makeup out, and hardened into a flat web of interconnected transmitters." There was still no censure in his voice, and I was thankful for that.

"That's how she found me at Master Comics," I said, trying to think back to all the times the compound had itched, indicating the feed was live. "And tonight."

"Where else did you apply it?"

"My calf," I told him, then froze. Oh shit. "The back of my thigh."

He lifted his gaze to mine, and for a moment wickedness lived in his smile. "Bend over, baby."

"Ah, maybe I should do it myself," I said, holding out a hand for the knife.

He sobered immediately, shaking his head. "You have to be sure to get it all, or else she might be able to lock in on you using the remnants."

He wasn't angling, and he wasn't flirting. It was fact, and we both knew it, so I sighed and began taking off my clothes—including my tattered turtleneck—while Hunter went to retrieve a solution he said would neutralize the compound and a wide-angle edged scraper used for sculpting putty. "Is there a toy you don't have?" I called as he retreated, but he dismissed me with a wave and kept walking.

The intervening minutes gave me time to order my thoughts. It was good that I'd come here. Warren might have had a few choice words to fling in my direction, but Hunter hadn't gone on attack, and his words *had* loosened a knot that'd been forming inside me. I still needed to take responsibility for the results of my own actions . . . but I didn't need to weigh myself down with Regan's as well.

And as for Regan . . .

"Time to pay a little visit to the state prison," I murmured, folding my pants. Because if Regan wanted to play hard and fast with lives she had no right to touch, then I would match her move to move. I'd attack her next by honing in on her soft spots, and when I reached the bruised center of her life?

I'd *push*.

Hunter returned with a vat of what looked like water but smelled like petrol. He carefully sat it on the drafting table, then stood back to regard me in all his cotton- and denim-clad glory while I wore nothing but two swaths of silk and lace, utterly exposed but for my scars.

Turning my back, I decided, would at least hide my nervousness. So would being a smartass. "Geez, Hunt. Taking quite a chance being alone with the girl who spawns heart-eating look-alikes, allows herself to be tagged by a Shadow, and unwittingly injures mortals. Aren't you afraid of my ill *chi* too?"

"You didn't murder Jasmine," he reminded me lightly, as if that would make up for the rest. "And I'm not afraid of much."

I released a breath I hadn't even known I'd been holding, and didn't even mind Hunter scenting my relief. It was going to be okay. He was the one person who'd been inside me in all ways but the physical, and he thought I was fine. He always had, and though I was grateful, I still didn't understand why. I hadn't been exactly stable to begin with. But that wasn't something I wanted to get into right now. "But you're afraid of me working at Valhalla, right?"

"Worried," he corrected, without looking up. The scrape of the blade gave way to a gentle tugging, the compound being removed. "For you."

"I can take care of myself," I said, still wondering why he was so against it.

"Clearly."

Okay, so I deserved that.

Hunter placed a warm palm on my back as he deposited a skin-colored strip into the vat. It bubbled, disintegrated, and dissolved. The remaining solution looked cracked. It was the exposed wires of the tracer now that the makeup had been destroyed. Damned clever.

"The tracer was itching while I was here. Will Regan find the warehouse?"

He shrugged and dropped another strip into the steel vat, then moved up to begin work on the back of my thigh. "I'm neutralizing them pretty quickly. I can't imagine she'd get an immediate bead on your location, but even so, this place has more traps than even your body could ever hold."

I glanced over my shoulder at him and sneered. "Nice."

He smiled now that he'd forced a fighting response from me. "She'd never get in, but I'll lock the wires in the tool chest if you're worried. The reinforced steel will interfere with the reception too. Here, I need you to move."

He lowered the stool I'd been sitting on to knee height, then pushed me forward so I was bending over it. There was nothing sexual in the movement, but I caught our reflection in a pair of safety goggles across from us—Hunter bent over me, the muscles twitching beneath one of those gorgeous round shoulders as he did his exacting work, and me in pink panties and a bra—and knew the scene would replay itself in my midnight memories, but with a different ending.

"She might wait for you to come out," I said, voice lower than I intended it. *Think of Ben. Think of anyone and anything else. Just don't think of the man behind you, whose touch makes you totally insensible.*

"Worried over my welfare? Touching," he said, as he gently touched me. I braced my hands on the drafting table, trying to get my equilibrium back.

"Hey, she knows about you too, Hunter." I shifted, sounding calm again as he pushed at my thigh. "She's not one to easily forget."

"So I'll have to make sure I don't accept any cover-up from her in the near future." And before I could respond, he whipped his hand up to place a finger against my mouth, and smiled as he leaned close. "I know. Fuck off."

But I was very suddenly aware of the length of him curled around my half-naked body, and the slight pressure against my lips didn't make me want to either shut up or return the smile. God help me, it made me want to give that finger one good long lick, and suckle it until he brought me something more satisfying. My lips, pressed together and readied for a hard retort, softened at the thought, and Hunter's eyes flashed dark. Humor fled us both, and the pressure against me increased fractionally.

"Do you remember before? When I was telling you about my templates and the way I fashion the conduits for individual agents?"

I'd have thought he was trying to redirect the sudden intensity, except he hadn't moved; he was still too close and warm and overly physical, but I let him talk, mostly because I was afraid to move more than I had to. If I did anything more than nod I might just loosen my limbs, throw my legs around his waist, and rock.

"Well, there's another reason some conduits feel like they're made for your hand and others don't." And his left palm was suddenly warming my side, gliding, smooth-tipped. "See, your crossbow has a catch mechanism and lock, so when you're controlling the conduit you can feel all manners of ripples and bouncing waves and vibrations."

"And if there aren't any catch mechanisms?" *Like on your whip*, I wanted to say, but even the thought of that slim piece of leather sent heat through me.

"Then you feel the lack of them, and for some, that's the right fit. Either way, when the right tool meets with the right person, there's a natural harmony of body and spirit. It's so simple. And complex. It's chemistry."

"Hunter—"

He spoke over me. "It's the same with people. Two people meant to be together will be drawn together again and again like they're caught in a magnetic field. And every time they interact, the energy changes between them. They change each other. So while the elemental forces that initially drew them together are reinforced, others are deconstructed to alter into something new."

I swallowed hard. I couldn't argue because our chemistry *had* had physical consequences. We'd once fired the night with a single torrid kiss and created thunder between us.

"And when the two join, like conduit and controller . . . well, it's not just the way they move together, the friction or the taste on the tongue or the sigh meant only for the other to hear . . . it's how one single body affects the other. It's elemental and—"

I knocked his hand aside, and tipped the stool to get away. I was breathing hard, the drawing table between us now, arms propped on it for support, head lowered as I kept my wary gaze on his.

Hunter righted the stool, straightened slowly, and after a moment, shook his head. "What are you so afraid of?"

I thought of the tattoo on his shoulder, the one stating fear was the opposite of desire. If I said I was afraid of him, he'd know I wanted him as well. And I did. My mouth watered with it.

"I fear myself," I finally whispered. "You should too."

"Yes." His eyes did a slow crawl down my body, pausing in all the right places. Heat rushed through me. "Very scary."

The taunt had me pushing away from the table, and I found that the momentum I carried inside me, that constant blind run away from him, still had some steam. "Are we done?"

"The compound is gone, if that's what you mean."

I began to pull my slacks back on. The turtleneck was ruined, but maybe I could temporarily knot the pieces together. I turned away from Hunter, hands shaking.

"I wouldn't hurt you, you know." His voice was a whisper, one I could've chosen to ignore, but doing so might make him think he had a right to say it, and he didn't. Not with Ben and my long-standing *no* and little more than silk standing between us. It was an opportunity he should have let be.

"No," I replied, gathering my shirt in front of me, "but you might charge me by the hour, and we have a long night ahead of us."

"Ah, the bitch is back," he said wryly, but didn't defend himself as he cleaned up, lifting the wires from the bowl with metal tongs, depositing them in the tool-box as promised.

"I'd like to look through the panic room," I said, ignoring the fat spears of guilt stabbing at my chest, and the spicy evidence of our lust hanging heavily in the air, threatening to choke me if I took too deep a breath. I took one anyway, looking right at him so he knew my mind was in control here, not my hormones, and told him how I wanted to study the map of breaches the doppelgänger had made in to our world so far.

The change in topic worked, or so I thought. He dumped the toxic solution into the floor drain, sprayed and wiped it clean with a red shop rag, and nodded slowly to himself. I didn't expect anything more, so I turned toward the panic room . . . and was ambushed by his next words.

"You should let Micah erase his memory," he said, and I froze in my tracks. The statement was bolder than his flirtations, and blunter than I'd have expected.

"I don't want him to forget," I said just as bluntly, without turning.

Because Ben would have to forget it all—me, our past, our potential future. All memories would stop the night I was attacked a decade ago, and Micah would rebuild a history for Ben that had me languishing in a forgotten childhood . . . and one that didn't include me in his adult world at all. I would cease to exist for the last person on earth who'd truly known me as me. "We have a child together."

"And you think that's reason enough to hang on?"

I still didn't turn around. "I do."

"You sound obsessed."

"I don't expect you to understand," I said, and though I did turn my head and meet his eyes, it was a dismissive gesture, my mind made up. "Why should I have to lose him just because I've found my true self?"

Laughter barked out of him, his bluntness turning cruel. "Because that's what we do. We live *for* them, Jo, not with them . . . and not for ourselves." He wiped his hands on another rag before tossing it on the floor. "You ceased doing that the day you metamorphosed, and the sooner you accept it, the easier it will be. For everyone."

Like Hunter gave a shit if life leaned a little easier on Ben. Superhero, I well knew, didn't mean saint. "I won't ever accept it."

I turned away before he could respond—because what I was saying was *I won't ever accept you*—but not before I saw an emotion abandon his face, one that apparently had been holding it up. I hesitated in the wake of that broken emotion, feeling victory and loss at the same time, before walking away. There was no call from behind me asking me to return, no apologies or explanations or footsteps across the floor to stop or help or seize me. I reached the panic room and flipped on the light, but all it did was illuminate the silence. I hesitated a second more, then closed the door firmly behind me.

18

I remained locked in the panic room for most of the night, knowing—sensing—Hunter on the other side of the door, my mind flitting unbidden to the warmth that'd seeped from his body into mine before I'd pushed away. Again. After refocusing on the reams of maps for what must've been the hundredth time, I finally recognized that Warren's tight handwriting wasn't going to reveal any additional secrets to me just because I was the targeted double.

Yet there was an additional key located to the left of the map, where yellow, red, and green dots spelled out suspected activity, but this was in Hunter's slanted script, probably marking for Warren his suspicions about how and where the doppelgänger would cross into our terrestrial plane next. The known entrances were yellow, and seemed to be mapped down to the square foot. The red dots represented places Hunter believed were most susceptible to the doppelgänger's future breaches, and the fewest dots, represented by green, were a mystery entirely. No matter how long I stared at them I couldn't decipher their meaning, and after the way we'd parted, I couldn't exactly go out and ask Hunter.

I followed the green dots once more with my finger, tracing them in what appeared to be a written chronological order, then gave up and left the room long enough to brew a pot of coffee, to make a call to the hospital to check on the mortal woman, and take another from Warren—whom Hunter had phoned after our nonargument—before returning with a high stool to sit while I tried to predict where the doppelgänger might pop up next. The red dots ran right through the center of town, one right in the middle of Valhalla itself, which I thought was poetically ironic.

I finally found a secondary key to overlay the primary map. It contained all the suspected locations of Shadow entry into our alternate reality, though why Warren wanted that studied was beyond me. I pored over the maps so long my eyes blurred, and eventually even the insistent throb from the injury to my thigh couldn't keep me awake.

Hunter's predawn rap on the door had me jolting from my slumped position before I even knew I'd fallen asleep. He'd given the steel door an extra hard knock and I cursed him as I wiped drool from the map, then gathered up my things. I collected the copies I'd made and rolled them to fit in my bag along with my mask and manual—feeling a sharp pang of loss that I wasn't also carrying my conduit—then put the originals back in place before whipping open the door.

Hunter's eyes only grazed mine before he wordlessly whirled toward the south bay. I followed him into a cool predawn glow punctuated with the city's fading lights. He waited as I buckled up, eyes hidden behind mirrored lenses, thoughts and emotions equally veiled. We found Gregor, and crossed realities in a hard, cold silence.

Yet we didn't part ways once inside the sanctuary, instead heading straight to the lab. Chandra was already there, partitioned off from the rest of the room and bent over her baby, an ornamental rock garden composed of the same porous sandstone that gave the nearby Red Rock Canyon its name. She was dressed in sweats, her hair haphazard at best, as she measured from three pails of grit, sand, and peat for layering among the sandstone crevices. A steaming cup of joe was perched on a rocky red outcrop, but I could tell it hadn't hit her yet. She even snapped at Hunter before he explained about Regan, the compound, and the tracking device, though he left out the details of my run-in with her the previous night, which had me softening toward him all over again.

Toying absently with the ornamental grass fountaining from the terraced slope, Chandra confirmed it was indeed possible to bury a tracking device in a synthetic blend of tinted putty, and though expensive and time-consuming to design, the technology had been around for some time. At least among the supernaturals.

"Get undressed," Chandra told me, switching shoes as she jerked her head toward the sterile half of the lab, and regarding me like I was the biggest ass she'd ever met. It was hard to argue. "We have to be sure it's entirely gone."

Hunter left without another word and I disrobed again, though unlike his examination the night before, Chandra's clinical stare left me cold. She wore gloves as she scraped my skin, and said nothing more. As chagrined as I was that she knew I'd been played by Regan once again, I was still relieved to know the cause of Regan's near-constant presence. A tracking device I could understand. I could even respect the balls it'd taken to trick me into accepting it. It was certainly preferable to thinking she'd developed some sort of ability to be omnipresent in my life.

"I attributed the itching to the doppelgänger," I told Chandra, speaking aloud while I worked it out for myself. "She scratched my chest, and that's where I first felt the tingling."

"Because you applied more makeup there than anywhere else." She paused, fingers light on my arm, before continuing without meeting my eye. "It makes sense you'd be focused on that instead of your arm or leg."

I caught myself before I drew back in surprise, but Chandra felt my muscles tense beneath her touch. She kept her eyes on her work, double-checking my arm as I continued to stare. Had she just stood up for me?

She cleared her throat. "Where were you when you felt the device go live?"

Everywhere, I thought, glancing around the sterile room. Other than the bright rock garden behind the glass partition, it was all white and chrome and flat, open spaces. "I'll have to think about it. I've been wearing it for two weeks."

"Write it all down. We'll triangulate your locations. Maybe Regan has positioned herself, or at least the equipment used to find you, square in the middle."

In the middle of the city. In the middle of my life. I sighed, not caring Chandra was close enough to scent my fatigue. Regan had attacked my body and tricked me into doing the same to an innocent. Hunter had all but obliterated me emotionally . . . it was nice to be somewhere safe and let someone else make the decisions for a moment. I closed my eyes and listened to the soft scrape of the blade, knowing even though she didn't like me, Chandra wouldn't hurt me. Not right now, anyway.

In fact, she was being unusually gentle. "Turn left. Into the lamplight."

My thoughts blared in the deep silence, and they weren't even proper thoughts, but fragments and images warring for space in my mind. I needed some real sleep to push them all away, but I'd settle for something to beat against. My eyes slitted open and I regarded Chandra coolly. She smelled like linen, as sterile and lifeless as the room, and with no emotional peg to hang my hat on. I'd make do.

"So, what?" I said, clearing my throat, setting the bait. "No lecture on how wrong and screwed up and impulsive I am?"

The tweezers faltered, her lips thinned as she fought the retort that wanted to come, but she swallowed it down.

"You did talk to me about a compound for the injured changeling, and you even mentioned Regan had made you think of it. You didn't know about this technology, but I did, and I should have put two and two together. Here, you moved again. Back to the left."

Okay, I thought, my frown falling into an open mouth, someone had obviously spiked Chandra's coffee with a passive pill. Because she never, ever conceded shit to me. And while she hadn't come right out and apologized, it wasn't far off.

So maybe if Chandra was going to take baby steps toward reconciling our partnership—or at least try being civil—I could too.

"Can you still do it? Duplicate the sample, I mean?"

I explained about Li, and how she'd looked the day before at Master Comics. That led to her questioning what I'd been doing there to begin with, which led to the revelation that Dylan and Kade had suggested I kill Jasmine . . . and if I'd started off well, the tightening of her jaw as I continued to speak let me know she was beginning to rethink her open-mindedness. But full disclosure—or as near as I could come—was needed if I was going to convince her to help. Besides, as soon as the manuals of Light started appearing again, she'd find out anyway. If I held back now, it'd be worse when she did.

But the roundup didn't sound so good. And I hadn't even included my agreement to work with the Tulpa, my latest run-in with Regan, or how I'd nearly killed an innocent.

"Look, before you can say it, I know I screwed up with Jasmine. I'm trying to figure out what I did wrong so I can fix Li and bring the manuals back to their original state, but in the meantime I could use some help on this. You didn't see her, Chandra. That little girl was falling apart before my eyes. Like the Tulpa's touch had infected her and the poison was spreading. It was awful, and she's just a baby."

Chandra watched me, saying nothing, and I looked down at my linked hands, finally allowing myself to feel the guilt coiled up in my gut as well. I swallowed hard so my voice could be heard. "I'd switch places with her if I could, take it all on myself. I'd die if it meant this little girl could have her life back, but I don't know how to do any of those things."

She drew back, her hair still fucked up, but her eyes less blurry, and her expression nonplussed. "You would, wouldn't you? Even with all . . . this." She motioned down the length of my body, indicating the glossy package.

I laughed wryly. She was talking appearance. I was talking life. "Of course. Wouldn't you?"

"Yeah. If I were given the chance."

And so the invisible elephant in the room reared its head. We met each other's eyes, acknowledging it from across the vast expanse of our separate experiences. My existence had usurped her place in the Zodiac, and nothing short of my death would alleviate that.

"The redness will remain for a while," Chandra finally said, turning away. "For now, we'll just take away the sting."

She turned back to the partitioned room with its greenhouse lighting and drip system, a little bit of life sprouting in a concrete underground. I had time to think how nice it was . . . before my eyes grew wide. Chandra waved her hand over a bald spot among the pink sandstone, and seconds later the stiff rosette of an aloe plant appeared. My mouth dropped open as she pulled a straight-edged knife from her pocket and sliced a spiny leaf. Sensing my awe as she returned, she shot me a satisfied smile as she sheared open the fleshy middle and scooped thick aloe like honey into her palm. "Another lesson on vibrational acuity, though smaller in scope than what the doppelgänger's been providing. Duplicate it in front of Tekla and you might get extra credit. Vibration is matter, and, after all, matter is all that matters."

I ignored that for the time being. "But how did you—?"

"Do something we all can do? Well, that the Light can do, anyway. Shadows can't create life . . . even their off-spring are born half dead. On the other hand, we can't create man-sized black holes the way the Tulpa did. That skill requires a lack of Light. After all, a black hole is the opposite of light, right? Nothing living can exist in such absolute darkness." She waved her hand in the air, and behind the glass the succulent again disappeared among the rocks. Show-off. "I may not be a hereditary star sign, but I know how to maximize my gifts."

She was applying the pure aloe to my chest and arm as she spoke, and when she was done she stepped back and wiped her hands on a nearby towel. I was looking at the rock garden with renewed interest, but if Chandra noted it she said nothing. It made sense, of course. I could create walls out of nothing other than my mind, but for some reason I'd never thought my mental powers extended to living things.

So did they also extend to black holes? The question hung there, unvoiced by both Chandra and me.

"You wear this well," she finally broke the silence, mo-tioning down the length of my powder-soft body, from the bright blond locks to the French-manicured toenails. "This body. Your sex-kitten image. I fell for it at first."

"I know. You called me names." She'd called me a cream puff, a bimbo. A life-sized Barbie.

"You called me names back," she said flatly.

"Only the ones I knew would piss you off." I'd long ago learned that every criticism said more about the critic than their subject. She'd attacked my looks, which was how I'd known what her sore spot was, and where to push in return.

"But you're not what you seem," she said hurriedly, like she was a cliff diver and might lose her nerve if she thought about it too much. "I know that now. And you're not . . . petty."

That statement confused me, but I shrugged it away, flush with her implied apology. This was acceptance from a quarter I'd never expected. Tension drained so that I actually slumped a bit, but as I opened my mouth to thank her, she shook her head.

"Look, there's something you need to know." Chandra hesitated, and I felt the tension return as I suddenly realized I was on the receiving side of a confession. And from her body language, I gathered I wasn't going to like it any better than she did. "It's about the animist's mask, and what you see. You don't have bad *chi*, or if you do it's not like . . . a head cold."

A head cold? "What?"

She sighed, her usual self-assurance gone as she cleaned off her instruments without looking at me. "What I mean is, it's not catching. Kimber lied about seeing her own destruction in the mask. She didn't see anything. I thought it was a joke when she told me, she said she was just playing a bit . . ."

I fell stone-still. So that's what she meant about being petty.

"But you let them all believe . . . ?" I couldn't even finish the sentence. After all the effort and trouble I had fitting into this place, all the time and energy spent convincing these people they could trust me, that despite my Shadow side I belonged in this troop . . .

Holding her hands up in front of her, Chandra did look at me now. "I just found out, I swear. I thought about telling Warren, but he didn't seem too concerned to begin with, so instead I decided you might want to take care of it yourself. I know how you are when someone—"

"—is petty?" I asked bitterly.

She nodded, biting her lip as she looked at her fingers again, at the floor. Anywhere but at me.

"You're starting to know me well."

She did look up now that my voice had gone flat. "Just don't go overboard—"

"Wow, you *are* starting to know me well."

She winced. "She was just having some fun . . . in her way. It wouldn't have come to anything. The danger to you from the doppelgänger is still real, so I mean, it changes nothing, right?"

She was already regretting telling me, and I put a hand on her arm—comforting, not threatening—so she wouldn't have to second-guess me, so she knew exactly what was coming. "No, Chandra," I said, very clearly. "It changes everything."

Chandra was wrong about something else as well. I *could* be petty, and had metaphorically tweaked her nose enough times that she knew it. She was hoping I'd take the high road here, but there was a difference between a joke and a malicious rumor, and Kimber had crossed that line without even knowing me. I didn't know if her assumptions matched Chandra's original impression of me, if this glossy exterior had her convinced that nothing of import or use lay inside, but she'd clearly decided taking the Kairos down a few notches would be a good way to establish a foothold in the troop. *My* troop.

One thing I'd learned in my short time as a Zodiac member was that while we were all capable, we were also all proud, and since we had the same essential hierarchy as a pack of wolves, the internal battle for position was as bloody and fierce as our wild counterparts'. When a combatant threw down, the issue wasn't resolved until one agent had clearly, if figuratively, pinned and submitted the other.

And that's what I planned to do to Kimber now as I snatched up the animist's mask from its wall peg in the astrolab, and headed to Saturn's Orchard, where I knew Kimber spent every morning honing her kata.

She was still warming up when I entered, sitting lotus-style on the mat in the middle of the pyramid-shaped room, using meditation to bring her mind in balance before she engaged her body. Her image was reflected back on itself in the mirrored walls, and I had a moment to consider how serene she looked sitting there, almost like a monk with her hands splayed over her knees. Then the door slammed shut, her eyes winged open to find me, and the peaceful image was ruined.

Her upper lip curled in a sneer and she shut her eyes dismissively, though her countenance held a stiffness it hadn't before. Her spine straightened, her awareness of me making her self-conscious when what she really needed to be was wary. Ah well, I thought, turning my shoulders. Live and learn.

I unfurled the mask, whipping it like a skipping stone so it clattered across the floor and struck her thigh hard enough to leave a bruise. She yelped, eyes flying open as I began my slow stalk, keeping to the perimeter of the room. To her credit, she stayed where she was even though my heart rate was up and my fury scented the air. I kept my stride even.

"You want what?" she said, still dismissive, pale dreads standing out like long corn husks against her loose black clothing.

"Some quality time with my newest, bestest girlfriend," I said in Olivia's highest dulcet tone, throwing in a breathy sigh to punctuate the difference between my soft words and my aggressive actions. An invisible wall soared high and solid in my wake. I could feel it like it was tethered around my waist, beginning to take on drag. My goal was to make it around the entire room before Kimber realized what I was doing. My voice, my words, my looks—all the things she'd underestimated—helped. "After all, you're the only one who understands what it's like for me under that mask. You're the only one in this big ol' world who shares my ill *chi*."

All right, so it was a bit of overkill, but she'd fall for it a little longer. I cut my fourth wall short, reinforced them all with a quick pulse of my thoughts, then cut a direct path to Kimber, where I hovered too close, too long, before lowering myself into a mirrored cross-legged position. Our knees touched. I smiled sweetly. Kimber scowled, pushed back fractionally, and handed me the mask.

"I don't think so."

"Just put it on. Just once. I want to know what you see. Is there ash raining on the city as it goes up in a conflagration? Is there mutiny among the remaining citizens? Wait, I bet it's the way they've turned to cannibalism, right? You look like you've seen the absolute worst of it."

Her serene expression had been blighted, and her lips had thinned into nonexistence. "I said no."

I thrust out my bottom lip. "Please?"

She cursed under her breath, stood smoothly, and tossed the mask onto my lap. "Begging," she said as she turned toward the door. "You're fucking pitiful."

By the time she hit my first wall, my pitiful self was standing as well. She reared back—confused, shocked, pained—and turned to me holding her nose.

"Come," I said, motioning her way, all the pleading drained from my voice.

"No." Her voice was strained now; she was trying to push down her panic, still holding on to her low estimation of me. "I'm not going to—"

"I'm not talking to you." I cut her off, still motioning, still concentrating. The wall behind her struck her backside first as it continued its slow glide my way. I hadn't learned to control the speed yet, but I could erect them, I could move them, and I could shrink the space inside them so thoroughly they could crack a nut. I smiled, and the other three walls shimmered as they began to close in.

"What are you doing?" She was panicked now, pushing back with her weight, heels stuttering as the wall continued inching forward.

"Don't be afraid. We're in the sanctuary, after all. Someone will be along to help you . . . shortly." Chandra hadn't tried to stop me, but she knew when I left the lab I hadn't intended to make nice with Kimber. "Maybe I'll even let them."

She was fighting it fully now, all that arrogant Zen master bullshit absent under the realization I could do something she could not. What can I say? Surviving something like walls materializing to trap you inside them, which I had, made the mastery of the skill a priority. I stopped all four walls when we were only feet apart, where they vibrated with an intensity that raised the hairs on my arms.

"Pretty, aren't they?" I said, voice breathless again as I admired my work, my bald appreciation causing them to materialize, though they still flitted in and out of view like a cell phone gaining and losing reception. "But of course they're more than they seem. Their outward beauty belies their strength. Geez, that reminds me of something else, actually." I tapped my chin, like I was thinking about it, then snapped my fingers. "Oh, I know what it is . . . me."

My voice dropped, my chin lowered, and I took three quick steps forward. Kimber's arms went up, but she struck out too soon, and I kept coming. I thought her shock might give me a greater advantage, but she had good instincts, and didn't roll readily. Her forward kick to my solar plexus landed squarely, but as I flew backward the wall behind me absorbed my impact, bending with my weight like a cushion, and I was bounced forward again to return the favor with twice the force. The wall behind Kimber didn't bend, bow, or break, and the impact rolled through her body with a force that caused her heart to momentarily stutter.

It would've been enough—she was pinned and practically submitted—but I wasn't feeling merciful. Yanking on her conveniently swinging dreads, I clamped the mask over her face with my other hand, muffling her protests.

"Tell me what you see when you look at me now, Kimber. Because I'm not begging, and I'm certainly not pitiful." She shook her head, pushing against me, then tried to shake it faster when I stilled it, hand on her chin. "Tell me!"

The sound of the world rupturing came on the heels of the impact that knocked me down. Cowering on my knees, I wrapped my arms over my head, the pain inside so great, my gray matter must have swelled in seconds. As vessels throbbed against my skull, and the ripples of vibrational impact ate my scream, I thought of death, wished for it, because nothing could hurt as much as being caught in the lengthening furrows of destroyed sound.

Concussion after concussion beat at me, each stronger than the last, but relief never came. It was at the precise moment that I gave up, blind with pain, deaf and mute and numb all over, that silence crashed over me. I must have been screaming the whole time because my vocal cords were sore, but nothing came out now but a guttural squeak.

A voice sounded next to me, sweetly. "She can only speak if she puts the mask on willingly."

I jolted on the ground, whirled despite my body's protest, but when I saw the doppelgänger, my empty hands fell limply to my side, and my mouth dropped open.

"Force it upon someone and they can't speak or reason," she said, froth spewing to the ground as she took a step toward me, her mouth moving to imitate mine and speak at the same time. The grotesque and smooth mutation would have been fascinating if not so worrying. She had, I realized, begun to look like me. The *me* beneath Olivia. "Or breathe."

But I wasn't listening to the words. In fact, I'd forgotten Kimber entirely.

"How did you get in here?" I whispered . . . barely.

The doppelgänger smiled with her razored teeth, motioning to my walls. "You left an opening. I walked through it."

She certainly had. And she sealed the opening behind her. Whatever it was making her my ethereal twin also allowed her to manipulate my thought matter. I swallowed hard.

Not, I thought as she took another step forward, a comforting thought.

19

Okay, so I wasn't entirely trapped. I could dissolve the walls I'd made with a directly channeled thought, but all my energy was understandably concentrated on the being in front of me . . . too strong, too unpredictable, and far too close for my comfort.

"I meant how did you get into the sanctuary?"

"I'm everywhere you are. I'm like the air you take into your lungs and the carbon dioxide you breathe out again. I'm a part of you."

"And let me guess," I said wryly, gaining my feet and backing away as far as my walls would allow. "You want me to be a part of you too."

She thrust out her bottom lip, chagrined. "You're referring to my little slip in control, aren't you? I was rushing things a bit, I know, but sometimes it's easier to take what you need. Devouring a still-pulsing heart is like mainlining pure power. It would allow me to hide in plain sight, or appear and disappear without restriction, heedless of worlds or planes or boundaries. Like you, I'm impulsive sometimes. That . . . and so goddamned hungry."

Her voice dropped, and my mind flitted to the conduit I no longer possessed . . . not that it would work on a partially materialized doppelgänger. Besides, what would happen if she *was* a part of me? Would I suffer if I shot her? I covered my confusion with a snarl. "Stop licking your lips. It ruins the apology."

"I don't expect you to forgive and forget. I never do, and we're made from the same cloth, so to speak." She chuckled at that, though I had no idea what it meant. "So I've decided to appeal to your reason instead. We should do this properly."

She tilted her luminescent head, the curve of her skull shaping and reshaping itself in layering bubbles. Even her skull was morphing more quickly in approximation of the old me. Her snapping, effervescent hair had shortened, the droplets releasing themselves above the shoulders, and she looked taller, her build paper-thin, but taking on more substance with every passing moment as the gaseous sheen shifted over, around, and through her frame. It was eerie to see my features taking shape in a pearly phosphorescent ooze. The Tulpa's words slid through me.

Wait much longer and you won't even have the ability to choose . . . She'll just take over your life.

So should I be thankful that her teeth were still blinding white and unnaturally sharp? I didn't know, so I continued keeping my eyes on her when Kimber groaned wordlessly behind me.

"She told me you were a smart girl, a nice girl. Well, not nice. But good. Good-ish." She was still drinking in my features, her own shifting so that even the words ran over themselves with that rippling voice.

"What are you talking about? Who?" I said sharply, though more out of a need to buy myself time than any real interest. I was silently repeating the Tulpa's mantra to myself, though having trouble remembering it now that my impulsive and dangerous double had broken into my sanctuary. And he'd been adamant that it needed to be exact.

"I'm supposed to be patient and wait for you to offer your energy to me," the doppelgänger was saying, interrupting my mental gymnastics. "Then I can return to where it will redouble upon itself, assimilating so that flesh and bone knit together in strong mortal weave . . . but that all takes so much time. That's why I stumbled before. And why you need to help me."

"Okay," I said, playing along. I had the mantra now; I just wasn't sure I wanted to use it. If I did, I'd belong to the Shadow side . . . no turning back. For the time being, I was just glad I had it at my disposal. I was shit at multitasking multiple attempts on my soul. "Just tell me exactly what you want."

That had bubbles blowing off her like steam. Her teeth, the only solid thing about her, snapped together in a cruel parody of a smile. "Don't be a fucking idiot, Joanna!"

Oh God. How did she know my real name?

"You're supposed to be smart! She said you'd understand!" She was whining now, alternately furious and desperate, exasperation making her sweat so perspiration rolled like pearls down her face. "Everything we say and do and think is channeled into one thing. Vibrations. Energy. I'd burn the energy, the magic in it, if I even suggested it. I'd touch on the exact same vibrational matter I need you to, but in a different way."

"And matter is all that matters." I was murmuring Chandra's words to myself, but the doppelgänger heard.

"Exactly so! So if you would just *think*. Then you could do it now and I'll be stronger, faster, more, real, him, me . . ." Her entire face flashed, like lightning trapped in a bottle, and layers of light bled in her gaze, white orbs rolling like marbles. She was becoming frantic, and had almost lifted her arms, reaching out to me with razored nails before catching herself and pulling back. She wrung her hands, and bubbles frothed between her palms. "Do it properly, okay? It'll be faster that way, almost instant. Formal isn't necessary, no, but proper. Informal, common. That's a given."

She tilted her head to the other side when I said nothing, airy eyes swirling with mist, earnestness making them wide. "I won't kill you, and we'll be friends. Because friends give, and given is best. Anyone can inherit it, so inheritance means nothing."

I licked my lips, not relaxing even if she didn't look like she was going to kill me at this moment. Another moment was coming on fast. "I just need, um . . . a little plain English here."

That didn't piss her off like I thought it would. "Plain English! Exactly so!" The doppelgänger licked her beautiful lips, and I took a step backward. She still looked hungry. "I need a noun. One noun, two aspects, right?"

I half expected her to pull on her ear and say, *Sounds like* . . . So I waited for the pantomime to play out. And waited. I swallowed hard. "Come again?"

She ignored me, still rambling. "The first aspect is the sense—you know a lot about senses, right?—and then there's a referent . . . but of course that's already inside you. Your Shadow side . . . but you still need another . . ."

And it was all going so well until her words trailed off in a hiss. Her teeth elongated in her mouth, saliva dripping, and she looked right through me like I was nothing more than a bag of bones.

"Flank her," came the order from behind me . . . and I realized she was looking at Warren, who'd burst through the Orchard's door, the rest of the troop close behind.

"Not yet, *Phantom*," the doppelgänger snapped at Warren, and he looked stricken at her tone. She turned back to me, eyes fierce white marbles. "Just give it to me. One noun, two aspects, a sense and a referent. All you have to do is think! Quick!"

Oh yeah—that was going to happen with my fanged and clawed double salivating in front of me. I shook my head, swallowing hard. "I'm sorry. I don't know—"

"Idiot! Stop apologizing." She no longer looked like me.

Her face was almost roiling, it was morphing so quickly into different oval, heart, and square-jawed aspects. Her eyes alternately slanted and rounded, and her skin looked thinner, weaker, in some places than others, like a balloon squeezed at one end. "Do it now, or I'll tell everyone here your real name."

I narrowed my eyes, and my fingers flexed automatically. "Don't," I said coolly.

"Olivia!" Warren had moved into my peripheral view, but I didn't dare take my eyes off my doppelgänger. She was boxed in, but I was boxed in with her.

"I'll let you say mine," she cajoled, drowning out his voice, ignoring him completely. He was behind her now, but couldn't get at her through the walls, and she knew it. The rest of the troop had spread out evenly around the perimeter, but she didn't spare any of them a glance either.

I shook my head. "I don't know yours."

"Olivia." Warren's voice again. "Break down your walls on my go."

He began to give the others orders, I saw all conduits lift—Vanessa's steel fan flicking open, Felix's edged boomerang, a flanged mace, hooks, and a short pole that flared into a four-tined military fork with the press of a button—but my double still didn't seem concerned. Her liquid tongue darted out, and her gaze no longer rested gently on mine. "If you're not going to soldier toward your destiny, then I'll do it for you, but one way or another, you're going to give me what I want."

I narrowed my eyes. "Don't hold your breath."

And as Warren raised his arm, I closed my eyes and wished the walls away.

Her response was a bubbling whisper. "You mean like her?"

I opened my eyes in time to see Warren tackle her, but he fell through her body like it was made of mist. An instant later, all that remained of her was crazed, bittersweet laughter.

"Dammit, Vanessa! I told you not to break the circle!"

But Vanessa was kneeling over Kimber, wrenching the mask from her face. It gave in her grip with a sharp popping noise, and then Kimber took the deepest, loudest, greediest breath I'd ever heard. I winced. The mask couldn't kill her, so she'd been suffocating all this time. It must have felt like eternity.

Felix turned to me while Micah and Chandra tended to Kimber. "Are you okay?"

"I'm fine. She didn't do anything." Though the conversation had left me more confused than ever. What the hell did she want from me? A noun? Two aspects and a referent? At least it was no longer my heart.

"How can you say that?" Vanessa said, turning to look up at me so her long ebony curls whipped around her face. "Look at Kimber."

"Oh." I swallowed hard, looking at the blue-lipped, pale-skinned initiate. "That."

Kneeling on her other side, Micah looked up at me in disbelief. "Don't tell me . . ."

So I didn't. But once Kimber had finally regained her color, her breath, and her wits, she made sure not to leave anything out.

I was duly reprimanded for forcing the animist's mask upon Kimber, even though no one else had known doing so would trap her breath inside it either. I would've pointed out Kimber was uninjured—even initiates couldn't be killed by anything fashioned by a mortal's hand—and that she'd only fallen semi-immobile because it was hard to think when you couldn't breathe. Yet that would've brought her absolute vulnerability to the doppelgänger to the forefront of the conversation, something I wasn't especially anxious to point out.

Of course, Kimber pointed that out for me as well . . . and was summarily reamed for pretending to see portents of evil and unmitigated horrors when she clearly had not. Warren stripped her of the right to leave the sanctuary again until after her metamorphosis, and as far as I was concerned, we were even. Yet one look at Kimber's sullen face and it was clear she didn't feel the same. Fine. So I knew she'd continue working to usurp my position in the troop . . . and she knew I'd be ready.

"But how did the doppelgänger get in?" Tekla asked, once only she, Warren, and I remained in the dojo. Warren was staring up at the apex of the room distractedly, clearly wondering if its pyramid shape had anything to do with it. I just shook my head because the more pressing question was *What did she want?* "One noun, two aspects . . ." I wrapped my arms around my middle and shook my head. I had no idea what that meant.

"Nouns have two functions," said Tekla, standing across from me. "They describe and they refer. She mentioned your senses, and that your Shadow side was a referent, what lives inside of you. Does any of that make sense to you?"

"Nothing. You?"

"No, but I'm not the one a doppelgänger broke into the sanctuary to have a chat with."

"Because she's a part of me," I murmured, running my hands over my face and hair. "At least that's what she said. Made from the same cloth. Everywhere I am."

Warren put his hands on his hips, still straining as he gazed at the pyramid's apex. He was clean-shaven, clothed in white . . . obviously taking the night off from indigence. "You know, for the girl who's supposed to be the savior of the Zodiac, you're pretty high-maintenance."

At least he sounded more bemused now than angry. I watched him bend to pick up the animist's mask, groaning softly as he put all his weight on his good leg. "I want you to keep this," he told me, holding it my way. "Put it in your room, lock it up. I know you won't put it on, and I don't want to risk anyone else"—and here he looked sharply at Tekla—"being tempted to do it."

"Including yourself, I presume?" Tekla said, coloring slightly. I'd seen her in a rage before, and the stillness surrounding her now, like a vacuum opening up around her, was the calm announcing that storm. I swallowed and shot Warren a hard look, but he knew Tekla's moods too, and had already looked, and moved, away.

"Yes, including me," he conceded, and the air loosened again.

Great, I thought, glancing down at the painted face as a stonelike dread settled in my belly. My horrific visions and Xavier's stolen soul essence had been enough to skeeve me out before, but now the mask could endlessly suffocate an agent as well. No way would I be able to sleep if it was secreted away in my room. The best place for it would be back outside Xavier's office, in the reconstructed stupa. That would keep it out of the hands of those who wanted to use it as a supernatural bong for their next visionary fix, and it would also give me an excuse to once again visit, and study, my dear old housekeeper, Helen Maguire. It was the only cause I had to smile as we all exited the Orchard.

20

There was no time to return the animist's mask to Xavier's the next day. Instead, I went to visit one Laura Crucier, a coma patient at Sheep Mountain Medical's ICU, who lay completely motionless, just as she had days earlier when someone had left her unconscious at the hospital's entrance. Apart from the machinery angled around her bed like electric sentinels, the main difference now was the clustering flowers and frames and stuffed animals adorning every available flat surface. Asleep, she was an island unto herself. In the living world, she was deeply loved.

"The Archer Foundation has found itself in the enviable position of a budget surplus this year," I told the hovering hospital administrator, without removing my eyes from Laura. I could envision her greasy hair shining and swinging. I wanted to bulldoze some color into her cheeks. The man remained behind me, giving me room, but I could scent oiled anxiety leaking from his pores. It battled in the air against the dozens of waterlogged roses. "I heard from a friend of a friend of Ms. Crucier's story and the wonderful job you've done with her."

"Well, we have hope that, with time and continued care, she'll recover."

"Fully?" I asked, turning to face him for the first time.

He looked for a moment like he'd been blinded by a camera's flash, and his smile stuttered over his face as he backtracked. *Olivia*, the heir and benefactress and social-ite, blinked. Waiting. "Well, no one can say for sure, but we certainly haven't given up hope."

I turned again to face the unconscious woman, the silent moments counted off in Laura's heartbeat. I knew the man was waiting for me to speak first, that the hope and time and continued care he'd spoken of would be made infinitely easier with what he wasn't asking. And while he continued not asking for money, and I continued staring, and Laura's heart kept beating, I couldn't help but think, *How could I have not been able to tell the difference between a Shadow and a mortal?*

These bodies, these mortal shells, were as fragile as blown glass, accumulating nicks and scratches and chips in the surface over the years, unless like Olivia, they were carelessly dropped, allowed to shatter into pieces. I, of anyone, should've been able to tell; I'd lived as a mortal, had the aspect of a Shadow, and possessed an alleged Light facet that should've been able to stop that blow before it landed. Regan was right; I had to start taking responsibility. I was almost a year in the Zodiac, a year without my sister, whose life and body was also destroyed because of me, and I wouldn't believe I'd learned nothing in that time. I couldn't keep accidentally chipping away at other people's lives. Otherwise, it'd all been for nothing.

I finally turned from Laura's bed, checkbook in hand, my answer as silently bold the man's question. I decided it needed further clarification.

"Make sure she's cared for," I said evenly, and held out my hand for a pen.

* * *

The second stop of the day, the second reason I couldn't return the animist mask to Xavier's mansion, was prompted by my twisted paranormal attempt at being the good Samaritan. I'd decided I wasn't the only one who needed to start taking responsibility for her actions. Regan was going to as well. It was a two-hour trip out to the Desert Valley Correctional Center, but on the way there I had plenty of time to rehearse my cover story—I was a reporter for a true crime magazine doing a feature on recovery programs for pedophiles—and I also had time to figure out what I was going to say to Regan DuPree's mortal father. I wasn't exactly sure what to expect. On the relatively rare occasion an agent of Light had turned to a mortal for companionship, they'd done so out of love. However, Shadows scoured humanity for a vessel where their own dark attributes could stew and spawn and therefore be given additional purchase in the world.

So I wouldn't have been at all surprised if the guards had brought me a being with horns and a tail, but the thin, blinking, and bespeckled man who dropped into the plastic chair across from me had me blinking back. He picked up the wall phone with a hand that would have been elegant were it not for the scars scoring his wrists and palms. I might have felt some pity for him then, except the cross-hatching of scars on his fingertips were especially thick. The former Father Michael had worked hard, and with some degree of success, to rid himself of his fingerprints. I had a feeling the wounds on his palms and arms had been due to slips in concentration rather than any deliberate attempt to harm himself.

There was also an odd angularity to the man's face, and after a moment I realized it was because his features—jaw and cheekbones and brows—should've been placed on someone larger. The rest of his face was sunken, aged before its time, though unlined and pale from the lack of sun. His deep-set eyes sat passively on mine, though it felt like they looked everywhere at once. I saw another scar on the hollow of his neck, a perfect square raised so thickly and neatly, it had to have been traced by a blade over and over again. I realized it represented the collar on a priest's frock and thought of the nerve it would take to cut so deeply and precisely right next to one's own jugular. Father Michael, for all his humanity, had the grit of a Shadow.

"You're one of them, aren't you?" he asked in a silky voice, when we'd finished looking each other over.

I neither agreed nor disagreed, in case this call was being recorded. "I know your daughter."

Something akin to emotion passed over his face, and his lids flared a bit, nostrils widening as his tongue darted out to wet his lips. "Did she send you?"

"She's why I'm here."

He smiled now, and his cheekbones rose into sharp angles. It was like his face was made of putty; the grin changed him entirely. How many faces, I wondered, did this man have? "It's amazing you found me. I know I'm not in the manuals, I'll never be worthy of that, but it's important that you know, that she knows, the human element weakens nothing. In fact, knowing my weaknesses has made me a master at pinpointing them in others. Like my daughter, I bet. She probably has incredible focus, right? An uncanny ability to wait out even the greatest threat to her survival?"

I thought of the first time I met Regan, how she'd betrayed a senior Shadow in an elaborate effort to get to me. How she'd risked even the Tulpa's wrath. How she was stalking me through Ben. "Actually," I said softly, "she's a lot like her mother."

He let out a wistful sigh as he remembered the woman who'd steered him directly into lifelong incarceration. "A great beauty, then, but with no patience for sentiment. I often think about her. Not Brynn, she always took care of herself, but my daughter. I always wondered how she fared growing up under the care of a woman devoid of sentiment."

That little nugget snagged my attention. "What do you mean?"

Father Michael's eyes blazed again as he realized he knew something I didn't. I had a feeling it'd been a long time since he'd been able to talk about our world with someone. Good.

"Brynn DuPree only had passion for one thing. She was determined the Cancerian star sign stay in her direct bloodline. She wouldn't even entertain the idea of it passing on to her younger siblings, much less anyone in the extended family. That's why she didn't mate with a man of the Zodiac, choosing instead to propagate with a mortal of the same sign. Thank God she settled on me." He crossed himself in a sincere mockery of piety.

"Why would that cause Brynn to turn to you?"

"The men of the Zodiac actively court a woman who can improve their lineage, but because the line is matriarchal, the women can turn to a human for their needs . . . if they find one worthy of them, someone whose humanity provides them with an even greater strength of will and resolve than the male members of the Shadow Zodiac."

Which was exactly what Regan had said about Ben. I fought off a wave of fear so strong it felt like nausea.

"Like you?" I asked, but Michael interpreted it as a statement of fact.

He inclined his head. "As we don't possess the more obvious physical skills of our supernatural counterparts, the chosen must work to turn their weaknesses into strengths. From that, true greatness is born. Of all the chosen, I worked the hardest to curry her favor, and she repaid me by allowing me to share in her illustrious bloodline. I am humbled that I could serve. Honored I gave her a daughter of the Shadow."

I glared at the top of his bowed, balding head, and saw my eyes darken in the glass between us. "You lured two girls and a boy from a elementary schoolyard. None of them were ever seen again."

"There are casualties in every war."

"They were seven," I said sharply.

He looked at me like he couldn't comprehend what that had to do with anything, and it was all I could do not to dive through glass and pummel him with the phone still clasped at his ear. Of all the things I'd seen in both my mortal and supernatural lives, this man was one of the scariest. His expression wasn't bland; it just reflected a psyche void of culpability on the too-wide face of a mortal who cut down innocent lives without reason or care. I could attempt to make sense of the Shadows' purposes, but I could make no sense of this: a man who'd been birthed, suckled, cared for, and raised in a world he decided to destroy for others.

And that was what Regan wanted with Ben. To infect him with this stoic indifference. To turn him into a monster.

I sat back, needing a moment to compose myself. His vacuous eyes followed me, making me feel like he could shake my hand, kiss my cheek, and kill me all in the same minute. It was all the same to him, and I realized despite the benign appearance, Brynn had chosen correctly. How she'd initially seen past the simpering veneer and the priest's robes was beyond me, but right now—even through the pane of unbreakable glass—the stench of a man whose soul had shriveled like a dried acorn was strong enough to have bile rising in my gorge.

"Your lineage shows in her," I finally managed, truthfully. "Regan has many of your attributes."

She was also this vile.

"Regan," he whispered reverently, and I realized he hadn't known until now. He shot me a smile that was almost shy, almost kind. "Thank you. You've given me a gift."

"It's just a name," I muttered, pissed I'd given him even a second of happiness.

His too-wide lips pursed. "Oh, but a name is everything. A name is all. You know that."

I shuddered when he winked at me, and decided enough was enough. I felt dirty even sitting across from this man, and found myself wishing we were on some darkened street so I could take his scarred neck in my hands and squeeze. Instead I reached into my bag. "I have another gift for you as well."

I let the package drop from the sleeve of my cuffed shirt where it'd been tucked in the crook of my elbow. Michael's gaze lit on it greedily.

I put a finger to my lips, and let out a long, slow *Shhhh* . . .

He froze, eyes shining like marbles above the bulging cheekbones.

I erected a thin, mirrored wall, blocking the partition from the view of the guards and cameras, so they saw no movement between us. Then I put my hand to the glass with the package gripped in my palm, Michael mirrored me on the other side of the glass, and the barrier dissolved like steam. Our fingertips met, and I barely contained a shudder. It was like touching a cold slug, spineless movement the only thing giving it life. I'd never felt anything like it around a human before. I hoped never to again.

"What is it?" he asked, weighing it in his palm.

"You'll know soon enough. Just don't open it until you've received a clear sign."

He nodded. A man who carved his own flesh would have the patience to wait.

"Will she contact me this way? My girl, my Shadow, my *Regan.*"

"Oh yes. So keep it with you at all times. It won't be long, I promise."

"Bless you, child," he said, tears welling in his glacial eyes as he slipped the package away. From his lips, it was a curse.

I inclined my head and let the shielding wall drop. "And may you be so blessed in return."

* * *

My meeting with the prodigal father took longer than I planned, and the drive back into town was lengthened by the caravan of Californians making their weekend trek into Sin City, a ritual echoing the pilgrimage to Mecca in fervency. As Valhalla was known for being particularly hedonistic, most were also headed there, and all this combined to make me late for my first night of work. I'd convinced Xavier to give me the swing shift after explaining to him noon was too early to recover fully from whatever event I'd been attending the night before, and though he still didn't want me working there, he didn't want me appearing foolish in front of his employees either. Anything an Archer did in public was a reflection upon him, so while he expected—even hoped for—failure in what he'd termed my "occupational nonsense," it wasn't going to be because of him.

So as I stuttered haltingly down I–15 toward Valhalla, I tried to make sense of my jumbled emotions. I hadn't anticipated the visit with Regan's father to affect me so much. I'd planned to go in there, garner enough supplemental information about Brynn to help track down Regan, pass along my little "gift," and be done with it.

But more, I admitted, I'd gone there to reassure myself there were distinct differences between Ben and Father Michael, that there had to have been even before Brynn had gotten to the guy. I wanted reassurance that despite Regan's attempts to turn Ben into an accomplice and a murderer, she hadn't achieved the level of competence her mother was famed for. I wanted to know beyond all doubt that no matter how much time Ben spent in Regan's presence, there was an overpowering goodness in him that wouldn't allow him to deteriorate into a fleshy shell housing a heart no larger than a nut.

But it was Father Michael's earnestness that had me taking halting breaths, as if I was running, not driving. I swallowed hard as I swung into valet, and pushed the fear away. "It won't happen. It can't."

But anything could happen when a life was rear-ended by someone bent on destruction. An image of Laura Crucier attached to so many machines that she looked like a science experiment assailed me. I swallowed hard, guilt like granite in my throat.

I was slipping from the car when the valet attendant scurried to my side. I flashed him a distracted glance, but he didn't offer me a ticket and a spot up front. Instead he shifted on his feet. "I'm sorry, miss, but employees have to park in the back lot."

I tilted my head, which made the attendant swallow hard and lose eye contact. So that's how Xavier was going to play it, I thought, offering the poor messenger a reassuring smile. "Okay, so where's the back lot?"

Ten minutes later, after a long hike in impractical shoes, I entered Valhalla via the back of the house and took the service elevators up to the casino, then the private elevator to the executive offices. From there, the hits kept on coming.

"I'm going to work where?" I asked Xavier's secretary, who was waiting for me after her shift and was none too pleased about it. Glancing at her Chopard watch, she pushed back her shoulder-length pageboy and rose to straighten her papers. The activity didn't hide her smile.

"Gift shop," she said slyly, motioning to a white-collared shirt and baby blue polyester slacks. "There's your uniform."

I laughed, sobering only when she threw a name tag with the Valhalla logo on top of the pile. A security guard entered the smoked-glass doors of the executive office, and she motioned him forward, summarily handing me off. Without farewell, or even a backward glance, she sailed from the office, obviously pleased to be rid of this pesky duty, probably assuming I wouldn't even make it one entire shift. I glanced back down at the uniform, thinking the message from Xavier couldn't be any clearer:

there would be no free rides at Valhalla. Not even for the boss's daughter.

I excused myself and escaped to the ladies' room while the guard waited. One look at my sister's bunny body in the shapeless uniform and I laughed out loud again. I doubted she'd ever even worn polyester before, and wondered briefly if I'd break out in hives.

"Cher would be appalled," I murmured, and set to pulling my glossy mane back into a low bun, and lightening the color of my lipstick. I still looked like I should be walking the red carpet, though the name tag would've set me on the sidelines. The guard raised a brow when I returned, clearly surprised I was going through with this, but said nothing as he led me from the executive tower, down to the main casino floor, and into the corner gift shop. Looking around, I had to sigh. The place was more spacious than any art gallery this side of the Mississippi.

Within thirty seconds the store manager, Ginny—whose name should have been Attitude—halted in front of me with a dour expression and a readied lecture about being late and how all Valhalla employees were held to a higher standard than blah-ditty-blah-ditty-blah . . . I mentally tuned her out, philosophically deciding to make the best of it. Sure, I'd thought I'd be given some high-level position in the company. But my intentions in seeking employment were dishonorable, so it was hard to complain about this turn of events. At least I was in.

I'd make this work, and not just for the troop. I'd do it to spite Xavier and his lack of faith in my sister; I'd do it to annoy, and perhaps surprise, the woman across from me until she looked at me with something other than dismissive resignation. And even if that never happened, I'd let it go, accepting her prejudice as her shortfall and not my own.

But mostly I'd do it to vindicate Olivia. Sure, she was dead, beyond caring and probably having a pearly white cocktail at a pearly white party beyond the pearly white gates. But I still cared about her; she was alive in my mind. Fighting for her kept the past from being so bitterly final.

So I followed Janet, the sales clerk Ginny had ordered to show me around, and revved myself up to learn about the fascinating world of stocking baseball caps.

21

"Don't mind her," Janet said as we left Ginny and her grim disapproval behind. "She's been fixated on you ever since the article came out in *Desert* magazine."

The one detailing the perks and privileges of Las Vegas's glitterati. It was the last interview Olivia had given before she died.

"The columnist called me 'socially promiscuous,'" I said, baffled why a bad interview would interest, much less antagonize, anyone.

"Yeah, and she wishes she was getting some," Janet said, smirking as she began our tour of the storefront. Janet was a typical college kid with straight brown hair and the freshman ten. There was a hint of the right coast in her voice, buried beneath a sorority smile, and I felt myself nodding hypnotically as she droned on about layout, merchandising, and the importance of product location, all the while aware of Ginny's hard stare burning through my neck. I placed my hand there, making sure the obnoxious cocktail ring was in plain view as I pretended to rub my neck. Olivia had mentioned the ring in the *Desert* article. Let that fuel Ginny's raging schadenfreude, I thought, turning my attention back to the crowded mishmash of collectibles.

Just in case giving your money away to the casino didn't do it for you, I thought wryly, you could always throw it away. The shop was a monument to the unnecessary: T-shirts, stuffed bears, perfumes—*What did a Viking smell like, anyway?*—shot glasses, key chains, used dice and cards, snow globes, and a wall cooler filled with vodka . . . all stamped with the Valhalla logo. Xavier should've just lifted a leg to mark the place, and been done with it.

I let myself smile at that, but it fell when I spotted the two security guards canvassing the shop from outside the glass wall. Clearing my throat, I looked away.

"Is security always so vigilant about watching the gift shop?" I asked Janet as we headed to the back.

"They're probably checking out the new merch," she answered pointedly, causing me to blush while she shot the guards a cheery finger wave. I kept my eyes averted, relaxing only after we'd disappeared into the storage room, and away from Hunter's frown. "Or at least Kevin is. Even you wouldn't have a shot with the big one. He doesn't date Valhalla employees. Come on, we'll start over here."

With no way to immediately steer the conversation back to Hunter and his dating proclivities, I let Janet lead me through a maze of cardboard boxes.

"This is our stock area. Basically we're supposed to unpack, sticker, and shelve all items back here until they can be moved out front."

"Exciting," I deadpanned. I was surrounded by towering shelves of crap.

Janet smiled in understanding. "Everyone starts out in here. It's not all bad, though there is a solitary confinement feel to it. But it gives you a chance to know the inventory, the pricing—and believe me, you'll know it down to the last cent—before you get onto the floor. Besides, you can listen to some tunes if the radio is getting reception." She hit an old boom box on its side, and the tinny voice of early Madonna piped out at me, overlaid with static.

Screw Olivia. I was out of here.

"Here's where we stash our purses and totes." Janet opened a closet doubling as cleaning supply storage, and cleared some space on the floor with her foot. "You're supposed to have a clear plastic purse so security can see we're not stealing anything from the hotel. The Balenciaga will have to go."

She gave a wistful little sigh as I dropped the bag onto the concrete next to the Windex, and so did I. The animist's mask was still cradled in the bottom of it, and a clear plastic purse would raise questions about such unusual items, though Regan had relieved me of the burden of hiding my conduit. I'd taken to using an ankle strap to carry a few edged weapons beneath my uniform. They wouldn't kill an agent, but used right they could slow one down. So there was an upside to wearing this much shapeless polyester. Yay.

"So maybe that's why the security guard won't date employees," I said, angling under the pretense of a little girly gossip. "He knows all the secrets we carry around with us in our little bags."

"It's more like he doesn't want to mix business and pleasure," she replied, before a knowing glint entered her gaze. "Or business and business, in his case."

I raised my brows. "What do you mean?"

"It turns out our illustrious head of security has an interesting little hobby on his off-time," she said, and swung open a top cabinet containing office supplies . . . and Hunter's ad for adult entertainment taped to the door.

"That's, uh . . ." Not good. "Interesting."

Janet leaned against the wall, a dreamy smile playing on her lips as she ran a finger along the image of Hunter's bare torso. "It's Valhalla's open little secret . . . at least among the women. God knows what would happen if it got out among the suits." She straightened, looking stricken, as if I'd elbowed her in the gut. "You're not going to tell your father, are you? Oh geez, if I'd have—"

"Of course not. Relax." I angled my gaze back at the shirtless photo like I hadn't seen the real thing only a couple of evenings before. "Anyone ever try calling that number?"

"Anyone? Practically everyone. You have to leave your personal information—name, address, phone—on a machine and he'll call back after he's checked on it, on you, and everyone you know. A Valhalla employee has never gotten through, though I know of a couple friends of friends who did. They were all dark-haired and -skinned, though. He seems to have a type."

She looked at me apologetically, but I was secretly agreeing with her. He probably did prefer a certain type, though not for any reason Janet might entertain. If Hunter was only looking for a specific physical template, chances were he was also seeking a specific person. It was a she, it was someone who was involved in some way with escorts—my guess was a Shadow agent, targeting them—and, for some reason, she was important enough to have him creating an elaborate and very public persona that put his job at Valhalla at risk. Meanwhile, he was hiding it all from Warren.

So was this really why Hunter hadn't wanted me working at Valhalla? Was he afraid I'd come closer to discovering what he was doing, and why?

After a brief run-down of the inventory, Janet left me alone with a bar code reader and went back out front to help with the registers. I spent a mind-numbing twenty minutes scanning codes on the bottom of Venetian-style masks—big sellers back in the Viking age, I guess—before boredom forced me to practice my fight stances in the door mirror at the back of the room. Pretending it was my lost conduit, I whipped the scanner from my cleavage, my hip, from behind my neck, and I was practicing spinning to nail two attackers in quick succession when I heard a hushed but distinct "Psst . . . Archer."

I whirled, and the laser of the bar code reader landed square between the eyes of a five-foot human being, those eyes widening before he ducked. It took me a moment to recognize Kade; seeing him outside the hallowed halls of Master Comics was disconcerting. Stripped of context the visual no longer made sense. But, I thought, as Dylan popped up behind him, seeing the two of them together brought everything back into mental focus.

"What the hell are you doing here?" I straightened, running a hand over my hair, aware I was blushing.

"The Shadow Cancer was just at the shop."

"Regan?"

"No, the other Shadow Cancer," Dylan lisped, and ducked back behind Kade when I glared. "We tried to call you like Douglas calls her but you weren't answering."

I didn't tell them I'd been at the state prison. They'd read about it in the manuals soon enough. Maybe. "So what did she want?"

Dylan peered around Kade's shoulder again, and when he saw I wasn't going to zap him with the bar code gun, shrugged. "She picked up a manual from Dougie, flipped through it while he whispered in her ear, then ran out of there like her house was on fire."

Mind racing, I thought back over the events of the last few weeks. It was probably the manual that showed me trailing her after I'd discovered how she'd targeted Ben. I'd planted bugs in the townhouse belonging to "Rose" too. Dammit. One less resource at my disposal.

"Any idea what was in it?" Kade asked, when he saw my short nod.

"Some." I wondered briefly if I could get Zane to let me in the store after hours to see what the latest Shadow manual said, but decided it was probably against the rules.

"Who are you talking to?"

Panicked, I motioned for the boys to disappear. They

ducked back behind a stack of boxes containing Valhalla waist packs, and I skirted to the opposite side of the room, making sure Ginny could hear me. She did, and came marching that way.

"Nothing. No one," I said brightly, propping the scanner up in one hand.

Ginny looked around suspiciously. "I thought I heard voices."

"I think the radio is getting interference from the security tower. There was something about a guy passed out naked on the fifty-fifth floor. I thought that was kinda a weird thing for the DJ to say."

Ginny gave me the zombie stare. "All right. Well, we need these coffee cups dusted off and brought onto the floor. The shelf out front is starting to look spotty."

Oh, tragedy. "Sure. I'll be right there."

She looked at me a moment longer as if expecting me to stand on my head for her, and I stared back blandly as if expecting the same. After she finally disappeared, I let my expression fall and spun. "You guys are going to get me fired my first day on the job."

"I don't think she likes you," Kade said, stepping out from behind the boxes. "When you're as attuned to visual charges as we are, you can tell something like that. Her aura's all muddled when she looks at you."

"You guys can see a person's aura?" I asked, drawing back when they both nodded. I hadn't known that.

"Why you working in this dump anyway?" Dylan piped up, twirling a pewter thimble on his middle finger. "Next time she gets all tyrannical on your ass—"

"With that jacked-up aura—"

"You should say, 'Fuck you, lady!'" He waved his fist in the air, pointing at the shop door. The thimble went clattering to the floor.

Kade did the same. "Yeah, fuck you in the ear!"

"Hold it down!" I hissed, throwing a worried glance over my shoulder. "Better yet, get out."

"But we have more to tell you."

I sighed and rolled my eyes. Of course they did. "And you couldn't text me like any other tweener geek?"

Kade ignored that, his expression so serious it looked misplaced on a face still rounded with baby fat. "You haven't suddenly lost the ability to imagine plate-glass windows into existence, have you?"

I'd done it less than three hours earlier. "No, why?"

"Because Jasmine can do it now too."

"Yeah," Dylan added, "and she's using it to box in Li."

"What?"

My response was reflexive, but Dylan explained it like it needed repeating. "She's using your power to trap her sister in one corner of the comic book shop."

"But don't worry," Kade said, too late. "We spiked her Surge with sleeping pills."

He motioned me over to the far wall where a giant black silk bag tied with a white ribbon lay slumped against the floor. He untied the ribbon. Inside was a writhing, tied up, nonsleepy-looking Jasmine.

I was so fired.

I rushed over and ripped the masking tape from Jasmine's mouth. She howled in pain, and would have leaped to rip out Kade's jugular if I hadn't stopped her. They were right; she was getting stronger.

"Fucktard!" she yelled, nailing Kade with her gaze.

"Nubcake!" Dylan yelled back, inching away. I shushed him again, shooting him a warning gaze of my own, and retaped Jasmine's mouth. Then I shoved her back in the bag. She kicked out, striking a wall unit filled with pewter Valhalla replicas, and I struggled to catch them before they hit the floor. I wasn't going to make it through this shift. I knew it.

"Please kill her now," Kade said, once I'd returned them to their shelves.

Jasmine began kicking again.

"No." I kicked back, but just enough to still her. She

grunted, then curled into a fetal position. "I'm not going to kill her for something that's my fault. But I might kill you if you lose me this job." I tensed, hearing the clacking of Ginny's heels as she headed my way again. "Hide!"

They hid, I feigned dusting, and after a few terse, pointed, petty words, Ginny disappeared again.

"Dingy aura," came Dylan's muffled and disembodied voice.

"Lots of adults have that, man." Kade popped up on one side of me, Dylan on the other. "That's what happens when you grow up, right?"

The boys sighed, and for a moment I shared their despondency, knowing what they were in for—mortgages, nine-to-fives, credit card debt, two weeks' vacation a year. But no evil beings trying to steal their auras. That was a positive.

Finally Kade sighed and turned his head up to me, though his expression was still serious. "Look, Archer, you may not like it, but you have to do something, okay? She's growing in power every day. Soon even we won't be able to control her, you know?"

I sighed and put a hand on his shoulder. He was mildly sweaty from dragging Jasmine around behind him, and I removed my hand. "Okay, I'll figure something out, but you have to leave. Now. I need this job."

They began to shuffle toward the door, dragging Jasmine along behind them. I didn't know how they'd gotten in unseen, and I didn't want to know how they were getting out.

"Wait!" I whipped back around, mid-thought.

"Make up your mind," Dylan said, one hand on his hip. "This bitch is heavy."

Jasmine kicked at him.

"You guys are still looking for the manual about Jaden Jacks, right?"

A look passed between them, and for the first time they looked uncomfortable. Kade swallowed hard. "We're trying, but it's hard, okay? We can read the Shadow manuals, but every time I think of telling you the information, it all gets muddled in my head. I put the manual back, and five minutes later I can't remember where I put it."

"Our short-term memory is blitzed."

"Like Alzheimer's for kids."

I frowned, forgetting all about Ginny and coffee mugs and kids in bags. "That doesn't make sense. I can read any Shadow manual I want. It's just a matter of finding the right one."

"Maybe, maybe not. After all, how will you know if you never come across it?"

They were right. It was like the tree-falling-in-a-forest scenario. Would it make a sound if there was no one there to hear it?

"Either way, I don't think we're supposed to help you. Sorry."

"Wait, wait." I held out a hand, biting my lip. The boys looked at me attentively, and even Jasmine stilled. "Okay, try something else for me, then. I need to know if there's ever been a Shadow woman targeting men who . . ." How to clean this up for the preteen set? I wondered, and then really looked at them, two kidnappers with a girl in a bag at their feet. "Who sell their bodies for money. Call boys, if you will."

Kade didn't even blink. "We'll try, all right? But we should start charging you for this shit. It isn't like we don't have better things to do than babysit your broken changeling and research your sexual abnormalities."

Better things like plugging into their PlayStations. "I know. I appreciate it," I said, giving them a placating smile, which dropped as they grunted and turned toward the door. With one final thump, they lugged Jasmine around the corner and were gone.

I went back to gather up Ginny's precious mugs—three in each hand, eight more pressed between my arms and body—noting the closet containing our personal belongings was slightly ajar. I kicked it shut on my way to the storefront, but when I returned for more mugs a minute later, it was open again. A faulty latch? A coincidence? Even before I whipped the door all the way open, I knew I couldn't get that lucky.

Hunter's picture was still splayed lewdly on the door, the purses still slumped forlornly next to the cleaning supplies . . . but eyes like silver swirling moons blinked at me from the dark recesses of the back wall.

"Who's the hottie?" the doppelgänger asked, eyes going slanty as she shifted them toward Hunter's ad, her gurgling voice sounding hollowly in the closet. Because she didn't immediately lunge at me, I glanced behind me, and up, spotted the security camera, and figured the suds spilling out onto the floor could be explained away by the cleaning products. A translucent woman with marble moon eyes could not. I began to shut the cabinet.

"Shut that door and I'll scream so loud, that pudgy mortal will fire you on the spot."

"So do it," I said, stepping back, challenging her with words alone. "Because then she'll come running back here, and that's the last thing you want. Isn't it?"

I'd put it together after her appearance in the sanctuary. She'd fled both times my troop had arrived to save me, but not because she was afraid of them. It was because she couldn't take on my form when distracted by so many other conflicting faces and energies. Confronting me was pointless unless we were alone.

One side of her mouth lifted like it was unattached from the rest of her face, and as unnerving as that was, it was also confirmation I was right.

"So you do exercise that muscle in your head after all. Wouldn't know it by your flat-footedness back at your *sanctuary*." She sneered at the irony, and I didn't blame her. I'd been no safer there than I was now.

I took another step backward.

"Hey, if you want to soul-stalk someone else, be my guest." I had mugs to polish.

"It would be significantly easier on us both if you would just *figure it out*." She stepped forward, still all iridescent curves, though there seemed to be a sharpness of light that gave her a molten look, like honeyed chrome. She was getting closer to solidifying. "You wouldn't even try to give me a proper noun."

Couldn't, not wouldn't. The latter implied a choice, and I'd had too few of those lately. I blew out a breath, and she copied the look. "Listen, your attitude and your riddles annoy me. If you're not going to tell me straight up what you want, then lose my supernatural phone number. I don't want to hear from you again."

"I can't just tell you. It's a tandem law in both our worlds." She was annoyed, and it made her voice sound like static and crossed wires, turning her every syllable into a hiss.

"And exactly what other world are we talking about?"

"I told you before." Her marble eyes rolled a three-sixty. "Midheaven."

The myth. Great. My imaginary friend came from an imaginary world with imaginary laws. I felt a sudden urge for an imaginary cocktail. "Well, I'm still playing catch-up with our Universe's"—apparently flexible—"boundaries. Wanna run that rule by me again?"

Her frame was diaphanous in the harsh storeroom light, and parts of her body came in and out of view as she stalked back and forth in front of the closet. "Words, spoken aloud, are given life and vitality. The spoken word becomes record. Think of weddings or vows of office. Nothing comes into being until thought is given voice via the breath of a living being. That, and action."

It was the same thing the Tulpa had told me when giving me the mantra; why he hadn't wanted me to say it aloud then. Nothing happened if I merely thought about binding her. But if I spoke the words the power would be released, the doppelgänger would die . . . and I'd belong to the Shadows.

But maybe I could use it without using it.

"Action, huh?" I bit my lip like I was considering it, and the doppelgänger mirrored the movement, lips shifting, nose twisting, then twisting back. For a flash second, I recognized myself. "Action like tearing the veil between two parallel worlds?"

Her eyes blazed. "The right word from you and it'll all stop."

"Oh, I know." And I told her about the mantra, left out the Tulpa's conditions, and watched as color drained again. A tremor passed over her, the bubble wavering but not bursting. I smiled, and this time there was no mimicking movement. "I want the vibrational chaos to stop. Let our reality heal. And leave me alone."

I finally seemed to have an edge. Unfortunately, as with many, this one came with a steep fall.

"Leave you alone?" If she'd had brows they have risen up her forehead. "Darling, would that I could, but what am I supposed to do instead? Get a real job? Pimp drinks at the gaming tables? Entertain at children's parties?" She pursed her lips, and bubbles flew from her mouth by the dozens.

Irritated, I waved them away, and glanced over my shoulder to make sure we were still alone. All I needed was Ginny or Janet coming in to find me talking to the mops. "How about creating your own identity, like any other person?"

"Please. Most people don't even create their identities," she scoffed. "They just stumble upon them. Just like Regan stumbled upon the woman you attacked in that dark street."

I fell still. "You saw that?"

"I saw that, then Regan ambush you, and the way you cried like a baby afterward."

She'd been there, and she hadn't helped. "And let me guess? You wouldn't have cried if you were me?"

"It wouldn't have happened if I were you, though it did make me wonder." Shimmering color rose again like a wave inside her. "If you were that torn up over one person, how would you feel about thousands?"

I opened my mouth.

"Uh-uh," she warned, and lifted her arm to point one razored nail above the doorway. "One little poke, and Valhalla will crumble."

A fissure appeared above the doorframe, a slim almost-shaft of light lasering through the alternate reality and into ours, and I quickly snapped my mouth shut again.

"Don't even fucking think about it," she warned, voice as sharp as her nail. Above me, the building rumbled.

I cursed my stupidity. I shouldn't have used the mantra as leverage. "Okay, I'll try to figure out your little riddle, but you have to stop *that*."

The doppelgänger smirked. "You've got forty-eight hours."

Was that it? That would make it the day of Kimber's metamorphosis. "I'm kinda busy on Sunday. Maybe you could get back to me during the workweek?"

She didn't even dignify that with an answer. "Figure out my 'riddle' or give me your beating heart, it really makes no difference to me, but if I don't have one of those things by the end of that period, I won't just take down this hotel, I'll pulverize this city."

Her willingness, the easy way she said it, stole my breath. "You have no conscience, do you?"

"You could always give me yours." She batted her lash-less eyes prettily, before squaring on me again, all business. "No? Then let me be clear. I'll take the energy I need, one way or another, and I'll take more than your heart. I'll take over your *life*, and sweetie? I'm already close. One more viewing and I'll have you."

She *was* close. I could see it in the colors swimming

inside her, like concrete being mixed before it solidified, though this would form skin.

A noise sounded outside the room, and she glanced that way, orbs shifting oddly to give her a cross-eyed look. "I'd prefer the other option, if you figure it out. It's the most powerful, it'll mean we can coexist in this world, *she'd* prefer it, and—of course—it's something the Tulpa wants to prevent more than anything."

Before I could ask again who "she" was, the doppelgänger lunged close. I jerked back, but if she'd really been trying she'd already have me. "Just mark my word, Joanna Archer. I will survive, no matter the cost . . . and I know you understand the need to survive, don't you, dear?"

And her face suddenly morphed into an exact approximation of my younger one, streaming with imagined tears, and an unholy cry that ricocheted off the shelves behind me. Glass tinkled, my blood went cold, and the stack of masks on the shelves behind me clattered to the floor. But the sound was gone as quickly as it came, and all of her swirling color and power was gone in that same instant. It'd taken everything out of her, but it had also done the job. She had briefly become me, my history laid bare on her face, and I was shaken.

"Two days," she said, voice nothing more than a bubbly whisper, and then she swirled like a mini-hurricane taking form and flight, and whirled through the room, and out the vent near the doorway.

I exhaled shakily, then let my knees buckle under pretense of picking up all the masks. "Cleanup on aisle one," I muttered, but the joke didn't amuse me. Her point had struck as intended. I too had fought hard to survive. And now that I'd finally found a place, a home, within my troop and my city, she could take it all away.

Forty-eight hours.

She had a point about the Tulpa, though. What was he so

desperate to achieve that he'd blow his own hole through the fragile terrestrial plane? Why was he willing to work with me now when never before? And despite the breaches in reality, the claws and teeth and threats, and all those fucking bubbles, the question remained: who was the greater threat?

My phone trilled in my bag behind me, shaking me from my thoughts, and I lunged to turn it off, knowing Ginny would have some rule against that. But then I saw the number.

I lifted the phone to my ear. "Speak."

When I heard the voice, I also lifted my eyes, and while my gaze remained focused on absolutely nothing, after a brief moment a smile as wicked as the doppelgänger's spread over my face. And as Gregor continued talking, that smile widened.

22

If there was anything that visually spoke of the Las Vegas of my youth, it was the sleek mid-century modern homes built in the decades before my birth. The clean lines, decorative block work, and butterfly rooflines were cool and wildly futuristic for their time, and the desert sun reflected off walls of sheer glass—in some cases, bulletproof—as if to light the world stage.

Birthed in what was now the center of town, the Paradise Palms neighborhood was one of these aging beauties, with customized homes of sanded stucco and sweeping driveways, each at a respectful distance from its neighbor. The address Gregor had given me over the phone belonged to a lot backing up to what was now called the Las Vegas National Golf Club. But, I thought, as I started up the long walkway early the next morning, when Brynn DuPree had lived here the club had still belonged to the Stardust, and the contemporary glamour of its parent casino was reflected in the homes where Las Vegas's most sophisticated players once lived.

The lockbox was set aside, the Realtor had already been by to prep for the open house later that day, but I didn't worry about that. Stepping inside a foyer that opened directly into a sunken living room, it felt like I was stepping back forty years in time. The light bulbs didn't even appear to have been changed in that time. It was as if Brynn had stepped out for a liquid lunch with girlfriends and would be back any moment.

How many martinis had the Shadow Cancer imbibed in these rooms? I wondered, wandering over the high-gloss terrazzo floor. How many nights had she put on furs and heels to take in a post-hours set with the Rat Pack? How many men had she lured back here to show off her glass-top bar . . . to torture and to kill?

I sniffed, caught the skein of Regan's scent on the velvet fabric of a streamlined lounge chair, and knew she'd spent some time here. Not a lot . . . it wasn't saturated with her odor, but some. So why was she selling it now?

I stepped up into a wide dining room overlooking a sheltered reflection pool, thinking perhaps she'd realized I was closing in on her real life. I guess she didn't want me springing up behind her one night while she was propped on her vintage sofa with a bag of Cheetos. Or maybe my mention of an agreement between the Tulpa and myself had her second-guessing her leader, her place in the troop, and my place above her if I ever did switch sides. She could be selling this safe house for another, one even the Tulpa didn't know about. It wouldn't be the first time, I thought, remembering the underground lair I'd been trapped in two months earlier.

But whatever it was she thought I might do, it was spooking her enough to have her selling a family home she'd held on to all these years. Out of nostalgia for the mid-mod period? I wondered, or had a young Regan DuPree created a few memories here of her own?

I reached the kitchen, and it was all I could do not to let out a covetous sigh. Sure, these Shadow bitches were spoiling like soured herring inside, but damn they had good taste in homes. The cabinetry was sleek, white, and sliding, clearly custom-made. A futuristic metal vent hovered over what was clearly the original aqua-colored stove, which matched the empty refrigerator and built-in counter appliances. The ceiling angled sharply upward into the backyard, adding to the space age feeling of weightlessness and light. I sniffed and found no bottom note of cooked food to add weight to the air, but there were herbs lined in sharply angled pebbled pots, fresh dirt mingling with the mint and tarragon and basil to snag my sensory attention. It reminded me of Ben, I thought, looking past the plants and out onto the expansive lawn dotted with round stone pavers. But then everything did. Even the gardener, I thought, spotting a man kneeling in the hedgerow.

I froze as the man suddenly looked toward the house. Maybe the reminder was so pronounced, I thought woodenly, because it *was* Ben.

The sun was in his eyes, so even though he'd seen me through the kitchen window, I knew he hadn't made out my features. He lifted a hand, one stranger acknowledging another, and I hesitated before edging around the slick, white counter, and through the glass slider wall. The gesture was appropriate, I thought, swallowing hard. Sometimes I felt like we'd never before met.

He recognized me—or Olivia—as soon as I stepped out onto the stone patio. The curious expectancy left his face and as it fell, my own blood ran cold. I fitted on a smile, trying for friendly warmth, though the Olivia of old would've reached out and hugged him as soon as they met. I wasn't sure I could risk the pain if he turned away, so I didn't.

"Hello, Ben," I said, shading my eyes as I sauntered toward him.

"Olivia." He wiped his brow with a forearm, but otherwise left his hands hanging loosely at his sides. "Just in the neighborhood?"

"Sure. I saw the open house sign and thought I'd stop in," I said breezily, ignoring the censure that'd bubbled up with his words. "What about you?"

"This is my friend's house. You remember me telling you about a woman I met online a few months ago, don't you?"

"Oh, sure." *Too fucking well.* "I do."

He paused as if waiting for me to say more, squinting as the morning sun brought out the caramel in the waves of his hair. Oddly, it didn't soften him like it used to. "Well, I told Rose I'd plant some greenery for the open house, add a little color to the hedges and pots so it looks like an oasis in comparison to all the cookie-cutter properties out there." He looked around, and despite his stiffness with me, sighed wistfully. Ben loved old properties like this. "It doesn't take much."

It didn't; the landscaping had had forty years to mature, and had obviously been maintained by a professional both loving and adept. But Ben sighed again as he turned back in my direction, and I froze under the weight of his gaze . . . and his scent.

"What are you really doing here, Olivia?"

I didn't answer, eyes flicking over his face assessingly, pausing on the scar below his hairline, the dark hair long enough to curl over his nape, and back to his eyes, which seemed too deep and hard in the bright morning light . . . not that I was one to talk. But it wasn't his eye color that was bothering me. It was the smell I'd picked up beneath the clean sweat on his skin, something acidic that had sunk into his pores and was souring there. Like the fermenting of cider vinegar. *Like Regan.*

"Sorry," I said, shaking my head, trying to loosen the thought's hold. It wouldn't budge. "What did you say?"

"Why are you here?" he said slowly, as if daring me to repeat my first answer. The fingers of his left hand twitched before he placed them on his hip, and the look he gave me was as dark as any I'd ever shot.

I've come to kill the woman who's trying to turn you into a monster.

I smiled again, even though the emptiness of unanswered questions hummed around us like a dial tone. We were so disconnected, this man and me. Standing right in front of each other with an entire unseen world between us. Unseen by him, anyway. "I'm always looking to acquire new properties, Ben. This one is a masterpiece. The interior is flawless, the furnishings vintage, the flooring original. I wanted to see for myself if the foundation was sound, or if the structure had any problems. If not, I'll have the plumbing inspected," I lied and lied and smiled. "We'll see."

"High-rise living getting old?"

I thought of my sister falling to her death. "It has its down sides," I said softly.

"So thinking of joining us mere mortals on the ground, then?" He was teasing, but that sharpness was still there, like flint, indicating a spark of something more. The word choice was peculiar as well. What the hell had Regan been telling him?

"You takin' shots at me, Traina?" I pouted and turned away, ostensibly to study the kidney-shaped pool, the scattered light of the trees falling softly across its surface. "Never thought I'd see the day. Must be that new girlfriend of yours making you forget who your old friends are."

"I haven't forgotten anything," he said, the censure in his voice equaling my own. "But Rose is very selective, and she knows how to make a man feel special. For example, she only brings people here once she knows she can trust them. And once she's gained that trust, she doesn't blow it away with lies or abandonment."

The insinuation was clear, and I thought, *It was a mistake to come out here.* I looked around the cool, dappled yard like I was searching for escape. He looked like the man I loved, and smelled like the woman I hated. And he was probing at Olivia to see how much she knew.

I glanced back to find challenge blazing in his eyes, so fucking angry and righteous and cavalier, it made me want to run away screaming. But what about the scent that'd dusted his breath? How soon would it begin spilling from his pores? When would it be too late to save Ben from Regan's destructive grasp?

When they make love? When she really gets to him? When he reaches the point where there's no returning to you?

I should just allow Micah to erase some of his neurological pathways, literally changing his mind so my existence was forever whitewashed from his memory. Then Regan would no longer be able to use him as a weapon against me. But did reason ever prevail when the heart was involved? What would remain of Joanna Archer if Ben forgot about my existence? If no one retained at least a mental record of a life lived, then had it been lived at all?

They were important questions because the person I was becoming, through experience and the march of time in the opposite direction of that which I'd have chosen for myself, was a person even I had trouble believing could exist. A superheroine. The Kairos. An individual who controlled the destiny of thousands.

Which brought up an even more pressing problem: I had one day left to find out what the doppelgänger needed from me before she either devoured my heart or blew Vegas to smithereens just to spite me. I needed to go, but . . .

I looked down at the row of white peonies he'd been planting. They were frilly and fragrant, and their petals would turn crispy under the full glare of a relentless summer heat, but in late October when the sun's touch had gentled, they looked wispy and promising. He had an artist's touch and a lover's mind when it came to his gardening. I knew it offered him escape from whatever worries occupied his mind, and he was at peace when surrounded by a quiet landscape and rich earth. The fear that had been knotting up inside me loosened.

There were parts of Ben yet untouched by Regan's foul influence. There was still time. And, I thought, as I stared at those fragile white blooms, as any good gardener knew, you don't pull out the whole garden just because there were a few weeds. You uproot the dead stuff, prune everything back, and start again.

I looked back up at Ben, considered everything I'd given up to so convincingly become Olivia . . . my home and work and body and self. I thought of the parts of my new life I'd so completely embraced . . . my strength and powers and responsibilities and troop. I thought too of the extraordinary man I'd continued to reject, Hunter, and I suddenly knew what I needed to do.

I would tell Ben everything. It would be no different than the mortals we used to help hide our supernatural activities, no different than the mortal/agent love matches of the past, even if Warren did believe my kairotic state made it too risky. Because didn't *kairos* really mean "the right or opportune time"? And the time to save Ben—along with the rest of the world—was now. I had to do it immediately, before Regan's influence burrowed in so deep he'd end up in a jail cell with slashes over his wrists and fingertips.

And after I told him, I'd kiss him as me, I'd infuse him with *my* scent, my touch, my taste. And it would make all my past and present sacrifices worth it. I could embrace my new life while holding on to what made me care about humankind at all. My first love.

"Listen," I started, whirling back to face him. "I'm chairing a pre-Halloween party for the North Las Vegas Children's Fund tonight at the Viva Las Vegas Wedding Chapel. Know where it is?"

"The Boulevard."

I nodded, but had to pause to swallow hard. "If you want, if you show up, I can make sure . . . *she* shows up as well."

Graveyard silence spread over the yard, and Ben fell so still for so long that I grew afraid he wouldn't speak at all. "You *know*?" he finally asked, vocal cords tight in his throat.

"Of course." I looked away, and closed my eyes until my breathing normalized. Then I looked back, my own voice stronger. "Um . . . it's a costume party. So, naturally, she'll be wearing a mask—"

"Naturally," he said wryly.

I jerked, but then took a step toward him. "Look, Jo has good reasons for what she's done. You know her—"

"I thought I did." Folding his arms, he took a step back.

"Just give her a chance to explain," I said, advancing on him again, forcing him to meet my gaze, not begging, but damned close. He only shifted feet. "Just give her a chance."

Again that deathly stillness . . . and then, unexpectedly, he softened. "She left me."

I shook my head quickly. "She hasn't gone anywhere."

Just then, a voice cleared harshly behind me.

I whirled, automatically feeling at my side for a weapon that wasn't there, and squinted up at a bulky, badly dressed figure posed on the stone patio. I sighed, relief mingled with resignation. Chandra. Talk about bad timing.

"Who is it?" Ben asked, squinting also.

"My . . . Realtor," I said, turning back around.

"Oh." Surprise lit his face. "You weren't kidding about buying the place?"

"Ben," I said, putting my palm to his cheek, letting the warmth spread through me again. I waited until his gaze met mine. "Archers only lie about the important things."

That almost brought a smile to his face, but it died half formed. Bitterness was bright on the air, I could almost taste it standing this close, and I knew I was right to tell him. He was deteriorating, like a sandy cliff relentlessly pounded by the cold sea. Soon all that would be left were crags and crevices where his softer spots had once been.

"Please," I said, my hand moving to his shoulder. "It was a mistake, she knows that, but extreme circumstances require extreme measures . . . and eventually, forgiveness."

He looked down, and stepped back again so that my hand fell away. "Just make sure she's there. I want it to end tonight."

One way or the other. He left that part unspoken, but it was alive on the scented air.

Throat tight, I nodded shortly. "I'll look for you."

My "Realtor" cleared her throat behind us. I shot him one last uncertain smile, before I headed back into the house and out the front door with Chandra. Once there, I took a deep breath of the crisp morning air. Despite the world threatening to crash in around me, it almost felt like a fresh start.

23

It occurred to me as Chandra and I strode to my car that whatever corner we'd been about to turn in our acrimonious relationship was about to experience a monumental roadblock. I don't know how long she'd been standing on that patio, but the strained silence told me she'd seen and heard more than enough, and Warren would undoubtedly make up for her astounded silence once *he* heard of it.

"How'd you find me?" I asked, as my engine ignited in a sweet, low purr. There was no other car on the street, and I knew she hadn't walked to Paradise Palms from the sanctuary, so I wasn't surprised when she answered darkly, "Gregor dropped me off. He knew where you were, and Warren has decided he wants us paired up again. The doppelgänger created another portal this morning."

"I know." The vibrational percussions had had my Porsche shaking on its wheels as I drove to Brynn's. It wasn't as long and percussive as her last entry into this reality, though, which meant it had only been a nongentle reminder—and warning—for me. One day to go.

"You know I have to—" Chandra broke off, then took a deep breath before continuing. "*We* have to tell Warren

about this. What you've done. What you've shared with
that . . . mortal."

Ignoring that I was driving down I–15 at ninety miles
an hour, I squared in my seat on Chandra. "That *mortal* is
my life. He's everything to me. He's all I want, all I care
about, all I need. And if any of you ask me to give him up,
you can shove the third sign of the Zodiac up your collective asses."

"If Warren wants you to give him up, he won't ask."

I knew that. Warren would kill the President himself if
he thought it best for the troop.

"Turn off on Blue Diamond," she said, a few minutes
later. "We have to scout a location for Kimber's metamorphosis tomorrow."

I did so silently, whipping onto a road so straight and
long and narrow it eventually disappeared into the desert.
We'd already scouted at least a half-dozen locations, but
the senior troop members weren't going to settle for a spot
that might be compromised. Riddick and Jewell were older
than the quarter-century mark when they'd taken up their
star signs, so not counting my flawed transition into the
troop, it'd been almost two years since an initiate had metamorphosed, and nobody had forgotten the carnage that'd
ensued when the Shadows had learned of that location.
Tekla's heir, caught in the paralyzing moments of receiving
his powers, had lost his life. I didn't think that night would
ever stop fucking with her.

"We can't leave the city limits," I reminded Chandra as
I watched the buildings fall behind us, the streets dropping
away until there was only the one.

"We can't enter another city," she corrected, which was
what I meant, "and we'll be turning off well before we
reach Pahrump . . . not that it counts as a city."

She wasn't simply being rude . . . this time. There had
to be a large enough population to warrant a proper troop,
and Pahrump wasn't there yet. Soon, though. People had
been pouring into Vegas for almost two decades now, an-

nually making it the fastest growing city in the nation, and Pahrump was getting a lot of the spillover.

We drove forty miles into what looked like nowhere, flat expanses of desert flanking both sides of the two-lane road with stubbled brush and crippled cacti jutting from the earth like a marine's botched crew cut. I was surprised when Chandra had me slow for no apparent reason, and totally astonished to find a badly paved road veering ninety degrees south, even farther out into a very literal no-man's-land. However, I wasn't surprised to hear the telltale bluster of Soulfly's "Corrosion Creeps" emanating from my phone, though I only gave it a cursory glance before setting it aside, smiling.

"Aren't you going to get that?"

"Not yet."

We drove for another five miles, the paved road giving way to gravel before a giant pole appeared out of nowhere, stretching into the desert sky like it was flagging us down. It was only as we got closer that I realized it wasn't just a pole; it had an unshielded light affixed to its apex. A beacon, then.

I pulled into a lot cleared of all natural brush and stone, still so taken by the sight of the pole, I would've plummeted over the cliff in front of us if Chandra hadn't jerked sharply on the steering wheel, causing us to swerve.

"Watch it, will you?" She closed her eyes, hands fisted on her lap as I pulled the car to a halt. "Just because I can survive a thirty-foot fall doesn't mean I want to."

"Well, shit," I said, climbing from the car so I could peer over the cliff. "I didn't know it was here."

"Not many people do," she replied, coming around to stand next to me. "Which makes it perfect for our purposes."

It was a small arroyo, proof water had once run through this area; probably around the same time greenery had flourished and giant creatures had yet to become extinct. "What is it?"

"Cathedral Canyon," Chandra answered, heading back toward the light pole, and motioning for me to follow. "Nature made it, and man improved it . . . or one man did, anyway."

She went on to point out a sign welcoming visitors to the tiny canyon, a wooden box next to it soliciting donations, and a rickety staircase leading into the crevasse, with a platform situated at the halfway point, directly in front of a giant sculpture of Jesus. We continued all the way to the bottom under his watchful eye, and that's when I saw the pottery and statues situated in surprising little clearings, and the drawings and quotes encased in Plexiglas stands, many dedicated to a deceased relative or someone who contributed heavily to the canyon's creation.

I glanced up to spy a rickety footbridge linking the two sides of the narrow grotto, and below it, where we were, a well-marked pathway curled along the canyon's base. A waterfall, currently off, was tucked at one end, and a bathroom was hidden in a natural alcove at the midway point. Most important, however, were the dozens of tiny stained glass windows fitted into the natural outcroppings, glinting impressively even in the full day's light. Chandra explained at night the colorful windows exploded with light, thus giving the cherished little canyon its name. Classical music would pump from hidden speakers, and water would again fall where it once had. Somebody loved this little place dearly.

"It's open air," I said, pointing out the obvious. Metamorphosis from initiate into star sign always took place in a secured indoor environment; the more elements the troop could control during the process, the better. "Unless there's an underground aspect to this canyon you're not telling me about."

"No, this is it." She turned around herself, the choppy layers of her hair striping her face in the slight breeze. She shook them away. "And the closed environment didn't serve us very well before. Warren thought we'd try something new. Something the Shadows would never suspect."

And a place of worship and respect and peace dropped into a crevasse in the middle of the Mojave would pretty much do it.

Soulfly's groove metal sprung from my pocket again, Chandra looked at me, and this time I answered it.

"Give it back."

I smiled again as I tucked my cell phone between shoulder and ear, not even pretending not to know what Regan was talking about.

"No. It's mine, I bought it, actually signed the papers and closed on it last night, sight unseen. God, you've gotta love the way money talks in this town." I heaved a happy sigh. "Hey, I have an idea. Next time you don a new identity, you should make her rich instead of cute."

Wow. Grinding teeth sounded a lot like sawing logs over the telephone line.

In a reasonable tone, I explained I wasn't going to actually live in her mother's old house. That wasn't the point. It just felt good for a change to possess something I knew Regan cared about. I didn't need to say she wouldn't have kept or maintained the property if she didn't care about it, or that that's what had exposed the weakness to me. She knew that, so I merely added, "The perks to my Olivia identity are starting to grow on me. I'm becoming quite the materialist. I've decided to start a small, but elite collection. I'm going to call it 'All the things Regan loves most.'"

Her breath hitched on the other end of the line but it didn't stop her ragged threat. "And do you think it'll ever rival mine? I call it 'All the ways I could maim Ben Traina.'"

It was the expected rejoinder, but I saved my own comeback for later. By now Chandra had realized who I was talking to, and was glaring openly at me. I batted my lashes but, like Regan, she had never fallen for that. "I understand from the changelings that you've seen something in the manuals exciting enough to have you running from the shop like your life depended on it."

This time there was no hesitation. "And I understand from my changeling that you had a run-in with the doppelgänger. Of course, being a loyal underling, I had to tell the Tulpa. He's pissed you didn't kill her when you had the chance."

Preteens were the biggest gossips, I thought, sighing as Chandra's eyes grew wide. She was making no attempts to hide her eavesdropping, but I shrugged her concern away. Whatever the kids could relay to my enemies wasn't anything that could affect the larger battle, anyway. Otherwise it would've been like Kade had said; the information would've slipped from their minds even as they tried to recall it.

"If he were truly upset he'd have sent a message-by-minion so he could tell me himself. Or didn't you feel like showing your innards today?" I gestured toward the restroom, turning, knowing Chandra would follow, still listening. As soon as I pushed open the door and daylight spilled into the cavernous darkness, there was a burst of frenzied squeals, and I ducked as my hair was rustled by hairless wings. Chandra yelped behind me, and the bats narrowly missed the canyon walls as they swerved blindly out into the sunlight. I ducked back out into the canyon, knowing Regan would try to make sense of the noise coming over the line.

"Never mind," I said, a smile in my voice. "You're probably depressed after having to sell your sole physical birthright to me"—I just had to rub it in—"but you can tell the Tulpa there was no way to harm the doppelgänger in the sanctuary. She was invulnerable to everyone who tried to stop her."

"And was your friendly neighborhood call boy one of those to try?" she asked, as I wandered directly beneath the sagging footbridge.

I snorted, feeling Chandra on my heels. "Still going on about Hunter? I'll have to let him know. He'll be so pleased."

"I'll let him know myself as soon as I find him."

The thought of Regan tracking Hunter made me laugh aloud. Even Chandra scoffed at that one. "Careful, Regan. You're starting to sound obsessed. Aren't you the one who once told me being a Shadow agent was a job like any other? You're just an underling, remember? An evil man's flunky . . . and an evil man's daughter."

"Your point?" she asked tightly.

"None," I lied, still leading her. "Other than you should be so proud of being sired by a mortal who can rival the Tulpa in atrocities."

She snickered, and I could envision the accompanying eye roll. "I can't muster interest, much less pride, in someone I've never met. I don't even care about most of the people I see every day. Affection is a supremely bad habit," she said, reinforcing what I knew of Brynn's legacy to her daughter.

"Then why would you suppose I care about what the Tulpa thinks of me?"

"Because you think of him, my dear Joanna. More than you'd like."

"I don't want to talk about my father with you," I said curtly. That was no lie.

"Fine," she said quickly, because she didn't want to talk about him either. "Then let's go back to talking about first loves."

I paused for effect, mouth winging up in a sly smile. "About that. Don't be expecting Ben to tend your garden anymore, or even returning your phone calls. In fact, don't be surprised if he's already left a kind but firm message on your machine canceling whatever plans you two made for the weekend. He'll be with me tonight . . . and every night thereafter."

I wiped the dust from a plaque memorializing a long-lost

child. Regan finally ended the silence. "I'll expose your world to him and tell him who you are, *Olivia*."

"I plan on telling him that myself tonight, *Rose*, and he's always been a part of my world. Always will be too." My smile was so wide it could be heard in my voice. "I told you he'd never be with you as long as I'm alive. So game over. I win."

"You think I'll give up that easily?"

"Why not?" I straightened, meeting Chandra's eyes as she shook her head, warning me off from baiting Regan. Too late. "I thought you didn't care about most people you see every day?"

"Oh, but Ben's different. He's special. In fact, I love him to *death*." And with that I heard a distant beep pass over the line, an innocuous enough sound immediately followed by a sonic boom, the way the air cuts beneath a speeding jet. Chandra jumped across from me, looking up, and even though I'd been expecting it, I couldn't help my sharp intake of breath. A part of me hadn't believed she'd do it. When the sound faded, Regan's laughter chimed over the line, genuine joy blooming where silence had reigned before. "Oh and now . . . there's so much of him to love."

I was no longer surprised at the unadulterated evil living in that sparkling laughter, but I closed my eyes, dipping my head. Regan, and those like her, would never stop. What scared me about that was I could never stop then either. Meeting evil head-on meant cutting it off, and preemptive strikes needed to be as vicious as the machinations of the Shadow side. So where and when did it all end? Or was this some sort of endless universal treadmill, where showing fatigue meant falling off into oblivion, but speeding up got you nowhere? The peace I'd felt upon entering the canyon dissipated, and I shivered in its wake.

"Your mom was right, Regan," I said softly, and the way my voice shook with the words wasn't an act. "Love *is* a weakness. But, as you know . . . we all have 'em."

Then I hung up amid the confused silence, Regan no doubt wondering why I wasn't out of my mind with grief for the life she'd just ended. But Father Michael's life, I knew, had ended the day he'd met Brynn DuPree.

"Tell me that vibrational chaos was the doppelgänger again," Chandra said, when I'd finally opened my eyes. I shook my head and looked up at the giant statue of Jesus, one hand held up in welcome, the other folded peacefully in front of his robes. I half expected a reaction out of him, a lashing with his olive branch, a stern look that would have the sky falling down on my shoulders. But the other half thought he might thank me. Too many alleged holy men had used his name for atrocities. I wondered briefly if he'd ever felt this sort of conflict, if dueling sides had ever warred inside him. I wondered if those upturned palms had ever wanted to curl into fists.

"You," Chandra said, pointing at me before I turned my back on her, "just killed an innocent, didn't you?"

"I wouldn't call him that," I murmured as I began walking back to the staircase. The canyon was half shadowed, and it was getting cool.

"I knew this was coming," she said, following closely. I walked faster, reaching the steps and taking them two at a time. "First you broke the changeling, you ruined the manuals of Light, and I tried to tell myself that Warren was right, and it was all an accident . . . but this wasn't. And the small things lead to the big, and your plans to tell that mortal who and what you are is big enough, but this—"

I whirled, halfway up the stairs, so we were staggered as we faced off against each other. "This is nothing like that! Don't you ever compare him to that . . . that pervert, that meat suit! They were both mortal, but the similarities stop there. Got it?"

"It's the rise of your Shadow side!" She was quivering, eyes wild beneath her choppy bangs, and looked on the brink of hysteria. I rolled mine.

"You're the only one who thinks so, Chandra!" Then I bent at the waist, tilting my head. "Or perhaps it's because you want to believe it?"

"Or perhaps," she articulated, leaning forward as well, "It's because you just killed a mortal man!"

I threw up my arms. "Regan killed him with her twisted need to continue hurting me. Excuse me for protecting myself and those I love. Apparently nobody else will."

"Don't." She reached out when I tried to turn away, and I slapped her hand out of my face. She grabbed for me again and kept talking. "Don't make excuses for what you've done. You need to take responsibility and respect that biology has made you different from the rest of us. This just proves we can't ignore that fact any longer."

"Ignore this," I spat, extending my middle finger so close to her face she went cross-eyed. I whirled, and this time her hand on my arm had my vision shifting to red.

"Look at you! You've got smoke coming from your ears! You try to downplay your differences but now we have to go back to the sanctuary and tell Warren you've done something none of us would even consider. Then he's going to change your identity, and hopefully your personality, so that—"

"Oh, shut up, Chandra," I yelled, and took out my anger on the scuttling movement I spotted from the corner of my eye. I missed my mark, due to temper and haste, and the sand scorpion froze, feeling the vibration of my foot slamming on the dusty desert shelf. Then it sped off, as blindly as the bat, to hide in the desert sand.

"You don't know anything about me," I told her, pissed that I couldn't stop the whimper escalating in my voice.

Nothing of importance, I told myself as I wiped at my face. Nothing that . . .

Matters.

My head shot up as an image of Chandra causing life to bloom from a rocky outcrop with just the wave of her hand hit me hard. She was behind me now, bitching about the acridness of my anger spicing the air, but I barely heard her over her memory-voice telling me creating life was something we all could do. A static buzz swelled in my ears, the doppelgänger asserting that with my help she'd be unrestricted by worlds or planes or boundaries. Synapses fired with almost audible pings, and sizzled as they finally connected. Every thought, every word, every action given voice. It's all channeled into one thing. Vibrations. Energy. Chandra had said it herself . . .

Matter is all that matters.

I blinked hard, as my own scattered thoughts began to crystallize. Then I turned to Chandra, frowning. "Have you ever heard about the boy, blind from birth, who gets around using echolocation?"

"What?" She shook her head, more in surprise at the topic shift than in negation. "No. Okay, yes. I think. Why?"

I began nodding to myself, the crystallized thought hardening into a stalactite of certainty. "Well, it proves a person, a mortal, can use vibrations to navigate the world like the scorpion, the bat." The doppelgänger, who circumvents the proper channels in order to access our reality.

"So?" Chandra asked, holding up her hands.

I squared on her, and bit my lip. "So close your eyes."

She did, exaggerating the action, half laughing as she lifted her chin. "You want to see if I can get around using echolocation?"

"No. It just makes it easier to do this."

The blow was one of the hardest I'd ever delivered, and it not only knocked her backward, but flipped her over the wooden railing as well. Maybe it was because of what she'd said before—we both knew a fall wouldn't kill her—and maybe it was because my anger still burned like a warm coal in my chest. But my fist caught her in the side of the head, and she was out before she stirred the dust on the canyon floor. I followed at a brisk pace, ignoring the Savior this time, and trailing a wispy thread of black smoke behind me. I confiscated her cell phone, used her belt to tie her hands together, and locked her in the cave doubling as a bathroom, lights off.

"Fine, so you're right," I muttered as I returned to the top of the canyon. "Biology has made me different."

But I'd just figured out why the doppelgänger was blowing holes through our reality, and Chandra was only going to get in the way. I needed to find a way to stop those cosmic breaches, and after I did, I swore, nothing would come between Ben and me again. Not a Shadow, I thought, huffing dismissively. And not a Light.

I later learned the screams of rage could be heard for ten square miles around Ben's house, which was where Regan had been when she placed her call to me. As for the explosion out at the correctional center, nobody other than Father Michael had been injured. It wasn't my fault Regan's homemade bomb had been designed for a slow kill, a poison meant to delay death, impart suffering, and burn a man from the inside out. It took five doctors, ten hours, and a strict quarantine, but even all that couldn't save Regan's father. Within the passing of a day, Father Michael was face-to-face with his Maker.

I'd heard the death of a parent could be felt by members of the Zodiac like a bullet to the breast. I'd never experienced it—my mother was still alive, and unfortunately my father was also—and I wondered if Regan had recognized the sensation immediately this second time, and how quickly she'd realized what I'd done with the bomb she'd placed in Ben's home. I wondered what she'd felt when she discovered she'd murdered her own father.

Not that I got a chance to ask. She didn't call again and wasn't answering the number that'd shown up on my phone's caller ID. But the subsequent eruption of destroyed window fronts and car windshields in Ben's neighborhood spoke of a rage just winding up, telling me I'd hit the jackpot when guessing who her love and weakness and regret and hope was centered around. I reminded myself she'd been the one to throw down first. She'd targeted my first love, and had, over the past few months, attempted to wrench away every foundation—both supernatural and mortal—that'd stabilized me.

But who would've guessed even a month ago that she was the one with more to lose? And now she had, I thought, the flats of the desert a buttery blur as I sped back into town. Gone was the house her mother had bequeathed her, the father she denied, and the man she'd targeted because she was so covetous of what belonged to me. Not wanting to face Warren yet, I called Gregor and said we'd need to place extra surveillance on Ben's home, though I didn't say why. Then I disconnected and settled in to wait for Regan to show herself. It was only a matter of time.

I'd be ready.

24

The city's annual benefit for the North Las Vegas Children's Fund was always held two weekends before Halloween. Though it was a costume party and ostensibly linked to the popular holiday, the timing meant there'd be no competing events to distract the city's moneyed and elite. Not that it mattered. This benefit was Vegas's premiere fall function, and this year would see practically every major headliner on the Strip contributing performances. None of that made a difference to the kids at Master Comics, but they acted suspiciously like normal children when costumes and candy were involved, and since the event fell on a Saturday, Zane decided to close the shop early so the little rugrats could get their Halloween groove on early.

And so it was shortly after one, an hour after I'd left Chandra unconscious and tied up in the middle of a barren desert canyon, that Zane toddled up the spiral staircase to his personal living quarters above Master Comics to find me squatting in his flat.

"About time, dude," I said, flipping through what looked like an original script to Whedon's *Serenity*. My esteem for Zane grudgingly rose a notch. "I was beginning to think you never took a break."

Comics, mail, graphite pencils, and pads went flying, and a steaming cup of black tea dropped to the floor in an impressive crash. Zane flung his arms out before him as if to ward off laser beams that might shoot from my eyes, and I lifted a brow and flipped another page. Man, I really missed Malcolm Reynolds. Zane stared at me a moment longer, then down at the luxury Persian rug, soaked with tea and studded with shards of expensive porcelain. He opened his mouth.

"Don't blame me for that, man. It's entirely too weird that you drink your tea like a prissy old Englishwoman."

"Fine china elevates the experience," he replied through clenched teeth, then bent over with a huff to collect his papers, slapping those that'd gotten soaked against his thick, jeans-clad thigh. His microwaved pot pie had landed facedown on the floor, but he flipped it back over and it looked salvageable. "That was my favorite cup and saucer."

I straightened, impressed by his recovery. I didn't know if an agent had ever broken into the shop before, much less his private quarters, but he seemed almost bored by my appearance here . . . and that just wouldn't do. "Nice selection," I said, motioning to a squat bookshelf with rare printings of every major graphic series ever written, including the script I'd pulled down.

He drew back at what he perceived was a verbal attack. "Entertainment reading isn't a crime, and Whedon's instinctive grasp of the primeval laws of the Universe is revealed as clearly in his 'Verse as any 'true' manual written throughout the history of—"

"Yeah, yeah." I stood, waving off the rest of his explanation. I swear to God, get the guy started on the mythos of any particular worldview and he might never shut up. "I just have one question to ask you, and then I'll leave."

He looked at me like he'd bitten into something sour.

I leaned over and patted the platform of the nearby bed, inviting him to sit. Zane slouched on the edge like he was

being told of his imminent execution, and listened list-
lessly as I explained how the doppelgänger was stalking
me, but had been told by someone to wait for me to offer
my energy to her, so that she could return to where it would
redouble upon itself.

"So she hasn't been creating the breaches in the fabric of
our reality just for the fun of it." I settled back, draping my
arms across the sides of the afghan-covered armchair, and
crossed my legs. "There's something that keeps drawing
my double back to the flip side of this reality, and do you
know what I think?"

"I know you're going to *tell* me."

"It's Midheaven."

"The myth?"

I raised a brow. "Is it?"

He shrugged. "They say so."

"What do you say?"

His turn to raise a brow. "You're asking the record
keeper for his opinion? That's a first."

"So?"

He stared for a long moment, then huffed. "I know
there's something."

"How?"

He leaned forward, palms splayed on his knees. "Because if the original manual was somewhere in this city, on
this plane, I'd have found it by now, and I'd have my ticket
out of this adolescent hellhole."

The original manual—a.k.a. Zane's obsession—docu-
mented the split between Shadow and Light, foretelling that
troops would one day be located in every major city around
the world, as well as predicting the rise of the Tulpa. The
means to killing the Tulpa was also supposed to be inked
in its pages, but no one could confirm that because our
city's sole copy had been lost. Agents kept looking, though,
because the knowledge in that one manual was so great it
could forever tip the scale of power in favor of the troop
that possessed it.

So Zane's point was valid. If the original manual still indeed existed, it certainly would be well hidden in a land everyone had dismissed as a myth. But what interested me more right now was his ending statement, so I watched carefully as he crossed to his bookcase where he pulled out a lighter and cigar I recognized as a Graycliff. Xavier smoked the same. And suddenly it was as clear as day. He no longer looked like one of the iPod people. He had the hunched-over mien of either a street fighter who'd been tapped too many times . . . or an octogenarian.

"Exactly how old are you, Zane?" He looked no more than twenty-seven, but the books and furnishings and comforts he surrounded himself with put him closer to . . .

"Seventy-three last March." He sighed, blowing out a thick stream of fragrant smoke. "I've been this valley's record keeper for almost half a century."

That explained a lot. "Made a deal with the devil, huh?" I said wryly, nodding when he pointed to a cognac decanter. "Did the original record keeper trick you into it?"

"Oh no." He poured two snifters of honey-gold liquid, and crossed to hand me one. I didn't even have to taste it to know it was quality. I could smell the silky finish from across the room. "He laid it all out, my obligations, my restrictions, my abilities. We're required to tell the truth to any potentials we have in mind for the job. I just haven't found anyone in the last half century as stupid as I was to take it on."

"And you can't just leave it?" I asked, sipping lightly. Zane was more relaxed, friendlier now that he had someone to talk openly with. I could imagine it got pretty lonely being the only person in a group who remembered World War II. Or even the Looney Tunes.

"I can't leave this building, Archer, never mind the city or state." He snorted gruffly, and scratched at his chin. "The voices would drive me crazy."

No wonder he was always in such a bad mood. There

was a cantankerous seventy-three-year-old in that non-aging body.

"About Midheaven, Zane," I said, more softly this time.

"Why are you asking?"

"Why aren't you answering?" I shot back, before sighing and running a hand over the top of my head. "Look, I understand you've taken an oath of omerta that'll probably result in some sort of terrible death if you were to break it, but I'm not asking you to divulge anything that isn't already widely known on both sides of the Zodiac. If you hadn't noticed, I'm a little late to this game, but I can't really afford to be red-shirted. The doppelgänger said she needs a word, some sort of proper noun from me, but she can't tell me what it is because it would break some tandem law in *both* our worlds. Where else would that be but Midheaven?"

Zane blew out four perfect smoke rings as he considered that, licking his lips as he watched them, waiting until they'd all dissipated. Then his eyes again found mine. "In astrology, Midheaven is where our actions reflect our true selves. Circumstances naturally arise there to—how do I put it?—bring your deeds into alignment with the seat of your emotions. Ultimately, you gain the trust of those around you, as well as reputation and fame."

"Sounds like a nice place to visit," I commented.

"But you wouldn't want to live there," he said immediately, and returned to the bed, leaning forward, elbows on knees. "See, in the Zodiac's mythos, Midheaven was created for one of the twin First Mothers."

I shivered at that. A twin. That at least paralleled the Tulpa's words. And a woman . . . a "she" had told the doppelgänger to come to me, that I was smart. That I would help. "Go on."

"The First Mothers were sisters, complete opposites, and eventual enemies. The original manual details what happened between them, but since most cities' manuals are long lost, including ours, the story has been passed on orally. Obviously there are a hundred different versions about what caused the rift, but what's important— and what remains unchanged in all tellings—is that one sister was banished to a sort of purgatory, a place where things get twisted. If you're at all divided in your ambitions, unsure of what you really want, it can be sensed in that other world. Used against you. The worst thing you can do is cross into Midheaven with a divided heart or mind."

A person cannot be divided against herself.

"Why is this considered a myth?" Because, like a chord being plucked inside me, it rang true. I knew it like I knew my own name.

"Maybe because nobody who had ever crossed into Midheaven has returned."

Except for the doppelgänger, I thought with certainty.

"See, you need a soul to enter Midheaven. If your theory is right, and the doppelgänger originated there, then she's made of the same material stuff as that world and can exit at will, but—"

"The Tulpa can't follow her there." *You'll never touch her in Midheaven.*

"He can't even access the normal portals. He was created, not birthed, so he's—"

"Soulless," I whispered. So was she. Thus the breaches in lieu of regular portals. I bit my lip, mind turning to Xavier. Was Helen forcing the mask on the Tulpa's mortal ally so he could steal Xavier's soul energy for himself, then follow the doppelgänger over? I ran the theory by Zane. "Because the only way to get to her there is with soul energy, right?"

"Another person's soul sacrifice is sufficient for passage, yes." He slanted a look at me then. "So is a stolen aura."

"A stolen aura," I repeated slowly as all the warmth of the cognac fled to my toes. "You thought I was going to . . . with Jas . . ."

He shrugged. "I didn't know. I still don't. All I know is

the last time an agent took off with a changeling's aura, the child went missing from this plane."

He meant dead. "It was Jaden Jacks, wasn't it?"

Zane shook his head immediately. "The answer's in the storeroom, but you'll have to find it yourself."

"All right." I sighed, not sure I even wanted to do that.

"But Archer? You should keep in mind that just because this doppelgänger is an enemy of the Tulpa's doesn't mean she's a friend of yours. Doppelgängers can't spring from nothing. She's pure energy, but it's energy that has been pooled. She smells like you, and alternately targets and helps you, which is the mark of an opportunist. Something or someone has set this thing in motion."

You're the golden ring . . . in both my worlds.

"One of the First Mothers?"

Zane shrugged. "I don't know, but I wouldn't trust her. And I suggest you don't let her get that final viewing of you either. Hide. Anywhere you can."

I made a face. Like I needed him to tell me that. But I couldn't hide. I had a city to save.

"Are we done?" he said, turning away to stub out his cigar. "Can I eat my pot pie now?"

I rose, and though nothing had changed, the room appeared entirely different from when I'd walked in. This wasn't the pitiful apartment of some man-child who spent his time, Pan-like, in the company of children. Zane was imprisoned here, trapped with his visions until he could foist them off on someone else, an old man whose generation had moved on without him . . . who'd found the elixir of life, and knew it to be bitter. I'd never look at the droll shop owner the same way again.

I'd only gotten halfway back to the bathroom and the skylight I'd used to break in when I drew up short. "Zane. What's supposed to be in the original manual that will release you from your duties?"

He looked at me like it should be obvious. "Their names,

Archer. The true names of the First Mothers. Names have power, and if I have theirs, that power will shift to me."

Because he'd speak them aloud, and like the mantra the Tulpa had given me, like prayers, like spoken thought, there would be energy, alchemy, and power in the spoken word.

"So what are you going to do now? I saw that your conduit was stolen, you know. It's not like you have a lot of options." Despite his caustic words, I caught the bald curiosity in his expression. It made me smile grimly, because the next time I saw him—in the shop, surrounded by children—he'd pretend we'd never had this conversation. "I'd tell you but . . . you'll see anyway."

I leaped back up through the skylight, and quickly dropped into the alley opposite the street, head ringing with all my new knowledge . . . and no idea what to do with it.

Whatever it was, it wouldn't include stealing human auras to attain Midheaven, and my greatest desire. But would it entail working with the Tulpa?

All I knew for sure was that it was a sick world when siding with the leader of the underworld looked like the lesser of two evils. But I'd worry about that later. Right now I had a benefit to attend, and a long-lost boyfriend to reclaim.

There was a recurring dream I had in the early years after my rape. In it I was always cradling a child as Ben and I sat in the middle of a dried lakebed, alone for miles but for the cracked earth surrounding us like dusty, peeling tiles. But that baby was deformed. When swaddled, all I could see were these perfectly formed facial features; a tuft of dark hair whipping up from her crown, a pink bow-pinched mouth, and one brow that winged up in either concentration or confusion. But loosen the swaddling, and the child literally fell apart. She was a fragile china doll that'd been dropped, thin shards of fine porcelain chunks jumbled in the center of that blanket. At first I was afraid of her. Every move I made caused her to rattle . . . and me to bleed. If I tried to coo or smile at her, she'd squinch up that perfect little face, and a tiny limb would flail up to nick me, scoring my face from the corner of my mouth to my ear.

But as the months went by, I began to ignore the pain—or at least get used to it—and I pieced the dream child back together, over and over again. A shard here to reveal the tender curve of a downy soft shoulder, or an aligning of pieces that had the chubby fingers suddenly snapping into place, gripping mine so the edges dug into my skin and blood ran into that bowed hungry mouth.

The baby changed in time; sure, she was still sharp and brittle—a face only a mother could love, I remember thinking—and she was beautiful in the way broken glass is as it catches the light of the morning sun, but most importantly, she was whole. And the very last time I'd had the dream, though bloodied and stinging from her sharp little kisses, I was whole as well.

It was when I stopped having that dream that I knew I would survive. It'd taken time, but the broken pieces of me, like that child, were put back together too, though I'd also become a mosaic, a mishmashing of parts from the earlier incarnation of me.

The only person who didn't change in all the months of dreaming was Ben. He simply sat beside me, smiling down at the shattered infant, saying nothing as he gazed into her lovely face. If the babe reached out to touch him, I'd smack her hand away, sending pieces of her palm skittering across the floor of the lakebed, her cries rising in the dry wind like razors to cut my cheeks to ribbons.

But nothing touched Ben. I wouldn't let it, and now, as I readied myself for the Halloween benefit, I knew why. He was more to me than a mortal, or the boy I'd once loved, or the father of my child. I'd remained next to him in my mind all these years, mentally molding my existence into alignment with his. His heartbeat was like the thrumming of strings across mine, and though time and circumstances had altered, the comfort I received just from his being in this world remained untouched. He was still the same person who'd smiled unflinchingly at me in that cutting dream. The difference, again, lay with me. Now, finally, I could smile back without bleeding.

25

The wedding chapel was located on the north end of the Las Vegas Strip, bordering the no-man's-land called Naked City that lay like an open wound between the gross affluence of the Strip properties and the dogged redevelopment of the downtown area. Squeezed in between were pawnshops outfitted like jail cells, an infamous strip club, and the now condemned apartment buildings where the showgirls in the forties would sunbathe nude on the rooftops, thus giving the area its colorful name. Criminal activity still flourished in the area, but the drug dealers and addicts were slowly being squeezed out by high-rise developers—the city's modern-day prospectors—and had begun oozing into other parts of the city. I'd canvassed this area many times when I was a photographer, before most of the flophouses were razed and the low-income housing relocated. The poor had no place to go even then, and despite the progress in the area, or because of it, their options looked even bleaker now.

With tonight's much-hyped gala, and police presence in strong evidence, the scariest obstacles on my walk to the chapel were the crater-sized potholes angling for my low heels. And *chapel*, I thought, finally reaching the front door, was a bit of a misnomer. Viva Las Vegas was huge. The largest chapel in Vegas, it specialized in themed weddings, boasting one traditional cathedral and a half-dozen fantasy chapels. The attached hotel and B&B was a natural outgrowth of the chapel's success, and the establishment now took up an entire city block, with an open-aired courtyard linking the two enterprises. It was kitschy and clever, and the owners had thrown caution to the wind with typical Vegas flair.

Tonight the doors to all the themed rooms were flung wide open to the autumn air, space heaters anchored between doorways like toasty sentries, and a red-carpeted catering tent set up in the middle of the courtyard. Though two weeks early, guests were clearly in the Halloween spirit, and some had even gone as far as costuming themselves for a particular room, though it was a bit disconcerting to see Al Capone wandering from the Gangster Suite into the turrets of Camelot.

A good deal of the women, unwilling to muss their hair or makeup, were dressed in half masks, and quite a few men had donned full-faced disguises as well. These unnerved me the most. Fortunately, as we were in Vegas, most of the guests had decided to dress up as pimps and hos. There seemed to be some sort of unspoken contest to see who could wear the least amount of clothing without getting arrested.

I smiled as I passed a bevy of Elvi and Priscillas lounging on a pink Cadillac bed, but moved onto the DooWop diner, where honeymooners could spend their first morning as a couple sharing coffee and Danish and gazing lovingly into their inbox via the hotel's free Internet access. Tonight the diner was being used as an open bar, but I didn't see Ben there, so I moved on.

And stumbled over a handful of ankle biters.

"You little fuckers just keep popping up everywhere, don't you?" I said, my gaze narrowed on a pint-sized Grim Reaper.

"You can't talk to us like that." The Reaper's voice was muffled beneath his rubber skull, but I could tell it was Douglas. How fitting. He looked a lot like the Shadows. "We're kids. We have rights."

"You're mutants. You have tentacles," I said menacingly. I watched him take a step back, then turned to Carl. I'd been right; his costume was that of a normal kid. "Where's Jasmine? And Li?"

"Jas blew us off for some school dance. Li isn't feeling so hot. She's staying home." I stared at Carl a moment longer, then closed my eyes, feeling myself go dizzy at the sudden sadness glossing his gaze. He saw it and his voice brightened in a deliberate attempt to sound cheerful. "You look good, Archer. Better than Angelina even."

I glanced down at my ensemble and murmured my thanks. My costume was tame compared to most. I'd chosen an outfit that seemed like a good blend of both Olivia's sensibilities and mine. The amalgamation of our personalities was, I noted with some surprise, becoming increasingly comfortable.

I'd chosen to come in the not-so-discreet guise of video game vixen Lara Croft. Or at least a highly improbable Vegas version of her. There would be no jungle adventures or treks through a muddy swamp for me, most notably because I'd taken her latex tank top and khaki short-shorts and recast them into racing-stripe red. It made it a bit hard to blend, but then this *was* the neon-zapped concrete jungle on a slamming Saturday night, and blending wasn't the point. So I'd accented the outfit with a black leather utility belt and a rhinestone buckle to match the jewels glued into my blond fall. Red leather cut gloves complemented my knee-high, lace-up hiking boots, which had been streamlined for less bulk, though I'd seized the opportunity to keep the lower heel.

"So what do you guys want?"

"Oh, because it's all about *you*?" Douglas snarled, leaning on his scythe. "We're here for the free treats, man.

Screw that slogging from door-to-door thing. The owners are giving out super-sized chocolate bars."

Dylan—a zombie—snickered and elbowed Kade—a pirate—who elbowed me. "Super-sized, get it?"

I didn't smile. "Fine. Then you'll have no problem staying away from me. I'm here on official . . ."

I trailed off as a woman dressed like a naughty nun began waving madly at me from the Egyptian Suite. I knew her, I thought, tilting my head, though I wasn't sure how. It was hard to place her beneath the satin veil. It came to me as she reached my side, though, and I found myself smiling back at her, and a man who was obviously a little starstruck where Olivia Archer was concerned.

"Hey, Janet," I said, as she adjusted her lace bandeau. "Sorry. It took me a moment to recognize you outside the gift shop."

"That's okay. It's probably the habit that threw you." She motioned down its length—about two inches; it ended just below her butt cheeks—then elbowed her companion. "See, I told you I knew her, Ted."

I offered Ted my hand, aware I had a very captive audience in the kids as well. They hadn't seen me in Olivia mode before, and it was probably like laying eyes on Diana Prince. Janet's date—a clearly defrocked priest—pumped my hand earnestly. Ted grinned, showing perfect teeth. "It's a dream come true, Ms. Archer."

The Grim Reaper mimed impaling himself on his scythe. "I think I just threw up a little in my mouth."

I took a large step to the side, my heel grinding into his toe. He howled, and I whirled immediately, simultaneously freeing my hand from Ted's clammy grasp and acting surprised. "Sorry, little one," I said, ruffling the hair tufting from Douglas's pointed hood. He jerked away. "I didn't see you there."

"Isn't the kiddie section set up over in the main chapel?" Ted asked snidely, clearly having heard Douglas's comment.

Janet too was piqued. "I didn't know they had a romper room in this place."

Okay, it was one thing if I picked on the little brats. It was something else entirely if two grown adults, exactly whom these kids loathed and feared becoming, did the same. "It's a benefit for the Children's Fund. These are some of the youngsters we're helping."

Carl didn't seem impressed with my attempt to defend them. "Yeah, well, we're going to take our homeless little asses over to the Alamo now. Maybe they have some brand-new cardboard boxes for us to live in."

I gave him an imploring look, not wanting him to be angry with me, but he'd already turned away, the three other boys following behind. Creepy little Douglas took up the rear, walking backward as he pointed at me with his scythe, totally scary up until the point he tripped over his robe and fell into the zombie.

"Guess who else is here," Janet said once the kids were gone. She paused dramatically, sipping white wine before continuing in an exaggerated whisper. "Mr. Security himself. I think he's on one of his 'dates.'"

"You're kidding me." But I could tell by the animated look on her face she was not. Hunter was here, and I bet he was watching me under the pretense of being on a date.

Unless he wasn't. I glanced around the open-air diner as discreetly as possible. It wasn't impossible he'd known I was going to be here tonight, but would he show up in top-secret call boy mode if he had? It might be a good opportunity to reverse our roles, spy on him instead of the opposite . . . except it was a rather inconvenient time to actually be doing my job. Tonight I wanted escape from all the intrigue and the disguises and the lies. I only wanted my lover back. I wanted Ben. "Where did you say you saw him?"

"He was in Camelot," she said, pointing at the upstairs walkway. "But I think they were headed to the Gangster Suite. They're doing palm readings there."

Of course they were. I nodded my thanks to Janet, excused myself, and headed in the opposite direction. By the time I passed Egypt, the Blue Hawaii Suite, and a disturbingly accurate replica of the *Star Trek* main bridge, I was feeling slightly traumatized, and there was still no sign of Ben. It was possible that he'd stood me up, I thought as I extracted myself from yet another boring conversation on philanthropy, but I didn't think so. He'd been as anxious for a reunion as I was; I'd seen it in his gaze.

Just before nine everyone began heading over to the main chapel for the charity auction. Olivia had been chairwoman for the North Vegas Foundation for the past five years, and I'd scrambled to keep up her work, though it was harder than I'd initially anticipated. She'd schmoozed half the glitterati in this city out of time and money at one point or another, and keeping up those contacts was a full-time job in itself. I needed to make an appearance at the auction; smile, shake hands, nod and bid on a few items, and then I could get back to searching for Ben. If he was here.

Yet one look around the packed chapel, one sniff, and my heart plummeted. Damn, I thought for the first time, maybe he really wasn't coming. Maybe, I thought as I leaned against a fiberglass pillar, he was still pissed at the way I'd disappeared on him, and this was his way of getting back at me. Making me feel what he had. Making me see how abandonment could cleave your hope in two.

"Hey, Archer." The whisper came from my left, behind a cluster of plastic potted plants. "There's something you need to see over here."

I moved only my eyes, then sighed, making my disinterest obvious. Douglas had removed his mask, and his sweaty head sprouted from the foliage, eyes shining.

"What is it?" I murmured lowly, tossing a nod and a smile to the governor and his wife as they passed. "Another message-by-minion?"

I saw him motion to me from the corner of my eye. "It's a surprise."

"A surprise like a party," I muttered, pushing off the faux Roman pillar to follow him, "or a surprise like herpes?"

He didn't answer, just disappeared around the back door, which led into the outdoor gazebo, moving so fast I caught only a glimpse of his black shroud as he slipped back over to the themed rooms. I tried not to look rushed as I followed, smiling at stragglers in the outdoor tents, and discreetly rushing past a couple making out in the pulsing light of the Disco Suite. More mirrors, please, I thought sarcastically, as I averted my eyes again . . . and again.

I finally caught sight of his tattered hem disappearing around the corner, and called out for him to slow down, but my voice was drowned out by the organ music straining from the Gothic Suite. A fog machine had mist snaking from beneath the closed door, and when I tried the handle I found it locked tight. No telling what Our Gang was doing in there now. I moved to the window to peer into a replica of Dracula's castle, replete with leering gargoyles and the flicker of medieval sconces, but my gaze was immediately drawn to the coffin-shaped bed centered beneath a werewolf's moon.

And to Ben on that bed, satin red sheets pooling around him like blood.

I was there too. My old bob swinging down around my cheeks as I rose and fell above him. The muscles in my arms flexed as I rode him. My small breasts strained through the soft chemise Ben had neglected to remove as he gripped my hips, both of us moaning. A mask like the one Hunter had designed for me lay snug against my cheeks.

Her cheeks. Regan's.

A keening wail spiraled out of me and I rushed the door, only to be yanked backward. The arm wrapping around me was as unyielding as concrete.

"No," Hunter said, repeating it when I jerked against him. "It's what she wants!"

"Oh, it's what I want too." I slammed my heel into his foot, and his grip loosened momentarily, but he pulled me back to his body before I'd taken three steps.

"You have no weapon. Breach that door, and Ben will be dead before you touch her."

The truth in those words had me sagging. Hunter's grip relaxed, released, and I lunged for the whip at his side, and raised it to the level I'd seen Regan's head through the window, but he wrapped his hand around the steel-tipped length so that I'd have to cleave through his flesh in order to wield it. "Think, Joanna. Think what it'd do to him to see 'you' slaughtered on top of him. It's what she wants. She'll break him through his mind rather than his body, and in doing so she'll still get to you."

Because mortals were so easy to break, especially when you didn't give a shit about any of them.

It was masochistic, but I leaned forward, looked through those cobweb curtains again, hoping against hope I hadn't seen what I knew I had. That maybe Ben would open his eyes at any moment and throw Regan from his waist, re-alizing his mistake. But he was too far gone, lost in an ecstasy that was supposed to be mine, spending himself inside her even as I blinked, and causing another blade-sharp wail to rise from my throat.

Hunter wrapped his arm around me again. Regan threw back her head. And I swore she looked right at me as she climaxed.

26

The voice that had begun screaming inside me the instant I'd seen Ben pinioned beneath Regan fell silent as we sped away from the chapel. I was suddenly icy with calm, but the accompanying silence was that of a hurricane's vortex. It must have frightened Hunter, because he kept one hand on the steering wheel as he drove, the other poised on the console between our seats, tensed. His eyes were on me more than they were on the road, but I didn't care. I was playing and replaying everything I'd said and done and missed, piecing together the puzzle of how Regan, once again, had gotten to Ben. Gotten, this time, inside him.

Closing my eyes, I leaned back against the leather headrest. I'd told Regan that Ben would never be with her as long as I was alive. So instead of wasting time or risking rejection, Regan had chosen a more effective tactic in making him her own. She'd become me. And that was my fault too. Hadn't I taunted her less than twelve hours ago? Hadn't I told her straight out that Ben knew who I was, and we were going to be together tonight, and every night hereafter?

I'd handed him to her on a silver platter, I thought

numbly, opening my eyes to watch the zigzag of street-lights flaring before us, disappearing behind. By confirming to Ben the truth of my dual existence, or at least part of it, I'd given her leave to fill in the blanks. And she had. She'd pretended to use a changeling to turn herself into the old me—as Ben knew I'd done before—and with the mask on and the mannerisms she'd studied so closely, and a scent she'd manufactured and bottled after scrutinizing my own, she'd recreated the woman who spoke to Ben's soul. And he was expecting me, after all. He wanted me. He thought he was making love to me.

None of that lessened my desire to throw myself from the speeding car.

The bay door to Hunter's warehouse was lifting even as we rounded the final corner, and he pulled in smoothly, then waited for it to close again. He unlocked the car doors and got out. I remained seated, the cabin's silence a cushion against my senses, only vaguely aware when Hunter lifted me from my seat and carried me through a narrow passage-way I'd never even noted. We continued up a flight of stairs that ended in the crow's nest where I'd sat with Warren a week before. Hunter deposited me on the corner of the desk, studied my gaze as it lingered on the black depths of the workspace below, then lifted me like I was a rag doll, and dropped me to the chair, away from the railing.

"Don't try to escape the warehouse," he said, closing the door to the hidden passageway so it melded back into a rickety wooden wall. It was almost pitch-black up here, and I looked around for the utility lights that were casting his outline in relief, finally glancing up to find a low-slung ceiling angling over the bed's raised platform. It glowed with an elaborate universe of stars. I'd have thought it was some cheesy attempt at turning the crow's nest into a love nest, but all the Zodiac members had a weird obsession with the solar system and the stars freckling its face. Raised outside the troop and inside a city whose skyline obliterated the night sky, I harbored no such affection. I'd have asked him to turn on the lights, except I preferred not to be seen right now. "It's rigged, alarmed with trips and snares. You won't even make it onto that concrete floor."

"You can't trap me here." My voice was scratchy with the screams that'd escaped me, and thick with those still caught there.

He folded his arms and leaned against the wall, putting himself between me and what looked to be my only escape. "I just did."

And he probably thought it was for my own good. He always thought he knew better than I did; that he was right just because he was stronger, had more knowledge and experience in death dealing and demon fucking, and creatures who used sex as nothing more than a sport or a job or another weapon in a superhero's arsenal. Just like him. Just like her.

I narrowed my eyes, feeling anger heating again like the core of a nuclear reactor, though this time I had a new target. Hunter felt it too, but he couldn't back away . . . the arrogant, sanctimonious, merciless . . .

"Why are you pissed at me?"

"Because you're always there!" I screamed, twisting the last word into an ugly growl, throwing my arms wide to send a stack of books skittering across the ground. I stood, squaring on him. "Always watching me, stalking me! Just like *them*!"

That wasn't fair; he had saved my life more than once, but none of that mattered now. My lover was with Satan's spawn, and instead of helping me—rushing the room, securing Regan, saving Ben—Hunter had dragged me to a location where only he knew the hidden passageways and alarm trips.

Worse, he wasn't even defending himself. He shifted so his legs were spread apart, defiant as his regarded me from that not-wall, absorbing shock after shock of my anger like he was an emotional sponge. I rose with the need to claw at someone, rip at them with my teeth until blood filled my eyes and I no longer saw that damned image of Ben pumping and pumping, ecstasy etched on his face. But Hunter was the only one in front of me, and he was as calm as I was frenzied. Which pissed me off even more.

And then he opened his fucking mouth.

"Should I put on a mask? Because the death breath is getting a little thick."

My vision had gone red, and the sheen reflected back in the corrugated roof slats, smoke pumping through my pores without me willing or controlling it. My father's temper was getting the best of me . . . and I didn't care. I cursed Hunter so loudly the furniture shook on its legs, and an alarm sounded from somewhere below. Still calm, he leaned over in the billowing smoke and pushed a button on the outside of his squat headboard to silence it, his other hand covering his mouth. But he still watched me with that patient darkness.

"Fuck you!" I repeated, over and over again, the inflection altering in my throat, scratching it raw as it grew deeper and more fibrous, and feeling good. The part of me that always had a sarcastic comeback told me I was having a major paranormal shit fit, but I just screamed louder. A desk lamp went over the railing, triggering another alarm, and I heard the whizzing of deadly darts cutting air, fired pellets that joined my voice in the ringing chaos. I screamed some more.

I don't know how much time passed before the breath simply wouldn't come. One minute I was standing in the center of the crow's nest, wolf-mad with howls, the next I was mewling on the bed, slumped up in the corner like a patient in a nuthouse. Finally deeming it safe, my sarcastic bent popped up its head again. At least I wasn't drooling.

"I hate you," I told Hunter, as he stepped through the thinning smoke, his indistinct form solidifying again. It felt like the only solid thing around me.

"I know." His voice was gentle, still absorbing the after-shocks of my tantrum as he lowered himself to a crouch in front of me.

"You should've let me kill her."

He put his hand over mine. "You would've hated your-self later. It would've fed into his destruction. Just like Regan is doing."

"Stop that!" I jerked away, sick of people bringing up my Shadow side, as if I was any more treacherous than anyone else. Like Hunter wouldn't have felt or thought the same things if it was his lover being fucked by a rotting corpse! "Stop using me against myself!"

"I'm not." He laid his hand on my arm again, but this time its solidity balanced me in a world gone formless and faint. "I'm pointing out a strength that makes you better than them, or any of us who make flawed decisions even without a lineage that puts us in opposition with ourselves. Regan mistakes your Light for weakness. But it's a greater strength than I've ever witnessed in any person . . . and any man, at any time, should be able to recognize it."

A tremor shot up my spine, like the carnival game where the smash of a mallet sends a bell ringing above. I sud-denly realized the silent knot coiled inside me was really a choked-off thought, one I'd strong-armed into silence so I didn't have to admit the selfsame thing. Leave it to Hunter to come along and clobber that bell square. I wiped at my eyes with the backs of my hands.

"She looked like me," I said weakly.

Silence reigned. I dropped my legs to the floor, shifting uncomfortably, and I found myself unable to meet his eye in the wake of that feeble excuse.

"I'd be able to tell it wasn't you."

I looked up into Hunter's face to find his steady, assured patience coupled with a fierce tenderness. And the knot that'd already been dissolving in steamy corkscrews gave way to scalding tears. My shoulders shook.

How? I wondered. I wasn't male and couldn't know if one woman's flesh beneath a callused hand felt much the same as another. Could a man distinguish between two women—by the way their hands moved over his body, how their tongue tasted in his mouth, how their thighs warmed his as he pressed them apart? I'd have gone on wondering, and weeping, if I hadn't accidentally spoken the word aloud.

Hunter's palms stilled my knees, his smooth fingertips pressing lightly. He leaned forward slowly, until his breath was in my ear, shifting the hair at my neck in the slow, calming beat of his pulse. I turned to him, our faces inches apart as I studied him studying me, and breathed in deeply. A gentle fizzing on the air, the Light in him straining to comfort me, an enveloping warmth like a hot spring in a hidden cave, something wanting to warm and secure me all at once. Overlaying it was the sharp, depthless need I always tried to ignore, and the poised flint of his banked gaze, ready to spark to life. Oh, I thought breathlessly as we locked eyes. I'd forgotten. Hunter felt like lava-licked sea water and smelled like ozone, and yes, it was totally different from any man I'd ever known.

"Because once he's been inside you," he whispered in the breath of a scalding ocean, "how could any man mistake you for another?"

A final sigh stuttered out of me, my defenses unraveling, and I lowered my gaze to his sea-swept mouth.

Ah, I remembered now. He tasted different too.

His strong, solid face blurred as I leaned closer, then reappeared touching mine, lips soft and warm and waiting. The kiss started out uncertainly, a meeting and parting, desire squared and split in two. Then, the smoothest flick of his tongue and heat shot through me, a slide that numbed, like bubbling champagne hitting the tongue.

With the gentlest press of printless fingertips, he lowered me to the bed, and this time—as never before—I let him, watching the faux stars spread out overhead as he loomed above me, the glow of distant planets and forgotten origins the only witnesses to my acquiescence. They grazed my irises before I closed my eyes, winking their approval.

Five minutes later he rose to his knees, stripped off his shirt, and unbuttoned his jeans. Tenting his body over mine, he held his weight on his arms and I ran my hands along his tight biceps, over the dense rounding of the shoulders I'd been wanting to caress since seeing him shirtless, and traced where I knew that enigmatic tattoo lay, marking his back. Meanwhile I branded him with my tongue, wet warmth sliding over his chest, crisscrossing the peaks of his nipples as I pushed his jeans down using my instep. We kicked them away together, a little more rushed, slightly frantic now, and I gazed up at him, down at him . . . and wished for more light.

The removal of my clothing went a little more slowly, more considered as his hands worked over and down, between and in, his warrior's artistry turned soft, but still relentless as he shaped and pressed and molded me as he pleased. My focus faded and sharpened in turn, as did my breath as he licked me into place, pressing kisses just so to ensure I stayed there.

By the time I lay naked beneath him, my body was dewy from openmouthed kisses, mind numb from those electric fingers, and my legs curled lightly around the backs of his thighs. He bent, found a breast, performed the lazy crisscross I'd fired across his nipples, and I arched back, hooked my ankles in on a moan, and rose to him.

He slid inside me like he'd been there before, like I'd drawn him a map he'd committed to memory, tracing memorized pathways on my bridging body so he could find his way there in the dark. Though coming to it late, I began to study him too.

But Hunter saw me looking, and offered a swollen smile before slipping his thumbs over my eyes, sliding his tongue between my lips, rocking forward to rest solidly at my core. All my senses shorted out as I curled around him, tightening inside. My hearing dimmed, sight snuffed, taste melting on a moan. My fingertips curled like talons on his naked back, and the safety he offered, that steady peace, the barrier between me and the rest of this heartbreaking world swept over me like a gauzy net.

And that was when his need reached in to kindle the remnants of our once-shared aureole. I hadn't known it was possible, but there it was still living between us, sparking to life. What I thought was dead had only been banked, and I saw the same surprised realization flash across Hunter's face before he plunged into me again, mouth and middle, separating those soft places while I simultaneously opened for more.

The connection was like electricity surging across naked distance to collide with a bolt of lightning; one force instantly recognizing the other. Seconds earlier I was wishing he could go deeper, and now he did . . . into my thoughts and knowledge, my experiences and past, the flash of a hard memory causing a tear to fall over his cheek. This both was and wasn't the aureole we'd shared eight months earlier, more of an apparition born of our need, stark black and white line drawings blurring as one rushed into the next.

Our individual memories of the last few months fused to make a new story. My knowledge of how he felt about Marlo's death was no longer empathetic. I owned it now, and gave him my recollection in return, our shared guilt shorting out as the memories repelled one another. There was a flashback from the last time we'd kissed, tucked in the shadows of a boneyard maze, and the power we'd denied then flamed to life now, redoubling itself so we both stiffened in the wake of its current. My memories differed from his only in that they appeared in boldface, but otherwise we shared them, like we were both scales, and the aureole the beam balancing out the raw power streaming through our split pulse.

But it wasn't a bridled thing. The power turned on us suddenly, pulsing and alive, and we groaned together, bartering for breath as those shared memories fragmented into incomplete and current thoughts.

More . . . love this . . . can't stop . . . thank you . . .

And, finally, *Fuck. Now.*

His orgasm drenched me in his aura, I could see it in our joining, and the syllables of my name arched gold across his tongue, into my mouth and down to warm where my bruised heart slammed mercilessly in my chest. When I cried out, sending my red aura channeling across to saturate his soul, it was in the tongue of the same ancient power that caused stars to shatter in the sky, elemental chaos reigning, the rich twining of color trailing behind like the tail of a shooting star.

I opened my eyes in the last moment, Hunter clasped close, and stared at the stars above. Each one looked cocked and ready to shoot. Yet as I gloried in the rightness and oneness and random perfection of an observable universe, I knew even celestial bodies were subject to certain laws. Strongly opposing elements only came together, brightly, because of so many other far-off deaths.

"Your map is fucked up." My voice was disembodied as we lay in the near darkness on that narrow bed, and raw from the yelling I'd done before we made love. Hunter had gone downstairs to retrieve some bottled water—hadn't even gotten shot in the ass by fatal arrows while doing it—but I didn't attempt to escape or follow. I was boneless and numb, parched from my loss of breath and dizzy from the gift of his.

"No," he said, reclining beside me as he took a long swig from his bottle, one strong thigh bent and resting against mine, the other hanging off the bed. "The constellations are correct. The rest are frozen stars."

I glanced back at the sky and only then noted the stars I'd thought were positioned incorrectly were all blazing more brightly than the others. I should have known I'd never catch Hunter making an astronomical mistake. He took the reading of the sky far too seriously. I was a novice, and that was being generous. "Frozen?"

"Black holes. All that's left of giant stars that have evolved, contracted, and died."

I shifted, trying to make out his features, but I was prone, and much of his face was hidden by my pillow. But his silhouette showed he was gazing up at his treasured re-creation. "You track the death of stars?"

"Only the large ones." He paused uncertainly before continuing. His voice rumbled deeply; I could feel it vibrating through the pillow beneath my head. "They have the shortest lives."

I had enough trouble remembering the days of the week on the Western calendar, so while I didn't know exactly what he was talking about, I did detect the sad undercurrent to his whisper. "Why?"

"Why do I track them?" I felt him shift, and nodded. He returned his attention to the heavens with a sigh, but not before I smelled myself on his breath. I warmed again like he was still in me. "The irony, I suppose. The idea that something so enormous, that once gave off such heat and light, can collapse in an instant, with such force and density even light can't escape . . ."

I sat up on my elbow, and did study him now.

His eyes flicked to me, then away again, and he brought his bottled water up to his lips self-consciously. "It fascinates me."

"It should frighten you," I said sharply, because we obviously weren't speaking of frozen stars anymore. Hunter, sensing my mood shift as clearly as if it was his own—and, who knew, it probably was—inched away and didn't answer.

"I don't understand," I finally said, shaking my head as I sank back down, resting as my eye traced the pattern of the black holes. I didn't explain what I meant, but I didn't need to. He'd been so deep inside me he could probably explain me to myself.

"It's simple," he said after a time. "The Light in you is magnified because of your darkness. I'm like a child pressing my nose against a windowpane, seeing the source of the light and wanting to warm myself with it."

"I don't see it."

"Because for you it's like the sun. You're blinded when looking directly at it."

"But for you?"

Warm breath passed again over my skin, then the cool slide of one fingertip tracing my hips. Bumps shot along my thigh, tightened my nipples, raised hairs on my arms. Hunter's whisper was steady as always. "It's like the touch of twilight, a fleeting and beautiful thing. Even now, in the dark, it feels like waves rolling over my ankles. It makes me think a peaceful balance between the two really can exist."

I didn't know what to say to that. I didn't feel beautiful or rare. But I couldn't deny the peace slipping over me, coaxing me to release my questions and sorrows for now, and steal this sliver of time while I could. If I let my vision blur, it even felt like I was floating in that wrongly marked sky, weightless and buoyant amid the remains of dead stars. The power I'd felt before, the aureole obliterating the skin that separated us, was fading. And now, I thought dizzily, I was just tired. So I curled up and finally closed my eyes, drifting off at some point before sunrise, still blind to whatever it was Hunter saw as he continued to stare down at me.

Chandra had been the one to tell Hunter where I was. She'd awoken in the cave at Cathedral Canyon, untied herself in short order—as I knew she would—then hiked back to town, which wasn't as bad as it sounds. She wasn't a star sign, but she could still move four times as fast as any mortal on foot. Once there she'd contacted the one person she knew could save me from myself. I suppose I should've been grateful. If she'd contacted Warren instead of Hunter, I'd be in a secret hospital, unconscious, and wearing someone else's skin by now.

However, I doubt Chandra had predicted this turn of events, I thought, rising to dress at some point the next afternoon. It was Sunday—the day of Kimber's metamorphosis and the doppelgänger's deadline—and I knew I wasn't the only one in Vegas waking with the distressed realization of what they'd done the night before. Despite the aureole we'd shared, and the solace I'd taken in Hunter's bed and body, the morning after any ill-considered knee-jerk response was bound to appear sordid in the light of day. It seemed sadly appropriate that Hunter's makeshift sky had been whitewashed into oblivion in the day's light.

Hunter wasn't stupid; he had to suspect I wasn't making love to him as much as I'd been escaping the haunting image of Ben and Regan together. At least, not at first. Worse, he'd been willing to settle for it, which meant it was less a matter of him taking advantage of me than my exploitation of the perpetual state of hope I knew he lived in. I had exposed that hope. He had let me.

Of course, he also knew the moment I rose from his bed. He didn't try to stop me, though I felt his gaze on my back and heard the bedcovers rustling as he shifted. I didn't want to turn around and risk seeing anger—or worse, foolishness—stamped across those stoic features, but I owed him enough to at least look at him. So steeling myself to the expected hostility, I masked my own features and whirled.

He was sitting up, propped where the two walls met, the white sheet draped over him from navel down, though one leg was bent, exposed from thigh to ankle, his foot disappearing again under the covers. He watched me without blinking, everything he'd done and said the night before naked in those dark eyes. He didn't look ashamed or foolish or apologetic, or anything you'd expect of a man who'd caught a woman sneaking from his bed. And with one short word, he opened to me again.

"Stay."

My knees almost buckled.

"No," I said quietly. I laced up the boots to my ridiculous costume, fingers trembling slightly. "I have to make sure he's okay."

But we both knew I was lying. If there'd even been a chance of Ben being killed or mortally wounded the night before, we would have both worked to save him then. But Regan hadn't been killing him. That wasn't what she'd wanted me to see.

"Why?"

I skipped past the stock replies and straightened to give him the real answer. "He makes me feel soft."

The dark eyes narrowed. "I thought you didn't like that."

But I wanted it all the same, I thought, wincing. How fucked up was that? "There's a strength in being vulnerable."

"I know," he said sharply.

I swallowed hard. He did. He was doing just that by showing me into his workshop via his secret passageway. By lying naked—literally and figuratively—in a bed he'd allowed me to share. By opening his body and mind to me so completely I'd momentarily forgotten myself. But . . . I sighed.

But Ben.

"I know what you're thinking, Jo," Hunter said, his voice so reasonable I was sure he'd rehearsed this during the night. "Peace and quiet sounds good. Some harmless little mortal sounds safe. But it won't satisfy you for long."

I wanted to tell him he didn't know what would satisfy me, but after last night I couldn't even think it. "Don't push me, Hunter. I'm being pushed from too many sides right now, and I don't need it from you."

"No," he said evenly. "It's exactly what you need."

I covered my face with my hands, slumping slightly, just for a moment. "Please. Just stop."

He paused . . . but he didn't stop. "So what do I make you feel, then? Because it's something."

Guilt. Chaos. Divided.

I looked him in the eye, needing to prove I too could be strong and vulnerable at the same time, and thinking the truth would settle things between us once and for all. "Whenever I look at you I feel at war with myself. You make me think of need, like there's something lacking in myself. That, and violence."

He winced before he could help himself, looking sad, like he'd trusted me with something fragile and I'd responded by smashing it at his feet.

"Look, Hunter—" I was reaching toward him, but he squeezed his eyes shut and jerked his head.

"You'll make it worse."

My frozen silence was making it worse anyway. I glanced down at the workshop floor, the organized clutter of tools and chests and tablets and books. Foam templates spilled from his waste bin, crumpled papers drooping over the drawing table and onto the floor. Chandra's arrival had obviously interrupted his work. And he'd dropped everything to come to me.

"You know it's not out there, right?" He huffed humorlessly at my returned look of incomprehension. "The lack you're talking about. It just goes on and on. And one day you'll be cruising along, doing the work you've championed for years, and suddenly it'll rear its head, and your conviction fails. *All this time*, you'll find yourself thinking, *I've been a fool*." I swallowed hard as his gaze skittered past me, unseeing before he blinked. "But when it happens? It's actually a relief. You'll recognize yourself in the mirror again. It's the epiphany you've been seeking laid out right under your nose."

"I don't know what you're talking about," I murmured.

"I'm saying you don't have to do what you've always done," he said, voice snapping sharp. I swallowed hard, and stepped back. "You can just forget, drop off all the memories that make you *you*, and give yourself leave to *feel more*."

"I don't want to forget him."

"You don't want *him* to forget you." He shook his head in disagreement. "You're holding on to a Ben that doesn't exist because you're holding on to a Joanna that no longer exists. *You* don't exist."

I straightened on the spot. "I'm right here!"

"But you're not present! If you were, you'd stay with me!" And he pounded his bare chest so hard the echo thudded through me. He ran a hand over his hair, pulling at it in frustration. "You want everything to be like it used to, but it's okay to change, Jo. Growth doesn't have to be painful. It's natural for a person to change their mind. Even to admit they were wrong." A humorless snort escaped him, but I only stared, and he fell back against the wall again, deflated. When he next spoke, his voice was again soft. "You can even change your heart. You can do it in an instant."

I didn't believe him. Certainly not in this instant. Because *You don't exist* still hung on the air. "Maybe you can. I can't."

"Won't."

"Semantics."

"Truth."

"Hurts!" I countered, yelling suddenly. He should stop. Now.

"Maybe," I said, after a hard swallow, "I just prefer him."

He scoffed, expression shuttering again. "You prefer the idea of him . . . but the white-picket fantasy will never be yours, *Archer.* Your fence will always be coated in blood. Don't drag him into it."

I smirked. "Your concern for him is touching."

"I'm concerned for you."

No. Like everyone else, he was concerned for himself.

"I love him."

The words didn't even faze him. "If you did you'd never have let her near him."

That mobilized me. I clamored down the rickety staircase in haste lest I really think about what he was saying. "I just hope you find someone who feels this strongly about you someday. Then you'll understand."

Let him sulk and scheme alone, I thought, kicking a foam template out of my path as I headed across the vast open space of the warehouse. Because that person couldn't be me. My mind had been made up long ago. It wasn't a matter of just doing something new or dropping treasured memories like they were refuse. It was a matter of following through and sticking it out and making the life you wanted—and *needed*—for yourself. My life. With Ben. Period.

Hunter was at the railing now. I could tell because his voice shot over the empty warehouse like it was fired from his body. "I doubt it. Your *violent need*," he said, throwing my words back at me, "has completely *fucked* me."

I stopped in my tracks, the warehouse too silent after the sure-footedness of my heeled boots. I wanted to keep walking but I couldn't leave him like that, not after what we'd done and shared and knew.

"Don't," he called from over the balcony, a warning and a command. "Don't you look back now."

"But—" I was already half turned and could see his strong naked silhouette from the corner of my eye.

"You've made a commitment with your head and your heart. A backward glance is an apology. And an insult. Better to stick with your bad decisions."

And I *had* made my decision, long before he'd ever come into the picture. So despite the waves of pungent bitterness assailing me from behind, I began walking again. I needed to compartmentalize if I was going to effectively go after

Regan . . . and Ben. I'd bottle this night up and let time wash it away, because there was only one way to fill the lack creating that hole inside me, and it couldn't be accomplished with another man's body.

So I strode out into the crisp autumn day, turning into the chaotic center of my hometown, the sharp scent of Hunter's hostility lessening the farther I walked.

I didn't look back.

27

Regan didn't bother taking Ben hostage. She didn't need to. He'd probably risen like the dead from that coffin-shaped bed and followed the crook of her little finger as she led him away from the chapel and sheets the color of blood. I followed their olfactory trail— rot and smug satisfaction mingling with the scent of their lovemaking, a figurative and conspicuous middle finger in my direction—until his vanished through the threshold of his modest home, and hers disappeared altogether.

She'd gotten what she wanted from him, and injuring him was unnecessary. Not to mention too easy. She'd rather do as her mother had before her, and let the man corrode from the inside out, a slow corruption of his mind that would torture him and me both. And watching him deteriorate, growing shifty-eyed as he began smelling like something rotted and rancid, was much more fun than a swift death. So she'd simply left him at home to sleep off their lovemaking, disease incubating inside him.

I left him there too and headed to the Strip to begin my search for Regan. It was the most populous, transient area of town, and if I were she, this is where I'd hide from me. I started at the north end, closest to the chapel where I'd last seen her, and started walking south. Tourists streamed around me like bright, chattering banners, but I never veered from the stiff, almost militarily precise stride that took me down the center of the walkways, my senses thrown outward, searching, but my gaze straight ahead.

Usually the dusky autumn afternoons distracted me. I always felt on the precipice of something profound in October, like I was walking a tightrope in the thin light between the past and the future, suspended over the unknown. This had never been truer than it was today, but unlike Octobers past, my upended hourglass into the future was now a ticking bomb. And when a breeze swept across the sidewalk in front of Planet Hollywood, skittering leaves and dust from City Center, it was accompanied by a rush of static bristling across the power line overhead. The sharp crackle followed me across Harmon, growing louder until the line sparked and sizzled overhead. When the mortals started noticing it, heads and hands pointed upward, I altered course to end up behind a strip mall composed entirely of souvenir shops. The last grain of sand had fallen in my hourglass. I'd cleared the tightrope safely, and now my unsafe future was here.

A click, more solid than static, sounded behind me.

"You're early," I said, without turning around.

"I'm hungry."

I opened my mouth, the Tulpa's mantra ready to trip from my tongue, but a sliver of sound shot past me and the air between me and the back of the pink stuccoed strip mall splintered like a web. I held my breath lest reality fracture on my exhale.

"Don't even think about it."

I did turn now, and found the doppelgänger dressed like me in dark jeans, a long-sleeved black tee, with a messenger bag slung across her body from her right shoulder. Of course, her dark clothing was relative. Layers and layers of the same mutable substance composed her body and clear face, and her outline now darkened into near-opaqueness, though anyone could still see she wasn't human. Yet her hair no longer bubbled from shaft to end. She'd found my old style and copied it precisely. I was getting so tired of people doing that.

"You're depressed." Her voice no longer rippled in long echoes from that see-through throat, and I wondered how she'd managed to copy my tone, my cadence. Of all things to imitate, voice had to be the hardest.

"I'm tired." And maybe a little depressed. The desire to curl into a fetal position was almost palpable.

"No, it's more than that." She tilted her head, eyes catching in the thin light. Those hadn't changed at least. They still swirled like clouds caught beneath glass. "Could it be because the Shadow Cancer has your mortal lover?"

"Why bother asking the question if you already know the answer?"

She shrugged a slim, muscled shoulder and casually perched a hand on the bag at her side. Like we were just chatting, I thought wryly. As if she wasn't here to kill me. "I wasn't sure you knew about their carnal escapades . . . the way he took her on the park bench. How she opened to him on that rooftop."

I closed my eyes. Regan was "marking" the city so no matter where I went, seeking her, I'd smell them, and I'd know.

"You two collected famous quotes as children, didn't you?"

My eyes flipped open like shades. "How'd you know that?"

She ignored the question, continuing her dramatic monologue. "You swapped them back and forth in a secret language all your own, an ode to the love blossoming between you like a rose. And as we know, 'A Rose by any other name . . .'"

Smartass. I waited for her to finish the quote, but she suddenly looked distracted, head twisting slowly from side to side like she was trying to work out a kink, or dislodge a thought. The drawn-out silence continued until I finally realized that no, it hadn't. Buzzing, so faint at first it was like a swarming hive approaching from a distance, grew louder, but then the doppelgänger shook her head violently, her neck stretching so thin it was no wider than a candy cane. I thought, and was hoping, it'd snap, but then the buzzing dropped off like a switch had been flipped. The doppelgänger's skull righted itself, a bit bobblehead-esque at first, but normal enough once she'd stilled.

"If she hasn't gotten it by now, she won't," she muttered, like someone was standing beside her. She caught my raised brows, and almost looked embarrassed. "Give me your heart."

Surely I'd known it was going to come to this? Otherwise why leave Ben with Regan last night? Why leave Hunter, who could have helped, today? Wandering the world in search of Shadows was only possible if there was still a world to wander, and sacrificing myself was the only way to ensure that. So I'd go down in the manuals as a hero, my death would return Jasmine's *chi* to her in full, and it would certainly put a definitive ending to the question of the suspected "rise of my Shadow side."

Still, fighting to the death was one thing, but simply lying down and submitting? I'd sworn that off a decade ago. "I don't know why you can't just tell me the answer to your riddle. A sense and a referent. One noun, two aspects. Especially now, when you're going to kill me anyway."

It'd be nice to know what—other than the city's survival—I was dying for.

"That's right. You don't know. That's exactly the problem." As she took a step closer, the planes of her cheeks rippled, then settled into an unsettlingly familiar upward curve. *One last viewing, and she'll have you.* "Look, if I could have told you before now, don't you think I would have? You'd have figured it out long ago, we'd both have what we need. But like anyone, my actions must speak for themselves."

"Your actions?" I scoffed, unable to help myself. "Well, let's see. You're unforgivably careless with the vibration of matter, and you want to kill me just so you can gain more power. So, all in all, your actions tell me you're no different than the Tulpa."

She froze at the insult, lips trembling slightly before they clamped shut. I stared at her. She stared back. Oddly, it went on this way for a while. When I still said nothing, she finally sighed. "I can't wait any longer. I *am* sorry."

The static sounded again, which would've been telling if I'd recognized it early enough. Before that could happen I was sprawled on my back, breath knocked from my chest, shocked that someone who had yet to take full corporeal form could weigh so much. The doppelgänger's eyes glittered as they bored into mine, then raced over my face, seeing past the breathy, soft Olivia exterior to what was beneath. There was a slight adjustment to her nose, I saw it shift and stick, her heart-shaped chin squaring, the eyes deepening. When they darkened, the clouds disappearing in a pupil of black—literally the eye of the storm—I knew I was fucked.

She licked her lips, and I saw her teeth had squared in her mouth, the middle two slightly crooked, but only if you knew to look. I swallowed hard. Almost there. Almost me.

"I know it doesn't seem like it, but I really am on your side. I have been all along. But another agent of Light will figure it out. Eventually." She sighed, like she was imagining things differently, then sighed again. "Maybe it's like that mask. It's just too close to your face to see it clearly."

I turned my head to find the animist's mask sprawled right next to me. I hadn't yet gotten a chance to return it to Xavier's and had forgotten I even had it with me until now. It must have fallen out of my bag when she'd tackled me, and it stared up at the sky of splintered reality like it saw something I couldn't.

I had a thought, smiled slightly, and gazed at the fragile webbing above us, as if at the same spot the mask had pinpointed. The doppelgänger, looming over me, frowned. Then she turned her head to see what I did, which gave me my chance. "You can eat my heart, but you're not going to become me."

I'd had enough of people doing that, and I slapped the mask over my face before she could turn back around.

I jerked beneath her, head flying back to hit the concrete with the g-force of pure chaotic violence. The doppelgänger howled above me, but the mask was already fusing greedily to my skull. The synthesis happened in the snap of fingers, and colors too bright to see swirled behind my lids like whipping snakes. I couldn't see out, and felt for a moment like I couldn't breathe either. I concentrated on that alone, breathing in and out, and eventually the dizziness lessened, colors fading until I was deathly calm and the mask only pulsed gently against my cheeks.

Then it all ceased, and this time there was no vision, no dream, to replace it. My mind was whitewashed, shallow breathing echoing loudly in my ears, punctuating the silence, my thoughts lost even from myself.

"Olivia?" the doppelgänger asked, then "Joanna?"

"What?" Hollow . . . like the mask.

"What do you see?"

She meant what did I think about what I saw . . . but I saw nothing. "J-just so you know, you can't remove this mask. It has adhered to my face." Better. Almost like myself.

"No shit," she said, her weight shifting as she fell back on her heels. "Not until the trapped stream-of-consciousness has played your future out in full. After that it will release, and I can look until my little heart is content . . . no pun intended."

But her black humor didn't interest me. It was what she'd said before that, revealing a purpose to the animist's mask that no one had correctly guessed.

"It tells the future," I whispered. But that meant my future was blank. I sat in the silent wake of those punishing sheets of light, in total solitude, without even thoughts to keep me company. I'd seen destruction to the city before, death to the inhabitants, my troop, the being on top of me, along with the Tulpa and my mother. So maybe that had changed? Either I was really going to die now, or maybe . . . "It's mine to write."

Or rewrite. I took a deep breath, and thought back on the chain of events since I'd last donned the mask, all the things that could have altered the destiny I'd viewed before. The past twenty-four hours alone was enough to send me reeling. There was my visit with Zane, discovering Ben with Regan at the chapel, my night with Hunter, and the single-minded search for Regan that had finally landed me here. I recalled, and followed, my own progress down the Boulevard, and when the static overtook me this time, I let go of the thought thread, and freefell into my own mind.

Lightning punched a blackened desert floor and I was streaming out to Cathedral Canyon, meeting the others for Kimber's metamorphosis, biting down on ozone as the world readied for another star sign. Next I flashed to an image of me standing over the fractured gorge, buffeted by the vibrations of impending violence, much of which I would cause. It went on this way until the blank slate reappeared, and my future lay unwritten again. Then my breath again filled my ears, harsh and rattling, but not with fear this time. With excitement. I glanced up, and this time I could see out the slits of the mask to the wide, blackened eyes staring back at me.

"Oh," I whispered, as my fingers blindly found the mask again. But what I meant to say was *Oh fuck*. Because I knew then who had set the doppelgänger on me. I knew it like I knew my own name.

The mask released me with an audible snap. The doppelgänger reached for it.

"Not so fast, Hannibal."

I slipped the mask from my face myself, easy now that it'd already told me its story, and ran a hand over my sweat-dampened hair. "What would you say if I told you the third sign of the Zodiac was about to come to pass?"

She didn't look as impressed as I thought she should, and smiled wickedly, teeth bared. "Same as before . . . I'm hungry."

I smiled back. "And I'd say come and get it."

It took some time—too much of it—to collect what I needed and put my plan into action. Namely, one Zell Trexler, for whom we had to wait for over an hour before he came sauntering around the back of Master Comics, a freshly lit cigarette flaring between his lips. The smoke only blunted his senses for a second, but if I'd had my conduit with me it would've been enough to kill him. In the next second, his head shot up and his hand found his ax, which he could fling with such deadly accuracy I quickly jerked back behind the illegally parked van where I'd been hiding. Fortunately, due to the prophecy that he was to die at my hands, my disembodied voice was all the weapon I needed. "Thank God you're here. I was afraid the Tulpa really had tipped you off."

The cigarette was discarded, red ash burning down to nothing in the gutter. "Tipped—?"

"He told me about your little penchant for frightening the changelings as they leave the building," I interrupted. "You're such a dick."

"I'm brokenhearted that you think so," he said, sounding more like himself. Defensive, but still arrogant. "I suppose you're looking to score another meeting with Daddy, huh? Too bad he's no longer taking your calls."

Because, I knew, the Tulpa had what he wanted. He'd given me the mantra that would trap the doppelgänger, call him to finish her off, and place me in servitude from now until eternity's end. Using it would be icing on his cake-o'-death. Still, I had to be sure.

"I guess I'll have to use his answering machine like everyone else."

Zell just scoffed as he backed down the alley, returning the way he came.

"Hold up. What's the rush, Zell? Hot date?" I tapped my fingers on the hood of the car so he could tell I hadn't moved. "Just remember, bite the pillow and you'll be fine."

"Fuck off," he shot back, unable to help himself. "You only wish you knew."

Which told me all I needed to know. "Oh, but I already do. Haven't you heard? The Tulpa's given me a way to join the Shadows." I peered through over the driver's side mirror to find him looking skeptical, though he was no longer moving away. "I thought I could ride with you to the rendezvous point for tonight's ambush."

He was silent for so long that if I were still hidden, I'd have thought he really had left. But I was watching, and saw the uncertainty, followed by resignation, creep over his face. "How 'bout I just give you directions?"

"That's nice of you," I said, my tone companionable.

Zell sneered in his reply. "I'm bighearted that way."

"But I'd rather come with you anyway. It's a long drive, I could use the company . . . and you drive a Prius, right? So practical."

"No."

"Hm, that almost sounded definitive." Taking a chance, I did step into view now. His eyes traveled over my body, encased in unrelieved black, and lingered on my mask. "I guess I'm going to have to force you."

"Force me? Honey, you don't even have a conduit anymore, and by the way, Regan has been bragging for days about the way she tricked you into attacking a mortal. You're the laughingstock of the Shadow side."

That did it.

"You're right," I said after a moment, voice deadly soft as I lowered my head, stepping closer. "I no longer have a conduit . . . but I do have a friend with very sharp teeth."

The doppelgänger landed so softly behind him, he didn't even hear her. But as he turned again to leave, her grin verified my claim. "How big did you say that heart was?"

28

Despite Zell's resistance—his conduit, his cries, his fists, his blood—my next great feat actually took longer . . . probably because I couldn't just whip Chandra into doing what I asked. I found her huddled over a microscope at the Sky-Chem drug testing facility, her cover in the mortal world and where she snuck in on the weekends to do the reconnaissance we needed while not surrounded by curious coworkers and bossy supervisors.

I knew she'd be here, distracting herself with work to keep her mind off where the rest of the troop was, what we were doing, and how badly she wanted to be a part of it. It was for that last reason only that I eventually succeeded in convincing her to go along with my plan.

"It's too risky," she still argued, but she was locking up as she said it.

"It's the best way, Chandra. And if we succeed, *when* we do, we'll have done something previously unimagined. We'll topple a troop." I smiled grimly as she turned to face me. "It'll be in manuals in every city the world over."

"I don't care about that!" she snapped so quickly I almost believed her. I kept silent as she whirled away, afraid one more word would have her reaching to call Warren . . . and then I really would have to hurt her.

She paced, biting her bottom lip, running her hand through her hair so much it stood up like a troll doll's. Finally she jerked her head, and I followed her to the parking lot for the long drive to Cathedral Canyon.

Blue Diamond Road was markedly different at night than during the day, and as we left the city glittering behind us, we fell off into disembodied blackness, only the cab of our car lit by the steady glow of our console, silence as deep as the night.

I'd once thought myself a stranger to darkness. Growing up in a twenty-four-hour town was a lot like going to bed with the ultimate nightlight on. Sure, there were untouched parcels of desert still sunk like inky pockets within the sprawling city boundaries, and the terrain surrounding that shiny core fell away abruptly into an inflexible vacuum of time and space, but that only made Vegas appear all the more like an island unto itself. Because on that island was undying luminosity. You could make your way across the valley simply by following landmark after shining landmark alone.

I first went camping when I was seven, an event fueled by my own incessant nagging and questions about why we never left town on family trips. Of course, now I knew why. As a full-fledged Zodiac member my mother could no longer physically cross state lines, or even enter another town, but she did her best to fulfill my wish, taking us to a campground in mountains I didn't know existed so close to the desert. The camping trip was a resounding success, but on the way back I cowered in the backseat of the car as we hurtled into a darkness cut only by the beam of our headlights. Olivia slept soundly beside me, her breathing drowned out by the speed of our wheels on the asphalt road, and the report of other cars as they rocketed by us in the opposite direction. I watched them disappear through the back window, their taillights growing smaller until they popped like the dot on an old television and disappeared completely. It was, I remember thinking, as if they'd never been. There were houses in those mountains too. I saw a chimney smoking, a strong rooftop peeking out from the firs, and the occasional light winking in some far-off window, looking lonely and too isolated to stand for long.

"Why," I had asked my mother, greatly concerned when we passed yet another one of these disturbing homes, "do these people live in the dark?"

"Humans are creatures of habit," my mother said, her voice a comfort in that small heated space. "People do what they know, what they've always done, because it's a comfort to them. Perhaps they live in a dark place because that's where their parents lived, and their grandparents, and theirs before them."

"I would never live in the dark. No matter where you used to live."

She turned in her seat, hands upon the wheel, the lights from the dashboard illuminating half her face, lengthening the amused smile that lingered there. "Yes, but if you were born in darkness, born *to* darkness, you wouldn't know the difference."

"I'd know there was no light," I said, as she turned back around. I heard a sigh stream from her chest.

"The absence of a thing doesn't tell you about its nature, Joanna. Its lack robs you even of a comparison. You'd have no idea what you were missing; you'd only know that there was . . ." She paused, searching for the right word, then gestured to the landscape hidden beyond the sweep of our headlights. "A void."

"A void?" I repeated, frowning, not sure of the word, much less if I agreed. But my mother was wrong about few things. "Well, do you think people who live in the dark want some light?"

I couldn't see her face, just the outline of her shoulders as she slumped against her seat and stared out into the night. Her voice, however, went soft, almost like she was afraid of the sound. There was no force behind the words, as if whispering them would keep them within the confines of this car.

"Yes, Joanna," she murmured. "They covet the light more than anything."

It was one of those answers a child was ever frustrated in understanding. One of the ones that, if pushed, would be explained away with an unsatisfying *You'll understand when you're older.* I knew I was missing something important, something she wouldn't explain to me, and that made me sulk.

"Well, I'm never going to live in the dark. I'll live in Las Vegas forever!"

She turned again, and this time her face was absent of all humor. "No matter where you live or how many street-lamps there are, no matter how many hours of sunlight there are in the day, or neon bulbs torching the skyline, every place at one time or another is touched by darkness. And every person."

Well, she knew better than most, I thought, as Chandra and I hurtled forward on a similar journey. A lesser person would've been consumed by all that darkness too. I couldn't help wondering what would've happened to me, what path I'd have chosen, if I'd been through all my mother had before me.

At least I knew Warren was right. My mother *was* still out there. Somewhere. She was working to do what she could to help the troop, and me, fight the Tulpa. And she'd go on doing it too, all the way up until her death. I would do the same, I swore, fists clenching on my thighs. Even if that death was only minutes away.

It didn't matter how warm it was on any given October day, by the time midnight came around, the desert air crept in like an invisible fog to send residents and tourists alike scurrying for the indoors, its icy fingers pulling the heat

from the city's sizzling lights as it swept through the
streets. It was even colder out where the wild desert air
originated, the brittle breeze snapping over cacti and
bramble in the same way reality could snap in the palm of
an uncaring being.

It was this thought, more than the biting cold, that
caused me to shiver as I stepped from Zell's car at Cathedral Canyon. The other agents of Light were already
waiting in the shimmering little gorge, the scent of their
initial impatience crowded out by a greater worry, and finally relief as I appeared over the lip of the ridge. Just as
I'd seen in the mask four hours earlier.

"I'd have called," I told Warren as he met me at the top
of the rickety wooden staircase, "but you said no cells."

We only spoke about these locations face-to-face, usually in the safety of the sanctuary. The life of the agent
being reborn into their star sign depended on the security
of that information. During the metamorphosis itself, the
rest of the Zodiac troop also formed a circle around him or
her, partly for ceremony's sake, but mostly for additional
protection. The circle had been breached before, and if my
mental dip into the future was right, it would be breached
again tonight.

"We'll talk about this later," Warren said impatiently.
"Here are your robes. The others are already waiting."

I ignored the censure in his voice and draped the robes
over my arm as I wordlessly made my way down the zigzagged staircase. It was a time for picking battles, and I
needed to save my energy for the one to come.

Tekla was overseeing the troop formation and Kimber
was already centered in the widest part of the canyon, the
initiate's gold robe shimmering spectacularly even among
the chips of stained glass and stars. Everyone else was robed
in white, and I slipped mine over my head as I passed by
Hunter . . . not a coincidence. It would be hard to face him
at any time, but right now I had to focus. I halted on the
spot indicated by Tekla, immediately recognizing that we

were arranged in the order of the Zodiac wheel. First came Hunter, the Aries, joined next by Warren, our Taurus. Then Jewell, Gregor, and Vanessa, all evenly spaced and somber. Micah was next, though there was a large gap next to him where Kimber would stand as the new Libra when her metamorphosis was complete. Tekla and I were followed by Felix and Riddick, with the empty Piscean spot our only weakness. Warren had been trying to fill it for months, and I eyed the dusty ground nervously. It was the one spot that could be tested.

"Star signs, draw the line of defense."

Every fist, save Warren's and mine, suddenly held a weapon; a whip, military fork, mace, clawed hand fan, surgeon's steel, palm-sized grapnel, edged boomerang, and a shiny new dental saw. Warren hadn't used a weapon beyond his own body and mind for years, ever since he'd had to draw down on his own father. But I slipped my hand beneath my robe . . . and pulled out the animist's mask instead.

Jewell, opposite me, was the first to notice. "Olivia, what are you doing?"

One by one the other star signs turned my way. I glanced up as the roof of the sky suddenly lowered, cirrus clouds clamoring for prime spots over the little canyon. "Putting on the only weapon I'm going to need."

Though I was expecting the kick of power this time, the mask still knocked me back a few steps as it bound itself to my skull. Pure power pooled through my temples, divining my purpose, my expectations, my future actions . . . starting with those I'd take in the next second. I relaxed, calming the breath as it ran through my body, and waited for the chaos to settle. Finally the inner world fell silent and the slate blank. Power rumbled through the canyon, but that was only the thunder gathering overhead, sending ozone to slip through the mouth hole and lick at my lips.

As much as I wanted to, I couldn't tell the troop what I was seeing. The future assailing me behind the mask was too near, and it'd be too easy for them to lose perspective. The same sort of revelation was what made amateur fortune-tellers and going to psychics so dangerous. It wasn't that their advice was evil or wrong, but even the right information doled out in the wrong moment led to poor decision making, or in some cases, no decision at all. The agents of Light needed to *act,* and do so in unyielding agreement according to the knowledge they *currently* possessed, and no more. If the vision in the mask was to come true, I had to be careful about exactly how much I revealed.

Yet my pulse jumped once my vision cleared and I caught the stares of disdain and surprise—coupled with a skein of burgeoning fear—all of which made me itchy with the need for action. But it wasn't time; it wasn't the kairotic moment. Not yet.

Kimber's somber piety fled her and her head snapped up over the golden cowl of her robe, hood slipping back so her hair looked star white in the deepening night. "Goddammit, she's trying to make this about her!"

"I've already metamorphosed once and it was enough, thank you." They couldn't view my scowl behind the mask, but it couldn't stifle the sarcasm.

"Then what are you doing, Olivia?" Tekla said sharply. "Metamorphosis is a sacred ceremony requiring the troop to act as one. You're to do what you're told, remain in formation, and never, ever act or speak out of turn!"

"Uh-huh," I said absently, as color flared behind my eyelids. The mask was agitated, fate momentarily unwritten— destiny up in the air—but then it settled and I breathed a sigh of relief. As the blinders of the future lifted, I swiveled to regard Tekla. "Do you happen to have the time?"

"*What?*"

"Never mind." I glanced up at the sky to find a perfectly formed hole in the clouds, a funnel revealing a ringed moon on the high side. The air was thicker than it'd been even a minute ago, and farther off, a giant nexus of thunder began rolling our way. Time, and other fluid, manipulative elements, were drawing nearer. Deciding to err on the side of caution, I put my fingers to my lips and sent a piercing whistle knifing through the canyon.

"Are you nuts?" Felix asked, from my other side. "Do you want the world to know we're out here?"

"Which world?" I muttered darkly, as I lifted my head to the two figures stepping onto the lip of the ridge above us. Feeling the air current, sensing the motion, the rest of the troop whirled as well.

"Chandra?" said Micah, because she wasn't supposed to be here.

"Archer?" Warren growled, demanding an explanation through the question. Again, as one, the troop whirled my way.

"You told us to partner up." I shrugged. "So we have."

Chandra managed a nervous smile as she held tight to the bound Shadow agent, but I could see she was already faltering. I'd only told her enough to convince her to help me, but even that would doom us if she revealed it too soon. Zell groaned, eyes edging my way before rolling to white. His shirt was a mess, ripped and bloodied from his earlier struggle against us, and his labored breathing infused the air with the acrid scent of his pain in sharp, floating puffs.

"This is a metamorphosis," Tekla said lowly, and her outrage seeped like oil into the briny air. "It's not meant as a kill spot."

"No, but as you know they're sometimes one and the same," I answered just as coldly.

There were a handful of gasps, and Tekla blanched at the untimely reminder of her son's death. Despite her shocked wobble, I kept my eye on her. She had more usable power in her pinky finger than I did in my entire body.

"You're grandstanding," she managed in a ragged whisper.

"I'm not." Without taking my gaze from Tekla's, I said, "Tell them, Zell."

Zell swallowed hard, like his throat was working against the rest of his body, and blood bubbled from the side of his mouth as his eyes rolled again. "They're coming," he croaked.

"Who . . . ?"

But the chaos I'd been privy to in the confines of the mask suddenly made itself known in a resounding crack, and the thick sky still gathering to welcome Kimber into the Zodiac was rent apart by a new splintering power. And when every single glyph in the circle flared to life, they all knew *who*.

Kimber whimpered in the center of our circle, her face turned toward the unnatural roil of smoke as it filled in the gaps between the battered clouds. The furious expression that'd met my appearance was gone, and in its place was stark, palpable fear. "Oh God."

"Stay centered." Warren put a hand on her shoulder as she started to move, but removed it immediately. Ozone was gathering around her, and enough elemental power would soon assault her body that it could kill even him. There was nothing she could do, and nowhere to run or escape. At her moment of metamorphosis she'd be frozen where she stood, easy pickings for the swarm headed our way. And it was too late anyway. The clouds pinpointed her location, revealing her existence to the heavens . . . and anyone else who might be watching. "And stay low. It'll be better that way."

"But the Shadows . . ."

The Shadows appeared over the ridge of the bright little canyon, glyphs smoking on their chests as they circled us in a living ring. We turned outward as one, backs toward Kimber, moving in as tightly as we could. There were a number of Shadows I'd never seen in person before, ones who'd gradually taken the place of the four I'd sent to an early grave. Ronan was the new Aries who, for some reason, had an affection for dressing as a modern-day pirate. Too much Jack Sparrow in his cinematic diet, I gathered. Harrison was the Shadow Virgo, and like Ajax before him, he had a build to match his slim, sharp weapon, a fencing sword. En garde. Little was known about the Aquarian, Tariq, who, as the Shadows' newest member, had replaced my former mortal enemy. On the other hand, I knew everything I needed to about the Piscean Shadow. I'd encountered Adele spiking the drink of a sorority sister weeks earlier, then setting the poor girl loose in a notorious "gentlemen's club." She'd obviously escaped me then, but not unscathed. The new limp would've gone better with Ronan's disguise.

Regan had taken up the five o'clock position, and though her stance widened, her arms were crossed as if the outcome of this contest had already been decided. Yet, as alert as I was to her presence, nothing about her called to me, and I knew she hadn't brought my conduit. She wouldn't risk losing it to me or her ally agents, who wouldn't hesitate to seize the opportunity to steal it from her. The chance to erase the Kairos's existence from the earth was too great to resist. Yet, in the next pulse-pounding moment, even that concern, along with Regan, was forgotten.

He appeared directly opposite Chandra, positioning himself above the statue of the Christian savior . . . and well above all of us. This time he wore the flesh suit of an absentminded college professor, his day-old stubble and haphazard hair accented by loafers, a vest, and the expression of someone who'd just looked up from a particularly engrossing text. It was all at once thoughtful, faraway . . . and calculating.

If he were mortal, I thought, he would've been called slight and almost considered handsome. But with liquid power causing his hair to stand on end and kindling his eyes into fiery silver and onyx globes, what he looked was invincible.

"Well, what have we here?" His voice was almost gentle. "A familiar scenario, it seems. An agent of Light, about to kneel before me."

Lightning drilled into the dry ground next to Kimber, searching for her, and she yelped while the rest of us drew closer, the bolt jumping like an electrical current to run through the tight circle, tying us together in purpose. In duty.

In the kairotic moment.

The Tulpa laughed . . . and I inhaled deeply, swallowed hard, and stepped forward, breaking the circle.

"Joanna, no!" Though he barked out the order, Warren was careful to use my real name in front of the Shadows, but the air around me still shook with the shock of my ally agents. My identity beneath Olivia's soft shell had been a mystery among our agents from the first, so they couldn't help themselves. The air was so heavy with storm clouds and humidity you could almost take a bite out of the emotion, and I knew the Tulpa felt their surprise because of it . . . and because he laughed again.

"Another secret revealed among the troop." He lifted his leg as if to take a step from the gorge's rim . . . and gently floated to the canyon floor instead. His flesh looked like a lustrous silver parachute, unlined and glowing, as midnight air rustled his clothes. Once his feet touched ground, he asked, "How long before the new mole inside your sanctuary shares it with us?"

"There's no one else," Micah said, calling his bluff.

"So confident," said the Tulpa, tilting his head, electric eyes firing. "So sure. I guess that makes you suspect number one."

"There's no one else," Warren said, backing Micah up, and I wondered if he was even aware of how the circle tightened around Kimber at his words, with me on the outside. No one seemed to note it, though. No one but the Tulpa.

"Ah, except for the sole agent who remains now, as always, divided between us."

"I'm not divided anymore."

"Step back, Joanna," Tekla commanded, deliberately

making room for me next to her. It temporarily loosened the ring, creating an obvious breach among them, though the Piscean gap between Riddick and Hunter still stood out more. Even linked, there was nothing they could do about that, and I knew the Shadows, whispering and shifting up on the canyon's rim, saw it too. Adele, as the opposing Pisces, would be particularly drawn to it.

A second bolt of lightning suddenly speared at Kimber's feet, sizzling as it lifted the hairs on our bodies, showing off the depths of its immense power, though it was just the warm-up act. I closed my eyes, steadied myself on a breath, then looked straight at the Tulpa.

"No." The dense air thickened even more. I licked my lips and tasted sky. "As you said, Tekla, this is not a time for grandstanding. But it isn't just a metamorphosis either. This is the third sign of the Zodiac come to pass. Tonight marks the rise of my dormant side."

The ring instantly tightened around Kimber, my spot again swallowed by their bodies.

"I know what fate awaits me at the end of this night, and where my future lies." I chose my words carefully, raising my voice so it could be heard over the storm already railing above us. By the time those swollen clouds broke it'd be too late. "While my fellow troop members have seen only success through the eyes of this mask, I see the truth."

The Tulpa smiled wryly. "You figured it out."

I waited until the sky had finished crackling. "What? That you've planted masks all over the city to draw on the power of the public?" Shrugging, I lied. "It was easy."

"Tell that to Warren."

I did. "It's how he's been getting energy," I said, though it looked like Warren had figured that one out for himself. "At one time he would've forced people to don the masks, stealing their soul essence to yield energy for his animation, but he knew you'd be looking for that. What you *wouldn't* be looking for was a souvenir sold in the Valhalla gift shop, one worn to every Las Vegas event imaginable."

One quick phone call to Janet had confirmed all the masks worn at last month's Swingers' Ball had been generously donated by the Valhalla gift shop. And all the power in the wearer's thoughts and emotions and soul had been ferried right back to the Tulpa.

"All this time . . ." Warren began.

But time was short. I looked up as the sky fell unnaturally still, and even though the clouds could be seen spinning and roiling via the bolts firing within, the silence was the same that waylaid the land before a tsunami. So I kept my eyes on the sky, and finished for him.

"All this time mortals have been wearing these masks willingly, their vitality leached from their body in bundled packages of soul power. They'd stumble home in a fog, wondering why they had a headache at the end of the night—if they'd drunk too much, if it was just jet lag, or if it was Vegas working its late night magic." Still others, like Xavier, put on the masks in worship, and who knew how many of those willing victims were out there, giving up bits of their soul they could ill afford to miss? "But an animist's mask, like this one, is even more powerful. This is a weapon that was designed with superheroes in mind, right?"

The Tulpa inclined his head, and in that same unnervingly gentle voice, took up the telling. The absentminded professor schooling us all. "It shows an agent of Light exactly what they hope to see of the future. It gets them to let down their guard, then it feeds their thoughts directly to me."

Now Chandra, who'd stolen the mask, looked guilty, and Warren looked positively ill. He'd willingly donned the mask, and from the way he began to sway, I had a feeling it was more than once. He'd certainly done so after choosing Cathedral Canyon as the site for Kimber's metamorphosis, thus the Tulpa's appearance here. The only thing to be thankful for was that the mask only revealed the future, not the past. Otherwise the Tulpa would already know of my transformation into Olivia, and I wouldn't be standing here now, alive, the only one still able to spin lies and hide thoughts.

Hunter was the first to find his voice after I'd explained all this to them. "Why did the mask adhere to your face? Why'd it choose you to reveal the future to?"

"Because you're the Kairos?" Micah guessed.

"Because you're part Shadow?" said Regan from the ridge.

"No." Though those things were undoubtedly a part of it. "Because I'm the only one in a position to do something about it."

The Tulpa began to laugh, his voice no longer gentle as it boomed over the canyon to equal the power of the thunder roiling above. "Your position, darling, is at the bottom of a canyon, surrounded by enemies, with no conduit, and a troop of agents facing imminent death. Or so I saw from this end."

"And when's the last time you checked?" I snapped, unable to help myself. "Fates can change quickly . . . and I'm the only one wearing a mask now."

"And what, pray tell, do you see?"

"I see, I see," I sang in a childhood rhyme, before my voice fell to a growling scratch. ". . . something bloody."

The energy in the mask wobbled, the Tulpa's spike of concern a sudden factor. It was too early yet for either of us to act, so I whirled to face Warren, again playing the traitor's card. "I'm sorry, but our fate is already written. I told you the first time I put this thing on that destruction awaits the agents of Light."

Micah whirled toward the top ridge, and the woman he'd counted as his closest friend. "And Chandra? You're helping her?"

Chandra couldn't look at him. "Trust me . . . it's for the best."

"Chandra's the one who told me I had to respect that biology has made me different," I said, because we could all sense her wavering. "She's the one who made me face the consequences of my Shadow side."

"So it seems you *do* have some betrayers in your troop after all." The Tulpa's grin widened so far it was beyond normal, and no longer handsome. "My daughter and the girl you betrayed for her. Too bad your Kairos is really my Kairos."

I shook my finger in his direction like I was chiding one preschooler for swatting at another. "Not so fast. Shadows never do anything unless there's a trade involved. If I'm to come stand at your side, I want something in return."

"Name it."

"I will," I said, smiling at his word choice. "So . . . anything?"

His inclining head fell well short of a nod, the only outward sign of his hesitancy. "You're my daughter. I want you on my side."

"Yet there's something else you want more, isn't there?" I said, and he suddenly looked less comfortable, though he hadn't moved at all. I had to risk it, though. A mean game of push-and-shove would be more believable than a total and abrupt turnaround. Changing the subject before he could answer, I feigned ease. "Well, this mask has shown me that if things go your way, five minutes from now the entire troop of Light will be nothing more than a memory, but at least one of your agents will die with them. It'll either be Zell . . ."

And here Chandra pulled out Zell's ax and pointed the weapon at his back.

"Or Regan."

I saw her jolt on the shelf above us, her mouth falling open before she knew what she wanted to say. Her attempt to catch the Tulpa's eye failed because his were glittering excitedly, pinned on me.

"Trades are always tricky, and fraught with risk. Zell believes himself destined to die at your hands anyway. He almost deserves the fate; a belief that strong can only come to pass. Why would I exchange a perfectly solid star sign for him?"

Exactly the question I wanted him to ask. The mask hid my smile, and I held my breath until I was sure I could neutralize my voice. "Because Regan knows who I am beneath this mask. Beneath all my masks. She's known my secret identity for months. She just hasn't shared it with you."

Truth rode over some people like a stampede. Confusion marred their brows like new thoughts were trying to break out in Braille over their foreheads. Then their expressions, their bodies, would slacken with lost hope. Yet other people, those who held little hope to begin with, didn't move at all when their ideals were shattered, and not surprisingly, the Tulpa was this latter sort. Minus the "people" part. Because no mortal's bone would've flashed like quicksilver to match his eyes, his hair, the nails that had spontaneously lengthened into honed points beyond the silvered skin.

Black mist, opaque against the stormy desert night, formed in half a dozen tendrils snapping to wrap around Regan's body. They coiled like sinewy lassoes, jerked her half a foot into the air, and tightened so quickly, the plea forming on her lips was thrust from her body in a terrified gasp.

"Come." It was said almost sweetly.

Rain began to drench the tiny canyon as Regan floated to him, like rope drawn through a pulley designed of his will.

"You've been given an inordinate amount of freedom, Ms. DuPree. From the time you were small it seemed to have been an expectation of yours. I blame your mother for that. How fitting that we should be reminded twice in one night that despite a matriarchal hierarchy, the mother's lineage *isn't* always dominant."

"Let me explain—"

"It's a lucky turn of events for the Archer, but . . ." He raised one pronged hand in the air. "Not so much for you."

With a mere jerk of his wrist, the coiling mist yanked from Regan's body, taking her clothes with it. The bonds dissolved immediately, and her clothes fell haphazardly across the dusty ground, like they'd tried to run off on their own. Before shock could set in at her nakedness, before she could even cover herself, the Tulpa also began stripping her of her identity.

Literally.

Raking his fingers through the air, the man who'd been dreamed into being flayed a woman born of this world. Five solid slashes formed down the front of her body like thick paper cuts, from her hairline all the way to the cracks between her toes. She went stock-still, momentarily wide-eyed, until the skin lifted and began to curl back from all edges on her face and body and limbs. Even her screams turned tattered, the cut muscles of her throat causing the sound to overlap in deep and anguished waves, while the Tulpa only watched, his face again lengthening into that unnaturally wide grin. He gave another finger wave, and muscle tore from bone.

"You took a vow—all of you!—to follow me and obey me in exchange for my patronage and power." Despite the pattering rain and rising wind and twisting bolts firing above our heads, despite Regan's screams of agony, the Tulpa's voice remained conversational, slipping around us from every side. The ultimate ventriloquist's trick. I hated it when he did that. "Have I let you down in some way? Have I not delivered all I promised and more? Have I failed to bring the agents of Light to their knees time and again?"

"No!" The Shadows yelled it as one, living up to their name, nothing more than a series of blurred outlines above us. Their sole distinguishing feature was the smoke billowing from their chests, refusing to be extinguished in the heightening torrent.

"No . . ." Regan's pain-filled wail sounded a moment too late, a belated attempt to return to her leader's good graces despite the flesh hanging from her in ribbons.

"Then please recall that while your service to me is voluntary," he said to the rest of the troop while he continued gazing at her like she was a beetle under his boot, "once committed, your loyalty is not."

He beckoned a final time, and Regan screamed until her vocal cords either snapped or split, and even the thunder couldn't drown out the fracturing of all two hundred and six bones in her body.

I wanted to look away. The mask had merely revealed a truncated version of these events; it hadn't shown the blood puddling beneath her bare heels or the carved organs peeking through her pink, tattered skin, or the way dust and grime and rain pummeled that brutalized flesh, each drop of rain a world of agony on its own.

"Vanity is something I normally endorse. But yours, Ms. DuPree, has been your downfall."

Her downfall, but not her death. She wouldn't expire from these injuries . . . but she wouldn't recover from them either.

"Lindy. Dawn. Escort Regan to the other side of the ravine."

"Halfway is fine," I said, unable to hide my revulsion. He smiled.

Despite the carnage done to her body, of the humiliation of being reduced to nothing more than a lesson in subservience, and of the downright cruelty of his actions, Regan began to shake as she found herself suddenly flanked. "Sir, if you'll just let me—"

"One more word and I'll rip that lying tongue from your mouth with my teeth."

The only sound she made after that was a soft squeal as her two guards grasped her tattered wrists. Chandra leaped from the canyon's edge to drop with Zell behind me, and I almost began to breathe normally beneath my wooden guise. It was going to work.

Yet as Regan neared, the mask surprised me by flaring to life. Something was fluid in this situation again. Some decision had been made that could put my plans in jeopardy.

Wishing for my conduit despite its absence in the mask's vision, I glanced sharply at Regan, but she was beyond any ability to form expression or thought, her glassy eyes fixed on Dawn. The Shadow Gemini had paused, searching the discarded clothing long enough to locate Regan's conduit. She laughed as she threw the ice pick at the Tulpa's feet, and Regan jolted, though her gasp was lost in a clap of thunder. I couldn't help but empathize. I knew how it felt to have your conduit taken from you. It was like losing a limb.

I was watching Regan so closely, I almost missed the stare of the other Shadow, Lindy, as she and Dawn dragged the former Cancer closer. The mask suddenly sang to me in colors, obscuring my peripheral vision and admitting a sound as shrill as a home alarm. This wasn't good.

I widened my stance, readied for a physical attack, but gasped when Lindy's hooded eyes met mine. Thank God the mask concealed emotion as well as thought, because Lindy was none other than my longtime malevolent housekeeper, Helen Maguire. I hadn't recognized her because I'd never seen her dressed in anything but frumpery, and was surprised to find she actually had a figure hiding beneath those loose black dresses. Blood pumping hard in my chest, I wondered how greatly it would screw things up if I reached out and snapped her neck.

My vision clouded again, but this time with a smoky heat that hardened my gaze. I glared at her with my father's eyes, and suddenly the color in the mask died. Whatever thoughts she'd been having, any recognition or speculation she'd been entertaining, had suddenly been redirected. I still had an edge.

Time to hone it to a point, I thought, the exchange made, Zell safely behind the Tulpa, Regan held at arm's length by Chandra behind me. "One final thing," I told the Tulpa.

"Of course," he said wryly. He was losing patience.

"I want your pledge that none of your agents will touch Kimber for as long as she's immobilized by the impact of metamorphosis. The rest are fair game"—I shrugged—"as is she the moment the paralysis leaves her, but I'm Light enough to still want an even playing ground."

"Joanna!" Warren's voice was curdled with disbelief. His fear stank. "Think about what you're doing!"

But the Tulpa already had. "I swear it."

The remaining Shadow agents dropped to the ground, fanning around the Tulpa in a half moon but for Zell, who fell back as if afraid his leader might turn around and punish him for his capture. But the Tulpa's eyes were shining, brightly fixed on the agents of Light, who continued to hold their circle around Kimber. Stubborn. Loyal. Practically helpless.

Just as I'd seen in my vision.

29

I centered myself with a breath so deep I felt like an athlete preparing for an impossible physical feat. Then I squared on the Tulpa, strode two feet forward, and looked directly into those swirling silver eyes. "And I, Joanna Archer, pledge to use the primordial force of universal life to bind together the roots of your origin, faster than light, the whole to the half, reclaiming the essence of your original mind and subjecting it to my own."

It was the spell he'd given me, twisted back upon himself, and I recited it precisely three times, just as he'd ordered, right down to the inflection he'd used in relaying it to me. He was a tulpa, not a doppelgänger, and therefore too strong for the spell to hold for long, but it would secure him long enough for the troop to realize their advantage, at least if the glowering Shadow agents didn't catch on first. Their leader had fallen unnaturally still.

"Not too long ago you spoke to me about a legend," I said loudly, stalling for time, and motioning meaningfully in Chandra's direction. Regan stilled beside her, the only one to note it, but Chandra felt her stiffen, and responded swiftly by whirling and burying Zell's ax in her tattered thigh. That took care of that. Regan crumpled to the ground, sobbing again, but nobody on either side of the Zodiac protested. The rain drew down more relentlessly now and I had to yell to be heard. "A person born equally of the sun and moon who could freely choose her fate, her allies. The first sign that this person and her allies would come to power was her discovery—the Kairos actually exists. The second was a plague in her city of birth, which she would overcome with the help of her troop." I inclined my head. "Anyone care to tell me about the third sign?"

Chandra, steadier and with Regan at her feet, spoke up. "The third was the reawakening of her dormant side. For the bearer of the Archer sign there would be a death, a rebirth, and a transformation into that which she once would have killed."

"Her Light eclipsed, her solitary descent into darkness, an ability to see the unseen." Dawn's words were loud as the rain suddenly shuttered off. She looked at the sky as she untied Zell's hands. He continued staring at me, unblinking, as if in a trance. "Tell us something we don't know, please."

"All right," I said slowly, watching her bend to unbind Zell's feet. Lindy was snapping her fingers in front of his face, frowning as he stared through her. I smiled, not because of his lethargic response, but because they were both so preoccupied with him that they'd taken their eyes, their energy, off their leader. The Tulpa, however, was watching me closely. He was furious, eyes charred marble, hatred rolling from him in bilious waves to join the low ceiling of clouds, but otherwise totally incapacitated under his own spell. "That sign has nothing to do with me."

Dawn's head shot up as Zell flexed his fingers and shook away the numbness that had them tingling back to life.

"*Dormant* doesn't merely mean lying at rest. It can also mean lying in *wait*." A small shiver rolled up my spine as elemental madness funneled into a fat, swirling vortex above us. The crackle of lightning and growl of thunder streamed into it, and I had to yell again. "The third sign of the Zodiac heralds the return of my mother to the paranormal battlefield. The death you speak of is the decade-old loss of her otherworldly powers. Her rebirth came when she fully embraced her mortality and all its gifts. But time is fickle and fluid, and her full transformation has taken until now to complete."

"She's a mortal. She no longer has any influence in our world." Lindy turned to the Tulpa for confirmation, but he could only glower in return. She took it as chastisement, swallowed hard, and turned away.

I smiled.

"It's true that at their worst mortals are simply pawns, fuel to be thrown away when their useful resources are depleted. But at their best?" Pride and anger powered my words, and I paced like a caged lion between the two opposing factions. "They're agents of free will, and the mortals who know what that *really* means are also purveyors of energy through the power of thought."

Spoken words, written language, action—and my mother, Zoe Archer, was most certainly a woman of action—could all be channeled into visualizing matter into life. She would be conscious, as most mortals were not, of moving through this mortal plane both physically and mentally, constantly creating and recreating her world, building on what was already constructed or tearing it down. Either way, the constant flux of reality was an opportunity, and like my mother, I saw it all as I never had before. We could all mentally manipulate different aspects of vibrational acuity. Because wasn't vibration nothing more than matter?

And wasn't *matter* all that mattered?

"A tulpa is made from thought," Chandra provided, and I could hear the smile in her voice.

I smiled too, and this time the animist's mask responded to my will by tilting evilly, cheekbones flaring with the grin. "And so is a doppelgänger."

Lindy's expression blanked. The others shifted on their feet, still waiting for the Tulpa's orders. My troop had gone still as well, sensing a shift as imminent as the sky's eruption. I looked up to see a visible mass of power swirling in the funnel, looking as if it was ready to fall in around our ears. The animist's mask didn't contradict the thought.

"A newly born tulpa gains power in one of two ways. The first is by consuming the heart of someone with a concentrated amount of will and mental strength."

A gasp from someone in my troop's circle. The Shadows shifted, almost as one, again, but the Tulpa still didn't move. I hurried on before he did. Not long now. "Eat enough hearts and their strength becomes boundless. The only upkeep required? A regular diet of soul sacrifice.

"Yet there's a second, less bloody, but more powerful way to do this. A means by which you can instantaneously create a strong, fast, smart, and *fully realized* tulpa. And that is done simply by bestowing a name."

Not a formal name, but a proper one. Informal. Common. Given.

The Tulpa's fetters began to loosen. Color flashed across the pane of the animist's mask, and a rumble escaped the funnel, a fractured warning from the sky. I paused, the mask fell blank, and I remembered to pace myself. The exact moment of Kimber's metamorphosis. Not a moment sooner or later. *Not yet.*

"My mother has spent the past decade channeling the fuel of her mortality into the creation of a doppelgänger, the evolutionary predecessor of a tulpa. She could have been the one to provide it with a name, but she's patient and she's good. Well . . . good-ish."

Tekla was up to speed now, and she joined me to face the Shadow warriors. "And a name would be so much more powerful if provided—"

"By a living Zodiac member," Warren finished, and he

too stepped forward, next to me. The agents of Light flanked me, save Kimber, who was oath-sworn as off limits. "One with the same blood of its creator, no less."

"One little noun," I said to the Tulpa, watching as the body he'd donned began to shake. Silver zigzagged so furiously beneath his eyes that it leaked from his tear ducts and into the watery-thin layer between muscle and flesh, causing him to shine, and it wouldn't have surprised me if his physical mold exploded into a million splintering pieces. "Two aspects, a sense and a referent. Something you were never given."

The Tulpa's face twisted as a lightning bolt escaped the sky's low funnel, and a howl tore from his throat, probably ripping it from the inside. The Shadow agents jumped as if waking from a trance, and fire erupted in the sky, lightning searching out Kimber like she was a living rod. Agents, both Shadow and Light, shifted on their feet—my allies automatically pulling in tight as the Shadows bent their knees, weight shifting to the balls of their feet—but still waiting for their leader's command. And when my pulse was so strong I tasted the bloody beat in my throat, I opened my mouth.

The first arrow of heat lightning struck Kimber, searing her image on the canyon floor—back bowed, limbs twisted awkwardly, mouth open and splayed to the sky. I screamed, but my voice was lost in the hail of lightning ripping at Kimber's prone form.

Nobody heard.

My mask burst into a kaleidoscope of color. I felt, rather than saw, the Tulpa draw on the reserves of power he'd stored to chase the doppelgänger—power afforded him by the loyalty of his agents, the soul energy of his mortal worshippers, and the lives he'd stolen to fortify his own—and suddenly, on the back of the mask's face, screaming into my own, was an image of him finally, painfully, willfully opening his mouth. "Kill them!"

Lindy was the first to move, barking out a command as she unsheathed an edged weapon and lunged at Vanessa. Our Leo's bladed fan whipped open and they were off in a shower of sparks and smoke, cold darkness gobbling them whole. Felix and Riddick and Gregor all lunged, clashing with the other Shadows in the center of the canyon. Warren, more circumspect due to the lack of a conduit, took a more circuitous route, weaving between bodies before pouncing from overhead. Chandra ferried blows from behind with Zell's ax, while he continued to cower behind the Tulpa.

I too hung back until my allies could clear the path to the Tulpa, and they did gradually break up and scatter—sparks flying every time one conduit met another, glyphs fired, battling mano a mano, like we were in the Dark Ages all over again. The charged sky continue to pummel at Kimber, but no one took note, limbs and cries and weapons whipping in martial fray.

"Joanna!"

I'd been so focused on securing a defensive position that I didn't hear Chandra until she used my real name. "Jo!"

I whirled to find her alone in a rain-drenched crevasse. "She's gone!"

Regan.

I glanced back at the Tulpa, whom I could see staring at me, silvered eyes unblinking in the whipping gale, and as yet, unmoving.

I can have them both, I thought, and the mask stayed still. *I can have it all.*

I charged—three running steps—and leaped to the ridge of the battered little canyon, following the trail of blood until the storm wiped it away. Then I used my nose to scent out Regan's desolate agony, and chased her farther into the darkness. My glyph lit up a mile into the chase, lighting my way only enough to see one foot in front of the other, though if Regan looked back, I knew the wobbling light would alert her to my approach. And I was gaining on her.

I could taste the coppery rawness of her blood in my throat. After another half mile, the scent was so strong I knew she was only feet away.

But in those few feet between us dropped a fully animated, and thoroughly pissed, Tulpa.

I skidded to a halt, backing up in almost the same motion. "Um. Hi." I kept backing up, ankle twisting sharply as I tripped over a boulder, though I righted myself in time to see a figure limping away into the inky night. "Can you just give me a minute here?"

I don't know what reserve of strength he'd drawn on, but his response was to bellow so loudly he counteracted the gale all around us. My hair blew back from my face, and I tripped backward again. Okay, so he was more than pissed. I'd ruined everything for him, revealed what must have been long-held plans to both the Shadows and the Light, and pulled Zoe from his reach once more. I wondered if there was a chance he'd let me live in spite of it. The way his hands fisted kind of made me doubt it.

Then a circle of calmness surrounded us, stillness falling like an A-bomb, unnatural after the gale whipping around us. The enclosure—for I had no doubt that's what it was— was large enough to allow movement, though still not wide enough for my liking. My glyph lit the whole thing like it was a mini-amphitheater.

"Call the doppelgänger to you."

Oh, I thought with some surprise. A reprieve.

"Why?" I asked, licking my lips, the image of Regan being shredded like paper reliving itself in my mind. "So you can use her to locate Zoe? I don't think so."

Regan had gotten off easy compared to what he had in mind for my mother.

I swallowed hard and backed up, though I didn't run into a wall of resistance. The invisible enclosure of calm simply moved with me. Fuck. "Besides, calling her would mean I'm working with you, and I've already told you the third sign of the Zodiac is not the rise of my Shadow side. If you haven't noticed, there was nothing wrong with it to begin with."

"Brave words, Joanna. And brave actions too. But I can taste your fear. So let's skip the formalities and just give you what you expect. A beating . . . Tulpa style."

He raised his claws like he had with Regan, and I winced as I turned away, putting my hands out in front of me even though it wouldn't help. I thought he was stalling—playing up the anticipation—but when the moment lengthened into seconds, I couldn't help but crack open an eye. Frustration twisted his face as he gazed down at his upturned palms.

"She doesn't belong to you, tulpa," came a voice from the darkness, and then Chandra sidled up next to me, Zell's conduit clenched in her fist. She said his title like I'd instructed, as if he was a thing and not a person, and with more than a little disdain. The Tulpa still wasn't moving well, most of his energy yet bound by the spell he'd given me, and the rest expended on the boundary of stillness around us. The one Chandra had just waltzed through.

I stared at her in wonder . . . as did the Tulpa.

It didn't take him long to figure out what was happening, and when he drew himself upright, settling in, I realized he was going to try and keep me talking long enough for the rest of the spell to wear off and his full powers to return. It was an obvious ploy, but as Zell slid up beside him to face off against Chandra, I let them both have their way.

"How long have you known?" The Tulpa asked with forced calm. It fooled nobody. It was the same calmness that encased me against my will.

"That my mother is the doppelgänger's creator? Or that a doppelgänger is a precursor to a full-blown tulpa?" My narrowed eyes were sharp as they ran back and forth between him and Zell. "All that matters is I know it now. But you've known it all along, haven't you? You said the double-walker smelled like me, but what you really meant was similar. You also said she was a twin . . . but I didn't understand until later that you didn't mean my twin. You meant yours."

"She tried to eat your heart," he reminded me, like my defensive position was her fault.

"You tried to microwave me and throw me into a black hole." My voice deepened at the memory. Zell inched closer to his leader.

He shrugged one slim, scholarly shoulder. "Think of it as a little belated parental discipline."

"Then this would be my adolescent rebellion," I said bitterly. "Now, Chandra!"

Chandra whipped back the ax and sent it whistling through the air, head over tail, in a move so quick, you'd have to be superhuman to even spot it. Zell lunged in front of his leader to take the blow beneath his breastbone, and staggered backward, mouth falling open in a cry that was lost in another crack of thunder. I shifted my attention back to the Tulpa, but even though Zell had just surrendered his life for him, even though being impaled with his own conduit would erase his existence from the entire annals of our mythos, the Tulpa ignored the sacrifice.

Thus he saw Chandra hand signal me, and watched us both lift our arms while imagining the same thing into existence. The lesson she'd given me as we left the city was still fresh, but she was the experienced one and did most of the work. I was just here to reinforce her imagination, to believe in the strength and height and solidity of the giant cacti spearing from the ground like Jack's beanstalk. Tit for tat, I thought, as the Tulpa and Zell were enclosed in a sharp jutting circle of imagined life. Zell fell behind his leader, still clutching his chest. Meanwhile, the Tulpa's face finally betrayed alarm, then a confusion that lasted only moments before shifting to amusement.

"A mind can create life. You know that better than anyone, don't you?" I said as the sky above paused to take a breath between rounds. The Tulpa looked a little less amused as thistles from the wall of fleshy giants corralled him into the center of the circle, a bleeding Zell edged in tightly behind him. "And, in some cases, two minds are better than one."

The only reason he hesitated to blow the thorny barrier apart was because it would deplete the precious energy he'd been rebuilding to turn on me. His pinched expression betrayed his impatience, though, and I knew that when he finally did get free, there'd be no more chatting.

"Now where were we?" I hurried on, drawing as close as I could to the ring of cacti and still remain in his line of focus. I needn't have worried; my words were compelling all on their own. "Ah, yes. A name. Proper, informal, common, given; one noun, two aspects, a sense and a referent . . . a name like . . . *Skamar.*"

Rain gusted around our tight rings, the sky fired above, and smoke ballooned from the Tulpa's feet like he was a shuttle about to rocket into space. It had been a jolt, probably because it was what he dreaded most, but nothing else happened, and he lifted his chin, straightening again.

"I looked it up," I told him, before he could interrupt. "I took it from the Tibetan language. It means *Star.* You told me when you gave me the mantra that a name wasn't needed, but you lied. A name is everything, isn't it? A name is all."

In spite of my important and devastating discovery, he actually relaxed. "Fool. She has to be here to receive it."

While the sky erupted behind me again, where Kimber was still pinned to the canyon floor, I inched forward until all that separated me from the Tulpa was a single jutting thorn. In the pause between fire and thunderous crack, I tilted my head. "Fool. She's right behind you."

And Zell rose up behind the Tulpa, yanking his ax downward so that flesh fell open in a perforated line all the way from his pubis to his throat. Fresh blood poured over his chest, and a hand that was only partially materialized—the lower half still shining like the light off an iridescent bubble—reached out to strangle the Tulpa. The doppelgänger—now a tulpa via the power of a given name—shed Zell like a snakeskin . . . then leaned over the Shadow leader to take a ravenous bite.

She had the advantage of position, surprise, and the power of a recently consumed organ to give her strength . . . even if the heart had belonged to a Shadow. Yet experience, a violent will to live, and, yes, finally fear, powered the Tulpa into action. The bubble of stillness around us popped as they fought for the offense, blood flowing from the fleshly bodies they'd been so sure they wanted.

The succulent wall didn't hold for long; the cacti ripped away in fleshy chunks, barbed darts impaling themselves on wheeling limbs and soft cores. Chandra and I backed up as the two tulpas whipped past us and back toward the canyon now flooded with water and blood . . . and unfortunately, Kimber.

We glanced at each other, then bolted after them.

The Tulpas fought like snarling dogs, whipping over their own malleable bodies to re-form in superior position. Evenly matched, they fell into the gorge and churned across the canyon floor like a snarling dust devil, so out of control that our fear was realized just as we skidded to a stop at the canyon's lip. They careened into Kimber so hard she was knocked from place, and the bolts of lightning were riveted to them instead. Screaming in liquid voices of agony, they loosed themselves, then continued their homicidal tumble through the arroyo, around stained glass bends, leaving only shards in their wake. The lightning found Kimber again, and Chandra and I breathed a sigh of relief.

The Shadow and Light had scattered, no one left in the crevasse of earth where the fight had originated. I pulled off the now-useless animist's mask, gasping as cold stormy air whipped over my sweaty face. Chandra licked her lips, her own face pearly with rain, hair plastered to the sides of her head as she squinted against the whistling wind. I real-

ized, too late, she was watching the metamorphosis she so
longed for, and she turned in response to my stare.

"You should go." She had to yell it, and I nodded to let
her know I'd heard.

I should. Skamar would take care of the Tulpa. The
other agents were battling elsewhere, but if any Shadows
returned I'd have no way of defending myself. Yet . . .

"Kimber—"

"I've got her."

And I knew she did. With nothing but a stolen conduit,
dreams of a future in this troop, and a whole heap of imagination, Chandra had helped to save us all. So I nodded,
then ran, leaving her as the protector of the canyon, and
letting her go down in her rightful place in the manuals.
The last woman standing.

30

One would think with the birth of the new tulpa, and the rebirth of my mother's influence in the paranormal plane, that everything would have changed. Yet in the days after Skamar's nascence, life remained remarkably normal. It was a relative term, to be sure, but my daily routine, my duty to society, and the way I interacted with the world remained exactly as before.

With one giant exception.

The Las Vegas valley was going through something of a crisis weather-wise. The Tulpa and Skamar continued to battle, one or the other disengaging only long enough to catch their breath, before launching themselves at each other anew. Their progress through the valley was marked by distant roars, whipping dust, and a city-wide blackout when they careened into the power grid. The meteorologists were agape—and even more mistaken than usual—and over the next few months scientists would travel from all over the globe to study a weather situation sporting elemental chaos more commonly associated with tropical depressions.

And still they fought.

It occurred to me even as I fled on that stormy desert

night, that if the Tulpa had been pissed at me before, there'd be no mercy now. He'd never really wanted to join forces with me, anyway. All he'd yearned for was a way to annihilate the agents of Light. . . and find Zoe Archer. Daughter or not, I'd shown three times now exactly whose lineage I intended to follow. It was also painfully clear that I could have given the doppelgänger a name immediately upon figuring out who and what she was behind that souvenir shop off the Strip, but I'd waited until she was in a position to engage and kill him, and by introducing a third party into our troops' sick little dance, I'd also caused the destruction of the Tulpa's long-held dreams of retribution and revenge.

A little "parental discipline" couldn't be far off.

For now, though, a reprieve. His hands were full with Skamar . . . another living tulpa. And while he possessed experience and a reserve of power, she was hungry . . . and she was *named*. And really, I reasoned, it was his own fault. He'd taken the wrong approach when trying to make nice with me. I was always suspicious of overtly friendly gestures, the fallout of a life lived looking over my shoulder, so after he so blithely handed me a spell he claimed would kill the doppelgänger, I couldn't help but wonder: Why? And how had he even come to know about it?

The answer was obvious now. He knew what she was because he was the only being in our city to have ever walked the same path into existence. Blowing holes in our reality was the only way she could escape him, though now that she was fully realized, that was no longer an option. Giving her a name had elevated her on a vibrational level that was incompatible with other realities. Besides, one needed a soul to access the regular portals, and neither of them had that.

As for Skamar and her cold-blooded attempt on my life, she'd been truthful in claiming impulse had caused the behavior. A new, undisciplined tulpa was like a toddler exercising her free will. Zoe had given her everything a mortal mind could manage, but Skamar wasn't just hungry for life, she was ravenous. And trapped in a no-man's-land between her creator's control and own free will, with the world cracking and the Tulpa getting closer, time was also short. Becoming me, taking over my life, eating my heart, would've solved all that, despite my mother's attempts to restrain her.

In a way, I didn't blame Skamar. Zoe had initially sent her after me so that someone in the Zodiac, and of the same blood, could provide her with a name. A name giving that would be as powerful as if the creator was still a troop member. But the naming had to be given, not coerced or forced. And while she couldn't come right out and say what she needed from me—not without negating the energy in the spoken word, and diminishing the power Zoe had spent a decade amassing for her creation—she could provide hints, like offering the parts of a noun that make up a name . . . like saying we were cut from the same cloth.

Birthed from the same woman, one physically, the other solely from thought.

It was how she'd known things about me, including my real name and that Ben and I used to talk in traded quotes. She'd also kept referring to a cryptic "she" who was feeding her info. That "she" told her I was smart, good. Well, good-ish. I'd thought for a brief while, especially after my conversation with Zane, that she was referring to the First Mother. The one who existed in a place of exile and myth. Yet perhaps the others were right, and Midheaven really didn't exist but in the minds of a few who needed it to, like a very desperate record keeper.

Well, I knew about desperation, didn't I?

Because it was desperation that had me driving to a nondescript home in a guard-gated community on an iron-leafed autumn afternoon, a day after retrieving an address I'd secreted away in the sanctuary. There I put up a wall to shield us from mortal eyes . . . and introduced Ben to the daughter he never knew he had.

We watched her play in her front yard, an ungainly colt of a child with shining curls that caught light like her father's, with a ferocious knack for concentration, and a grudge she was taking out on a battered soccer ball. She wasn't one of those children whom eyes followed, already marked with beauty or physical attributes that would lead her into adulthood. She was one of the plain ones whose defining features would mushroom at puberty, surprising everyone, particularly themselves.

But we were watching her, each trying to locate the best, possibly lost, bits of ourselves in her, and we were silent for so long, the sun finally dipped behind the rose-tiled rooftops, and the girl fled the accompanying chill by escaping indoors to a warm cup of cocoa, and a mother who slung an easy arm over her shoulder. Ben and I were left staring at the ball as if it was a magical relic just for belonging to her. I'd had more time to grow used to the idea of a daughter, so I was the one who found my voice first.

"She has your hair." It was the same exact color, with the same gorgeous unruly waves, but given leave to grow, those curls softened with length and snapped when they bounced. I had seen them so clearly, even through unexpected tears, that I could bring the exact way they fell over her shoulders back to me now.

"And Joanna's eyes," he said, taking my hand in a brotherly touch, gazing down at "Olivia" with a fierce and blindingly pure happiness. I held tight to his hand, my chilled palm warming beneath his grip, but I didn't return his smile. She did have my eyes. They'd blackened to obsidian depths when her goal attempts flew wide.

Yet even seeing that, I still had a hard time thinking of her as mine. There was a disconnect there, probably because of years of refusal to acknowledge her existence. Yet I didn't allow myself to feel guilt over that. I'd believed she was the offspring of a killer, and the only true memory of her I could dredge up was a nurse's half-horrified whisper at her grossly premature birth. *A survivor, like her mother.*

I hoped so. Because even with the time-induced disconnect, it was clear I could no longer pretend this child didn't exist. She'd been born on my birthday in late November, an Archer, like me. She was as much a child of the Zodiac as I had been, and I couldn't let her remain ignorant of that fact for much longer. Another year, maybe two, and her pheromones—and lineage—would begin asserting themselves. Puberty would mark the onset of her second life cycle, and then *everyone* would know of her existence.

Ben interrupted my thoughts, his sigh suffused with such contentment, a sharp pang squeezed an extra beat from my heart. "I bet she protects the smaller kids on the playground. Just like Jo and I did."

I'd told him that Jo was away on business, but that she'd wanted me to show him this. She'd wanted him to know.

"You can't know that," I said softly, thinking of schoolyard bullies, thinking again of Ben's way of dealing with them. "You can never really know what's going on inside a person."

"'Who knows most, doubts most,'" he quoted before smiling fondly at me. Of course, he didn't expect Olivia to know Browning. "But we don't have to worry about that, do we? Jo and I are going to make a go of this, and somehow, deep down, I always knew it. Because I've always known her."

It was the wrong thing to say.

I shut my eyes at the moment of impact, so that the image that would forever linger was his misplaced serenity. But the sound of my blow connecting with the side of his head still shocked through me. I caught him as he crumpled at my feet.

Gently, I lowered his head to the cool, dusk-damp grass behind the imagined walls still shielding us from sight, and whispered, "I love you, Ben."

But love came with a price. The cost was knowing one woman's touch from another's. It meant searching your heart so an impostor could never insinuate herself into your life, much less your body. Maybe a part of me continued to be piqued that he'd known I was alive, and had still gone out with "Rose" to spite me, the supposed great love of his life. In a way, he'd left me again, as he had the first time, unable or unwilling to trust and understand that I had reasons for my actions. But more than anything, after the years and the emotion and the heartache that had piled up between us, I was tired and burned out. My words, *that* quote, were the most honest thing I could say to him . . . but not without adding, "But you should have known . . . and you didn't."

Hunter had been right about that. Right enough that I'd also begun to question the other theory he'd so desperately put forward . . . that I wouldn't have ever let Regan near Ben if I'd really loved *him*.

"I do love you," I repeated, as if he'd heard the thought and I had to argue against it. "But no matter what's going on inside of me—this war of Shadow and Light—some things just need to be a little more black and white."

I packed him up in the Porsche then, and drove to the Bonanza underpass, where I'd asked Warren to meet me. As I pulled to a stop along a clearing next to the Art Deco bridge, I saw Micah and Gregor exchanging looks. They scented the mortal. They said nothing as they lifted Ben from the car and loaded him into the back of Gregor's cab. It was fast, less than thirty seconds. He was with me, then he was not, and I was left staring blindly in the direction the cab had sped off.

"I didn't give up on him, you know," I told Warren, as he came to stand beside me.

He put a hand on my shoulder as cars raced beneath the underpass, engines both hollow and loud, exhaust choking me and making my eyes water. "I know."

I turned to find him watching me with a kind sadness, like he really did understand the final act in a long good-bye. "He's a good man. He just needs to remember it."

Which could only happen if he forgot the rest—a man

named Magnum, a woman named Rose. A girlfriend who was also a superhero. I knew now that mortals had no place in our world. One disturbing conversation with Regan's father had taught me that.

So I wished goodness for Ben, so much so that I was willing to let Micah rewire large chunks of his memory and restructure his neural architecture so that Ben's original personality could rise to the forefront of his mind. He wouldn't be the boy I fell in love with, but he'd have a chance at becoming the man he would have been if horror and savagery hadn't entered his life. And that's who I wanted him to be. Unscathed. Unharmed.

An innocent.

"You knew it would come to this, didn't you?" I whispered, swaying slightly in Ben's wake, his sudden absence devastating, even though he was still alive. At least he had a better chance of staying that way now. "That's why you didn't pressure me."

A half-dozen cars raced by before he answered. "I didn't want you distracted."

That made sense, I thought, turning to head back to my car parked on the shoulder, in the shadows. Then I paused, lifted my gaze from the concrete, and felt Warren hesitate behind me.

I whirled suddenly, not caring who saw it or what someone might make of Olivia Archer kicking the shit out of some homeless guy underneath a concrete bridge. But Warren blocked my fist, grinned apologetically, and blocked again.

"Joanna," he chided, sounding disappointed with my predictability.

"How long have you known?" I said coolly.

"You mean what the doppelgänger was? What she wanted? Who was behind it?" He smiled, and I thought of hitting him again, but knew he'd be expecting it. "Since her appearance in the sanctuary for sure, but I suspected it as far back as our talk in the warehouse."

Up in the crow's nest, where he'd already been trying to convince me to release Ben.

"How? What tipped you off?" *Why didn't you tell me?*

"For one, you couldn't describe what she smelled like. Yet when we encountered her I realized she smelled exactly like you." No agent could smell themselves. The inability was an evolutionary defense, though this time it'd been a liability. Warren went on, obviously relieved now that he could speak of it. "Then, in the sanctuary, she used a nickname on me that only Zoe had known. Once she fled I also realized she'd been less physically stable under the collective stares of the entire troop. She was morphing under our influence, which told me she didn't leave because she was afraid of us, merely because she couldn't become you in our presence. The Tulpa too has trouble materializing under the influence of multiple stares and expectations."

I felt my face crumple with confusion. "And you didn't help me?"

"It wasn't my help that was needed." The calmness in his voice didn't transfer to me. Instead it infuriated me, driving home how at odds his personality was with his deceiving appearance. He looked like a have-not in a city built for the haves, and beneath that, a leader bowing to the wishes of his troop. But looking even deeper, I saw the craftiness accompanying his words, his every act. "I needed to stay out of your way. I cleared a path by ordering Chandra to let you go out alone, then I sent you out into the world so Zoe, or her creation, would continue to reach out to you."

He sounded so fucking proud of it. "You used me as bait."

"It was necessary to see if she'd contact you."

Yes, but would you have let her eat my heart if it came down to that?

"It was ruthless."

"She was getting desperate."

And it was telling that he didn't know I was speaking about him.

"What about the mask? Did you know what it could do as well?"

His pride, even his features, sank at that. "Of course not. I really thought we'd stolen that mask out from under his nose. The visions of victory seen by our troop while wearing it made me believe it was the tool allowing the Tulpa to anticipate and counteract so many of our actions."

Our visions of victory?

What about my visions? Or didn't I count because I was still part Shadow?

"You fucked up, Warren," I said, wanting to be hurtful and harsh.

"Big time," he freely admitted, which pissed me off all the more. I held my breath, bottled my emotion, and looked away.

And after a minute, I softened. I knew as well as anyone that we all acted from the information we had at the time. The thing that made us most like the mortals we sought to protect was that despite our abilities and powers, we could still only choose rightly, work blindly, and hope for the best. My own actions—seizing the kairotic moment—had required not the work of the body I'd honed for years in anticipation of physical battle, but faith, and the work of my soul.

But as for Warren . . .

"You let me keep Ben," I said in a whisper, "merely so I wouldn't be distracted."

It meant he'd have taken Ben from me earlier if it wouldn't have interfered with my focus on the doppelgänger.

"I bought Skamar time to form, to contact you, and gave you the opportunity to bring the third sign of the Zodiac to life. Of course that backfired a bit. The Tulpa couldn't wait for you to act, so he began to draw on his mortal beards for more power in tracking and fighting the doppelgänger."

"Like Xavier," I said, remembering the thin frame on the giant man.

"How is Mr. Archer these days, anyway?"

I looked at him sharply. So he knew I'd gone to check.

Warren always knew far more than he ever let on. Why hadn't I kept that in mind?

"Better. Still an ass." And undergoing his own meta-morphosis. Xavier Archer appeared to be giving Howard Hughes a run for his reclusive billions. He wasn't even leaving his house for meetings anymore. But I pushed that concern out of my mind. "He's not my responsibility."

"As much as any other mortal."

I stared at the man who demanded so much of me, who pulled levers and pushed buttons behind emerald green curtains, and he shrugged. But it was true enough. I thought of Helen, a.k.a. Lindy Maguire, and knew I'd have to take care of Xavier's pushy, bitchy, stank-ass housekeeper sooner rather than later. But it wouldn't have anything to do with Xavier Archer's well-being.

"Yes," I said, taking my cue from him, deciding to hide a little more of what I was all about. "But no more."

"No less."

Despite Warren's words, the urge to fight drained from me. Did I really have a right to be angry with him? I'd known he always put the good of the troop above that of the individual. I'd been lucky my desires had coincided with that thus far. God help me if they ever did not, I thought, and couldn't contain my shiver as I watched him recline against the concrete hill, the duster of his coat flapping as cars and an errant gust from a far-off battle sped past. I was glad I hadn't told him of Ashlyn's existence.

I'd hate to go to war with you, Warren.

But I'd do it if he took one limping step near her.

"I'll see you tomorrow," I told him, turning again.

"Dawn or dusk?"

"Dusk." Loneliness suddenly gored me, expelling breath from my gut, and as it passed through my chest, by my heart, I thought I felt a crack. I glanced back, knowing Warren had scented it, but he must have interpreted it, and my expression, as regret over losing Ben. He was beside me before I blinked.

"It's the right thing," he said, strong hand on my arm.

I shook off his touch and wrapped my arms around my middle in the encroaching night. I felt the sudden need to go somewhere safe, but we'd already missed the even splitting of this day's light, so crossing into the sanctuary was out. Cher and her mother had only returned from Fiji the day before, but they weren't too far from here. It'd be good to forget about supernatural politics for at least a little while. Perhaps it would even distract from the loss of Ben. No matter what, I had to get away from Warren.

"No," I told him, turning my mind back to the image of Ben lying crumpled at my feet, second-guessing the wisdom in handing him over to Micah. He hadn't looked like the man I'd wanted him to be, the one I'd been desperate to save and love and live the picket-fence, one-point-two-children, nine-to-five lifestyle with. Instead he'd looked like a cutout of himself, like the paper dolls I'd played with as a child, imposing the clothes and background and life I wanted them to have.

Had I become that already? I wondered, thinking of the last mortal I'd struck on the head. Since I was the primary benefactress of the head trauma unit, the hospital director had kept me apprised of Laura Crucier's condition. She had emerged from her coma the previous weekend, and with time and patience and care, was expected to make a full recovery. I sighed in relief at that, though it still didn't answer my question.

Was I really someone who so easily plucked others from their chosen existence because it suited my own needs? Someone who so quickly accepted it as my right just because I was stronger and could do so? Because that would mean I was like Warren, moving people around like pawns, though he did so with superheroes as well as mortal men.

"No." I sighed again, the question still brightly unanswered in my mind. "But it's the wrong thing for the right reason."

31

"Hey, asshole," I called out the next day, banging the handbell on the glass countertop at least a dozen times. The pitter-patter of giant, corn-riddled feet thundered down the hall, and I smiled wryly to myself. Seconds later, Zane trundled into the comics shop, sneer already in place.

"Get out. We're closing early."

"Because it's Nevada Day?" I asked, eyes all wide, blue innocence.

"Because it's Halloween."

"All the kiddies run off to play with friends their own age? I guess trick-or-treating gets old after seven or so decades." I slapped a Shadow manual onto the countertop, and Zane flipped it around to stare at the cover like he hadn't been the one to create it. It showed the Tulpa ringed in giant saguaros, a marble-eyed woman poised to take a bite from his shoulder. I waited for him to mention the manuals of Light—or lack thereof—but he was studying the cover, expression as alive as any changeling's.

"This was a great issue to interpret. The Archer of Light always comes through."

I blinked, surprised. "Thanks, Zane."

"I'm not talking about you." He scowled up at me, and slapped the comic down. "I mean Zoe Archer's successful entrée back into our world. Despite her humanity, she's still a force to be reckoned with, with a mind and will so strong she created another living creature."

I listened to his speech, and drew back from the counter as realization dawned. "Ew. Do you have a crush on my mother, Zane?" I asked, making a gagging noise when he colored. "Isn't she a little young for you?"

Not looking at me, teeth clenched, he asked, "Is this going to be all?"

"No, it's not all," I snapped, suddenly tired of being treated like a gaming piece on some paranormal chessboard. My mother, Warren, now Zane . . . all moving me around at will. "How about acknowledging that I gave that doppelgänger a name, turned it loose upon the Tulpa, and brought the third sign to life? I mean, I just annihilated every threat to my life, but I suppose that doesn't warrant mention in here, huh?"

"Is the Tulpa still alive?"

"Yes, but—"

"And did you ever manage to track down the former Shadow Cancer?"

"No."

"And has the fourth sign of the Zodiac been revealed?"

He already knew the answer to all these questions. "Your point?" I asked tersely.

"The point is that nothing's changed. The Tulpa still wants your life—"

My turn to interrupt. "He's busy defending his own."

"Regan still knows who you are . . . *and* she has your conduit—"

"*And* she couldn't sneak up on me if she were as well-wrapped as King Tut. I'd scent out her blood a mile away."

He pinned me with his gaze then, eyes gleaming. "And even when the fourth sign of the Zodiac comes to pass, nobody will recognize it."

My mouth stuttered before it fell shut. There was that. Jasmine still thought she was a superheroine in the making. Li was still deteriorating by the day. "I'm working on it," I muttered, unable to keep the guilt from coloring my words. Hearing it, Zane pounced.

"Well, work harder. That changeling isn't going to heal herself!"

"Oh, are we exchanging advice? Fine, then don't forget to take your fiber, and the Fixodent should be applied liberally."

Zane grumbled but rang me up, and I snatched the plastic back out of his hand. Later, Gramps."

"Wait until you're my age," he called after me. "You won't find it so funny!"

"Zane." I turned, back against the door. "Do you really think I'm going to live that long?"

"Good point."

I was too apathetic to let the comment bother me, and too late in meeting Gregor for the crossing to immediately rip into the manual. As soon as I was tucked in the back of his cab, though—and alone for a change—I flipped through it to relive the Shadow version of the events at Cathedral Canyon. I glanced up to find Gregor observing me through the rearview mirror, curious as he studied the flash of color and light rising from the manual to wash over my face.

"Learn anything new?"

"No," I lied and looked back down. The manual shook in my hands. The cryptic ending was clearly meant "to be continued," but that's not what was most confusing. I'd simply never expected to see Hunter Lorenzo gracing the pages of a Shadow manual.

His expression held the same resolute calm it had when I'd left him at the warehouse, though it sat on his face like a sunken stone, like he'd settled something for himself inside. He was obviously in a building of some sort, but it had been drawn intentionally obscure, and all that was visible was yards of concrete and four slim windows that allowed a full moon to fall on that disturbingly peaceful face.

"People should have their greatest desires," he told someone, and his voice lifted from the pages to wash over me, causing chills to break out along my spine.

I looked up, but Gregor had turned his attention back to the road, and clearly hadn't heard. Disturbed, confused, and inexplicably sad, I flipped the manual shut just as dusk split down its thinning middle, and we rocketed through the wall and into the boneyard. The dust from our impact into an alternate reality hadn't even settled before a strange pulsing glow seeped into the cab. For a moment I thought the Shadow manual had fallen open again, the recorded events springing to life once more on my lap. Yet in the next, I realized the light was coming from outside the vehicle, and I automatically reached for a conduit I no longer possessed.

I glanced at Gregor to find him half-turned, observing me again, but this time with an air of expectation, not curiosity. I frowned my confusion, but he merely smiled and jerked his head toward the center of the boneyard. Pushing open the cab door, I stood, then cautiously edged toward the glare. A few yards in, I entered a clearing of pulsing, streaming, gas-infused light. And Light. I turned around myself in the middle of the clearing to find agents gazing at me from varying vantages, their smiles as bright as the dilapidated signage they were perched upon.

Except none of it looked dilapidated with bright, flashing bulbs and streaming neon tubes, a carnival of the city's history: Aladdin's lamp, the marquees from the Frontier and Maxim, café arrows . . . and the Silver Slipper looming over them all. Its chipped paint flashed in the puncturing glow of hundreds of bulbs, the first time they'd been lit since 1988. It took my breath away.

My lower jaw had just swung shut when I saw Dylan and

Kade waving at me from the tail of a neon yellow shooting star. The other changelings were fanned around the clearing's perimeter, some with other agents, others with initiates of the same age, who'd obviously been let out for the night. But why?

"Wha—?"

Reaching my side, Gregor put an arm around my shoulder. "Now, Vanessa!"

A mishmash of individual lettering from the Dunes, the Landmark, the Hacienda, and the Sands sprang to life across from me, and my breath caught on a surprised, and touched, sigh. "Oh."

Welcome, Joanna.

"Oh," I said again, tears stinging my eyes. "It's beautiful."

"Skamar's not the only one in possession of her true name now. We thought it good cause to celebrate."

I sniffled, unable to say anything. But he was right. I'd felt it inside, like an inaudible click, as soon as the troop had learned I was Joanna beneath Olivia. It had been the power, the magic, the alchemy of being recognized.

A part of me was concerned, I admitted, watching the young initiates swing from the old Stardust constellation. They streamed past me, glowworm faces flashing with their laughter. If the secret of my identity was out among my troop, *would* it be long before the Shadows learned of it as well? After all, we'd been infiltrated once, and despite Chandra's actions, she was still bound to be discontent at her displacement in the troop. And, of course, there was Kimber to consider. I scanned the boneyard, not finding her. She was a new and certainly antagonistic X factor.

Zane had also made more of a point than I'd wanted to give him credit for—Regan was still out there. She knew me as both Olivia and Joanna. The question was, would she use that knowledge as a bartering chip with the Tulpa, or would she come after me herself?

"Hi, Archer . . . I mean, Joanna."

I looked down, smiled, and sank to my knees. "Li. How are you feeling?"

"I'm okay." The makeup Chandra had made her had evened out the cracked egg aspect of her face, and she almost looked healthy in the fresh autumn night. She was dressed as a black cat, and it was all I could do not to reach out and scratch her behind the ears. "Aren't the lights beautiful?"

I looked around again, catching sight of Jasmine talking to Rena, ward mother to our initiates. Even Jas looked impressed tonight . . . though she was wearing a typically angsty T-shirt that read, THIS *IS* MY COSTUME.

"They are," I agreed, straightening.

"I don't think I could ever live in a place of darkness."

I sighed as I looked back down at her. "Yeah, I know what you mean."

Kylee and an initiate named Elena arrived just then, pulling at Li's arm, chattering excitedly about a maze that'd been turned into a haunted house for the night. They were both in costume, both superheroes, and they rushed away so quickly, she barely managed a backward wave. Seconds later, thrilled screams of terror rolled over the boneyard. I smiled grimly, knowing I had to help Li, and soon, but for tonight she was happy and safe.

"Happy Halloween, Archer."

My brows winged up to find an Autobot Transformer. I tilted my head. "Carl? Is that you in there?"

Earth's protector nodded.

"I thought you didn't dress up for Halloween."

He shrugged. "It's not every day you get to turn into a semi."

"This is true. Though I'm not sure how safe all this is." I jerked my head toward the boneyard's perimeter.

"Oh, the mortals . . . the *other* mortals, I mean . . . they can't see us. Tekla put up a shield. Didn't you notice? It isn't storming inside the boneyard."

I did now that he mentioned it. The serenity hovering over the boneyard wasn't due solely to my surprising contentment. Only Tekla could shield such a large space from the fallout of battling tulpas. Yet one thing remained unsettling. "I don't see Hunter."

"Hot date," Carl muttered, watching one of the initiates glow with more than a little envy. "You know how those working men are."

I suppose I did, though of course the question remained: what was he working on?

Not your business, quipped a voice loitering inside me. Besides, it was probably best he wasn't here. I needed time and space to figure out who I was now that Ben Traina wasn't taking up so much real estate in my head. And my heart. Immediately filling that space with another man was a mistake . . . and wasn't even possible. Maybe in time it would be, but only if that person fit well and wholly with the woman—the superwoman—I was today.

And that was my most pressing problem. Ambivalent in my self-awareness, I was no longer the person I used to be but still unsure of who I was to become. It was as if I was still composed of two halves: the mortal me, who'd used logic and determination to power through life, and the new one, who had to accept there was a place for magic alongside the practical. I was surrounded by people who could conjure plants and storms and walls using nothing more than thought; I could do the same. My birth father had been wrought into being by the same applied mental power, and my mother had just spent the last decade creating a being that could take him down.

Yet whenever I considered these things together, along with my future, my destiny as Kairos, I had trouble seeing from here to there. It was like the fourth sign. Delayed, yet to be revealed. And there was no path to follow, no book to read, no great teachers who'd come before me, leaving scripture like bread crumbs trailing behind them. My path to becoming me, I now knew, would have to spring wholly from myself.

But for now, in this exact moment, Li was safe, Ben had a chance at a normal life, Regan was defeated, the Tulpa was on his heels, my mother had succeeded . . . and for the first time since Olivia's death I had people who knew me. It was with a surprised jolt that I realized I was relatively happy. I really had a place in the Zodiac now, in this world, and whether anyone liked it or not, no one could question it. I had an identity.

I had a home.

But what about Warren?

That voice again.

What about the way he ruthlessly played us all?

What about it? I mentally shrugged. I knew where he stood, and now knew the extent he'd go to protect his troop. Would he sacrifice me, and along with me, this life I'd carved for myself in the troop? Not any faster than he'd sacrifice himself. And not if he thought he needed me, the Kairos.

Besides, I'd discovered, when it came to protecting what was mine, I could be ruthless too.

"Yo, Archer! So what do we call you now?" Felix yelled from the top of the maze. He was sweaty from chasing changelings and initiates, and looked like a statue standing tall in the flashing, pulsing glow that chased darkness from all corners of the boneyard.

"Yes," said Tekla, folding her palms before her, similarly lit. "What'll it be? Joanna? Olivia still? Just the Archer?"

I thought of what I knew of the power of names, how they claimed a place for you in this world, how people could seek them out in order to use them against you . . . how powerful they were when you claimed them for yourself. *A person cannot be divided against herself.*

Then I looked into the sky where the stars snapped sharp and clean, and thought of my sister. My heart pinched so hard that I momentarily lost my breath. Almost a year gone now, and still the look on her face at the time of death haunted me. It always would.

And yet.

"Olivia is fine," I finally answered, turning away from the desert sky and back to all the lights that burned so brightly for me.

And it was.